THE NINTH SORCERESS

THE NINTH SORCERESS

THE PRICE OF MAGIC: BOOK I

BONNIE WYNNE

TALEM PRESS

Published by Talem Press, 2020

An imprint of Writer's Edit Press

www.talempress.com

First printing, 2020

Print ISBN 978-0-6485342-2-8

Ebook ISBN 978-0-6485342-3-5

Cover design by Deranged Doctor

For Mumsy.

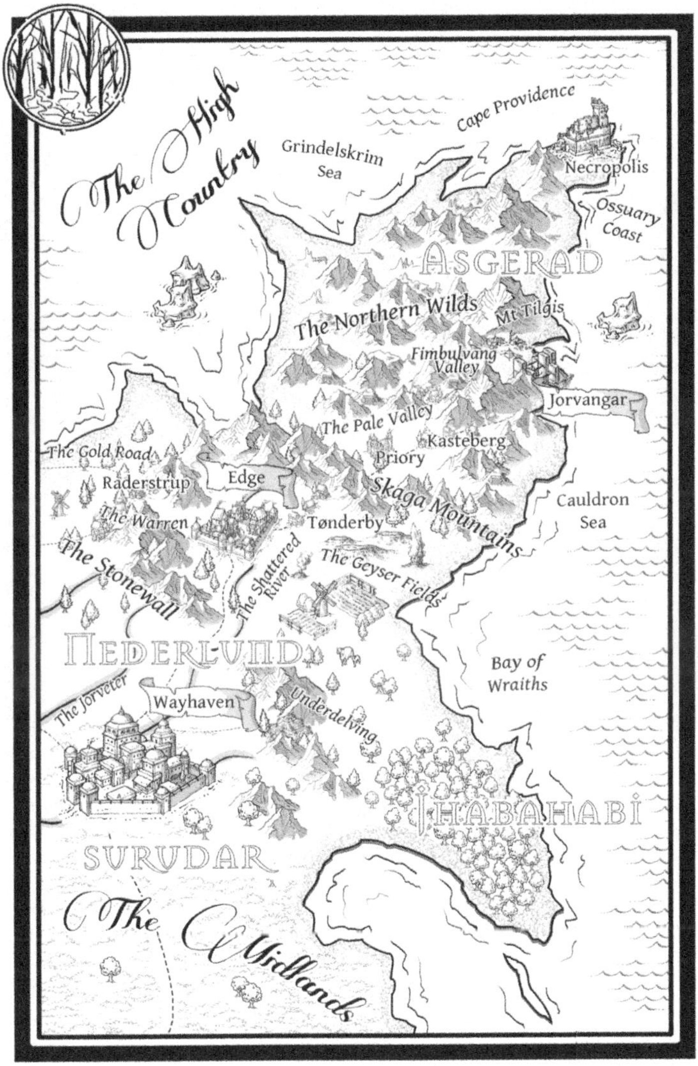
The High Country
Grindelskrim Sea
Cape Providence
Necropolis
Ossuary Coast
Asgerad
The Northern Wilds
Mt Tilgis
Fimbulvang Valley
Jorvangar
The Pale Valley
Kasteberg
Priory
The Gold Road
Raderstrup
Edge
Skaga Mountains
Cauldron Sea
The Warren
Tønderby
The Stonewall
The Shattered River
The Geyser Fields
Nederlund
Bay of Wraiths
The Jorveter
Wayhaven
Underdelving
Jhabahabi
Surudar
The Midlands

PART I

PROLOGUE

THE BIRD TOWER

The bridge to the Bird Tower was slippery. For three months now, it had rained steadily, and today the wind had started too. As it howled up out of the rift, the wind snatched at the cloak of the slender man crossing the bridge, his broad-brimmed hat clasped to his head.

The mancer refused to think about the wind. There had been too much talk of that lately. Enoch marched with his head down, a battered leather satchel clutched under one arm. His worn-down boot heels clattered on the wet stones. To his left, the bridge dropped away into a chasm three quarters of a mile deep. There was no railing. If he fell, he would have plenty of time to scream. But he wasn't going to think about that either.

At the entrance, stepping out of the rain, he stopped before the guards. Their surcoats were emblazoned with the tower-and-moon emblem of the Paragon Holdings Syndicate, the same as the brand on Enoch's forearm, and they wore shortswords at their hips. Both snapped to attention to greet the mancer.

'I'm here to see the prisoner,' Enoch said, by way of introduction. Six hundred feet below, he heard the mighty support chains creak, felt the vibration in his feet.

The guards grimaced. The Bird Tower held cells for over a hundred prisoners, but there could be no doubt which one he meant.

'Has she been giving you more trouble?' Enoch asked.

'No, m'lord mancer, no more'n usual. Nobody else's lost fingers, far as I know.'

'Good.' The rain lashed in sideways at him, and the wind made the roof tiles rattle like corn husks. 'I'll try to keep it that way.'

The guards chuckled and stood aside. Through the second doorway, torchlight illuminated the stone stairs that curved down into the belly of the tower, into deeper shadow. The air was tight and scentless. Enoch's footsteps rang hollowly as he descended.

The stairs opened onto a dank, windowless hallway, and beyond, a tall door strapped thickly with iron. Through the grille Enoch could see a group of guards crowded around a knife-scored table, their game of Tact seemingly untouched. One was honing his shortsword, watching the door with haunted eyes.

Enoch lifted the clapper, but the guard had already risen. He peered at Enoch through the bars. Behind him, the other guards reached for their swords.

'I'm here to see the prisoner,' Enoch said again. When the guard didn't move, Enoch flipped open his case, fished out the topmost sheet of parchment, and pressed it to the grille so the Archmage's seal was visible. A few moments later he heard the first bolt slide back, then the second, then the third. The door swung open.

'Apologies, lord mancer. We've been having some ... uh, unauthorised visitors.'

'Still?'

'Oh, yes.' The guard led him beyond the table to the second door, this one crisscrossed with – Enoch blinked – *six* padlocked iron chains. 'It was worse the first weeks, of course. We had to move the other prisoners to the Charnel Vaults. The ones we couldn't release, that is. Scullions couldn't get across the bridge with food, on account of the mob outside.'

Enoch had been in Chastis then, acquiring new books for the library, so he had missed the excitement – if it could be called excitement. He would still be missing it, and gladly, thank you very much, if not for the Archmage's orders. Though why Ravenmarsh thought a librarian would succeed where the Inquisition had failed, Enoch couldn't guess. Perhaps he was still being punished for supporting Suswara in the Ascension.

Well, it made no difference. Enoch was a Mancer of the Fourth Rank, and when the Archmage said *toad*, Enoch hopped.

He waited as the guard grappled with his brass ring of keys; waited as he heaved the bolts back, one by one. Beyond the door, torchlight showed a narrow corridor and rows of more heavy wood-and-iron doors, padlocked, with barred windows and slits for passing through food. None were marked, but Enoch knew where he was going.

'Knock thrice if you need us, lord mancer,' said the guard. 'Thrice, mind, else we'll not open it. Archmage's orders.'

Enoch had no chance to reply before the door slammed shut behind him. He counted the bolts this time. One, two, three ... seven bolts slammed home, followed by the heavy clunk of the padlocks. Ravenmarsh must have called in a locksmith from the city. A locksmith! Enoch shook his head and reached for the oil lamp, hanging on a hook from the low ceiling. Apparently even the Archmage could fall prey to hysteria.

The last door in the hallway had only one lock, this one pure silver and etched with marks of binding. That gave him pause, more than all the other chains and bolts and padlocks. A shiver tickled the base of his spine. The cold air of the prison – nothing more. He fumbled for the key at his belt and unlatched the door.

The stink hit him like a mouthful of wet cloth. The mancer swallowed the urge to gag. Underfoot, fouled rushes scratched the floor, and an old slop bucket overflowed its contents – but the source of the smell seemed to be the small figure his lamp revealed, chained to the far wall.

She was skinny, ragged. The bones stood out against her fish-pale skin. A snarl of dull gold hair hung to her waist, obscuring part of her face. Her features themselves might have been pretty, once: broad across the cheekbones, with full lips and a small, firm chin.

Now the skin stretched tightly over the bones. There were muddy circles under her eyes, and the left was ringed in purple – a recent bruise. There were older bruises, too, on the long legs that stuck out from her sackcloth dress, and on her arms. The worst were at her wrists and ankles, where the heavy manacles had cut welts into the skin.

Both wrist and foot bore a second set of chains, attached to metal symbols – moons, stars, runes – and they jangled together as she stirred. Enoch recognised those chains, though he had not seen them used in many years. They were the chains forged to hold a mancer.

She was looking at him. Green eyes glared out

from under a lank fall of hair. Enoch raised the lamp, and for a moment, the eyes almost seemed to glow, like a cat's. He sucked in a breath – but, no, they were just ordinary eyes, slitted against the sudden light.

'So,' said the woman. Her voice was low and pleasant, though hoarse. 'Another little bird flaps his way in to gawk at me.' She gave a brittle cough, making the chains clatter. Even seated, she was slumped against the wall, as though too weak to hold herself upright. 'Go away, little bird. I have no seeds for you today.'

Her accent was hard to place. Enoch recognised the clipped, precise vowels of Aranor, his own birth country, as well as the lilting tones of rural Nederlund. She was much younger than he had expected; barely more than a child. *A child, in this place.*

'I'm here to ask you some questions,' Enoch said. There was a stool by the door, and he pulled it over and sat – though well out of the woman's reach. He had no intention of becoming the second visitor maimed in the course of duty. Perhaps she noticed his caution, for a little, secretive smile flitted across her face, and then was gone.

He set the lamp on the floor. 'This is inconvenient for me. I have a lot of work to be getting on with. If you cooperate, I can help make your stay here a little easier. Some blankets, maybe. Or I could ask that they take off some of those shackles – would you like that?'

'Oh, on the contrary.' She held up her hands, where the bruises were clearly visible, and rattled her chains. 'Why, I've never had so many men come to bring me jewellery in my life. It's quite flattering.' She chuckled humourlessly, which turned into another fit of coughing that lasted a long time. When she took her hand from her mouth, there was something dark on it that could have been blood.

'What would you like, then?' Enoch asked when she was done. 'If I can provide it, I will.' Judging by her appearance, she needed a casket more than a blanket, but he kept that thought to himself.

The prisoner gave him a speculative look. Her eyes were deep-set and hooded, a green too striking, too alien, to be considered truly beautiful. The harsh shadows cast by the lamp turned the sockets to black pits. He realised he was leaning away from her, and told himself it was just the smell.

'Well,' she said slowly, holding up her wrists again, 'you could take *these* chains off. The pretty ones, with the little moons on them. Silver does nothing for my complexion.'

Enoch forced himself to lean closer. 'You know I can't do that.'

She seemed to lose interest at that, turning her head away and pulling her knees up to her chest. The baggy dress only accentuated how gaunt she was, her limbs like a bundle of white twigs. 'Fly back to your nest, then. You'll get nothing from me.'

Enoch was undaunted. He had come prepared. He opened the clasp of his bag and pulled out a cloth-wrapped bundle that smelled of oats and honey. The woman had her eyes closed, but her head turned back slightly in his direction. She seemed to be trying not to breathe.

'Biscuits?' she said. 'You insult me. Do you think I'd sell my secrets so cheaply?' Her eyes opened. She still didn't look at him, or the biscuits.

Enoch shrugged, breaking off half an oatcake and popping it in his mouth. It was moist and crunchy, the inside still warm from the oven. 'Did I say they were for you?' he asked, swallowing.

'Please. You're as predictable as the rest of your Syndicate. Although I do prefer your technique.' The woman let out another hacking cough that might have been laughter. 'I wish all my visitors brought biscuits instead of pincers and hot irons.'

'I'll leave those to the Inquisition. I see no need to resort to barbarism.' Enoch had never had the stomach for the bloodier work of some of his colleagues. 'I'm aware they can be ... zealous. You mustn't judge us all by their example.'

'Mustn't I? No other, gentler wizards have come to rescue me from their care. In fact, the big quiet one suggested there were more good times to come.'

There was only one mancer she could mean. 'Saire Castlemaine?'

'He never bothered to give a name.' She shrugged, her chains clanking. 'More interested in getting straight to the hot irons, I suppose.'

'Castlemaine is the Exorcist-General of the Inquisition.'

She drew her brows up in mock surprise. 'Indeed? I had no idea I was in such fine company. The Exorcist-General himself! If I'd known, I would have worn cleaner rags.'

As expected, Enoch was getting nowhere. The junior Inquisitor the woman had maimed said she was insane. Shrieked it, in fact, cradling his ruined hand to his chest beneath a crimson-soaked rag. Enoch had seen that himself, as he passed by the infirmary on his way to evening meal. The blood had spilled onto the floor like wine from the god Yotha's drinking horn. Despite the healers' efforts, the wound had festered. A week later, the man still lay in his cot, clammy and pale, with the leeches growing fat off the poison in his blood.

Enoch hadn't spoken to Castlemaine himself – like most, he tried to avoid the Exorcist-General – but he had heard whispers in the library. They said the woman had laughed when they'd brought out the irons. Seeing her now, like this, he believed it. Few people laughed about the Inquisition. And nobody had ever laughed at Saire Castlemaine.

Now, sitting across from her, Enoch silently cursed the Archmage. He had no love for madwomen. Too chaotic; too unpredictable. All he wanted was to go back to his chambers, to the safety of his books.

Instead, he held out the package of biscuits. The prisoner looked at them for a moment, then reached out, slowly. Her knuckles brushed his hand, and the touch was cool and electric.

'I'm not the Inquisition,' he said. 'All I want is to talk.'

Her mouth twisted. 'Of course. Biscuits for me – maybe a blanket, if I behave myself. And for you? Two thousand years' worth of secrets. Power beyond your imagining. Answers to all your questions.'

'One in particular.'

She nodded, taking a bite of biscuit. She must have been starving, but she ate carefully, delicately. She didn't seem to spill so much as a crumb. When had she last eaten? There were a few little bones in the corner of the room. Had she been eating rats? The thought turned Enoch's stomach.

'I could give you the answer you want,' she said, when the biscuit was gone. Her sharp eyes met his. 'Though I doubt you'd like it.'

He frowned. 'Does it matter? Surely you must understand what's at stake.'

Slowly, her gaze vacant, the woman licked the last crumbs from her fingers. Her hands shook. 'I understand better than you. There are some secrets better left dead. Secrets your Syndicate should leave dead. You truly have no idea what's coming.'

With a sigh, she slumped further down the wall. The lamplight turned her hair to a wild blaze of copper. Rather than replenishing her, the food seemed to have drained the last of her strength. She looked tired, and sick.

'Wizard ... What was your name?'

'Enoch Arehi. Mancer of the Fourth Rank.' Then, after a moment, 'Librarian.'

She smiled wanly. 'Librarian. I see. He's clever, your Archmage. But the answer is still no.'

Enoch pressed his lips together. His next move was a gamble; one he'd been hoping to avoid. But she left him little choice, now. He clamped his bag between his knees and began rummaging, fingers seeking the small, cool object at the bottom. The woman watched him silently.

'Do you recognise this?' he asked, when his fingers had closed on it. He pulled it out.

Her control was tight. If Enoch hadn't been watching closely, he wouldn't have caught her slight intake of breath, the way her pupils narrowed, the tiny flexing of her fingers. She folded her hands in her lap, as though to stop herself from reaching out and snatching it.

'When you were taken, all your belongings were catalogued,' Enoch said, when she didn't answer. 'I've examined the list. Heavy clothes – furs and such – as though you'd come straight out of a High Country winter. New boots, only a little travel-stained.' He let the copper disc slip through his fingers, so it dangled at the end of its leather thong. 'This, though. This hadn't been recorded at all. At first I wondered if we simply overlooked it. But it was right on top of the pile – impossible to miss.'

She still said nothing, only followed the disc with her eyes, as though hypnotised. Her knuckles had turned white.

'It's not enchanted,' Enoch continued. 'That was my initial thought. Many of the standing enchantments have begun to fail, and if this was under some sort of concealment ...' He shook his head. 'But no. It has a residue of magic on it, but nothing recent. Nothing that would account for its sudden appearance.'

'Who have you shown that to?' she asked at last. Her voice was low and deliberately even, and Enoch smiled inwardly.

I've got her.

'Nobody,' he said. 'Yet.' He drew the disc back into his hand, and the expression that flitted across the woman's face was close to pain. 'I assume it's yours. Would you like it back?'

Her gaze moved from his hand to his face, searching. 'You would do that? Why?'

He shrugged. 'I'm satisfied it doesn't pose any

threat to the Syndicate. Any value it holds would appear to be sentimental. For information, I would consider it a fair trade.'

'Information,' she repeated flatly. 'Yes, that's the key, isn't it? You want to know where it is. More to the point, you want to get it back.'

It wasn't a question, and Enoch didn't offer an answer. He held his breath. Sweat pricked the back of his neck.

'I won't give Idris up,' she warned. 'Not for biscuits, not even for ... for that.'

Enoch cleared his throat to cover his surprise. *Did she just say ...?*

'I understand. Tell me what you can.' He loosened his fingers, so the edge of the disc flashed in the lamplight. The front showed a woman's face in profile, proud and queenly in a crown of laurel wreaths.

She nodded, gaze going back to his hand. Enoch swallowed. The prisoner held very still. Praying he wasn't making the biggest mistake of his life, Enoch handed her the disc.

For a moment, she only held it, the leather thong hanging loose from her hand. Her eyes fluttered closed, and he thought he saw her mouth something under her breath. Then she slipped the cord over her neck, tucking the disc underneath her tunic, so it hung just above her heart.

'Alright, wizard,' she said, after a moment. 'I'll tell

you what you want to know. If you're sure you're ready to hear it.'

'It's why I'm here,' Enoch said, hardly daring to believe. He reached for his bag, grabbing quill and paper with suddenly boneless hands.

'Some of your wizards want me dead, and for good reason,' she began. 'The rest would see me moulder away in this dungeon for the next thousand years. They think I stole your magic; gobbled it up, maybe, like a piece of candied fruit. They think they can cut me open to get it back.'

She closed her eyes. When she raised her head and looked at Enoch again, her gaze hit him, bright and deadly as a knife-blade. 'You want to know how I became what I am? Very well. Listen.'

Enoch listened. His quill trembled over the blank page.

And as she spoke, the first mancer to hear her story grew cold inside.

CHAPTER 1

THE MAGNIFICENT ASCEPIS MELM

The caravan had appeared before first light, slouched in a clearing on the outskirts of Vønnerlund. Its side was cornflower blue, its wheels red, and neither looked to have seen a lick of paint since the First Age. Remnants of what might once have been gold leaf clung to the door frame at the rear.

Striding up the main road from town, Gerlef Laursen's gaze fixed on the peeling walls, and his face was hard enough to carve stone. He had already driven off two bands of rovers this year. Those, at least, had had the sense to stay out of the town proper, away from decent folk.

But this! This was an insult. Right up to the town limits it had come, bold as you like. No doubt there were a dozen of them living in that hovel, crammed in thick as sheep thieves at a town fair. That thought made Gerlef's frown lines deepen into furrows. Likely they *were* sheep thieves; most rovers were.

Scowling, Gerlef walked up to the door – a garish yellow – and mounted the steps to rap sharply on it three times. A threadbare curtain fluttered in one of the small windows. Otherwise, there was no reply. Gerlef knocked again, more loudly, stamping his feet against the cold.

The caravan door swung open, nearly catching him flat on the nose. Gerlef jerked back, saving his face at the expense of his elbow. An old man came out onto the top step and beamed at him, rubbing his close-cropped white beard.

'Good morning to you, sir! A fine day, is it not?'

The fellow looked as shabby as his caravan, with robes that had been patched a few too many times, and a musty-looking book under one arm. His hair was thin enough to show his brown scalp. Gerlef scowled, massaging his arm where the door had clipped him.

'This land is under the jurisdiction of Thane Aalgen of Harloff,' he said. 'Rovers aren't permitted within town limits.'

'I'm not a rover. Nor am I within town limits.' A loopy grin split the stranger's face. 'The township begins at the far north of this clearing, does it not? I have maps, if you would like me to —'

'I know what the maps say,' Gerlef snapped. 'Who are you, if not a rover? Are you a tinker?' It looked like no tinker's wagon Gerlef had ever seen; not with those colours.

'I'm sorry,' said the old man, shaking his head. 'My manners must have deserted me. Allow me to introduce myself.' He gestured towards the side of the caravan. Gerlef leaned around and looked. Up close, what he had taken for flaking paint spelled out words, each letter two feet high:

The Magnificent Ascepis Melm

Herbalist, Doctor, Future-Teller

Then, underneath, in smaller writing and added more recently:

No magic – don't ask!

Not rovers, Gerlef thought. Fear wrapped cold fingers around his heart. *Worse. Molech preserve me.* He took a deep, steadying breath.

'You're with the Syndicate?' In his head, Gerlef began running through the list of possible infractions. The Widow Elst sold herbs, sometimes, for young women hoping to conceive: corn cockle and hawthorn, hazel and red snout. His wife had drunk the widow's tea every morning for three months, the year before little Pieter was born. And Rikkert tied prayer kites to his back fence year-round, not just on feast days. But that was a matter of faith; hardly worth the Syndicate's attention, and surely ...

Gerlef started. There was a face staring at him from the caravan window. A woman, or perhaps a girl, regarding him solemnly from beneath a fall of fair hair. As he turned to look at her more closely, she ducked away out of sight.

'Not the Syndicate,' the old man said. 'Master ...?'

'Laursen,' Gerlef said, shaking his head to clear it. Perhaps it was just the way the rising sun struck the windowpane, but for a moment the girl's eyes had looked green as agate. 'Gerlef Laursen. I'm the Churl of Vønnerlund.'

'Churl Laursen.' The man inclined his head, just enough to avoid rudeness. 'I am not with the Syndicate. My trade is in potions, remedies for sore knees and bad teeth; in card readings and meteorology.' He had the sound of repeating something by rote. 'No to exorcisms, communing with dead grandpappies, and any type of spellcasting. My work is completely by-the-book, and no transgression to Syndicate law.'

Gerlef pressed his lips together. It was too dark inside the wagon to make anything out, but he caught a whiff of burnt flowers. Witchcraft, and no doubt about it. This far from the centre of magic – and the iron fist of the Syndicate – there was a hedge-wizard for every hedge. His fear refused to abate; it only changed forms.

'Peddlers of witchcraft aren't welcome here in Vønnerlund,' he said, meeting the old man's gaze. 'The Syndicate has not called here in over a decade, and that's how we prefer it. We want no trouble with the wizards. You have to leave.'

Impatience flickered across the man's face. 'The Syndicate has little interest in small townships, unless they ride in Seeking. But they have been known to investigate those places believed hostile to wizards.'

'You're not a wizard. You said so yourself.'

'No. But tales have a way of twisting in the telling.' He gave Gerlef what he must have considered his most winning smile. 'I understand that my presence here is ... distasteful to you. With that in mind, I'll not intrude long on your hospitality. A day to trade with your good townsfolk should be enough. At first light on the morrow, I'll be on my way.'

The face had reappeared at the window, still watching him. She was older than Gerlef had first thought, perhaps fifteen or sixteen. The old man had the dark skin of a Midlander and the clipped accent of an Aranorman, but the girl's colouring was northern.

'You have a child with you?'

The old man didn't look at the window, but the girl's eyes widened, and she slashed the curtain closed.

'My apprentice,' he said, taking a deep breath, as if to calm himself. 'She is of no importance.'

Gerlef looked back towards the window, but there was no sign of movement within. *A hard life for a child.* Pieter would be fourteen this winter, not much younger than the girl.

'You can stay until nightfall,' Gerlef said, turning back to the hedge-wizard, who was watching him closely. Strange – for a moment, Gerlef had been sure the man meant to strike him. 'If this wagon isn't gone by then, it will be removed.'

The hedge-wizard bowed. 'Of course. Your generosity is appreciated. I will ensure you are not inconvenienced.'

Gerlef scowled. He had already been inconvenienced, and it would be worse once the town council was informed. By midday, they would be shouting for his badge, if not his head.

'By nightfall,' he said. 'I'll be watching.'

With a final glance at the window, he strode away, his cloak drawn up around his ears against the morning chill.

Gwyn started laughing as soon as the Churl was out of earshot, but one glance from Ascepis and the laughter died on her tongue.

He stepped inside the wagon and closed the door behind him.

'I know,' she said. 'I know.' She clambered down from the window seat and sat on her bunk, hands folded. 'Don't be seen.'

'One rule,' he said. 'I have one rule. Only one, in

exchange for everything I do for you. For your room and board, for training you, for taking you in off the street and giving you a life. One rule.' His finger shot out to jab her, four times, right above the sternum. '*Do. Not. Be. Seen.*'

'He barely noticed me,' she said, rubbing her chest. His finger was hard and knobbly as an old twig. 'And I don't see that it matters. Why should anyone care if you have an apprentice? It's not forbidden.' Besides, she *was* seen, at least from time to time; it couldn't be helped. Not even Ascepis expected her to stay cooped up inside for days at a time. Sometimes, when he deemed it safe – which, she had to admit, wasn't often – he let her mingle with the customers; let her try her hand at haggling and bartering. Not an easy thing, with Ascepis fretting and hovering as though someone might snatch her up the instant his back was turned.

Ascepis sucked in a deep breath, and Gwyn winced, certain he was going to yell at her. But he only pinched the bridge of his nose and sighed, appearing suddenly ten years older.

'What more can I do?' he said, seeming to speak to himself. 'What more? I sacrifice everything for her, and she continues to spit in my face. Have I not given enough?'

Her rebelliousness subsided. She had gone too far, again. She looked at her feet. 'I'm sorry.'

She was used to his shouting; even shouted back,

sometimes. But the weariness and the disappointment – those were harder to deal with, harder to argue against.

He had plucked her off the streets of Til Iver when she was three. A threadbare foundling from the Crane's Hollow orphanage, so skinny and grimy it was impossible to tell at first glance if she was a boy or a girl. Why? He had never explained, even when Gwyn pressed him, and she remembered nothing of those early years.

Ascepis gave her a tight look that was not quite a smile. He only had one smile, and he saved that for customers and puffed-up town officials. It was warm and slightly bemused, a kindly old man's smile, though Gwyn had known him long enough – fourteen years, now – to sense the teeth behind it.

'*Salmo's Compendium, Volume I.*' He handed her the book from under his arm. 'I want it finished by the end of the week. You may begin now.'

Gwyn sighed, relieved. Her transgression was forgiven, and she hadn't even been ordered to scrub the stove in penance this time. 'Will you go down into the village?'

'There's no need. By mid-morning, the whole town will know I'm here. Although I expect it will take a few hours for any to work up the courage to call on me. I'm going back to bed.' There were circles under his eyes; he had driven late into the night to get here. 'Stay out of sight, and wake me if anyone else comes by.'

Gwyn waited until he was settled in his bunk, snoring loud enough to rattle the windows, before she eased the door open and clambered onto the roof of the wagon, *Salmo's Compendium* tucked under one arm. The sun was brushing the tops of the trees, dissolving the morning frost so the leaves sparkled like dragonfly wings. She breathed the cold, clean air into her lungs.

But being outdoors, Gwyn discovered, lying flat on her belly on the caravan roof, did not make *Salmo's Compendium* one whit more interesting. The book was at least twice as old as Ascepis, a hundred and eighteen pages of cramped text on the thousand varieties of herb and medicinal flower encountered by the Simpler Salmo in his travels in the south. There were no illustrations, so she was left scratching her head over the difference between pilsroyal (dark green, striated leaf), and sweet roadweed (dark green, striped leaf). Most of the plants didn't even grow here in the High Country, which made the whole thing rather academic.

Someday, maybe I'll go to the southern lands, and I'll be glad I learned all these herbs, she told herself, not really believing. At least in the south she wouldn't have to be cold all the time, wouldn't have to shiver and huddle in her blankets through another seemingly endless winter. In the Slumbering Isles, there were beaches. Expanses of glittering white sand that spanned the horizon, the water clear and so blue it hurt the eyes. You could walk through fields of sugarcane taller than a man's head, could slice off stalks and chew on the sweet, milky insides. Could visit the markets at Port Corsair and buy coloured skirts of wispy cotton, and fruits so bright and swollen they looked ready to burst. Or so she had read.

Of course, Ascepis always said the south was no place for a hedge-wizard. The Syndicate was jealous of its territory, and the lands surrounding the Clockwork City were a bad place to be accused of impersonating a wizard. Even with the sign painted on the side of the wagon, too many people made assumptions about Ascepis. And besides, he said, what use were herbs and philtres compared with true magic? There would be no business for them in the south; they would starve within a month.

Privately, Gwyn had her doubts. Would southerners go to the wizards for every bump and graze? Those with a lick of sense stayed well clear of magic. Wizards were wicked, tricksome creatures, according to Ascepis – as likely to strike you dead with a bolt of lightning as give you aid. He was full of those sorts of macabre stories, especially when he fell into one of his moods. Gwyn didn't fully believe some of the things he told her, but she still held a healthy northerner's suspicion of magic. Not that

Gwyn had ever met a wizard, or was ever likely to. They rarely came north, except to steal away children.

The pale sunlight cast little warmth. Gwyn wrapped her coat tighter. The beginnings of a cramp needled the base of her skull. She twisted her head, massaging her neck with one hand – and as she looked up, she glimpsed a flash of movement among the trees. It was gone a second later, so quick she thought she'd imagined it. But no, there had definitely been something, just beyond the tree line.

Probably a badger. Still, Gwyn's skin prickled, and her hand went unconsciously to the pocket of her sarafan. A badger, out in daylight? If so, it was the biggest one she'd ever seen. They rarely came this far north, for that matter, even in the summer months.

It was nothing, then. Just the shadow of leaves stirring in the wind. If someone had been there, she would have heard the crackle of branches. The woods stood still and dark.

So why did it feel like she was being watched?

Ascepis' paranoia must finally be getting to her. He was forever jumping at shadows, seeing phantoms from the corners of his eyes. She wondered, sometimes, if he might be a little mad.

Gwyn rolled over onto her back, closed her eyes and emptied her mind as Ascepis had taught her. From the town, she could hear the ring of a blacksmith's hammer. A gull cawed. The cold wind carried the scent of fresh bread.

Perhaps Ascepis could be convinced to travel south, at least for the season. Winter was hard in the north, the roads clogged with snow, or else axle-deep in melted slush. And the trading was poor. Folk hoarded their coin, in case the spring came late – as it often did – and they were forced to supplement their winter stores. To go south would make good financial sense.

I can convince him, she thought sleepily. Her mind was empty now, that was certain. Ascepis would be proud. *I just ... need to ...*

The tar-black sky yawned above her. Black, except for the smear of the nebula, purple and mottled as a bruise. The twin moons rode low in the east: Prior, silver and pale, drawing the grey clouds up around it, and Sadira, the dwarf moon, glaring down like a red eye. A light rain had fallen, and the ground was slick and muddy.

She kept running, breath coming in sharp gasps. The stone ramp ahead of her crept steadily higher, winding away into the darkness. There was a pain, white-hot, like a spear, under her ribs.

Up close, hundreds of windows pitted the sheer cliff like pocks on a leper's face. In one window, high up the mountainside, a single lamp burned.

Then the doors were ahead, with the ramp unfurling down from them, a wet, grey tongue. As she ran, the doors started to open. Red light poured from the widening gap. She skittered to a halt.

A hand on her shoulder. She spun around.

'Is it you?' he said.

The sunlight streamed onto her face, grey and steady. Gwyn stirred sluggishly and opened her eyes. It took her a moment to remember where she was. She sat up, blinking, and an engraved copper disc fell from her fingers to land with a *ping* on the roof.

She snatched it up at once and stuffed it back into her pocket, glancing around. Nobody was near. Nobody had seen. She took a few steadying breaths, waiting for her heart to slow.

I must have taken it out in my sleep. Careless. If Ascepis had come to check on her ...

Gwyn cursed silently and rubbed her eyes, trying to banish the fog from her head. From the light, it was nearing midday already. A bank of cloud had rolled in from the sea, and the air was chill as a knife-blade.

A face came into her mind, and she froze. The face of a dead man, swollen tongue lolling from his mouth, maggots moving under his skin.

Is it you?

Gwyn shuddered. She had dreamed of the man

before. Different faces, but the same man. Sometimes he was fair and smiling, green-eyed, with a sweep of gold hair. Other times ...

Ascepis knew how to interpret dreams. Folk were superstitious in the High Country, and reading omens and portents was a cornerstone of his business. No doubt he would have some piece of 'wisdom' to share. *A dead man speaking to you in your dream? That's a sure sign of congestion in the liver. Take a half spoon of thistleberry and call on me tomorrow.*

But although the dream had kept coming for weeks now, Gwyn had stayed silent. Even in the light of day, remembering made her skin crawl. Lately, she had found herself lying awake at night, afraid to sleep, long after Ascepis was gurgling in his rack. No wonder she'd nodded off before. She was exhausted.

The air was unusually still, and it took her a moment to realise she couldn't hear Ascepis snoring. Snatching the book, she leaped down onto the grass, just as the front door of the wagon swung open. Ascepis' head appeared, his remaining hair dishevelled, as though he'd just woken up too. When he caught sight of her, his face hardened.

'What are you doing out here?'

'Just checking on Pepper,' she said, nodding towards the horse that clipped the grass a few yards away. 'I heard her snorting. I thought she might have seen a badger and gotten spooked.'

Ascepis gave her a jaundiced look. Gwyn didn't

think he was fooled for one minute. 'No badgers this far north. Come inside. The customers will be arriving soon.'

'You know,' Gwyn said, stepping past him, 'if you let me help with the customers, I could be useful for once.' Her tone was light, though she was only half jesting. True, she hadn't quite mastered Ascepis' smooth salesman patter, but she had never embarrassed herself, or him. Surely she was old enough for some responsibility? At seventeen she was past her majority, almost a woman grown.

'You are useful,' he said, as he began pawing through the cupboards. 'But if you want to be very useful, you can cut up this cow-lily while I set up the stall outside.'

CHAPTER 2

THE HOUSE OF DEATH

Impatient, Gwyn twitched the curtain aside. The shadows had grown long now, but Ascepis still stood outside, deep in conversation with an earnest-looking young farmwife. He was smiling at her, which meant he must be trying to sell something.

She was the last customer of the day, not that there had been many to begin with. Gwyn doubted Ascepis had sold more than a few draughts of cough syrup. Most of the 'customers' were just busybodies, wanting to know if the Magnificent Ascepis Melm was truly a wizard, and could he call down thunder like the wizards in the stories?

Well, that was the trouble with these outlying villages. Half the villagers couldn't read, and the rest just let their eyes skim over the words painted on the side of the wagon. *No magic – don't ask.* As if a

Syndicate wizard would be trudging around in a second-hand tinker's wagon, two thousand miles from the Clockwork City, pulling people's rotten teeth. At least in the larger towns people understood the difference between a wizard and a common hedge-doctor. They didn't gawp at you as though you might murder them – though Gwyn had noticed they didn't bring their children around, either.

She sighed and pulled back the curtain. In a good year, Vønnerlund was far too small to warrant visiting. But this hadn't been a good year.

The door swung open, and Ascepis poked his head inside. Gwyn thought his smile had become rather fixed. Perhaps that farmwife wasn't as wide-eyed as she looked.

'Gwyn. I need to go down to the village. This ... customer wants to be certain the caterpillar repellent works on her pumpkins before she buys any.' Ascepis sounded like he was chewing glass. 'I'll be ten minutes –' He glanced over his shoulder out the door, and his expression hardened further – 'maybe more. Pack up the shop for me and bring everything inside. And don't go wandering off.'

Gwyn rolled her eyes, but he was already gone. She watched him retreating down the main road, gesturing to the farmwife, no doubt extolling the virtues of his one-of-a-kind caterpillar repellent.

Actually, Gwyn thought, as she started moving the displays from the stall back into the wagon, *it's* my *one-of-a-kind caterpillar repellent.* Adding the crushed eikelbloom had been her idea. The potion worked spectacularly now, though with the unfortunate side effect of filling the air with the tang of rotten eggs.

'Are you the wizard?' came a voice.

Gwyn, standing on the top step of the wagon as she folded the tablecloth, gave a start. She turned, heart hammering in her chest.

She noticed their size first. Gwyn was tall, like most northerners, but these two over-topped her by several heads. The tallest one had an unfortunate spotty complexion, and a glowering look that made Gwyn think he might be chancy to cross.

'I'm afraid the Magnificent Ascepis Melm is not in at the moment,' she said, swallowing. 'He's expected back soon.'

'Who are you, then?'

'I'm his assistant.' Gwyn gave a short bow. She kept her eye on the smaller one. He had a more pleasant face than his friend, round and ruddy-cheeked, though there was something about his eyes she didn't like.

The tall one jerked his head towards the side of the wagon. 'Says there that the wizard can do future-telling.'

'Master Melm is an expert at the subtle art of card-reading,' Gwyn said. 'Perhaps if you return in an hour or so, he will be available to do a reading for you.' She had already moved the stools back inside, but the table was still set up, and Ascepis would be furious if she let a potential customer slip away.

The man scowled. It made him appear older than his nineteen or twenty years. 'Don't have an hour. If you're his assistant, you must be able to do it too.'

'I'm not ...' Gwyn began – then stopped and looked more closely. She had taken them for farm boys at first, but they were dressed too finely. Their clothes were wool, yes, but well cut and richly dyed. Fur lined their coat collars. Snow fox, unless she missed her guess. Not nobles, perhaps, but well-to-do merchants' sons, at the least.

The shorter seemed to sense her regard. He smiled and reached into his pocket, tossing something into the air. She caught a flash of bronze and snatched the coin in mid-air.

'Another shill when you're finished,' he said, speaking for the first time. His voice was smooth and surprisingly high-pitched.

Gwyn hesitated. She did know how to read the fate deck. No thanks to Ascepis, of course. He never let her so much as hold the cards, not even to pack them away. 'Knowing the future can be a great hardship,' he would say, scowling. 'You're far too young to shoulder that kind of burden.'

That was the wrong thing to tell her. The fact that it was forbidden knowledge only made Gwyn want it more.

Still, Ascepis couldn't help teaching her a few

things, if only by accident. Peeking through the window, she had seen him do more readings than she could count, and she remembered everything she saw. Besides, these two didn't look sophisticated enough to notice any mistakes.

Gwyn looked up, shading her eyes against the sun. Ascepis would be back soon, and if he caught her ...

Well, he couldn't kill her in front of witnesses. And perhaps when he saw for himself how capable she was, he would finally start trusting her.

In the stories, good things never came to those who sat around waiting for them. Sometimes you had to take charge of your own destiny.

She bowed again, gesturing towards the folding table under the awning. 'Please. I'll bring you some chairs. Make yourselves comfortable.'

Seated at the table in the wagon's shadow, the boys looked awkward and oversized, maybe even nervous. Gwyn kept up a steady patter while she fetched the deck from inside and spread the tablecloth, hoping to put them at ease. But they just looked at her, giving curt, bitten-off answers, and her words trailed into silence.

The deck was heavier than Gwyn imagined. The cards felt strange in her hands, more like wood than paper. She took her seat and fanned the twenty-five cards out across the table, face down. Overhead, a slice of cold wind made the striped awning snap and shiver.

'Have you ever had a reading done?' she asked, playing for time. Ascepis usually started with a little speech about parting the mystic veil, but she couldn't remember how it went.

'Folk in the High Country don't hold much with that sort of thing,' said the tall one. His voice held a touch of disapproval. The other said nothing, but his eyes followed Gwyn's hands as they might a venomous snake.

Then why come? Gwyn thought sourly, but she kept her mouth shut and fixed a smile to her face.

She had guessed rightly about these two. They came from money, at least by village standards. They had told her their names were Horik and Davald, and they were apprentices to a well-off silversmith down in Til Iver, only in Vønnerlund for the summer solstice celebrations, five days from now. Their father, Jonas, owned the inn and sat on the village council, so they were used to lording it over others; used to getting their own way. That type usually had more coin than sense.

'The art is an ancient one,' Gwyn said, once she was ready to begin. Part of Ascepis' speech had suddenly come back to her. She selected the first card at random, then cleared her throat and tried to imitate Ascepis' plummy, oracular tones. 'Originating in the farthest southern reaches, some say, where the ancients built great step-temples to Umbrael, and the air is scented with jasmine. As to the truth of that, well, who can say.'

She turned the card and laid it down.

'Pestilence. The pawn of the House of Death.'

Horik scowled. 'You mean to say there's a sickness coming?'

Gwyn suppressed the urge to roll her eyes. Town folk. So literal. A few years back, she had seen a fur trader scared half out of his wits when Ascepis had drawn the Dragon. He had ducked and covered his head as though expecting the beast to fly down out of the clear sky and burn him to ash on the spot.

'No. The first card represents the present. Things that concern you now. And while the Pestilence card can represent an actual disease, what it really means is a time of trials. A difficult card, but it's important to remember that trials can also mean opportunities.'

The second man – Davald – smiled slightly. Gwyn took a deep breath before selecting the next card.

'This card represents the past. The figure you see here is the Executioner – the priest card of the House of Blades. He represents solitude. In this position, his appearance often points to a lonely childhood, or isolation following some type of tragedy.'

No response from either of the men.

'Now, the future,' Gwyn said. Turning the next card, she groaned inwardly. *Try explaining this one.*

'This card is the Gallows, the noble card of the House of Death. But, again, not a card to be taken literally. Its appearance heralds a sudden upheaval of some kind. This can be a very good omen, especially for those who find themselves stuck in a routine.'

She ventured a small smile. The men exchanged a quick glance, but Gwyn could read nothing behind it. She continued.

'The fourth card serves as a warning for the future.' She turned it face-up. 'Ah ... the Crone. Priest card of the House of Snakes. She represents deception. Her appearance is a call to beware of false friends and tricksters.'

'Very wise,' the shorter one muttered. Gwyn blinked, but he said nothing else, and she turned the final card, already feeling the second copper shill in her pocket.

'Our final card, with his tools laid out before him, is the king card of the House of Death – the Necromancer. While he may look an imposing figure, he represents independence. The fifth card signifies the potential in your future – the best possible outcome of the decisions you'll make.'

Gwyn sat back, quite pleased with herself. Ascepis couldn't have done it any better. Bad luck, though, to draw so many Death cards. Never mind how you explained it, most people just didn't appreciate all those hooded figures and grinning skulls staring up from their cards.

'I don't like all this talk of death and disease,' said Horik, echoing her thoughts. 'Gallows. Executioners. It seems a grim business to me.'

'And necromancers,' the other said, still smiling. 'Not a nice thing to mention, really. Not polite.'

Gwyn's mind flashed instantly to Ascepis, to the face he used for calming over-excited customers. It was similar to his salesman's face, and she hoped she was doing a fair impression of it now.

'I hope I haven't caused any offence.' She spread her hands, a placating gesture. They used to burn witches here in Nederlund; she'd just remembered that. 'The cards show what they show, after all, and none of these should cause you alarm.'

'I wouldn't say we're alarmed.' Horik cracked his neck loudly, making Gwyn jump. 'Might be we think all this card business is rubbish. Might be that folks like you just come around peaceful villages to stir up trouble.'

She could almost feel the copper piece slipping out of her hand. *I should have just made up the reading.* 'Not at all. The Magnificent —'

She broke off as the men stood, almost upsetting the table. Gwyn pushed her chair back, but before she could rise, Horik had seized the front of her shirt and yanked her forward, scattering the cards. A moment later she was on the ground, the taste of blood in her mouth.

Why am I —?

His kick caught her in the kidney and sent her sprawling. All the air rushed out of her lungs. Pain spread up her ribs, turning the world dark at the edges. Dazed, she pushed herself up onto her knees.

'I don't —'

A second kick. She heard something snap. Spots appeared in front of her eyes, red, green, blue, and Gwyn screamed. She tried to pull herself up, tried to crawl. For an instant, she thought she might get away, but the clumps of grass broke off in her hands.

Stop! Another blow sent her sprawling onto her back. She screamed. Or was it just in her head? The tiny whimpering sounds wriggling out of her throat seemed to be all she could manage. She brought her arms up to shield her face, and a boot caught her in the jaw. Her head whipsawed back and forth. She felt something tear. They were shouting, the men, but Gwyn couldn't make out words over the roaring in her ears. Her chest hitched uselessly. Impossible to catch a full breath. She choked on blood, and reached into the pocket of her sarafan, fingers closing around the copper disc.

'I wish —' Gwyn croaked.

A rough hand tangled in her hair, pulling her to her knees. She had been thrashing futilely to either side; now she went limp. Dimly she saw a man's face – the short one, Davald, she thought – an inch from her own. His eyes were violent blue, but everything else was soaked red. Her face felt wet.

'Witches,' he spat, 'are not welcome in the north. You hear?'

Gwyn tried to speak, but her mouth wouldn't form words. The crackling in her head sounded like someone scrunching paper. She coughed, spraying the man's face with blood.

The next kick took her square in the middle. He must have released her hair, or torn it out, because suddenly the world was tilting sideways.

Her head struck the ground, and all the light snuffed out.

She woke in darkness.

Her skull seemed stuffed with wool. A dull pain throbbed in her ribs, a sharper one in her nose. Both felt a long way away. She had the distinct feeling that she had been running. Running at night, her feet pounding ...

But no. That was foolish. She was in the wagon. Gwyn recognised the hardness of the bunk beneath her, the drawn curtain on the window letting in just a crack of light at the bottom. She tried to sit up, but her neck seemed made of treacle.

'— more than she can tolerate safely,' a woman was saying. Her voice was dry as old leaves and creaky with age. She spoke so quietly Gwyn could hardly make her out.

She tried to turn her head – *a stranger, in the*

wagon? – but pain lanced through her skull, making her stomach heave. Cold gripped her to the bones, though a slick of sweat covered her skin.

'It can't be helped,' someone replied. Gwyn knew that voice, at least. Ascepis. He sounded tired. She saw him clearly in her mind, pinching the bridge of his nose, a heavy crease between his brows. 'She's strong enough. Do as you need.'

The woman said nothing for a moment. When she spoke again, her voice was hesitant. 'She has no brand. Strange. I'd give a pretty to learn how you managed it.'

'I don't recall paying you to ask questions.' Ascepis sounded as cold as Gwyn had ever heard him.

The woman sniffed. If his tone alarmed her, she gave no sign. 'I don't recall you paying me enough. Five shills will buy you an ordinary healing. For this, well ... nine for the healing. Four for the risk. And a scupper to keep quiet about it.'

'Two scuppers and three? You must be mad.'

'I must be,' said the woman. There was a rustling sound. 'Well, I'm sorry to have taken up your time. You'll be wanting another whitehood, no doubt, if you care to see that girl walk again. If you can find one. Best of luck with that. I'll —'

'Wait.' Ascepis spoke quickly. If it wasn't desperation that strained his voice, it was something close. 'Wait. Alright. Two scuppers and three. If you can do this, Mistress Erna, then I'll consider it well worth the price.'

'Of course I can,' the woman said briskly. 'I healed Mancer Rainer, didn't I, when he took that fall from his horse? No, but you wouldn't remember. You were just a boy then, and your kind never did bother to tell one whitehood from another. Oh, calm yourself. I said the scupper was for my silence, didn't I? I'll keep your secret. And as for her, well, I don't know how you did it, and now that I come to it, I don't much care. I've been around long enough to realise when to keep my nose clean.' She seemed to weigh her next words carefully. 'You must know it won't last, don't you? They're going to come for her, eventually. Runaways never make it far. It's only a matter of time.'

'I can deal with them,' Ascepis said. His voice was like a stone sinking through clear water.

'Well. Just so as you know.' The woman clapped her hands together softly. 'Now, then. The patient.'

It took Gwyn a moment to realise the woman was talking about her. Everything was dim and muffled. She saw movement from the corner of her eye, and a cool, dry hand touched her brow.

'I suppose I don't need to tell you how hard this will be,' she said. At first, Gwyn wasn't sure if the woman was addressing her or Ascepis. She could just make him out, standing at the foot of the bunk, the curtain stamping a thin bar of light across his chest.

'You were there for Rainer. This will be worse. You'll need to hold her down.'

'I'll do it,' Ascepis said. He sounded sick.

'Very well. I hope those skinny arms are stronger than they look.'

Gwyn thought she saw his hands clamp down on her ankles, but she felt nothing. The woman's face swam in front of her, thin and swarthy and etched with lines. Her breath smelled of something sweet. Gwyn looked into her eyes, only inches from her own. Her pupils were very large, the corneas pale yellow, threaded with murky green.

And in the centre, in those deep holes, Gwyn swore she saw something move.

A shapeless horror filled her, more powerful than anything she had felt before. Her heartbeat slammed in her ears. She opened her mouth, perhaps to scream, but a moment later the world was obliterated in an explosion of light and pain.

CHAPTER 3

RADERSTRUP

A writer in the Second Era had called Nederlund the Dreaming North. Sparsely populated, the sleepy jarldom was all rolling wheat plains, tiny farming villages and scattered stands of autumn-bright trees. Its dark soil and neatly ploughed and harrowed fields made it the breadbasket of the High Country.

Raderstrup lay in Nederlund's heart, at the crest of the grasslands that rolled russet and golden down to the Grindelskrim Sea. Gwyn had spent most of her life in Nederlund, but rarely more than a few nights in any place. Raderstrup was big enough to warrant a longer stay, but since Vønnerlund, Ascepis seemed more obsessed than ever with staying on the move.

Gwyn pushed that thought away quickly. She heard the dim echo of her own screams in her head; tasted blood and bile on her lips. Her ribs ached.

You don't think about Vønnerlund, she thought fiercely.

And she didn't, for the most part. Except sometimes at night when Ascepis was asleep, and the wagon was in darkness. Then it seemed she could think of nothing else. Reliving that afternoon, over and over, as if hoping it might come out differently. She slept little, and when she did sleep, she dreamed. Of the gold-haired man, of course – what else? Gwyn still felt his hand on her shoulder.

Is it you?

Ascepis pulled the wagon up just short of the town border. She heard him unhitching Pepper, and Gwyn considered going outside to help. Instead, she tugged the curtain closed and lay back on her bunk.

Two weeks had passed now. Her side was still tender if she bent the wrong way, but the bruises had mostly faded. Gwyn supposed she had the healer to thank for that. The woman had been gone by the time she woke.

The week afterwards was a blank. Foggy memories of being propped up in bed, someone pouring warm tea down her throat. The curtains drifting in the open window. Dreams, reeling into each other, one after the next. But her memories of what happened in Vønnerlund were clear as glass, etched in full colour on her mind right up until the moment she lost consciousness.

Ascepis hadn't told her the extent of her injuries,

and Gwyn wasn't sure she wanted to know. The answer was there in the way he looked at her now – sidelong, wary, as though expecting her to come apart in the first high wind. She understood without being told that the old woman had saved her life.

Remembering the healing still filled her with that hot, sick, swooping feeling. She remembered the woman's eyes, and the sudden, irrational certainty that something lurked behind them. Something wrong. The memory made Gwyn feel unclean.

In the days after she woke, after the fog lifted, Gwyn had been sure the woman was a wizard. How else to explain it? It had taken her a week to work up the courage to ask Ascepis. He had been drinking hot tea at the time, and he had spat it almost clear across the room.

'A wizard?' he choked, loosening the top button of his coat. Gwyn thumped him on the back. His eyes looked wild. 'Why would you ask that?'

'She used magic on me.'

Gwyn half expected him to deny it. But Ascepis said nothing at first, and Gwyn began to wonder if he had heard her. Afternoon light streamed in the wagon door, casting long shadows on the wall.

'White magic,' he said finally. 'It's different. Wizards can't heal. They can only destroy.' He spoke the word – *wizards* – strangely, with a mix of reverence and disgust. Gwyn had recognised the finality in his voice, and hadn't asked again.

He had been distant since then, distracted. The wagon kept rolling, the towns came and went, and Ascepis moved through it all like a sleepwalker, bustling about with an absent-minded efficiency that was horrible to watch. For his sake, Gwyn feigned an interest in her books and in the world outside the window. The attack seemed to have broken something in her – something that the healing hadn't been able to touch.

Gwyn sighed, staring up at the roof. Her fingers toyed with the copper disc, still hidden in the secret pocket of her sarafan. By some miracle, she hadn't lost it that afternoon in Vønnerlund, and Ascepis hadn't discovered it in the days and weeks that followed. Touching it no longer brought that old giddy thrill of anticipation – just a heavy, numb feeling. She felt like crying, which was pure foolishness. She had nothing to cry over.

You survived, didn't you? And without using the wish. That should have been comforting, Gwyn knew, but she found it hard to care. She had the feeling of being submerged underwater. Worse still was the sense of something in the water with her – some immense, scaled thing, glimpsed out of the corner of her eye.

The door swung open, and Ascepis stepped inside. Gwyn snatched her hand out of her pocket, but he hadn't noticed. Mud caked his turned-down boots. He moved heavily, with none of his usual briskness, brown cloak closed against the cold. The look he gave her was tight and wary. She forced a small smile.

'I was thinking I'd go down to the village,' he said. He took his hat off and hung it on the peg by the door. 'Tell folk that the Magnificent Ascepis Melm has arrived.' He hesitated and took a deep breath, seeming to steel himself. 'But I thought ... Would you like to go instead?'

That wiped the smile away. Gwyn sat up in bed, staring at him. 'Me?'

'Of course. You know what to say as well as I. I know I can trust you.' He spoke evenly, but his face had the look of sucking on something sour.

'I took your fate cards and did a reading,' Gwyn said. 'Even though you told me never to touch them.' She wasn't sure why she was arguing with him. He knew what she had done, of course. The overturned table and the cards strewn across the grass told the story of her guilt. Later, when the healer had left and Gwyn had been sleeping, Ascepis had gone outside in the dark to gather them up. He found twenty-four of them, he said. The last was gone – blown away by the wind, probably.

'I know. You did it because you have a curious mind. Just as I've taught you.' He came and sat on the edge of the bunk. For a moment Gwyn thought he was going to take her by the hand, but he seemed to think better of it. 'I know I haven't always been honest with you. For your own safety there are things

I haven't told you, things I've kept hidden. I forget sometimes that you're not a little girl anymore. It's time I started giving you more responsibility.'

Gwyn wasn't sure what to say to that, so she said nothing. His serious expression made her uncomfortable. She cleared her throat. Since Vønnerlund, she had been outside to wash herself and to make water. The rest of the time she stayed in the wagon. She spent her days there, flat on her bunk, and in the evenings she took her meal on the top step.

Strange. Even a month ago, she would have been thrilled at the chance to go into the village by herself. But now ...

Don't be such a fool. Of course you can go outside. You can go outside any time you want. You just ... haven't wanted to, that's all.

Well, she wanted to now. The sick feeling in her gut had nothing to do with it. 'Alright,' she said at last. 'I'll go.'

As she stood, relief flitted across Ascepis' face. Guilt tugged at her, tiny hooks under her skin. She grabbed her coat and hurried out the door before he could say anything else.

Outside, the mid-morning sunlight held grey and constant. She glanced around as she followed the muddy road into the town, her heart beating a little faster than the exercise could account for. A damp, insistent wind lifted her hair, then skittered away. On the outskirts, herds of cattle scattered beneath the glowering sky. Miles to the south, she could just make out the tip of the Pyramid, daggering down through the cloud cover. That was unsettling, somehow. It rarely drifted this far north, even during the height of summer.

As in many of the bigger villages in Nederlund, the Gold Road ran straight through the centre of town. Now it was bustling, and in the press of bodies Gwyn felt a little safer, a little less exposed. Raderstrup was a stopover for merchants' wagons on their way to Til Iver, carrying trade to and from Edge, through the Nørregård Pass. The roads were wide, to let the wagons pass freely, and deeply rutted by wheels. She dodged stray chickens, children chasing a hoop, women with baskets on their way from the market. Aside from a bright-eyed hawk, perched on the edge of the bakehouse's thatched roof, nobody spared her a glance. In the smaller hamlets, people would look at her with open curiosity, as though unused to seeing strangers. Here, she was safely anonymous.

In the market square, a rail-thin priest, hands lifted to the sky, was giving a sermon to an indifferent crowd. Ascepis had little patience for gods and goddesses, and scorned the prayer books the street priests sometimes tried to press into their hands whenever they caught a glimpse of Gwyn's face at the wagon's window. *'Children need the guidance of Molech'* – it was usually Molech, this far north – *'lest they fall into sin.'* To which Ascepis would reply that *his* was the only guidance his apprentice needed, and only a simpleton would take lessons on sin from a bunch of gods-touched fools.

But Ascepis wasn't here now. Maybe that was why Gwyn stopped a moment, lingering at the back of the crowd, and listened.

'... Beheret the Mother, Beheret the Blessed, Beheret who shelters all of Caerwyn beneath her loving palm. To her do we give praise. She who stood astride the world at the moment of creation, who took up the burning sword of salvation and turned it upon the demons of the void. With her three children did she drive that darkness back, and with chains of silver did she bind the three demons of chaos and seal them away for all time. It is our faith that holds those chains fast, good people of Raderstrup! Our faith in Beheret, in our Holy and Blessed Mother, that —'

Gwyn turned away, shaking her head, and the priest's words faded. Maybe Ascepis was right. What use were gods and demons when the winter frost choked your crops, or your cows froze to death in their barns? At least the Molech priests sold prayer kites. Tether one to your fence on the storm god's feast days, and he would shelter your home from his wrath – or so the priests claimed.

Inns were the best place to spread gossip, and the

biggest one in Raderstrup was easy to find. It stood three floors high with white-washed walls, the only building in sight with a tiled roof. Above the door, a wooden sign painted with a plate and a bowl creaked in the wind.

The innkeeper's wife was an apple-cheeked woman with flyaway hair. Her apron was patched, but clean. 'Dorthe Lind,' she said to Gwyn, holding out a damp hand. 'My Frode runs The Plate-and-Bowl, or likes to think he does. He's upstairs, I'm sorry to say. A sore tooth that's been troubling him something fierce, and this morning he woke with a nasty cough – though he does complain.'

Before Gwyn could get a word in, Dorthe had started on about her Frode's cough in uncomfortable detail, about his mucus production and what herbs she was using to loosen his chest. When Gwyn finally mentioned her reason for coming, Dorthe shifted topics with hardly a pause.

'Goodness me! Master Melm, back in town after all this time. We were beginning to think he'd gone south to escape the cold! 'Tis hard on old bones, you know.' Dorthe laughed – a little shrilly, Gwyn thought. 'Well! Well ...' Her hands were scrunching the front of her apron without her seeming to notice. 'Truly, it will be a pleasure to see him again – Master Melm is well liked around these parts ... Helped my sister Bruna, he did, when she was first with child – but ...'

'Is something wrong, Mistress Lind?'

Dorthe hesitated. Her eyes darted around the inn, and she licked her lips, leaning closer. 'Nothing wrong, young mistress. Only ... well, I'm embarrassed to say it, being as how it's been such a time since he last came.' The woman swallowed. 'It's just, well, if you'll forgive me, Master Melm picked an unfortunate time to call into Raderstrup. We've a ... a visitor, at present. One that might not be best pleased to know a hedge-wizard's in town.'

Gwyn followed her gaze. She was looking at the corner of the inn – or rather, at the man sitting there, sipping on a cup of wine and staring into nothing.

Gwyn had noticed him when she came in, but now she looked more closely. A tall man of middle years, with dark olive skin and chestnut hair – not a northman. He wore an odd, divided coat, belted at the waist, with snug trousers underneath and a heavy chain of silver discs strung across his chest. The tunic did nothing to hide his well-defined muscles, and even in profile she could make out a broad jaw and dimpled chin. He looked rugged and capable, a man accustomed to sleeping nights under hedges and fighting off highwaymen. For all that, his clothes appeared spotlessly clean.

Gwyn turned back to the innkeeper's wife, who was watching the man as she might a dangerous animal. She kept trying to smooth her hair, without effect.

'Who is he?' Gwyn asked quietly. Dorthe didn't look at her, just kept staring at the man, chewing on her bottom lip. 'Mistress Lind?'

'What? Oh!' She turned back to Gwyn. 'Well, that's Mancer Dorin. He arrived two days ago. From the Clockwork City.'

Gwyn sucked in her breath as everything clicked into place. The Clockwork City! Gods below, but she knew what that meant, sure enough. She needed to tell Ascepis.

But it was too late. The man had seen her. In fact, although he hadn't so much as glanced at her, Gwyn sensed he'd seen her as soon as she walked through the inn's door. Before she could flee, he rose in a swift, fluid motion, placed his cup on the table, and crossed the common room towards her. Gwyn gaped, her feet rooted to the spot. Her hands went automatically to the small lump in the pocket of her sarafan. Could he sense it? No, surely not.

'Blessings of Aeshma,' he said. His accent was familiar to her ears: precise and clipped, the same as Ascepis. The same as her, for that matter. 'It is a pleasure to meet you. I am Dorin. Please forgive the intrusion. I overheard you speaking with Mistress Lind and felt compelled to introduce myself. This Ascepis Melm sounds a fascinating fellow.'

Gwyn's sense of danger warred with her curiosity. It was hard not to stare. He looked so ... ordinary. Nothing in those beetle-brown eyes spoke of fire and thunder. No lightning crackled at his fingertips. No unseen, eldritch wind stirred the hem of his cloak. He looked like any other minor noble or local merchant.

Any rich local merchant, she amended. Unless she missed her guess, that neck chain was real silver.

'Pleased to meet you, er, Master Dorin.' He hadn't introduced himself as *Mancer* Dorin – that was the proper way to address a wizard, wasn't it? – so Gwyn supposed it was safer to leave out the title. 'Ascepis the Magnificent and I arrived in Raderstrup this morning. I assure you, you'll find no better herbalist or augurer this side of the Iron River.' She kept her tone light, putting a subtle emphasis on *herbalist* and *augurer*. Those were safe things; nothing to do with wizardry. Everyone knew what happened to folk who played at being true wizards.

'You have an interesting corner of the world,' the wizard said. 'Tales of the bitter snows and winds were not exaggerated.'

Gwyn relaxed slightly. A Syndicate wizard wouldn't be discussing the weather with someone he meant to arrest as a heretic.

Would he?

'The Magnificent Ascepis is a renowned predictor of the weather,' she said. 'If you're wanting to know when the snows will be coming, he's the man to ask.' That would be for the best. Let the wizard come; let him see they were doing nothing improper.

'And this Magnificent Ascepis – does he know aught of dreams?'

The mention of dreams made her flash back to the previous night, and her neck prickled with gooseflesh. *Is it you?*

She pushed the thought away. 'He does. Dream interpretation is a favourite pastime in the High Country. Ascepis Melm is very well trained in the art.'

The man nodded thoughtfully. 'Then perhaps that is something to ask him, too. A dream has been troubling me these past nights.' His eyes watched her closely, and for a moment they seemed unnaturally bright. Did he have a touch of fever? 'Far in the south is a place called Harrowing, and there lies a mountain range, quite black, with parts of it shiny like glass. In my dream I am there. A door stands in the mountain, washed in red light, and everywhere else dark and silent.'

Gwyn schooled her face to stillness, though every hair seemed to be standing on edge.

Her dream. He was describing her dream.

A coincidence, she told herself, but she could hardly breathe for the premonition of danger than rushed over her. She wasn't sure if she wanted to faint or sick up.

'Harrowing?' she heard herself say. 'What place is that?'

'Once it was the stronghold of the sorceress

Ailbhe Ahriddin, though then it was called by a different name. Nobody has been there for hundreds of years. It lies in Ashsalem, beyond the Blighted Rim.'

They locked eyes for a long moment, and a smile appeared over the wizard's face. He was still watching her intently. Those eyes made it feel like he was trying to bore a hole right through her with his gaze. An icicle was crawling its way down her spine. All of a sudden, Gwyn wanted to be as far from Mancer Dorin as possible.

'Well, I'll be certain to tell Ascepis that you'll be calling, Master Dorin.' Her voice came out high and piping, a little girl's voice. She cleared her throat and took a step back, then another.

The wizard bowed again. 'Certainly. I won't keep you. 'Til next we meet.'

Heart hammering, she hurried out of the inn, still feeling the wizard's eyes stabbing into her back.

CHAPTER 4

THE ROAD

Outside of town, Gwyn found Ascepis in their wagon, grinding down a cluster of braighbur seeds with a pestle. He barely glanced up as she entered.

'More than enough to go around when —' He cut off short when he saw her face. 'What happened, Gwyn? Did someone see you?' His hand shot out and gripped her arm hard, fingers sinking into the flesh.

'What? No. I don't know. Nothing happened, really. But there was a wizard ...' She recounted the story quickly, and watched as Ascepis' face drained of colour. That frightened her all over again, far more than the wizard himself had done.

'You're sure he was a wizard?'

'The innkeeper's wife said so. A Syndicate wizard. And ...' She swallowed hard, remembering the way his eyes seemed to scorch her. '... and I believe her.'

Ascepis put down the pestle and, for a long moment, just stared at his hands on the table. His green-and-gold vermarine ring winked in the light streaming through the doorway. Then, turning on his heel, he pushed past her and out the door, almost knocking Gwyn into the spice rack. He didn't return, and a moment later Gwyn stuck her head out the door, only to find him hitching Pepper to the wagon.

'We're leaving?'

'Yes,' he said shortly. 'Get back inside.'

'But you said that —'

'I don't care what I said! Get inside and stay there!'

Gwyn went over to Ascepis' bunk along the front wall, sat, then stood again and started to pace.

Who was that man? How could he possibly know what I was dreaming? And why has it got Ascepis in such a panic?

There were no answers. She was sure the man had been lying when he talked about having the same dream. He was testing her – gauging her reaction. But why? What would that prove? Could he suspect Ascepis, after all, of pretending to be a wizard? True, villagers sometimes mistook him for a real wizard, but that was their own ignorance. Ascepis was always so careful, right down to the writing on the side of the wagon. The hedge-wizard the Syndicate arrested in Surudar a few years back was using smoke and flash-bombs in his shows and telling people it was magic.

The wagon started to sway. The pots and saucepans hanging along the wall clanged together, and the pestle rolled across the table and onto the floor with a heavy *thunk*. She heard Ascepis up in the driver's seat, cursing. They were on the move.

Gwyn clambered onto Ascepis' bunk and slid open the little window that looked out to the front of the wagon. 'Where are we going?' she asked, and Ascepis jumped.

'Don't sneak up on me, girl. I'm an old man.' But he didn't answer the question.

'Ascepis?' The scenery slid by: treetops, barn roofs, sky. They were leaving the way they came, along the south road.

'Ascepis!' she prompted again. 'What's this about? Why are we leaving? Do you know that man?'

She thought he was going to ignore her. But after a moment, he spoke, his eyes fixed on the road ahead.

'I don't know him. But he knows us. I knew this would happen. It was only a matter of time.'

The sun was well past its peak by the time the roofs of Raderstrup disappeared, swallowed up by the curve of the land. The wide plains opened up around them – an endless blanket of russet and gold, running rampant with poppies. As the wagon trundled on, neat fields gave way to wilderness, where clusters of tundra-wort crept up between the rocks, turning their star-shaped faces towards the sky. The clouds still hung low and heavy with the promise of rain.

If Gwyn expected a break for the midday meal, she was disappointed. Ascepis kept pushing onward, even when the clouds broke open and sheets of cold, grey rain started to fall. The light faded, and fields and forest both disappeared behind a curtain of fog. It was almost silent, except for the *rat-a-tat* of water on the roof, and far away to the north, the boom of thunder. When the wind picked up, it blew the rain into the caravan door, forcing Gwyn back inside.

She remembered the last time she'd seen a wizard – the only time, until today. It had been nine years ago, in a flyspeck town called Vonsted, not far from here. Actually, she hadn't really *seen* the wizard – or wizards; there had been seven of them – so much as glimpsed them from a distance, wending through the main street with their manservants and packhorses. And she hadn't known they were wizards – not until later, when Ascepis had explained why they'd hitched up and fled town on the spot. She'd wanted to turn around and go back, then, but Ascepis wouldn't hear of it.

Gwyn hadn't seen them take the boy, but by the time the wagon reached the next town, the story had already spread. The wizards had ridden straight to the boy's house, the townsfolk said, without even stopping to ask for directions. Had knocked on the door three times – that was one version; another said they'd blasted it down with wizards' fire – and asked to speak to the goodman. And when he'd come to the door, they had informed him, quite calmly, that his youngest son, no more than eight winters old, was to be taken to the Clockwork City and inducted into the Syndicate.

It was the only Seeking that Gwyn had ever seen, though sometimes they passed through towns where the wizards had already been; saw the hollow-eyed parents, the jumpy, ill-at-ease neighbours. There were times, too, when Gwyn had wished the wizards would come for her. But her tenth birthday had come and gone without incident, and by then she'd learned to be properly fearful of magic, and was grateful to have been spared.

Still, a sensible caution of wizards didn't explain Ascepis' sudden strange behaviour. She thought he'd moved on from that particular fear after she'd turned ten and become too old for Seeking. Only a few years ago, the mere rumour of wizards heading north into Nederlund was enough to make him turn the wagon down the nearest overgrown rabbit trail; to have them hiding out in the woods, eating boiled roots and catching rainwater in a bucket, until word came that it was safe again. He was better now, more reasonable ... or so she'd thought.

Gwyn threw herself flat across her bunk, scowling. *He is better. It's just ... well, he doesn't like it when I talk to strangers, and a wizard is doubly strange. That's all it is.*

She kept telling herself that until she drifted off into an uneasy sleep.

The wagon had stopped.

Gwyn sat up, blinking in the dark. The rain had eased, and outside was still and quiet. No light filtered in under the door. Had they stopped for the night?

The door banged open, and Gwyn jumped, smacking her head on the roof. Ascepis stood silhouetted on the top step, a half-shuttered lamp gripped in his fist. His boots tracked splotches of mud as he stumbled inside, but for once, he didn't seem to notice.

'Gwyn. Are you awake?'

'Of course,' she said, swinging her legs over the side of the bunk. 'What's going on?'

'Grab your coat. Put on your boots.'

A million questions sprang into her mouth, but she let Ascepis bundle her outside.

'Ascepis, what's —?'

'Shh,' he said, his eyes darting between the outlines of dark trees. The moons had not yet risen, and only dim lamplight shone on the wet leaves.

'Ascepis ...?' she repeated, quieter now. 'Tell me —'

A flash of movement in the trees. She cut off, hand going straight to the pocket of her sarafan, to the copper disc that still lay there. Beside her, Ascepis stiffened –

Then relaxed, letting out an unsteady breath. Gwyn squinted into the tree line, following his gaze.

A hawk. It sat on a low branch, head tilted towards them, citrine eyes flashing in the lamplight. Watching.

Gwyn swallowed and turned back to Ascepis. But he wasn't looking at her. His gaze was still focused on the hawk, and the expression on his face was mingled relief and anxiety.

'Did you see him?' Ascepis asked.

Gwyn opened her mouth – but he wasn't addressing her. He was talking to ... *the hawk?*

She turned, confused. And jerked back so suddenly that her feet, slipping in the mud, almost went from under her. She had to grab the back of Ascepis' coat to stop herself sprawling on her backside.

Because the hawk was gone. And in its place, perched on the tree branch with one leg dangling over the side, was a man.

He was young. A few years older than Gwyn, perhaps, and well built. His hair was a tawny brown, edging towards blond. But it was the tattoo that drew the eye, black and jagged, cutting the left side of his sun-browned face into uneven plains. Some

Asgeraders bore tattoos, but this ... She had never seen one like it before.

'He's ten minutes away and riding like there's a pack o' warglings on his tail,' the stranger was saying as he slipped down from the branch. There was no fear in his movements, but his voice was tight, the accent so thick it was hard to understand him. Not an Asgerader accent. Not any accent Gwyn recognised.

And Ascepis ... Her fist still gripped the back of his coat, and even through the thick wool, she could feel him shaking.

'There's more,' the stranger said, stepping into the circle of lamplight. Up close, his eyes were a honey-brown that was close to gold, with a ring of darker brown around the outside. A hawk's eyes. 'Two men have taken rooms at the Blessing and Club, in Hersted. No Syndicate robes on these ones, but it's plain enough who they are. And ... there are drakes, Melm.'

Ascepis jolted as though stuck with a hot poker. 'You saw them?'

'I dinna see anything, but I heard them. At least two.'

'How far?'

'Maybe ten miles west of here.'

Gwyn finally found her voice. 'What's going on? Who are you?' He wasn't a stranger to Ascepis, that much was clear. But ... Ascepis didn't *know* anybody;

not in that way. He had some regular customers, villagers and shopkeepers he would speak to each year when the wagon rolled around. But certainly no one like this man.

Both men looked at her, and Gwyn had to stamp down the impulse to retreat into the wagon. The reflex was that far ingrained. A stranger was *looking* at her. Seeing her!

'Gwyn,' Ascepis said, and his voice had the sound of barely held panic. That alone made her own heart gallop into her throat. 'You need to listen to me. Listen very carefully. This is Lucian. He's a friend. I need you to go with him. Can you do that?'

She shook her head, more confusion than denial. 'Go where? Ascepis, tell me what this is about —'

'There's no time,' he said. 'Run inside. Grab clothes, and ... just clothes. Hurry!'

The last was punctuated with a sharp *clap* of his hands, and Gwyn jolted into action, almost tripping over her feet in her haste to get inside. She blundered around in the dark, bumping into cupboards, stuffing clothes into her bag at random. That man ... He had turned into a *hawk.* Or was it a hawk that had turned into a man? She felt that, between one moment and the next, she had been set adrift in some fairy-tale world, where all the stories were somehow true.

Ascepis and the stranger were still talking when she stumbled back outside.

'... to Idris, he'll know how to —' Ascepis broke off

when he saw her, pulling her down the steps and shoving her towards the stranger.

'Ascepis ...' Gwyn began, but he silenced her with a furious shake of his head. The whites of his eyes were huge in the lamplight.

'Lucian will keep you safe,' he said. 'You can trust him. I'll catch up with you when I can. But you must —'

Somewhere deep in the woods, a long, ululating howl split the air.

Both men froze, lifting their heads. Ascepis' fingers tightened on her arm.

'Go now,' he said. 'Go, Gwyn!'

The stranger was hauling her towards the trees, and Gwyn didn't try to stop him. The habit of obedience was too entrenched. She turned in time to see the wagon and the lamp swallowed up by the dark.

Then they were in the woods, Gwyn tripping over roots and dead branches, over her own feet; the stranger light-footed and swift, a shadow glimpsed between shafts of pale starlight.

They had gone less than twenty feet before the stranger grabbed her, pulling her to the damp, muddy ground, his hand clapped over her mouth to silence her protests. But she fell silent when she heard ... Were those voices?

She held her breath. Yes. She recognised Ascepis' voice, low and insistent. And another voice, male, familiar.

'... wasted my time,' the other voice was saying. 'Better you had come to us and given the girl up willingly. The Great Lady might even have spared your life.'

In an instant, she recognised the voice. It was Mancer Dorin.

'Your Lady isn't known for her mercy,' Ascepis replied. 'Even so, I wouldn't give her up.'

'She isn't yours to give. You stole her, and you were lucky to keep her hidden this long. No more.'

'I wasn't lucky,' Ascepis said, calm and level. 'I was careful.'

'Not careful enough. Bring her out, Melm. Don't make this harder than it has to be.'

'I think not. You'll never lay so much as a finger on her – you, or your Lady.'

'And what will you do to stop me, old man? You have no power left. Your magic has been snuffed out, and your wits are wandering if you think to stop me.'

Gwyn sucked in a breath. *Magic? What magic?* She felt unmoored from reality. Everything was happening too fast. Maybe this was another dream. She almost expected to feel the fair-haired man's cold hand on her shoulder.

Is it you?

A sudden shout from the direction of the road, and the sound of fists striking flesh. Then a sharp, sizzling *snap* that made the hairs stand up on Gwyn's head. She gaped, but already the stranger – Lucian – was pulling her to her feet, dragging her deeper into the woods. Half sobbing, she followed him. Her fingers scrabbled bonelessly for the copper disc in her pocket. She could feel it, but it was caught under a fold of fabric, and her hands were shaking too hard to get a grip on it.

'Hurry,' Lucian urged, grabbing her elbow to steady her – the first word he had spoken to her. From behind, she could still hear muffled shouts. Then, after a long silence ... a *crack* that seemed to echo through the trees.

Lucian stiffened, hesitating for a moment. She could just make out his face, and for the first time saw fear flit across it.

Then it was gone, and he was urging her onward, deeper into the trees, into the darkness.

CHAPTER 5

LIGHT AND SHADOW

Gwyn woke screaming.

He was out there, seeking her. Green, laughing eyes; his touch on her shoulder. She thrashed wildly, but something held her down. Cool, unseen fingertips moved over her skull.

Run!

She struggled to rise, but her limbs seemed to move independently of each other. The hands reached out, soothed her, eased her back into a fitful sleep.

When she woke again, it was to silence. Somewhere in there was the echo of a scream, but it faded as soon as she became aware of it. Her clothes were damp with sweat, her chest and arms achy and bruised. She pushed herself up onto her elbows. Darkness. For a horrifying instant, Gwyn was sure she was blind.

After a moment, though, her vision cleared, and her stomach tightened. This wasn't the wagon; wasn't her bed. And the man sitting opposite her, across the low fire, wasn't Ascepis.

'Who are you?' Gwyn demanded, pulling herself upright. The world swam, and she had to swallow down a sudden surge of bile. There was no sign of the wagon, no sign of Ascepis. Trees pressed in on every side.

'I'm the one who just saved your life,' the man called Lucian said, still in that unfamiliar, lilting accent, as he stirred at the fire with a long stick. 'And carried you here after you fell down in a dead faint. You can thank me any time, mind.'

She shook her head. It was pounding, so sharp it made it hard to think. What had happened? She remembered blundering through the trees, and then, suddenly, the world fogging at the edges, the forest floor tipping up towards her ...

Gwyn jolted to her feet. 'Ascepis! Is he —?'

'I dinna ken where he is,' Lucian said carefully. 'He'll meet with us later, if he can. Dinna trouble yourself with that for now.'

'That man, that ...' Her hands came up to her eyes, heels pressing against the lids, as though trying to push clarity back into them. She felt her eyes moving frantically underneath.

'The wizard,' Lucian said. 'Aye. He'll be hunting you, if he lives. We can spare no time here.'

'Hunting me?' She lowered her hands and stared at Lucian. There was something important about him; something she was forgetting. A faint memory stirred: Ascepis, outlined in the doorway, the lamp swinging in his hand. Pepper, snorting in the dark, agitated and flicking her tail. And a few feet away, among the trees ...

'You turned into a bird!' she gasped. That hadn't been a dream, unless she was still dreaming now. Was she? Shivers wracked her body, and she found she couldn't stop them.

The man only smiled and pulled himself to his feet. 'You turned into a nuisance.' He scuffed the fire out with his boot and shouldered the pack that lay beside him on the ground. 'Come. There are worse things than wizards afoot this night.'

'I'm not going anywhere,' Gwyn said. She rose, brushing herself off. Gods, she wasn't going to cry. 'Not with you, at least. I don't know what this is about, but it has nothing to do with me, or Ascepis.' She sucked in deep, shuddering breaths, feeling the trees close in around her. 'I shouldn't have come with you at all.'

The man tilted his head, a strangely bird-like gesture. Clouds blanketed the stars above his head. 'Why did you, then?'

'Because ...' she began, then stopped. *Because Ascepis told me to,* she wanted to say, but that seemed suddenly inadequate. She had left Ascepis behind, left him to – what? Be captured by the Syndicate? Thrown in a dungeon somewhere, or worse? It had been a test of her courage ... and Gwyn had failed. She turned to go back.

'I wouldn't,' Lucian said. 'Ascepis kens what he's about. Will you not heed him? Believe me, lass, it's not my dearest dream to be killed protecting you. If you intend to get out of this place with your life – and mine – that means doing what I tell you. Now come. We've far to go, and these woods are scant refuge.'

Lucian muttered to himself as he strode through the forest, avoiding the main road. Gwyn had to half run to keep up. The trees huddled close on all sides, and though the moons had risen, the night was still black and bristling.

'Next time,' he said, 'next time, he can go himself. No trouble, indeed!'

'Who's "he"?'

The man looked back at her in amusement. '"He" is Idris. You'll meet him later. If we get out of these woods. Perhaps that's being a wee bit ambitious.'

'And who are you?'

He laughed outright. 'A little late for that, isn't it?'

Gwyn struggled to catch up with him and almost tripped over a gnarled root, catching herself just in time. 'I already asked,' she panted, steadying herself. 'You just ignored me.'

He turned and gave her another grin. 'In truth, girl, I dinna ken if I should trust you with too many details. If you should be captured – well, I'd rather the wizards not ken about me.' He held up a hand, forestalling her. 'My name is Lucian, and I'm a friend of Ascepis. I know you must have a lot of questions, but this isn't the time for them.'

A wolf howled somewhere, high and wild. Lucian's head whipped around as he came to a sudden stop. For a long moment, neither of them moved. Gwyn hardly dared to breathe. But the sound didn't come again, and at last Lucian gave a little shake and started to walk again, faster now.

'Come on,' he said. 'If you value your life, come on.'

There was nothing else she could do. Gwyn followed, her heart in her throat.

Their slow uphill journey led them onto the lower slopes of the Stonewall Mountains. The high peaks were still miles above, slowly becoming clearer, outlined in the faintest shade of grey. Gwyn could make out the dim shapes of trees hugging the black crags, and at the very top, the white gleam of fresh snow.

They came to the road so suddenly that she

almost didn't notice. One moment, leaves crunched underfoot; the next, they stepped onto hard-packed earth. It was a rude, unpaved road – slightly overgrown in places, but still showing signs of frequent use. It cut a deep swathe through the forest, disappearing into shadow only twenty feet away. Reddish moonlight glinted on the smooth, loose pebbles.

A pass lay before them, the narrow gap flanked by oaks on both sides, with the road slicing through woods and mountains both. Within, she saw only gloom, and the occasional dry tree making twisted shapes against the bare rock. But it was not the darkness that made cold hands clench around Gwyn's heart.

Three men stood there, their dark robes patches of rippling shadow. One wore a floppy, broad-brimmed hat in the northern style, pulled low over his eyes.

'The pass is blocked,' Lucian said, making her jump. He had seen them too.

'Are those ...?'

'Wizards? Aye.' He gestured her closer, drawing her back into the trees. They were downwind from the wizards, and hadn't been seen ... yet. Could wizards see in the dark? Gwyn thought she might faint from trembling so hard.

'Come on,' Lucian said. 'I ken another way.'

. . .

Gwyn's eyes followed the river as it flowed downstream, snagging hungrily on the rocks, making terraces of small waterfalls as it curved out of sight. Further down the mountain, it would join with other streams and flow southwest into Lake Hjolby.

'This is your other way?' she asked, shivering. They were well into the foothills now, but she had seen no sign of another pass, not even a rabbit track.

Lucian only smiled, a little tightly. 'There are caves and passages all through these mountains.' His gesture took in the walls of the valley and the high peaks above. 'That'll be our best chance to stay undetected. Even though ...' He trailed off, shaking his head.

'Even though what?'

'Ah. Well, I've a ... a contact, in those caves. I'd hoped not to involve him, but ...'

'In the Warren?' Gwyn asked. Lucian looked at her in surprise, and she flushed. 'I've seen maps. Nobody lives there, though. Nobody even goes inside. They say the Warren is haunted.'

'Haunted?' Lucian made a derisive sound in his throat. 'I've been in your Warren, more than once. I saw no ghosts or ghoulies. No, you've no need to fuss yourself over that.'

'But what about Ascepis?'

He squinted upstream, towards the mountains, and for a moment Gwyn was sure he was avoiding her eyes. 'As I said, he'll catch up with us when he can. He kens where we're headed.'

'Where?'

He did look at her now, his eyebrows slightly raised. 'To Idris, of course.'

'Idris?'

'He's a wizard. The greatest wizard. He can help you.'

'Help me?' She knew she was just echoing his words, like a fool, but she couldn't seem to help it. 'I don't want to go near any wizard! It's a wizard who's after me!'

'Dinna worry. He's not a part of the Syndicate. You can trust Idris. But first we have to reach him.' Lucian turned and began trudging upriver. After a moment, Gwyn followed, picking a path amidst the slick rocks and leaves that lined the bank.

Not Syndicate? Then he's a renegade. That was even worse. To flee the Syndicate ... well, that was a capital offence. If the wizards found her consorting with a rebel, they wouldn't even bother capturing her. It would be straight to the headsman's block. Oh, gods, what had she fallen into?

It took the better part of an hour to reach the caves, and though the sun was still trapped behind the mountains, the little triangles of sky above them were turning from grey to pink.

'You should turn into a horse,' Gwyn panted at one point, and Lucian smiled back at her.

'Why do *you* not turn into a horse? Then you can carry me for a change.'

She looked at him, puzzled. 'But I can't.'

'And there you go.'

The cave was a narrow fissure in the side of the mountain, half hidden by stiff thornbushes and widening into a low, dark bowl inside. At first it seemed like just a cleft in the rock, disconnected from the rest of the Warren, for Gwyn's hands met stone before she had walked even ten paces inside. In the corner, though, was another crack, this one barely wide enough to walk through, and beyond it, a long, sandy-floored tunnel.

'This is it,' Lucian said, picking a spiderweb off his coat. The narrow bar of light streaming through the cave entrance revealed a sliver of his face. 'We'll stop for food, at least for a time. You wait here.'

Lucian disappeared, and Gwyn sat alone in the half-dark, shivering. In time, he re-emerged, a dead rabbit flung over his shoulder and a bundle of sticks and tinder under one arm. His belt pouch held flint and a small blade, and it took no time at all to start a fire. Soon the rabbit was skinned and roasting. It was the best thing she had ever smelled.

As they waited, Gwyn opened her mouth to speak – once, twice. Each time she closed it again. The night had been a long, disorienting stretch of stumbling through the dark, of falling on her face in the mud, of choking down screams or sobs or both.

There had been no time to think, much less speak. Now, alone with this stranger, she felt oddly inhibited.

Lucian took a stick and prodded the rabbit, turning it in the firepit. Gwyn watched him from the corner of her eye. He had to be a wizard. Strange. Even after meeting Mancer Dorin, she had imagined a wizard would look ... well, different. Lucian looked only a handful of years older than herself. If not for the odd accent and the tattoo along his temple and cheekbone, he would have blended into any of the little villages in Nederlund. But she had seen him turn from a bird to a man, so he must be a wizard. How else to explain it?

'Breakfast,' Lucian said, and pulled the rabbit out of the fire. Gwyn forgot everything else as she tore into it, swallowing without bothering to chew. It seared her fingertips, but she hardly noticed. Fear and danger had made her ravenous.

'You probably have questions,' Lucian said, when they were done. He licked the last of the grease off his fingers, giving her a small smile.

Gwyn grew wary at once. 'I thought you said there was no time for questions.'

'There isn't much. But if you care to pick your most pressing, we've time for that.' He glanced at the crack leading to the outside, and his expression darkened. 'They'll not be far behind us, mind, so you'd best hurry.'

One question. Gwyn nodded, thinking hard. She had a *thousand* questions, but for the moment they all seemed to have flown out of her head.

'Are you a wizard?'

He gave a snorting laugh. 'That's a poor question, I reckon. Nay, I'm no wizard. I'm from Jhabahabi. Do you even ken what a wizard is?'

'Of course,' she said, bristling a little. She had read books; she was no fool. 'They live in Aranor, in the Clockwork City. They're old, and have beards – well, most of them do. And they steal children.'

Lucian covered his mouth and cleared his throat. 'Ah. Aye. That's mostly right. Though the women dinna have beards, for the most part.'

'I think a wizard healed me, once,' Gwyn said, remembering. 'After ... after I had an accident.'

'Wouldn't have been a wizard. Wizards canna heal.' At her quizzical look, he continued. 'There are two schools of magic: white and black. Opposing forces, like two sides of a coin. Nobody can use both. Healers, like the one you met, use white magic. The best place to learn is at the Lower City, right underneath the wizards' fortress. You follow?'

Gwyn nodded slowly. She had heard of healers. True healers – not just Simplers and hedge-wizards with their herbs and philtres, like Ascepis, like she was training to be. They could do incredible things, the stories said, miraculous things; could bring folk back from the very cusp of death. She had always assumed they were wizards, too, or some lesser type, at least.

'Good,' Lucian said. His eyes were gold and liquid in the firelight. 'Black magic, though, is different. For those who can use it, it's born into them. That's the wizards. And unlike the healers, they *will* use it, whether they want to or not, because the Syndicate tracks the birth of every wizard, and they never, ever let one go. Too rare, and too dangerous. To practise black magic outside the Syndicate is punishable by death.'

'If you're not a wizard, then how did you ...?'

But Lucian was standing up, brushing sand off the back of his trousers. 'You've had your question,' he said, smiling. 'But if you tear me off a strip from your skirt there, I'll give you one more for free.'

Frowning, she made a rip in the bottom of her skirt and handed it to him. He began wrapping the cloth around a short, stout stick, and when he held the end to the fire, it started to burn.

'Answer a different question,' she said. 'How do you know Ascepis?'

He nodded. 'That's a better one. Well, the fact is that your friend Ascepis was a wizard. A long time ago, but he was. But he was silenced. That's what they call it when a wizard gets cut off from the power. They're still sensitive to magic, but they canna use it again, not ever. There's no cure for silencing, no way to heal it.

'As to the rest, well, the reason Ascepis raised you the way he did, moving always from place to place – the reason he raised you at *all,* even though you were none of his blood – is because he was ordered to. In fact, a lot of people have been ordered to lay down their lives to protect you. Myself included.' Gwyn's mouth opened, but Lucian kept on. 'Why you need protecting, I couldn't say. What I do ken, or what I can tell you, is that Beheret has taken an interest in you. You've heard of Beheret?'

Gwyn blinked, sure she'd misheard. 'The ... the *god?*'

'The very one.' He saw her expression. 'Oh, she's real enough, make no mistake, though her divinity is a matter of debate. Some of the wizards are her servants. Not all, thank the Claw, else we'd truly be in dire straits.'

Gwyn wasn't sure whether she wanted to throw up or faint. A *god* wanted her? It made no sense. But it was too far-fetched to be a lie. And the rest, dropped in so casually ... *Ascepis* was a *wizard?* It was impossible. Wasn't it?

'Do you pray?' Lucian asked.

'What?' she said, starting. 'No. No, I don't. I didn't think the gods were ...'

'Real?' He nodded. 'Well. Maybe you should consider taking up prayer. You might need it.' He scuffed out the fire with his boot. 'Best be getting on. These passages come out the east side of the mountain, eventually, but it may take a time to find the path. The Warren's more than just a fancy name.'

Lucian turned away from the entrance and moved into the tiny passage at the back of the cave. The light of the torch disappeared as though it had been swallowed.

Gwyn sat for a moment, dazed, then climbed to her feet and hurried after him.

CHAPTER 6

THE WARREN

It was narrow inside the passage, and in several places Gwyn had to inch through sideways, glad she wasn't a big-breasted woman. Lucian went first, holding the torch. He stood a few inches taller than Gwyn, no more, but he was broad-shouldered, and only cracks of light squeezed past him.

Gwyn had never been afraid of small spaces. There had been a hollow under the floor of the wagon, a secret hidey-hole. She used to go there, from time to time, when Ascepis' smothering became unbearable. It was too dark down there to read, or to do much of anything, but the solitude made it almost her favourite place in the world. It had been her secret – until one afternoon she fell asleep. Ascepis had found her, after an hour or so, but he was near hysterical by then. The next day a lock appeared on the trapdoor.

This tunnel was narrower than her old hiding place, and Gwyn was conscious of the weight of the mountain pressing down around her head. As they moved deeper, the air grew moist and almost warm, with a mouldy, wet-fur smell that made her want to sneeze. Water trickled down the walls, collecting in little hollows on the floor.

The deeper she moved into the mountain, the more the hairs stood up on the back of her neck. She rolled her shoulders, uncomfortable, but the sense of menace remained. A cold sweat sprang up across her skin. Her heart seemed to be trying to climb into her throat. And strangely, from time to time, she was sure she heard a snatch of distant, familiar music.

'There's ... resistance,' Lucian said. His head tilted slightly, and shadows danced over the rock walls. 'These caves are warded. I should have expected it.'

'Warded? What does that mean?'

'Wards keep people out.' He gave her a sceptical look over his shoulder. 'You can feel it, can't you? Can you see anything?'

Gwyn shook her head, though the question made no sense to her. 'It's just a feeling of danger,' she said, and Lucian nodded thoughtfully.

'Aye. That would be the wards. They're set to slow, not stop, else we'd still be sitting at the entrance twirling our thumbs. And they're dampening me as well. I canna shift. Strange.'

The way turned to shallow, irregular stairs, their surface worn to oily smoothness. At the top, the tunnel widened and branched into two. Lucian stopped, and Gwyn stood on her toes to peer over his shoulder.

'Which way?' she asked. Her voice echoed in the dark. *Way, ay, ay.*

Lucian didn't answer at first. He stood very still, as though listening. Gwyn felt the frisson of a nearby ward on her skin, though she had no idea where it might be.

Finally, he pointed to the left tunnel. 'I dinna ken the way,' he said. 'But down there is something dead.'

Goosebumps stood up on Gwyn's arms. Before she could object, he had started down the left tunnel, and she had to run to catch up.

'Maybe we should go the other way,' she ventured, but Lucian shook his head. The torchlight picked out the red in his hair.

'This way is more heavily warded,' he said. 'Anything we're like to find will be this way.'

'You mean your friend?'

'I dinna say he was a friend.'

The floor turned craggy and uneven, pitted with deep fissures that Gwyn kept stumbling into. More turns, more wards. They leapt through a veil of icy water, spraying from a rift in the ceiling. They splashed through dark pools and scrambled up slimy rockfalls, where cords of mineralised lichen scoured the palms of her hands. The air smelled of bats.

Eventually, they began to take a right turn before every left, and Gwyn lost all sense of direction. Lucian, though, seemed to become surer as they moved deeper into the mountain, and his steps quickened, leaving Gwyn hurrying to keep up.

It was a shock, then, when the tunnel came to an abrupt halt, opening into a wide cave, the ceiling daggered with stalactites. Gwyn opened her mouth to ask why they had stopped, then forgot to close it, staring around the cave in astonishment.

The floor was scattered with furs and rugs. Torches cast flickering shadows on the walls, which were hung with threadbare tapestries. Flames crackled merrily beneath a stone chimney that must have opened out of the side of the mountain. There was furniture: a narrow bed, a table with elaborately carved legs – and a huge armchair by the fire, which held a man, frowning into his goblet of wine. He rose to his feet as they entered.

He was small, for a man; no taller than Gwyn, and snake-slim under his grey, high-necked robe. A curtain of dark brown hair fell sleek and straight to his chin. Though still young, his face was lined, like someone who had once been fat and lost weight quickly. His upturned blue eyes held a slightly amused expression. It was an ordinary sort of face –

not one you would remark on in the street, or remember when it had gone past.

There was something on his forearm, Gwyn saw. A tattoo? No, a burn scar – or a brand? She couldn't make it out.

'I thought you might have moved on,' Lucian said. His voice was strained, the torch gripped tightly in his fist.

The man spread his hands and gave them a guileless look. Or tried to. It was unconvincing. His mouth had a naturally sardonic twist, as though he found everything around him just slightly contemptible.

'Moved on? I live here,' he said, and, with a sad shake of his head, added, 'I would offer you a seat, but ...' His gesture took in the mostly empty room. There was something strange in the way he moved, as though he shifted from one position to another without really moving at all, leaving a faint afterimage behind. Gwyn blinked hard, and the impression faded. Perhaps she had imagined it.

Lucian's eyes narrowed. 'It's been three years, Faolan. Without so much as a report. Idris didn't ken if you were alive or dead.'

The man he called Faolan shrugged. Hands clasped behind his back, he began to pace the length of the cave. That afterimage followed him, a smudge, a barely perceptible blurring of the air.

'Alive, as you can see. Come, Lucian, you can

hardly accuse me of dereliction of my duty. Idris sent me to watch her' – one long, white finger pointed at Gwyn – 'some time ago. And so I watch her. There seemed little to report on.'

Lucian snorted. 'You expect me to believe you've been following Idris' orders these past years?'

'And why not? You assume me to be faithless, because of my ... occupation, mmm? Such prejudice.' He gave a quick, cutting smile. 'Do we not worship the same god? Umbrael loves all her children equally, you know.'

'You are what you are,' Lucian said, with forced calm. There was a hint of crackling, barely contained violence in the air. A *contact,* Lucian had called him. Well, they certainly weren't friends; that was clear. 'It's nothing to me, if you sit here doing your ... your ...' He wiggled his fingers in the air. 'Your *unnatural* things. But don't pretend you've been doing this for Idris' sake, or for hers. You've always been jealous of Idris, and you took the first chance possible to break free.'

'Jealous?' Faolan stopped pacing and laughed – a strangely pleasant sound coming from that drawn face. It illuminated his eyes and made him seem more likeable. 'Is the moon jealous of the sun? Oh, it's true enough; Idris can do things with the black arts I can hardly dream of. It rankled when we were both apprentices – I won't deny it. But I follow a different path now. And it suits me very well indeed.'

His way of speaking was the same as Mancer Dorin's: formal and precise. *He's a wizard,* said a small voice in Gwyn's head. If the robe had not labelled him so, the accent did. A wizard! Lucian's words about Beheret came back to her, a sudden splash of ice water down her back. *Some of the wizards are her servants.*

'I assume from your presence that events are finally in motion,' Faolan continued, sinking back into his chair. 'That would certainly explain why you have Idris' little whelp in tow.' Gwyn started angrily at that description. The man smiled as if reading her thoughts, though he didn't so much as glance at her.

'There are wizards behind us, and more ahead, like as not,' Lucian said. He seemed to be gathering himself, forcing his breathing to slow. 'I'd not have come here at all, had I any choice. But there are wings in the sky, and these caves are our best and only way to cross the mountains. My orders are to bring the lass to Idris. If you serve him still, as you say, then you'll help us.'

'You wish to pass through the caves?' Faolan tilted his head, seeming to consider. Then he stood, smoothing the front of his robe. 'Well. I will aid you. I can do that much, at least.' He crossed the room and drew back a tapestry of a hunting scene to reveal a long, black passageway. 'Quickly, now. If your information is correct, we should expect company before long.'

Gwyn suppressed a shiver and stepped into the tunnel after Lucian. As she did so, she thought she heard again that faint, discordant music.

They made their way through the heart of the Warren. More slowly now, for the tunnel sloped steeply uphill, winding back on itself and branching as it went. Lucian took the lead, then Gwyn, and Faolan behind, calling directions over their heads. The torch threw barely enough light to see the floor of the cave a few paces ahead. Moisture dripped continually from the roof.

It was quiet inside the mountain, except for the distant moan of the wind somewhere far off. Though the passage narrowed and widened periodically, there was something orderly about it – something that made Gwyn think it was built by human hands, impossible as that might be. She didn't realise she'd spoken the last aloud until she heard Faolan's melodious laugh behind her.

'Assuredly so,' he said. 'The ancestors had many abilities that seem incredible to us, now. But magic rose, and they fell, their arts lost – so it goes.'

'Speculation,' Lucian snapped.

A rustle as Faolan shrugged. 'You will see for yourself in a moment. I have made some excavations of my own since moving into these caves. Remarkable, the things that time can bury.'

'A shame it dinna bury you too,' Lucian muttered.

Faolan only laughed. He was nothing like Gwyn had expected a wizard to be. Certainly nothing like Mancer Dorin, with his bright, inhuman smile – but, she thought, just as dangerous.

A sudden cold breeze tickled her face. Realising Lucian had stopped walking, she peered around him, then clapped her hand over her mouth to stifle her gasp.

'Very impressive,' Lucian said quietly. Gwyn could only stare.

The tunnel opened up abruptly into a colossal cavern at least five hundred feet tall, though it was impossible to say for certain. The walls on either side curved up and away into impenetrable blackness. Shapes loomed up out of the dark ahead, silent and gleaming, and Gwyn realised after a moment that they were buildings. Some had collapsed, leaving twisted mountains of glass and metal. Others ended in saw-teeth, half buried under landslides of rock. The remainder stood, impossibly tall, flanking the wide black-topped road and disappearing into the gloom.

'It's a city!' she said, hardly believing.

Faolan came up beside her, and she thought she saw him roll his eyes. But he only said, 'Yes – one of the oldest settlements in the world, I suspect, save perhaps the ruins at Vertica. Certainly this is much larger. Built by older, stranger magic, like all the ancient cities.'

'How old is it?'

He shrugged. 'Two and a half thousand years or so. I can't say why they would build a city underground only to abandon it. I've found little mention of it in any records, save the name – Sonderby – which makes me wonder if it was ever occupied.'

'How far does it go?' Lucian asked. His tone aimed for nonchalance, but like Gwyn, he seemed unable to stop staring.

'Far,' Faolan said flatly. 'Much of it is inaccessible, of course. Earth tremors. But there are tunnels still open that stretch underground, almost to Waystone. From there, you could be back in the Tanglewood in, oh, twelve days?'

Gwyn thought she saw Lucian stiffen, but he said nothing. The Tanglewood? She had never heard of it, not even on Ascepis' maps, which were extensive. Lucian had said he was from Jhabahabi, which was south and east of here, in the Midlands. But that was a land of dense, impenetrable jungle, closed to outsiders and inhabited by beast-men – or so the stories said.

Suddenly, from somewhere in the tunnels behind, there came a long, reverberating howl. Lucian's head whipped around, and Gwyn saw his eyes widen.

'Warglings.'

CHAPTER 7

IN THE DARK

'They have our scent,' Faolan said. He shook his head. 'My scent, rather. I suppose I can thank you for that. I've spent years in these caves without the wizards noticing, and now you bring them down around my head. Poor form, Lucian.'

Gwyn felt the first stirrings of panic. 'What are warglings?' she asked. 'Can you stop them? Or slow them down? You're a wizard, aren't you?'

He gave her a strange look, and she wondered if she had said something wrong. 'I suppose I am, at that. But warglings are the hunting hounds of the Syndicate – bred to track down rogue wizards. They cannot be defeated, hindered or otherwise stopped by magical means. They soak up the power like a piece of bread soaks up soup. And there will be mancers with them. Warglings never hunt alone.'

'Then we should separate,' Lucian said. The

flickering torchlight highlighted the jagged black lines on his face, making him look more savage; more alien. 'They'll follow you, not us.'

Faolan sniffed. 'And let them tear me to pieces? I think not. Surely you do not imagine you can navigate these tunnels without me, hmm?' Lucian said nothing, and Faolan nodded curtly. 'We have some time yet.'

The path here was not the natural rock of the caves, but a kind of glittering black stone, presumably designed for cart wheels. In places, age and the tremblings of the mountain had cracked the surface, but for the most part it ran smooth and level through the gloom. The torch provided only a wavering light, reflected darkly in the glass buildings on either side. It was near silent, with only the slap of their boots, and somewhere in the distance, the faint drip of water. The road took a sharp left turn, then a right, narrowing into a switchback that took them up and out of the cavern. The walls closed in around them again, and they ran on in single file.

The caves were rougher here, more natural, and had the musty smell of a mouse's nest. Pale tuber roots, gleaming in the torchlight, spidered the floor, the ceiling. Faolan seemed to know where they were going, directing them to take a left here, or a right there.

'These are the old caves,' Faolan explained. 'Older

than the part I live in. There is a passage near here that leads to the surface – one of many.'

Gwyn was silent. The promise of fresh air after so long in the lightless black hardened her courage. But what of the warglings? The labyrinthine tunnels might slow them for a time, but she had no doubt they would be able to pick up Faolan's scent eventually. It would be better to leave him behind, if they could.

A left turn. Without warning, Faolan reached out and grabbed the back of Gwyn's coat. She jerked to a halt. Lucian stumbled on without noticing.

Faolan stretched his other hand towards Lucian's retreating back. 'Not that way,' he said quietly – far too quietly for Lucian to hear. Gwyn stared at him, uncomprehending.

There was a sudden gasp, and then a shout, quickly smothered. Gwyn's head whipped back around.

Where Lucian had been only a second before, there was nothing. No torch. No Lucian. She stood with Faolan in complete blackness, no sound but her own panting breath and the dim, distant chittering of bats.

Gwyn heard the man's robe rustle, and there was light again. She blinked, dazzled. In Faolan's hand was a ball of white fire, bobbing an inch or so above his palm. He raised his hand and the fire floated forwards, to where Lucian had been. Its harsh light illuminated a great hole in the floor, dark and almost perfectly round.

'He fell,' Faolan said, smiling.

Gwyn tried to back away from him, but there was nowhere to go. There was only the pit behind her. She was too afraid to take her eyes from him, from the dancing flame in his palm.

'You killed him,' she whispered.

He made an impatient sound. 'Don't be more foolish than you must, girl. I like the shapeshifter well enough. If I wished to kill him, I could have done so between one breath and the next.' He snapped his fingers to illustrate the point, then flicked his hand towards the hole. 'It is hardly any distance at all to the bottom. And from there, a dozen different paths lead out of the Warren – though none so quick as the way we shall go. The correct tunnel is just behind us. I must have missed it in the dark.'

'You knew!' Gwyn said. Her eyes were beginning to water from trying not to blink. 'You knew the pit was there. You let him fall!'

'And what is it to you, hmm?' His face, long and sunken in the cold light, loomed out of the darkness. 'You owe him nothing.'

'He saved my life.'

'Perhaps he did. But did you ever ask him why? Now, come. These tunnels are a labyrinth, but they will not stop the warglings or the mancers forever.' When Gwyn didn't move, he grabbed her wrist with one bony hand. His skin was surprisingly soft. 'Your feathered companion will come to no harm by my hand, girl. In truth, he is far safer than we are. My word as a mancer on it. Come!'

Faolan turned back down the passage they had come from, dragging Gwyn with him. There was little strength in his grip, but dazed and off balance as she was, Gwyn stumbled a few steps after him before wrenching herself free.

'No!' She massaged her wrist, glaring at him and shaking so hard she could barely stand. 'I'm not going anywhere with you. Not after ...'

The pit was at her back. She glanced down, but saw nothing in the blackness. It might have stretched forever. Was Lucian truly alive? Wouldn't he have called up to them?

'Very well,' Faolan said. 'Do as you please.'

She blinked, expecting an argument – but he was already gone, the pale ball of fire retreating down the passage until it was almost out of sight.

Gwyn stood alone in the dark.

What has Lucian really told you? She was breathing hard, the sound like ragged, claw-like scratching against the walls. *That the wizards are chasing you. That a goddess has marked you out.* There was no hint of a lie on his face when he spoke, but he offered no proof, either. Yes, he had saved her life, but did that mean he was a friend? He had certainly done nothing to help Ascepis, for all that Ascepis supposedly trusted him.

For all she knew, he could be working with Mancer Dorin. And if not – well, she hadn't asked for his help …

When Gwyn caught up with Faolan, he said nothing, only acknowledging her presence with a glance and a slight nod. That twisted a tight knot of anger – or was it fear? – in Gwyn's stomach, though she couldn't have said why.

They hurried single file through the long tunnels, following the white light that bobbed ahead of them – for how long, it was impossible to say. Behind them came the yips of the warglings, but more distant now. Gwyn could almost feel them sniffing around the rim of the pit. Smelling Lucian far below – alive, she hoped – but unable to reach him. But how long before the warglings came after Faolan instead? He was the one they were tracking. Perhaps it would have been safer to throw herself into the pit after Lucian.

Abruptly, the tunnel ahead of them met solid rock. Had they taken a wrong turn and come to a dead end? But Faolan dropped to his hands and knees, and Gwyn saw that the passage continued, in a muddy crawlspace barely wide enough to permit a man's body.

'No,' she said. Her heart had dropped into her stomach. The space was surely no taller than two feet.

Faolan glanced back at her over his shoulder. The

light bobbed just above his back like a pony's saddle. He said nothing, but his head, then his shoulders, then the rest of him disappeared into the crawlspace. The light followed.

Gwyn shook her head. 'No, no —' But there was nobody to hear. She stood alone in the blackness, again.

Cursing, she dropped to her knees, and stuck her head into the crevice.

The soles of Faolan's boots were a few feet ahead of her, scrabbling against the rock. The passage had lowered even further, so the wizard was pulling himself along more by his elbows than his knees. Gwyn slithered into the opening, trying to ignore the feeling of a mountain of rock teetering above her head.

It's just like being in the space under the wagon, Gwyn told herself wildly, but the thought gave little comfort. There was no Ascepis to pull her out this time.

She was so focused on staying calm that she almost didn't notice the familiar prickling along her arms and neck, and when she did, it took her a moment to realise what she was sensing.

'There's a ward ahead,' she panted, squeezing herself deeper into the tunnel. She felt like a smear of crushed berries under a pestle. *Gods, don't think about it. There's plenty of space. How long can this passage be? Oh, gods —*

Ahead of her, Faolan stopped dead. 'What did you say?'

'A ward,' she repeated, catching up with him and taking the opportunity to readjust her position. Her skirts were tangled around her legs, making it hard to find purchase with her knees. She was surprised at how calm her voice sounded. Inside, she felt like screaming. She forced herself to breathe normally. 'Ahead of us. Isn't there?'

A sound came from the wizard's throat. At first, Gwyn was certain he was being attacked, and reversed on her hands and knees before she realised he was ... laughing.

'What?' she said, baffled. 'What is it?'

His shoulders trembled, and when he spoke, his voice was thin and wheezy, the humour barely contained. 'My apologies to you, Gwyn. You have no idea what a gift you have given me.'

It was the first time he hadn't called her 'girl' or 'whelp'. That seemed ominous, somehow. 'What are you —'

His mirth cut off abruptly. 'Hush. I need to think.' Gwyn fell silent, and in a few moments, Faolan started to crawl again. Gwyn followed, more confused than before.

The ceiling grew lower. Gwyn sunk to her elbows, then to her stomach. Her nose was half an inch from the rock, and above, she could feel it scraping her back. There was hardly room to breathe.

She could no longer crane her head up to see Faolan, but she could hear the little grunts and scrabbling sounds that meant he wasn't far ahead. Against all her better instincts, she pushed herself deeper into the crawlspace, until her ribs were scored and bruised.

Then, suddenly, she realised she was stuck.

She jerked herself forward, but didn't move by so much as a fingernail. Her shoulders were wedged tight into the fissure. Fighting down a rising sense of panic, she jerked again. Nothing. She tried to go back instead, but couldn't.

Gwyn called out to Faolan, and was horrified to find her voice was just a dry squeak, muffled against the rock. She was stuck too tightly to fully breathe in. Spots swam in front of her eyes. Dust clogged her nose, her throat.

Near hysterical, Gwyn pushed the last breath of air out of her lungs and surged forward on her belly. She slithered the last five feet along the tunnel, and found Faolan squatting on his heels, glaring back at her as she caught her breath.

'You do make a fuss,' he said. 'Well, we've left the warglings behind, but it appears we have a much greater concern at hand, hmm? You have put me in quite an awkward situation. Very awkward. I suppose you leave me no choice, though it inconveniences me greatly.'

His words washed over her without meaning. 'What are you talking about?'

Faolan nodded, talking half to himself. 'Yes. I will train you. After I take a few precautions, of course. For your safety. And mine.'

The man was making no sense. Gwyn took a few deep breaths before trying to speak again. The cave was much more spacious here; enough for her to stand upright. Still, she was more shaken than she cared to admit.

'Train me to do what?' she said, when she had mastered her voice.

Faolan looked her in the eye, then, and Gwyn saw a spark of malicious humour. Her stomach tightened.

'To use your black gift, Gwyn.'

Gwyn stared at the wizard as if he spoke another language. The ball of pale fire, still floating at his elbow, cast strange shadows across the floor. Her mouth was suddenly dry.

'My ... what?'

'Your black gift. Oh, come, surely you must have known?' Faolan was looking at her, face sympathetic yet intent. 'I knew it as soon as you told me you could sense the wards. Perhaps I shouldn't be surprised – how could you be otherwise, with your uncle being who he is? And yet I sense nothing from you at all. Very mysterious.'

'I don't have an uncle.' Gwyn's voice shook, but

she didn't care. Mad ... The man was completely mad. And she was alone with him beneath the mountain.

'Well, you have two, in fact. Family is such a joy. But I mean Idris Whitemane, of course, your mother's youngest brother. Idris the mancer.'

'Mancer?' She shook her head. Her ears were ringing, a high, piercing sound like a fork striking a crystal goblet. Unless she had misunderstood badly, *mancer* was another word for *wizard.* Hadn't Lucian said something about this Idris? Her *uncle?* Surely not.

'Yes, mancer. Are you deaf, girl, or are you foolish?' It seemed she had been demoted to 'girl' again. Faolan shook his head, impatient now. 'Well, you can't put the milk back in the cow, as they say. You don't want me, and I certainly don't want you, but here we are.'

Faolan reached out, and before Gwyn could react, he had grasped her head between both his hands. She tried to pull back, but it was too late. Too late by far.

The air slammed into her, a clap of soundless thunder. The ground cracked. The dust around her and Faolan lifted and billowed away in a ring.

A rush of heat.

Cold.

Heat.

Faolan blinked, slowly, slowly, eyelids falling, rising, like the tide.

Time slowed, slowed, stopped, and hung suspended.

Silence.

Then the moment passed. Her hair settled back down around her shoulders, and Faolan reeled back, wiping his brow. He was breathing heavily. For an instant it seemed nothing had changed.

But it had.

She could sense Faolan where he stood, and knew that even if she closed her eyes, she could point straight at him. He was several feet away, but Gwyn felt he was standing right on top of her, breathing down her neck. Like his white hands were at her throat.

But, more than that, she could sense his will.

He didn't wish for her to speak, and without meaning to be, Gwyn found herself silent. His wishes, his desires, his commands were inside her head, as strong as her own. She was too scared to breathe.

Faolan was shaking his head. 'An apprentice, at my age. I must be mad.' He looked down at her and sighed. 'Well, no need to stand on formality. You can call me Faolan. I expect you to work hard, do as you are told, and not talk back. If you can do that, then we shall see if we can make a mancer of you.'

CHAPTER 8

APPRENTICE

Gwyn stood, still and shocked, as though the words had been followed with a punch to the gut.

Faolan, though, had already turned away. He flicked his wrist, and the torches around the walls sprang to life. Gwyn's stomach gave a sick swoop, and she clutched at it, feeling the hammer of her heart through the thick fabric of her sarafan.

She had assumed they were still in the caves, but now she saw the truth. This was a crypt. Rows of stone coffins lay recessed into hollows in the walls. The floor was dusty, and there were cobwebs in the high corners of the roof, but it was otherwise well tended, the coffins crowded with dry flowers and scraps of parchment.

Scanning the room, Faolan smiled. 'Catacombs.' He held out a hand for her. 'Come. It is not far to the surface. Come, I said.' Faolan gave an invisible tug on the strange new bond between them, and Gwyn found herself turning before she could object. It felt like someone was yanking on a yoke around her neck. He set off into the dark, the pale fire bobbing ahead of him, and in a moment, Gwyn followed.

'You know,' he said after a while, 'it is something of a mystery, why the Syndicate has not come for you yet.'

Gwyn licked her lips, which had gone suddenly dry. 'What do you mean?'

'You are – well, it must be seventeen, now, yes? Seventeen, and a mancer – and yet you have never been to the Clockwork City; never been initiated into the Syndicate. It is unheard of. Why have they not found you?'

'Because I'm not a wizard!' Her voice was too loud in the darkness, almost a shout, but she couldn't help it. Tears pricked the corners of her eyes.

Faolan shuddered, and she was struck again by the strange, delicate grace of his movements. 'Not a wizard? Do you imagine I could have bound a non-gifted person as my apprentice? It is your gift that binds you to me, not mine. No, you are a *wizard* – or at least you will be. The same as your uncle.'

'My *uncle*.' Gwyn gave a bark of near-hysterical laughter. 'Well, you're wrong about that, too. I don't have an uncle, and especially not a wizard uncle. I don't have any family. My mother and father died when I was a baby. I was a foundling – an orphan.'

'Idris is not just a *wizard*, apprentice. He is the best to come out of the Syndicate in a hundred years.' Faolan's eyes took on a distant, faraway look. 'Perhaps that's why the Syndicate has gone to such lengths to get him back. They don't look kindly on renegades at the best of times, but even less when the renegade is their finest pupil.'

The tunnel turned to stairs, leading upwards. Coffins lined the walls here, too, but these were pitted with age. Some had crumbled almost to dust. No dust on the stairs, though they were worn down by the passage of many feet. The air was chill and scentless.

'Alright,' Gwyn said. 'If that's true, why have I never met him, this *Idris*?'

Faolan snorted. 'What, and join him in exile? Being on the run from the Syndicate is hardly any life for a child. Idris gave you over to Ascepis. Nobody was looking for *him*. Nobody cares what a silenced mancer does, or where he goes, so long as it is decently out of sight. That was the beginning of it.'

'And how would you know all this?' She shook her head before he could respond. 'It's all lies. I don't want to hear any more of it.' Faolan was mad; he had to be. No wonder he'd been living in a cave.

But Faolan went on as though she hadn't spoken. 'A few years ago, Idris came to me with a rather unusual request.' Gwyn could feel, rather than see, the corners of his mouth curl up in a pensive smile. 'He said there was a girl, his niece, who needed watching. That one day, people might come looking for her. I knew better than to ask questions.' He hesitated. 'Perhaps I was still a little in awe of him. He has that effect on people. But I did watch you, from time to time. I never saw need to interfere. Ascepis seemed to be doing a good enough job of it, and I never cared for children, myself.'

There was silence, then, but for the scuff of their feet on the granite stairs, and the chirp of a rat, somewhere in the dank warrens beneath the crypt.

'So,' Gwyn said flatly. 'You've been spying on me. You and this Idris, both.'

'Protecting you, I should think. And as it turns out, you needed protection. A lot of people have given over years of their life for your safety, and you never even knew it.'

At the top of the stairs, they emerged into a narrow, torch-lined room. The walls and vaulted roof were panelled in dark-washed teak, and down the length stood fixed benches with high wooden backs. At the front of the room, surrounded by tall frosted windows, was a cloth-draped altar, with a statue of Molech Suun, dark eyes glittering, thunderbolt gripped in his left hand. Offerings clustered around his feet: dull coins, dried flowers, wooden beads, prayers written on scraps of linen and paper. There were candles, though most had burned down to stubs.

'We will rest here for the night,' Faolan said. 'Come. Start a fire, and I will find food.'

At the doorway of the chapel, Faolan left Gwyn alone.

She volunteered to go with him, thinking it might be a means of escape. But Faolan just laughed at her, knowing what she was about, and told her to stay put.

So Gwyn sat on the stone steps with her legs folded under her. Even when Faolan was out of sight, she could *feel* him moving away through the fading daylight, a little bundle of awareness at the back of her head. Gods, what had he done to her?

She waited until she felt him reach the town, then waited a few more minutes, in case it was some sort of trick. When she was sure he was gone, Gwyn rose and shouldered her pack, hands balling into fists at her side.

Keep me prisoner, will you? Well, she had needed his help in the caves; had needed Lucian to lead her through the woods. Not anymore. She was done with wizards – or *mancers,* as Faolan seemed to insist on calling them. Done with shapeshifters. No – it was time to find Ascepis, and figure out what in the gods' names was going on.

The chapel was set on a hilltop, and below, a patchwork of blue-and-grey fields rolled down to the east, where hundreds of thatched roofs spread out like a neat arrangement of doll houses. The air smelled of rain and deep, fresh earth. The first stars had started to appear, and the wind nipped at her, carrying the promise of snow. Hopefully she could reach the next town before full dark. Gwyn had no money, but she supposed she could sleep in a hayloft if needed. She stepped forward, pulling her coat tighter —

— and felt her knees fold under her. She hit the ground with a *humph* that made her teeth clack together.

Clumsy, she thought, once she had caught her breath. She was rarely clumsy – a few tumbles off the wagon roof as a girl had taught her to be careful where she put her feet. But the hill was steep, and she was exhausted, so maybe it was to be expected. She pulled herself up, brushing grass stains off her coat.

This time she made it one step before her legs collapsed.

The jolt took the wind out of her. This time she didn't try to stand. She sat, dazed and numb, her thoughts chasing each other around her head.

Faolan told me to stay put. That was why she couldn't leave; couldn't even take a proper step towards freedom. Her body wouldn't allow it. The realisation made her gorge rise.

She wasn't going to escape.

Ever.

Faolan had told her to start a fire, and though it wasn't a command, Gwyn was too shaken to disobey him. Once she stopped thinking about running away – once she half convinced herself that she didn't *want* to run away; not under any circumstances – she was able to stand. In a daze, her legs shaking so badly she thought she might fall again, Gwyn gathered a heap of dry grass and twigs and piled them together.

Then she sat and stared at the two stones in her hands. She had no idea what to do next. There was a potbelly stove in their wagon, but Ascepis had always been the one to light it. He'd never let her try – she might burn herself, he'd said. Gwyn threw the rocks aside, where they clattered down the hillside.

When Faolan returned, some time later, he had an earthenware container and several waterskins. With him were two horses with bulging saddlebags.

'Soup,' he said, handing her the container. 'The town is Bangstørp, if you wanted to know. We're not far from Edge. A day's ride.'

He glanced at the unlit fire and pressed his lips together, but made no comment; just took over the task himself. A click of his fingers was all it took to make the spark, and in moments, the twigs were blazing merrily. Gwyn's stomach lurched.

'It won't be long before you can do that yourself,' he said, misinterpreting her expression. Gwyn lowered her gaze, focusing on her hands folded in her lap. Faolan shrugged and turned his attention to the cooking. As it turned out, the jug contained spinach and sorrel soup with hunks of river crab. He rested it in the fire until the outside was almost too hot to touch.

'You still don't believe me,' he said, when they were both eating. 'You think it a mistake. I admit, I wondered the same thing. The Syndicate has never failed to collect a mancer.' He gave her a sideways, speculative look. 'It is a puzzle. But there can be no doubt. My wards were set against mancers, not common folk. When you sensed them, I knew.'

'Lucian sensed them too,' Gwyn said, poking at the fire with a stick. 'He's not a wizard.'

'No, he is not a wizard – but the shapeshifters are sensitive to magic. Light and dark.'

'So maybe I'm a shapeshifter, then.'

Faolan laughed. His tone was light, almost playful. 'Hardly. Unless you were born in Jhabahabi, hmm, and failed to mention it? No? Besides, the *shamaya* go through their first change long before they turn seventeen. At your age, you would be considered *heru* – ungifted.'

'It's still not proof of anything,' Gwyn said, turning her eyes away. She wrapped her arms around herself, though the fire had cut through the worst of the cold. 'You said the warglings hunt wizards. Well, there were packs of them hunting in the woods last night. If I was a wizard, they would have sniffed me out.'

'That much is no surprise.' He shrugged, fishing around in the container for the last piece of crab. 'When I look at you in my mind, I do not ... see you. How could the warglings sense you? Your ability is *masked,* somehow. Is it something Idris has done? I can't begin to imagine how, but ...' He shook his head. 'It makes no difference. As I told you, I wouldn't have been able to bind one of the common folk. Go ahead – stand up, if you don't believe me.'

Gwyn narrowed her eyes; tried to stand. Maybe this time ...

But the tiny iron fist in her mind that was Faolan's will wouldn't allow it. Her legs refused to obey. They barely even seemed to be her own legs. Abruptly, hot, furious tears sprang up in the corners of her eyes. She wanted to scream; felt it building up in her chest.

Faolan was smiling, now, and there was nothing kindly or playful in the expression. 'So you see, Gwyn,' he said, 'you and your gift both are mine. And I mean to shape that gift into something useful, even if I have to bludgeon you with it.'

All at once, a violent rage rose up and uncoiled in her breast like a snake. Hate filled her, hot and white and blinding. It seemed to come from some dark, animal place inside her. A voice in her head roared at her to reach out and strike the wizard across the face.

Instead, she clenched her fists, and turned away.

'I'm going to sleep,' she said dully, and at once, she heard Faolan laughing.

'Sleep? Do you think this is a holiday, apprentice? Come. Stand up. Hold out your hand.'

Gwyn obeyed, blinking back her tears, because there was nothing else she could do. The wizard stood, too, and they faced each other across the low fire. He took her narrow hand in his own, turning it over, inspecting the palm, nodding to himself. For the first time, she noticed a marking on his own palm – an intricate black tattoo of some kind. She thought at once of Lucian, of the jagged lines that traced the side of his face, and almost snatched her hand away. No matter what Faolan claimed, she was far from certain that Lucian still lived.

'It will do,' Faolan said, nodding. He didn't release her hand.

'What will do?'

'This.'

She began to pull away, but Faolan held her hand tight in his own, and there came an abrupt flare of pain, white-hot in her palm. The smell of burnt flesh filled the air. She wrenched her arm away, and this time he released her, still nodding to himself.

Gwyn looked down at her hand. Across her left palm, taking up almost the entire space, was a black tattoo. The lines were dark and bold as ink strokes, with no evidence of charred skin. The marking looked to have been there her whole life, though it still burned like fire.

'What have you ...?'

The round marking looked twin to Faolan's own: a series of concentric circles in different widths; circles inside those circles, overlaying a five-pointed star. Inside the star was another circle, then a triangle, a square, a circle – a dizzying spiral that seemed to go on forever.

'Here,' Faolan said, pointing to a place on the outer ring of the marking. There was something written there, something Gwyn had to squint to make out. A circle with a diagonal line slashed through it, lower left to top right. It meant nothing to her, although the sight of it filled her with a shapeless unease.

'I suppose Ascepis never explained to you how black magic works,' Faolan continued. 'No, he wouldn't have. A pity. Well, for now, know this: all black magic is channelled through five schools. Each school has six signs. That's thirty signs in total, in case you never bothered to learn your sums. This sign is the first and the easiest to learn. It is called *scinder,* or more commonly, *sever*. Think on it tonight while you are working, yes?'

He stepped away from her – and as he did, invisible cords leaped out and lashed Gwyn's hands and feet together, holding her, teetering, on her feet. She couldn't sit, couldn't walk, couldn't move. Her stomach clenched, and a spike of fear made her forget the burning in her palm.

'What is this?' she asked, through gritted teeth.

'This is how you will be spending the night, and every night after it, until you can cut the ropes apart yourself. I suggest you hurry. It will only get more difficult after each night without sleep.'

'Cut the ...?' Her mouth was dry. 'What? Are you mad?'

'Perhaps I am. In which case you would do well not to anger me any further.'

Then Faolan scuffed out the fire, leaving them in darkness.

In the morning, Gwyn took one sip of cold soup and immediately crawled away on her hands and knees to vomit it up. Faolan clicked his tongue in mock sympathy, and the horses stamped their feet.

'Lack of sleep? I know, it can upset the stomach. You will have to try harder tonight, girl, or you will be spending a lot of nights standing up like a plough horse. And I will be tightening the knots, in case you get any ideas about sleeping standing up.'

Gwyn, wiping the back of her hand across her mouth, could only stare at him, hate making a hot, tight knot under her ribs.

'Why are you doing this?'

He sighed. *'"Why are you doing this?" "Why won't*

you let me go?" Do you not think every apprentice asks the same questions? I'll give you the same answer my master gave me: because I can. One day, perhaps, you'll be stronger than me, and that's the day you no longer have to wear my leash.'

Again, she felt the stirrings of rage, dulled now under the blanket of fatigue. 'I don't want to be a wizard. I don't want your leash. I don't want anything to do with you. The *only* thing I want is to keep away from the wizards and the warglings and find Ascepis.'

Faolan sighed again – the patient sigh of a governess explaining a lesson to a naughty and none-too-bright pupil. 'And what do you think would happen if I let you go? You have mancers and warglings on your heels, and the vim only knows why they would be chasing you.' Seeing her flinch, he smiled coldly. 'Besides, they call it the black gift for a reason. Without my guidance, the power will kill you – burn you up from the inside. If you think I *want* an apprentice yapping at my heels, you're sadly mistaken. I'm doing you the greatest service of your life.'

He offered her a hand, but Gwyn clambered to her feet unassisted, though her stomach was still unsteady. The pain in her palm had faded to a dull ache. In the grey pre-dawn light, the hillside seemed shadowed and strange. Far below, the rooftops of Bangstørp were shrouded in mist.

'Here,' Faolan said, thrusting a dark bundle of

fabric into her hands. It was a cloak, scratchy wool with a deep hood that covered her face. It smelled faintly of horse.

'What's this for?' A few weeks past the solstice, the air was still warm enough that a cloak was unnecessary.

'You'll keep your face covered while we're in Edge,' he said. 'The Syndicate has spies in the city. We need to stay ahead of them.'

They saddled the horses. Faolan had a sleek, spirited gelding that must have belonged to a wealthy merchant or a noble; Gwyn, a light-footed grey mare whose placid temperament, the wizard said, would suit a novice rider. She mounted with some trepidation. She had done a little riding on Pepper, the mare who pulled the wagon. But Pepper was a draught horse, and her wide back was like sitting in an armchair.

'I had to pay a pretty for them,' Faolan said. 'Well, it could not be helped. I have no intention of trudging all the way to Edge by foot. The blacksmith said that one's name was Otani, though I expect you could call her whatever you like.'

Otani just stood patiently, rolling her eyes back at Gwyn. At Faolan's instruction, Gwyn used her knees to grip, and after a few false starts, managed to stay mounted without falling.

'Ready? Good. If we have to run, just remember what I told you. Reins, knees, weight. That's all you need to control her. Don't let your rump flap around in the saddle.'

Gwyn nodded. The wizard smiled grimly, apparently satisfied, and they made their way down the hillside. The wind brought the smell of damp earth.

'Where are you taking me?' Gwyn asked, though she wondered if it really mattered. She was trapped, as surely as if Faolan had fastened manacles to her feet.

'Edge, girl, were you not listening?'

'But why?'

He rolled his eyes, leaning back in the saddle as his gelding picked a careful path down the hillside. 'I intend to take you to Idris, plainly.'

That surprised her. 'We're meeting my uncle? He's in Edge?' She wasn't certain she believed in this uncle; not yet. But if it was a lie, it was a strange one.

Faolan barked out a laugh. 'Certainly not. Idris has not stepped within city walls for ... well, fourteen years, now. Not with the Syndicate still hunting him. No, Idris has a house in the north. A hidden place. A safe place, I would say, though no place near Idris is truly safe. But I think in this case we have no choice. Certainly it is not safe to return to the Warren. I have you and Lucian to thank for that. You have mancers after you, and it seems Idris is the only one who knows why. You are no good to me as a mancer if you end up a pile of ash. No, best we get to the bottom of all that as soon as possible. We'll stop in Edge for supplies.'

'Lucian was taking me to this *Idris* anyway. So why did you let him fall down that pit?'

Faolan smiled unpleasantly. 'I like the boy. He has a sense of humour. But that hardly means I want him nipping at my heels day and night. Oh, have no fear. There is nothing in those lower caves he cannot face. Perhaps some traps and snares left by the necromancer who lived there before me. I have been meaning to go down there and clean up some of her mess, but ...'

'A necromancer,' Gwyn repeated, quietly. Faolan gave her a sharp look.

'Shemeris Morga. She was an apprentice in the Clockwork City at the same time as me. When she fled to take up necromancy, it caused quite a stir. Many people saying "I told you so". There is a feeling among some in the Syndicate that women shouldn't be educated in the black arts. Leftover prejudice, I suppose, from the Sorceress Wars. When Shemeris abandoned the Syndicate, well, it just seemed to confirm what people had been saying.' He snorted. 'Pure ignorance. A necromancer is nothing like a sorceress, whatever those superstitious fools might believe. A necromancer is just a mancer who knows a little more; dares a little more. A sorceress – well, nobody knows what they are, save that their power is blood magic.'

A chill ran through her. 'Blood magic?'

'Human sacrifice,' he said, grinning, and Gwyn felt herself pale. *Sorceresses.* It was the second time she had heard them mentioned in as many days; Mancer Dorin had been the first, back in Raderstrup. Coincidence?

'I always thought the sorceresses were ...'

'A legend? I'm afraid Ailbhe Ahriddin was quite real. There have been others, but she is the one everyone knows. That was, oh, some four hundred years ago, now.' The wizard had a distant expression – the same Ascepis often had while puffing on his pipe as he sat at the front of the wagon. 'They say Beheret put a stop to Ahriddin, and saved the world from her tyranny. I have my doubts. Not many records remain from that time, but we know Ahriddin was on the cusp of conquering all of Caerwyn, with nobody to oppose her. Then, without explanation, she disbanded her armies, gave control of the conquered provinces back to the people, abandoned her fortress at Harrowing, and disappeared out of all knowledge. It was years later that Beheret moved against her.'

By now, the town was far behind them, sinking rapidly beneath the curve of the land. Swathes of poppies cut blood-red gouts across the plains. The sky was low and grey, ready to crack open like an egg. She could still see the glowering bulk of the Pyramid, hovering amidst the clouds, only its wedge-shaped lower third visible. That was unusual. It drifted, usually, on some arcane flight vector only its long-dead creators knew. Now it was in almost the same position as the last time she had noticed it, in Raderstrup, days ago. Maybe a little closer.

Gwyn couldn't muster up much curiosity. Lack of sleep had made everything too bright, too immediate – yet at the same time, strangely disconnected. She had the feeling of floating outside her own body. Maybe that was why it seemed she could hear again, as though from a great distance, that snatch of eerie, discordant music.

'I don't understand,' Gwyn said, shaking her head. The music disappeared. 'Why would it take a god to kill one woman? Is a sorceress so powerful?'

'Powerful, yes. Nobody really knows where they come from; only that there is never more than one sorceress alive at a time. Perhaps the power is passed one to the next. There's no record of Ailbhe Ahriddin having children, or any other sorceress. Perhaps, like mancers, they are barren, or perhaps our kind are simply not compatible with theirs. They are certainly not human. Every description of a sorceress is the same – unearthly beauty, unimaginable powers, eyes that glow like lamps in the dark. And evil, yes, each worse than the last. Since Ailbhe Ahriddin, there has never been another sorceress. There are rumours, of course, every couple of years. The Great Sorceress of the

Northern Wastes is the latest, but I've seen no evidence for it.'

Faolan slapped Otani's rump, and the mare surged forward into a smooth trot. Gwyn hung on, accustomed now to the up-and-down motion, though her muscles were already beginning to ache from the unfamiliar strain. Ahead of them, to the southeast, there was nothing but endless gold fields, dotted here and there with spruce trees and hedgerows.

'Beheret is a puzzle,' said the wizard presently. 'I would very much like to know why she is seeking you.'

Gwyn's stomach clenched. 'Lucian told me that. It doesn't seem possible.'

'Well, it is quite true. I do not know why, but Idris does, or he wouldn't have had me watch over you these past years. He was expecting this, mark my words. If you want answers, apprentice, Idris Whitemane is the one you need to talk to.' Faolan laughed, suddenly, that shocking, merry sound. 'If you can find him.'

It was almost nightfall when they reached Edge. The day had been quiet and uneventful, and Gwyn was nearly asleep in her saddle when the grey walls of the city reared up from the grass.

'Why do they call it "Edge"?' Gwyn asked.

His mouth tightened. 'Because you are pushing me to the edge of my patience.'

Guard towers were spaced across the crenellated wall. The great grey stones were spider-webbed with dew, and worn by the passing of centuries. Narrow, swallow-tailed banners, sporting the stag-and-poppies standard of Nederlund, draped the walls. Outside the gate stood two guards, their faces and tabards washed red in the last of the afternoon sunlight.

'Guards?' Gwyn whispered, puzzled. Ascepis had always steered them well clear of cities, but this felt wrong. The cities along the Midlands border might well keep their gates barred, but this far north ...?

'Problems with bandits, perhaps,' Faolan said – though she thought he looked troubled, too. They approached the gates.

'Your business in Edge?' The shorter guard's accent was a north country twang, roughly moulded into something more urbane. His eyes roved over them without interest, alighting briefly, with a leer, on Gwyn's gold hair. Belatedly, she pulled her hood forward, covering her face.

'Private,' Faolan said shortly. Gwyn hung back at his heels, uncertain.

The guard raised his eyebrows slowly, as though not believing his luck. She could almost see his mind working; guard duty was boring, and the chance to clap a traveller in irons came along only rarely. The other guard seemed to be thinking the same. His eyebrows had disappeared into his receding hairline.

'*Private,* sir? I'm afraid nobody in Edge has *private* business. What concerns you concerns the jarl. Now I'll ask again – what business do you have in Edge?'

Gwyn could only see the sleek back of Faolan's head, but she could imagine the little smile that was spreading across his face. She drew her arms around herself as if touched with a sudden, cold breeze.

'Private,' he repeated.

'*Well,*' drawled the taller guard, 'if that —'

His words were cut off as though by a knife. At Faolan's tiny gesture, both guards fell silently to the ground, though not a mark showed on them. They were breathing, but unconscious.

'What did you do to them!' It wasn't a question, and Faolan didn't bother to give an answer. Gwyn's stomach wobbled unpleasantly – all the answer she needed.

More magic. Gods help me.

The gates were closed, but with another casual gesture from Faolan, they swung open. The wizard trotted his horse through without looking back – confident, as always, that Gwyn would be following. She paused on the threshold, but there was nothing she could do.

She nudged Otani with her knees and followed Faolan, head bowed, into the great city of Edge.

CHAPTER 9

EDGE

Gwyn hoped, with night settling around their shoulders, that Faolan would lead them to an inn. She was so bone-weary she feared she might float up off Otani's back and drift away on a puff of air. But what did it matter? She doubted the wizard would let her sleep, inn or not. Far above, the stars dripped from the sky, streaks rather than distinct points, all tipping and swirling around her head.

Edge was a busy, working city, a place of farmers and traders. Shouting men, pushing carts piled with rough sacks and barrels, streamed in and out of the warehouses lining the thoroughfare. Only the wider streets were cobbled, the rest tracts of mud rutted by cart wheels. In the market square, the stalls were closing for the night, the remaining traders haggling furiously over last-minute purchases. The noise was incredible, and Gwyn pulled her hood lower over her face. Hundreds of voices. Shouts and curses from the hurrying porters and wagon-drivers, laughter and the reedy music of hornpipes drifting from inn doors. The squeal of cart and wagon axles. The thunderclap of hammers on anvils.

'You've never been in a city,' Faolan said, giving her a sideways look.

Gwyn shook her head, not trusting herself to speak. She had passed by Edge before, but never been inside. Cities were too crowded, Ascepis said.

He was right. I never knew there were this many people in the world.

'This one hardly deserves the name,' Faolan said, sniffing. 'It used to be a military encampment, back when Asgerad and Nederlund were at war.'

She looked up towards the hill, where the low bulk of Hedegaard Keep dominated the skyline. Gwyn had read about Edge. *Beggars and Slaves: A History of the High Country Through the Sixteenth Century* had been required reading. The city itself, she knew, had sprung up around the castle, as soldiers might rally to their general in battle. The walls had come later, marking out the perimeter of their encampment. But those days were long gone, and the smoke that rose above the rooftops now was the smoke of forges and soap-boilers.

They walked their horses the six blocks to the inn, through narrow, winding streets, between brightly coloured houses strung with lines of washing. Meaty smells wafted from yellow-lit doorways, but even hunger seemed too exhausting, and the aromas turned Gwyn's stomach. As the air grew more chill, people began to retreat into the warmth of their homes, leaving the streets quiet and empty save for the occasional stray, rangy dog.

They stopped beneath a swinging sign, illuminated in a pool of torchlight. A bushel of wheat, words scrawled above it: *The Wheaten Man*. It was a two-storey building, set back from the road on a grey stone foundation, with an overhanging balcony, the upper level painted a coppery red. The narrow windows were criss-crossed in black, spilling even squares of light onto the road.

They gave the horses over to the care of the stable boy who ran out to them. Faolan flipped him a copper piece, and was rewarded with a cheeky, gap-toothed smile. The purse Faolan slipped back into his robe was almost splitting at the seams. How did a renegade wizard make his coin, Gwyn wondered, spending all his time in a dusty cave? He could hardly advertise his services.

The common room was only half full, most patrons crowded around the small stage, where a performer plucked his lyre and sang a warbling rendition of 'Snow on the Belfry Tower'. Faolan made a beeline for the darkest corner, and Gwyn slid into the seat opposite him, wincing as her muscles screamed protest.

'Sore? Yes, it takes some time to grow accustomed to riding. We will spend more time ahorse before the week is out.' He must have seen her expression. 'Oh, you don't think so? Defy me, will you? And how, young apprentice, will you manage that? Or have you not realised that you do nothing, think nothing, without my permission? Do you know that, for now at least, if I ordered you to stop breathing, you would?' He sighed. 'But I am not without sympathy, whatever you might believe.'

Raising a hand, he beckoned one of the serving girls to the table. She scurried over, smoothing her apron.

'Two meals, bread, ale.' Faolan's eyes slid back to Gwyn, and he gave her a measuring look before turning back to the serving girl. 'Do you have a healer in this city, child? A Simpler, mind you – not a white-magic user.'

The serving girl's face grew as pale as his, no doubt at the mention of magic. Gwyn understood that. She felt like crawling under the table herself.

I wonder if I'll ever be as casual about magic as Faolan, she thought, then wondered where the thought came from. She didn't *want* to be casual with magic, or even hear it mentioned. She'd had enough of magic to last the rest of her life.

The girl nodded, braid bouncing on her shoulder.

'Yes, m'lord. Lady Lenna is the only true healer – she lives in the castle.' Her eyes widened slightly at that wonder. 'But we have several Simplers in Edge, m'lord. Ma Greta has her shop only a few streets away. She keeps her door open late, for travellers.'

Faolan dismissed Lady Lenna with a flick of his hand. 'Ma Greta, you say? Perhaps later I may call on her. But for now, we will be taking a room for the night.'

'One bed, m'lord?'

Gwyn's stomach clenched, but Faolan said only, 'Two, I think. My sister' – and here he looked across at Gwyn – 'would say we are a little too old to snuggle up together.' Gwyn's muscles relaxed, and the serving girl bobbed a confused curtsy.

'Certainly, m'lord.'

When she was gone, Faolan turned to Gwyn with a smile. Seeing her expression, he laughed out loud.

'Come now,' he said. 'You have nothing to fear from me in that respect, Gwyn. You are hardly to my taste.'

She trusted him less than she would a sheep thief. Trust would have been absurd under the circumstances. He had never harmed her directly – aside from enslaving her with magic, best not forget that – but Gwyn had no illusions. The wizard was her enemy, as sure as if he held a naked sword to her throat.

He does have power over me. I know that much. It's

because he thinks I'm a wizard. Well, I'll just have to show him I'm no wizard. When he grows bored, he'll let me go.

It was a poor plan, but better than going meekly along with him, even if he did claim to be taking her to her 'uncle'. He may have saved her from the wizards, but since then, he had brought her nothing but trouble. And he had hurt Lucian for no reason at all. She hadn't trusted Lucian, either, but he'd saved her life, more than once. And unlike Faolan, he hadn't used magic to fasten shackles on her mind.

The serving girl returned, and all other thoughts dissolved as Gwyn caught a whiff of the food. Perhaps she had been hungry after all. Chopped, jellied pork, with ground garlic and onions. A feast, it seemed. Ascepis knew how to make beef stew, and boiled cabbages, and a thin, watery porridge; little else. The bowl had hardly left the serving girl's hands before Gwyn was gulping the contents down, hardly noticing when it burned the inside of her mouth.

'There's no need for those nasty looks,' Faolan said, spooning up a piece of onion. 'Do you think my master was so kind to me?'

She was surprised at his tone, and at the whisper of pain that slipped from him through the bond. She hadn't thought him capable of any genuine human feelings. But perhaps this, too, was just an illusion; some kind of test or trick.

'Who was he?' She hadn't meant to ask, but it was too late to take the question back.

Faolan looked up at her, a faint expression of surprise on his features. Surprise at what? That she had bothered to ask him about himself? Or that she didn't already know the answer?

'Kagani Alvarez,' he said at last. 'He was not the best of mancers. Only of the Fourth Rank. I was stronger than him, almost from the beginning. But he was experienced, and determined, and he could draw power from me when I was sure I had nothing left. He was, above all, a moral man, with very certain ideas of right and wrong.' His spoon scraped the bottom of the bowl. 'I suppose that's why I had to kill him.'

'You killed your master?' Gwyn didn't try to cover her shock. Not that he had committed a murder – that was easy enough to believe – but at his tone. The feeling through the bond matched his voice: cold, without emotion.

'Plenty do. It's a tradition almost as old as wizardry itself, and protected under the Syndicate's laws, if not truly condoned. An apprentice only breaks free of the bond with his master when he becomes the more adept of the two. That's how they keep the Syndicate strong. Of course, most masters are happy enough with a simple test of strength. A duel, a challenge. But there are others who say the test is not truly complete until one of the pair is dead. Kagani was one of those.'

Fear tickled the inside of her chest, making the meal taste suddenly sour on her tongue.

'And you?'

Faolan paused, bread halfway to his mouth, and smiled, looking up at her from behind a fall of brown hair.

'You will have to do more than just kill me, apprentice. Trust me on that.'

There was little rest for Gwyn that night, not that she had expected it. No sooner had she limped up the stairs after Faolan and set her pack down in their little room than the wizard had her standing at attention. Here in the half-light, his movements were ghostly and blurred again. The tiny hairs on Gwyn's arms stood on end. Perhaps it was exhaustion, playing tricks on her eyes, but she didn't think so.

'You made no progress last night,' the wizard said, pacing. He had his hands folded behind his back – a schoolmaster's pose. Up and down the length of the room, his boots made a hollow *clunk, clunk* against the floorboards. 'I suspect you made no effort to break free of the bonds. Would I be correct?'

'There was nothing to *break free* of!' Gwyn said, her hands tightening into fists. 'It was ...'

He stopped pacing, looked up. 'Magic. That's the word you're looking for.'

'Yes.' She swallowed and closed her eyes, just for a

moment. The room was silent except for the hiss of oil in the lamp, and faintly, from downstairs, the rattle of plates. *Magic.* What would Ascepis say?

'Does it not stand to reason, then, that *magic* is the means to break free?' The wizard stepped closer, grasped her hand and held it up to her face, so the angry black marking was visible. '*This* magic. *Scinder,* the first sign of the first school.'

He released her hand and stalked away. 'I have some business to attend to. You —' he pointed at Gwyn, then at the single bed by the window. 'Go there. Sleep. Your training resumes when I return. I haven't —'

He paused, then, raising his nose to the air and sniffing, as though he had scented something. He took a step closer to her, and Gwyn edged backwards without meaning to. His gaze roved over her, prodding, searching, before finally coming to rest on the front pocket of her sarafan.

'You have something,' he said.

Gwyn reached into her pocket, and was stunned when her fingers closed around the tiny copper disc. *My wish!* She thought she'd lost it during her flight through the woods, or else later, in the Warren.

'Give it to me.'

She tried to pull her hand away, but Faolan had prised it open before she could stop him. He snatched the disc, holding it up to the light, and the expression of fury that crossed his face made her take another step back.

'Where did you get this, girl?'

'It's mine,' she said at once, then flinched at the look he gave her. 'I got it from a travelling alchemist. Months ago, when I was in Twisviken, with Ascepis.'

'An alchemist,' Faolan repeated, his voice flat. 'In exchange for what? Money?'

She swallowed hard. 'No.'

'What, then?'

'He wanted ... I gave him my blood. Just a little,' she added hastily, holding up her hands. 'For his experiments. It's a wish.'

'A wish?' Now his voice was thick with incredulity, and he took a step forward as though he wanted to strike her. 'Do you think this is some tale, girl? This is no wish, and whoever you spoke to was no alchemist.'

'Then what ...?'

'This has a finding enchantment on it, you little fool.' He shook the disc in her face. 'Whoever gave it to you wanted to make sure he could locate you again. I suppose he told you never to mention it to Ascepis?'

Gwyn's eyes widened, and her eyes went to the disc. In the light of the oil lamps, it seemed to gleam with a kind of lazy menace.

Faolan sighed and thrust it back into her hands. Gwyn yelped and almost dropped it.

'I've removed the finding,' he said. 'It's just a trinket, now. One I suggest you keep as a reminder.' He shook his head. 'A reminder never to be so stupid and trusting again. Life is not a fairy story. You had best learn that, and soon. Now go get some sleep. I'll be back before long, and when I am, I expect you sharp and alert.'

He left. Gwyn staggered over to her bed, still in a state of shock. The copper disc felt like a hot coal in her hand, and she slapped it down on the nightstand, unwilling to handle it a moment longer than necessary. The laurel-crowned woman seemed to smirk up at her.

A finding? She shook her head, struggling with herself. If the disc was enchanted, then the alchemist had been a wizard.

A wizard who, wherever and whoever he was, now had a tiny vial of her blood.

CHAPTER 10

A BARGAIN

Something was shaking her.

Gwyn clawed her way up out of sweet, blank sleep, eyes snapping open so hard they almost hurt. She sat up, and the world tipped. Her head was full of cotton. With effort, she focused on Faolan's face.

'Wake up, girl,' he said. 'I've found Ascepis.'

Their destination was a Simpler's shop, not far from the inn. The old woman was closing up for the night, but they barged past her. Gwyn took the stairs two at a time, but Faolan was faster, reaching the landing a few steps ahead. The Simpler's thin, outraged voice drifted after them.

'Hey there, now, my lord, you can't just —'

Gwyn ran the length of the corridor, coming to the room they sought at the same time as Faolan. Both their hands leaped for the doorknob. Faolan gave her a stern glare, and Gwyn withdrew. The wizard pushed the door open.

The little room reeked of sickness, a heavy, cloying scent as thick as a blanket. The drapes were drawn, and only a thin bar of torchlight from the street lay across the bed. A dim lamp in the corner cast strange, shifting shadows on the wood-panelled walls. On the table, an empty cup lay on its side, the inside sticky and gleaming. One of the cupboard drawers sat slightly ajar, but there was nothing inside.

In the bed, under a light sheet – the blanket had been folded at the foot – there was a little mound. As her eyes adjusted, Gwyn made out a figure, curled into a ball. He looked smaller than she remembered, but she knew him; would have known him anywhere.

'Ascepis!'

She rushed forward and knelt at his side. His brow was hot, crumpled with distress. He shivered from time to time, as though freezing, and Gwyn saw the hairs stand up on his arm. Even when she shook him, he didn't wake, didn't stir. His green-and-gold vermarine ring, now loose on his finger, glinted in the dim light.

'How?' she asked, turning to Faolan. 'The last time I saw him, we were with the wagon, miles from here.'

'So Lucian told me,' he said, then gave a tight smile at her obvious surprise. 'In the caves. You were too busy tripping over your own feet to listen. Lucian said Ascepis was likely dead; that he and the mancer had killed each other. I admit, I believed him. I thought he had sense enough to tell a dead man from a living one. Clearly not.'

Gwyn shook her head, disbelieving. 'He didn't die. Mancer Dorin came after us, and Ascepis held him off while Lucian and I ran into the woods. But he didn't —'

'Yes, yes, I've heard the story. But the fact remains: the Gold Road is miles from here. So how did Ascepis reach Edge ahead of us?'

Gwyn had no answer to that, and Faolan didn't seem to expect one. He frowned down at Ascepis, frail and ashen-skinned in the lamplight.

'Well,' he said, after a moment, 'it's clear he is not dead, whatever Lucian might have believed. Not yet, at least, thanks to the old crone's care.'

'Here, now,' the Simpler huffed, appearing at the door. 'You can't just —'

Faolan whirled and said something to her – Gwyn didn't hear what, didn't care – and the woman retreated.

Not yet. But he would die, wouldn't he? Gwyn understood sickness, in all its different guises; had brewed potions for breakbone fever and ague and palsy. This was something else. This was death, standing shoulder to shoulder with them in this tiny room.

What did that wizard do to him?

Faolan leaned over Ascepis, feeling his brow, pulling down his eyelids to examine the whites. His hands were steady and surprisingly gentle.

'Well,' he said eventually, and his tone held a note of slyness that made Gwyn look up. 'I see this as an opportunity.'

'What?' It was hard to muster much interest in what the wizard was saying. *Dying – Ascepis is dying.* What would she do without him? Where would she go?

'I can save Ascepis,' Faolan said. 'But in return, I want ... one year.'

Gwyn just stared at him, her expression blank. Shock and exhaustion had drained her. It was hard to focus on anything. The wizard's words were like shards of broken pottery, impossible to fit together in any logical way.

One year? What did that mean? But, no, that wasn't the important part. *Save Ascepis? Impossible. He's too sick. Nobody could be ill like this and live. And wizards can't heal – Lucian told me that much. There's nothing we can do. Is there?*

'You already know I can force you to obey,' Faolan continued. 'What I'm asking for is your cooperation. One whole year of it. One year, in which you become my apprentice in more than just name. One year of total and complete devotion to learning the black arts. One year in which you *want* to learn. And after that year, well, if you still believe

I've made a mistake with you, I'll set you free. No conditions, and no obligations. You can do as you wish. Go back to Ascepis, if it pleases you. Squat in a run-down wagon, skulking from town to town until the Syndicate or Beheret's pet mancers catch up with you again. But for that one year, you're mine.'

'One year,' Gwyn repeated dumbly – not agreeing to the terms, but simply trying to understand. 'And in return, you can ... save him?'

He gave the familiar flick of his hand, as though swishing away an insect. The movement left a faint, trailing blur in the air. 'Yes, yes. You'll find in some ways, I'm a better healer than any of those fools from the Lower City. You might say that life and death are my trade.' That seemed to amuse him. 'But the details don't concern you. Do you agree to the terms?'

Gwyn looked down at Ascepis, but he was no help. His face was a blank slate. Well, it didn't matter. There was no question in her mind. There never had been. Even if it was true, and he'd only taken her in under orders from some wizard ... he was her family. Her true family, more than this so-called uncle she'd never met.

She reached one hand up to Faolan, and, after a moment, he took it in his own. His skin was very soft.

'His life, in exchange for a year,' Gwyn said. He nodded, and they shook hands. She could almost feel the weight of the bargain settle around her shoulders like a cape.

A low moan from the figure on the bed broke the spell, and they both looked down at Ascepis. He hadn't moved, but a film of sweat covered his creased brow.

'Not much time,' Faolan muttered, releasing Gwyn's hand. 'Very well. Don't interrupt me. Don't touch me. Just sit.'

He glanced around the room, then, smoothing the back of his robe, sat down in the hard little chair by the bed. Gwyn settled herself on the floor. Faolan was staring at Ascepis, with a look that made the hairs rise on Gwyn's arms. The look was intent, razor-focused – but distant, as though seeing through Ascepis. Through the muscles and sinews of his chest, through the fibres of the bed, through the floorboards to the shop below. Through to the centre of the world, perhaps.

Slowly, Faolan's eyes closed.

At first, nothing happened. The wizard's eyes remained shut, his face serene. Night air through the window stirred the silk-straight hair framing his face. On the bed, Ascepis lay fevered and still, dying before their eyes.

The wind picked up, and Gwyn shuddered, rubbing her hands together. The room had grown cold. She looked over to the window, but the drapes were still closed, and no breath of air touched them.

Life and death are my trade.

The small hairs on her arms and neck stood up from her skin. Faolan still hadn't moved. He might have been sleeping, save that he sat alert and upright in his chair. Not even his eyelids flickered to betray that he was still alive.

In the corner, the lamp stuttered twice, and died.

'That was unpleasant.'

Gwyn sat up, blinking to clear her eyes. There was a wet spot on her arm where her head had been resting, and for a moment she had no idea where she was. Four walls, a chair, a bedside cupboard. Faolan, seated and rubbing his forehead, looking paler than usual.

'You ... you did it?' Her voice was thick with sleep. How long had Faolan been ... gone? She had no idea. It was incredible she'd fallen asleep at all. But now, if he'd returned, that meant ...

Her hand went to Ascepis' brow. Warm, but not fevered. His breath came heavy and regular.

Relief flooded her. *He'll live. Ascepis will live.*

'One year, girl,' Faolan croaked. He sounded awful, though he smiled at her when she looked over at him.

She swallowed, her mouth suddenly dry. 'I haven't forgotten.' How could she? The full weight of it was just beginning to sink in. 'Was that ...'

She couldn't say the word. *Necromancy.* She knew almost nothing about wizards, but oh, she knew about necromancers. The dark wizards, so dangerous, so evil, that the Syndicate sought them and hunted them down like rabid beasts. *Life and death are my trade.* Gods, what had she gotten mixed up in?

'Necromancy?' Faolan finished for her. He said it as casually as he might say 'fishing' or 'basket-weaving'. 'Yes. For many years I was just an ordinary mancer, studying in the Clockwork City. Until I started a different sort of study. When the mancers found me, well ...' He shrugged. 'Your uncle Idris was the one who helped me escape. We were ... friends, once. He said he didn't believe the charges against me. Perhaps he should have. But it's only thanks to Idris that I have my life at all. Of course, escaping was only half the struggle. Since then, I've had to hide, from the mancers and their warglings both.'

'How did —'

He cut her off. 'Enough for now. I'll answer more of your questions in time. Now that you're to be my apprentice in more than name only, you should feel free to ask questions. Knowledge is wisdom, after all, and wisdom is power. Not that you should be getting too much power, now.' He chuckled softly. 'Not yet, alas.'

He stood, smoothing the front of his robe. 'Well,

girl, the night is getting on, and I seem to remember promising you a few more hours' sleep. Come.'

'But Ascepis —'

Faolan held up a finger. 'I said I'd save him. Well, he's saved. But he won't wake up for, oh, a day or two at the least. I'll leave some coins with the Simpler for his care and board, but as to the rest – well, he'll have to shift for himself. Your care has passed to me now.'

Gwyn had almost grown accustomed to the feeling of Faolan in the back of her mind. But she felt it now – felt him *tug* on her, gently, to coax her towards the door, as a farmer might tug on the leading ropes of the goat he was taking to market. It wasn't forceful, but she found herself following anyway, and had only a moment to look back at Ascepis' small body lying in its bed before Faolan disappeared around the corner.

She followed the necromancer down the stairs with unshed tears in her eyes.

CHAPTER 11

THE VIM

First light found Gwyn and Faolan facing each other across a table in the corner of the common room. He was in high spirits, chatting with the serving girl, arm flung over the back of his chair. She was quiet, chewing thoughtfully on her heel of rye.

When they had returned to the Wheaten Man the night before, Gwyn had barely made it into their room before sprawling unconscious on the bed. Faolan hadn't even tried to tie her up – she needed strength for the road, he said.

For a change, she had been too bone-weary to dream.

It had seemed only moments later that Faolan shook her awake with instructions to dress and hurry downstairs. Now, in the common room, Gwyn yawned into her watered-down ale. She could easily have slept for hours yet. Faolan wore the same grey robe, but it looked to have been washed, and some of the colour had returned to his cheeks. His hair was straight and shiny and smelled faintly of pears. On his forearm, the brand stood out starkly – a tower and a moon. He wore a ring she hadn't noticed before, too, glinting in green and gold like Ascepis'.

Very like Ascepis'.

She gave him a sharp look, and he shrugged. 'Payment for my services. A small price for saving a life, would you not agree?'

'And that?' Gwyn asked, pointing at his chest. At the end of a leather thong dangled her 'wish', bright copper in the morning light. It hurt to look at it now, knowing what it was, or what it had been. *A trick, like everything else.* She had planned to leave it behind on the nightstand.

'A reminder,' he said with a cold smile.

She pressed her lips together, but didn't argue. Let him mock her, if he wished.

'I want to leave a note for Ascepis. For when he wakes up. He should at least know I'm alive.'

'There is no need. No doubt he will return to the wagon, and then he can make contact with Idris himself.'

'Make contact?' She narrowed her eyes. 'How?'

Faolan began to massage his temple. His expression was long-suffering. 'At times I wonder about your intelligence. Did you never notice that Ascepis kept a jar of ashes, hmm?'

Gwyn thought back, then nodded. The wagon was always full of odd things – hanging bushels of herbs, jars of mole teeth and crow feathers and dung-beetle carapaces, moth wings suspended in brine. Though, now that she thought about it, what potions used ash as an ingredient?

'They're from the hearth at Priory – Idris' house,' Faolan said. 'With those, he can send a letter directly to Idris.'

'Magic? But I thought you said Ascepis wasn't a wizard anymore?'

'You do not need to be a mancer to send a fire letter. Only to enchant the ashes to begin with. Now, enough questions. I want to be away from this place.'

They finished eating, and were outside with their horses saddled before the sun had cleared the city walls. A thousand smells assailed Gwyn's nostrils, sweet and sour. She had barely noticed yesterday, in her dazed state. Food, sweat, sewage. Coal fires and woodsmoke. Loamy mud and wet wool, courtesy of the recent rain.

Half the buildings lining the streets were stone, or at least had stone foundations, the top floors whitewashed and crossed with timber beams. There were shingled roofs everywhere she looked, steeply pitched with front-facing gables, stretching all the way up to the great castle that squatted on the hill.

The charging boar banner flew above the keep to show the Thane was in residence.

They took the east road out of the city, across a bridge over what Faolan called the Shattered River.

'May I ask where we're going now?'

'You may,' he said. She waited, but he gave no other response, and she sighed.

Before long, they left the city behind and came to the open plains, fields knee-deep in pale gold lousewort. The ground was rockier here, and nothing seemed to grow that wasn't red or yellow or somewhere in between, aside from the occasional thatch of wild summer pumpkins. For hours they followed the road as it sliced across the land, the flatness broken only by a few dry trees, and weathered barns with their sides bulging under low gambrel roofs. This was further than she had ever travelled in Ascepis' wagon. He had liked to stay at least a half-day's journey from the cities, moving between the larger villages in Nederlund, and along the far-north edge of Surudar.

'Faolan,' she said after a time. 'Who was my mother? And my father?'

He shot her a sideways look. 'What am I, girl, your family chronicler?'

'I thought you might know.'

'I wouldn't know your father if he came to my door selling buttons.' He paused, cocked his head. 'If I had a door, that is. Your mother I knew a little.

Aislinn Whitemane. She studied white magic for a time in the Lower City. Pretty girl, tall, skinny, white hair, green eyes. I heard she was quite good – though perhaps that was just brotherly pride on Idris' part.'

'She studied white magic?'

He nodded. 'It's common among those with mancer siblings. And the parents of mancer children, too. I wrote a paper on it, before ...'

Before you were chased out of the Syndicate for necromancy, Gwyn thought, rubbing her arms. They were angling north and east now, following the up-swell of the land. Shingle-clad windmills beat the cold air with their great sails. To her left, far in the distance, Gwyn could make out the purple haze of the mountains, distant as clouds.

'After your mother left the Clockwork City, Idris spent years trying to find her,' Faolan said. 'Instead, he found you, her daughter. You were three, or near enough, when he passed you on to Ascepis.'

And Ascepis' story, about finding her on the streets of Til Iver? Apparently it was just that: a story. Not even a very good one. The image of dour-faced Ascepis, scooping some bedraggled orphan out of a life of poverty – no, it had never really fit. In truth, she had been passed to him by Idris like a package for safekeeping. Strange to think of this uncle she'd never met, manipulating her life before she was old enough to even know of it.

I have some questions for this wizard uncle. And for

Ascepis, too, although it was hard to imagine she'd ever see him again. Perhaps when this year was done.

Before midday, Faolan found a copse of wiry yellow trees away from the road, and they let the horses graze as they settled in a patch of sun for lunch. There was white bread, cold dumplings with ground pork, stuffed cabbage, boiled eggs with a cloth-wrapped twist of salt, an earthenware flagon of ale. Apparently, the necromancer believed in eating well.

When Faolan had finished his meal, he took a sip from the flagon and turned to her. 'Now that we're better acquainted,' he said, ignoring her incredulous look, 'I feel I should tell you more of black magic. A youngling's first years in the Syndicate are spent studying theory. You never had that advantage, but perhaps I can cover the basics.'

She shook her head, smoothing the front of her sarafan. As though anything about magic could be called *basic.* It was the dark power that moved the world, that cracked open the earth, that shook the stars out of alignment.

'Why do you call them mancers, and not wizards?' she asked, meeting his eyes.

'"Wizard" is a northern word. The Syndicate considers it uncouth. When they take High Country children, they spend months beating the word out of them.' He sniffed. 'For my part, I don't care what term you use. Words have only what power you give them.'

She gave a slow nod. Ascepis had always called them wizards, when he spoke of magic at all – but there *had* been a small hitch in his voice, hadn't there? As if the word sat uncomfortably on his tongue.

'The first thing to understand is what, exactly, black magic *is*. There are many names for it. The vim, some say, or the power, or just magic.' A tiny blue fire sprang up in Faolan's palm, and Gwyn's stomach lurched. 'You can build your strength up with practice. To a fledgling, lighting this fire would be like lifting a wagon with one hand. To me it's like lifting a cup of tea.' He closed his hand, and the fire winked out.

'And this?' Gwyn asked, holding up her own hand. The marking on her palm no longer hurt, unless she gripped the reins too tightly, but she was startled anew every time she glimpsed it – an angry black stain where her own pale skin should be.

'The markings,' Faolan said, nodding. 'As I told you, we channel the vim through thirty signs. In the early days of magic, it was necessary for a mancer to write these signs every time he wished to use the power – on parchment, on objects, and so on. It was effective, but time-consuming, too, and posed a problem if, for example, the mancer's hands were bound.

'Eventually, it was discovered that by imprinting the signs on his own body, it was no longer necessary to write them each time. Thus, the markings.

Convention dictates that the apprentice should be marked in the same manner as the master.' He held up his hand, showing her his own marking.

'Yours is different. Your star only has four points.'

'How observant of you. You will also notice only one sign has been added to yours thus far, being *scinder.* Once you have mastered it, I will add more.'

She looked at her palm. In the border around the circle, there was still space for – well, twenty-nine more signs, she supposed.

Gwyn shivered. Perhaps this Idris would put a stop to whatever game Faolan was playing at.

But until then, she was alone. Hunted by wizards. Captive to a crazed necromancer. Her guardian had almost died. Her life had been smashed into kindling.

She stared into the blue, radiant sky; stared until her eyes burned. She couldn't escape Faolan.

The best she could hope was to survive him.

CHAPTER 12

A RECKONING IN TØNDERBY

Gwyn stood stiff as a tree trunk in the dark. Only the invisible cords pinioning her arms to her sides kept her from slumping to the floor. She couldn't see the knots, but she felt them against her skin, digging in like hardened metal spikes whenever she began to drift towards sleep. Across the room, Faolan breathed lightly in the dark.

Peaceful as a babe in its mother's arms, Gwyn thought sourly.

The shadows had lengthened by the time they'd reached Tønderby. It was a good-sized town, holding pride of place along the busy Hjolvangar Road leading to northern Asgerad. A slicing wind gusted down from the peaks, bringing the smell of snow. As they approached the town, Gwyn had pulled her coat tight, shivering.

The houses were built low, partially underground

to conserve heat. They passed a temple to Molech Suun, the Father of Storms – a squat, ugly building, its dark doors carved with twin lightning bolts. It was much larger than the little chapel outside Bangstørp. Dozens of prayer kites, tethered to the encircling fence, shivered and snapped in the wind.

There were four inns in Tønderby, the most Gwyn had ever seen in a single town. Faolan had led them past The Stormlord's Forge and The Silver Bolt, before settling on a smaller inn, its creaking sign depicting a sheep and the innocuous name 'The Woolly Wanderer'.

When they'd come upstairs from the common room after eating, the necromancer had told her, quite amiably, that her training would continue tonight, and that if she wanted to sleep she'd best learn to cut through the knots holding her up.

'But I agreed to let you teach me,' Gwyn had protested, as Faolan tightened the knots. Invisible or not, they pinched her skin, made her bones ache.

'And what do you think this is for, hmm? My own amusement, perhaps?'

She *had* thought that, in fact. Surely this couldn't be how apprentices were trained in the Clockwork City? She had thought it a test of some kind; perhaps his way of breaking her spirit.

But Faolan was quite serious. He really did expect her to cut the knots. With magic. Ridiculous! She'd been standing for hours now, rigid as a statue.

Faolan had gone to sleep right away, and for the first hour Gwyn had stood raging silently. The man was a lunatic! Making her stand in the dark all night like a fool. And in her smallclothes, too. What if one of the chambermaids came? The inn may have been the smallest in Tønderby, but there were always servants. Not that they were likely to come into the room in the middle of the night, but if they did ...

At least he had let her keep her shoes on. The floorboards were distinctly chilly. The whole room was chilly, in fact. *Cursed man.*

But there were only so many ways she could call Faolan a pig-brained, motherless wretch, and eventually Gwyn began to think of escape. The necromancer was mad, and possibly dangerous, but he didn't seem stupid. If he said it was possible to escape from these invisible cords, then maybe it was. But that meant using magic.

The thought made her skin break out in gooseflesh. Magic – what would Ascepis have said to *that?* But, of course, Ascepis had been a wizard himself. It was still so hard to imagine.

In the common room that night, over sautéed beef with sour cream, Faolan had shown her the tower-and-moon scar on his left arm. It was the Syndicate's mark, he'd said, branded into the flesh on the day a young wizard was apprenticed to his master. And then he'd asked, taking a casual swig of his ale, what

Ascepis had done with his brand, after the Syndicate had silenced him and cast him out.

Gwyn had been ready to say that Ascepis had no brand on his arm. Of course he didn't; she'd seen him every day of her life, and would have noticed something like that.

But then she remembered his burn. It was rectangular, angry-red and raised from the skin, and in the exact same place on his left arm as Faolan's moon and tower. Ascepis had said he'd brushed up against a hot stove as a young man, and Gwyn had never thought much about it. But if he'd ever borne a Syndicate brand, that rectangular burn scar would have covered it completely.

Gwyn didn't feel much like a wizard, but Faolan said she was, and if the Syndicate ever found her, maybe they would think so too. If they routinely went about branding young children, she doubted they would believe her denials. Better if she were able to defend herself. The past few days had been an ongoing nightmare. Mancer Dorin, Lucian, now Faolan – everybody wanted a piece of her, and she was helpless as a kitten as they tossed her back and forth.

No more. If learning magic is what it takes to be able to defend myself, I'll learn it. She'd take any advantage she could get. And then she would make Faolan sorry he'd ever breathed.

So now she stood, trussed like a chicken in the

dark. The ropes dimpled her skin, made folds in the fabric of her smallclothes. Otherwise, there was nothing to see.

But there *was* something there. She could feel it.

It wasn't sight, and it wasn't touch, either. Maybe something in between. She could run her mind down the length of the rope like running her hand down a banister. She felt the knots, too. Her mind kept going back to them, a tongue to a missing tooth. There were half a dozen knots, but one at the front seemed different. She thought if she could get that one undone, the whole thing would fall apart.

Easier said than done. She wanted to just reach out and grab it. But even if she could move her hands, she doubted anything would be there. She had to use her mind, somehow. Or was it her *vim*? What was the difference, again?

Faolan had said to use the *sever* sign, but of course, he had never deigned to explain how. She remembered the sign, even without looking at the marking on her palm. She could think of a line bisecting a circle until her face turned blue. But what good would it do?

Frustration made sweat stand out on her brow, and Gwyn schooled herself to calm. She could try, at least. That was more than she'd done the first time, in the doorway of the chapel, where she had stood all night, weeping and raging alternately, never even trying to touch the knots. Back then, she hadn't really believed.

And now?

She breathed deeply. Calm. Frustration was making it harder. Faolan had mentioned something in Edge about keeping a calm mind. She could do that, at least. Ascepis had taught her how to empty her mind. He had probably learned it in the Clockwork City himself. How many of his lessons came straight from the wizards? No, better not to think about that.

Gwyn let her awareness drift, trying to imagine the tension draining out of her, water poured from a stone urn. *Calm.*

Her attention roamed, and in the little corner of her mind still given to conscious thought, she realised her senses had expanded. She could sense the servants asleep in their rooms at the rear, and the innkeeper down the hall, and the horses, stirring dust as they stamped their feet in the stables. Her mind brushed past Otani, and she heard the mare whicker uneasily, sensing *something.*

Out, further. Her awareness took in the street outside. Darkness. Prior was waning, Sadira dark and hidden beyond the horizon. She felt the hard-packed earth and the grumbling river just a few houses away, beyond the low stone wall that marked the border of the town proper. There were no guards, not even in a town this size.

But there was a man, crossing the field towards the town. Closer, now. There was something *very* familiar about him. He had a fall of light-gold hair, and his face was covered by a silver mask, etched with symbols she didn't recognise. Only his eyes showed, and even through the darkness she saw they were rich, velvet green, the mirror to her own. Why would ...?

Her mind snapped back into her body with such violence that she reeled and almost fell. Her vision went red and jagged. Blood pounded in her ears.

'Faolan! Wake up!'

Faolan didn't respond. With a shock, Gwyn realised his bed was empty. And not just empty, but undisturbed, as though he'd never laid in it. And the world ...

The world had gone mad.

Colour was gone, and in its absence was a twisting whorl of light and shadow. She could make out the bed, the window, the walls of the room, but their shapes seemed to change before her eyes. The walls expanded, contracted, yet didn't move at all. The floor rippled like water. The drapes seemed one moment to gust inwards, wracked by fierce winds, then lay unmoving against the sill. The lamp was snuffed out, as before – no! The flame burned hot against the glass – no, it was dead; burned-out.

She wanted to pluck her eyes out of her head. She

wanted to vomit. The world writhed in front of her eyes like a nest of snakes.

Some kind of spell? An illusion? She didn't know, couldn't begin to guess. But the man in the mask ...

The window of their room looked west, towards the fields where she'd sensed him coming. Gwyn spun, raced for the window, almost tripping over her own feet. The street was too dark to make out anything but shadows.

The ropes, she realised, too late. The ropes were gone. Had she severed them? She didn't think so. Her muscles should have been screaming relief, but she felt nothing. In her gut, a shriek was trying to claw its way free.

She turned back to the bed. Empty, empty, how could it be empty? Where was Faolan? He had been there seconds before; she'd seen him kicking the covers, heard him sniffing and grunting in his sleep! Where —?

From the corner of her eye, Gwyn glimpsed somebody standing on the landing outside.

Faolan?

No. The figure filled the doorway – just a shadow, dark against the shifting grey of the surrounding world. A strange, fey light glinted off his silver mask. Those eyes ... She knew those eyes, knew the sweep of gold hair above them.

Is it you?

He made no move, but unseen hands grasped

Gwyn's shoulders, lifted her up like a sack of oats. She would have fallen, but the force holding her kept her steady, her feet hovering two inches off the ground.

'We meet at last,' the man said. His voice came out strong and clear despite the mask. 'Or should I say *again?*'

'Who ... who are you?' Her voice was raw and desperate, on the brink of panic. She struggled against the bonds, against the invisible force that held her, but it made no difference.

His silver mouth was carved into a genial smile, but she heard laughter in his voice. 'You don't remember me? I'm hurt. My name is Ygriel. I remember you well. Oh, you were a little smaller then, but not so different. You look more like your mother now. Bigger around the hips, though. She was always too small for the work they had her doing.' He laughed again, as though he'd made a joke.

Gwyn gaped, forgetting her terror. *Mother?* How could he know her mother? He was clearly a wizard, so perhaps he'd known her in the Clockwork City. Or ...

No – she dismissed the thought as soon as it formed. With the silver mask, it was impossible to be sure of this Ygriel's age, but he seemed far too young to be her father; surely not much older than herself.

'How would you know my mother?' she asked, her voice a hoarse near-whisper. The invisible ropes held her tighter than Faolan's had. Already her arms and legs were turning numb. Reaching out with her mind, she could feel the bonds holding her, but they were more like shackles than ropes, with no knots to untie. She tried to think of *sever*, the line and the circle – but it kept slipping away, like oil skittering across a hot pan.

'How could I not? It's been fourteen years or more, but I knew her, as I know you. Even if your name is different. Mine was the first hand you ever held, though I was barely big enough to see into your cradle. I know you better than you know your own reflection.'

Sever. She could feel the bonds that held her, but they were so different to Faolan's unseen ropes. They seemed to pulse, like dark veins. Gwyn tried to slow her breathing, the way she had before, but her heart pounded in her chest as though trying to escape.

'You're insane,' she said through gritted teeth. Empty bravado. 'Why have you been in my dreams? If you think you can scare me that way, you're wrong.'

'Scare you? Why should I? The Great Lady deals in love, not fear.' There was the light of fanaticism in those eyes. 'You have been honoured, Yennevere. To be given a message by the Great Lady herself? Men have died for just a chance at that privilege.'

Yennevere? The name meant nothing to her. Did he think she was someone else? Had this all been some kind of mistake? The thought made her want to break out in hysterical laughter. All a misunderstanding —

'My name is Gwyn,' she said. 'I don't know who you think I am. I don't have anything to do with your Great Lady. Please, just let me go.'

He laughed then – a brittle, cut-glass sound. 'Let you go? Free yourself, Yennevere. Come. Enough of this farce.'

But she couldn't free herself, no matter how she thrashed at the bonds; no matter how she reached for *sever,* reached and reached again. She would have screamed if there was any air in her lungs.

Ygriel's eyes narrowed, the amused gleam hardening into irritation. 'What good is there in this pretence? You refused to enter the Lurk to save Ascepis Melm, even when my riders dropped him practically at your feet. You preferred to send your minion in your stead. A cold decision, though practical. But now? We are the same, you and I. There's no need to dissemble here.'

His words were nonsense, but in Gwyn's fear, every one shivered with meaning. *Lurk? Riders? Minion?* She felt strangely untethered, a paper boat tossed in a roiling ocean.

The man moved faster than she could react. He crossed the space between them in two long strides, and his hand snaked out to grasp her arm. Gwyn cried out; couldn't help it. His touch was like cold fire.

'Is it possible?' he wondered, his fingers hard steel on her arm. He leaned closer, peering into her face, seeming to search for something. 'Do you truly not know?'

She leaned away as far as the invisible shackles would allow. 'Know ... what?'

His grip tightened. Eyes narrowing into slits, he gave a small shake of his head. 'No matter. You can make your pleas to the Goddess. Now —'

His words cut off. He looked – confused? There was no other word for it. Gwyn felt something *tug* at her, from somewhere underneath her breastbone, but she resisted it without thinking.

'How are you —?' he began, and the eyes that stared at her went wide with what seemed like shock, before his words dissolved in a corona of white fire.

CHAPTER 13

ASH AND EMBERS

Gwyn sucked in a sharp, desperate breath.

It felt like surfacing from underwater. The blood pounded in her ears, and she blinked, trying to clear her vision.

Ygriel was ... gone.

It was still night-time, but the room was solid now, shaded in blue and purple rather than grey. She stood alone.

Gwyn turned towards the beds – and almost screamed in frustration. Faolan's bonds were still there, pinioning her arms to her sides. She stood trapped, immobile.

'Faolan!'

But his bed lay empty, the covers half off as though he'd risen in haste. From somewhere outside, she heard shouts. A high-pitched scream, growls, something breaking. Then an explosion, shaking the boards beneath her feet.

Frantic, she turned her attention back to the bonds. These were definitely Faolan's, not the stranger's. She could sense the difference now. There was no pulsing darkness, no crawling *wrongness* creeping up her spine. And she could feel the knots, could almost see the way they were tied.

Was I dreaming? The colourless room, the strange, shifting walls. Ygriel. It hadn't felt like a dream, but how else to explain it? If it was real, why was she still bound?

More screams, closer now. Gwyn struggled until her muscles thrummed with pain, but it was no use. The *sever* sign burned in her mind, bright as a star ... and as distant as one. Panic made her clumsy, and the sign kept slipping out of her mind as though covered with soap.

Focus. I have to focus.

She was still grasping at the central knot when she noticed her shadow against the floor. It stretched out long towards the beds, flickering as though buffeted by a high wind. Had someone lit torches in the street? Why ...?

The smell of smoke came on the heels of the thought, and from behind her came a crackling *whoosh.* The back of her neck prickled with sudden heat. Red light bled across the floorboards.

Fire.

Outside, Gwyn could still hear shouts, muffled now by the low roar of flames. She couldn't see the fire, but the room had turned to red and yellow, as though illuminated through stained glass. The whole side of the inn must have been aflame.

'*Faolan!*' she screamed, again and again, until her voice turned to a croak.

No answer. He had left her.

Gwyn tried to wriggle free, thrashed and cursed and bit her tongue until she tasted blood, but the bonds held as tightly as ever. Again, she reached for the knot with her mind, and grasped nothing.

Gwyn didn't see where the fire got in, but when she caught sight of it from the corner of her eye, she almost passed out from terror. In the corner, the little table was burning. Flames licked across the wall, the roof. Smoke choked the air, burning her eyes, clogging her ears and throat. With her arms pinned, Gwyn had no way of covering her mouth. She started to cough. The air tasted hot and thick as tar.

The blanket caught fire, then the mattress. Straw stuffing went up with a sound like cracking ice.

Gwyn's chest hitched uselessly. Sweat plastered her hair to her face. No air. She had escaped the masked man only to die here, burned to death in an inn she couldn't even remember the name of.

Ascepis, I'm sorry.

And then ...

Perhaps it was the distraction. While her lungs

strained for breath, the rest of her mind kept working on the knot. The *sever* sign flared up in her awareness, a line and circle that burned hotter and brighter than the flames. The feeling in her head was of something *tearing*. A spike of pain, and a sudden warmth inside her head, like blood.

Then it was gone, and when Gwyn reached out she felt something touch the knot. Not to untie it, but to slice it apart. An unseen blade. A knife of pure thought.

Flex.

The bonds fell away like silk parting beneath a sword. Gwyn's knees buckled, and the floor rushed up to meet her. She hit the ground and lay there, too dazed to move.

Have to ... get out.

She couldn't see the door, but she remembered where it was – the general direction, at least. Were the stairs on fire? It didn't matter. She had to risk them. Half blind, Gwyn began crawling towards the hallway, sucking in deep, sawing breaths that made her throat feel choked with burnt wool.

Out of the flames, two cloaked figures ghosted into the room. The smoke eddied away as though swept with a broom, pressing up against the walls.

Exposing Gwyn where she lay, flat on her belly, blinking hot smoke out of her eyes.

'Is this her?' said one, grabbing the back of her shirt,

hauling her up so he could look into her eyes. His were dark brown, cold and savage beneath a wiry brow. The tower-and-moon brand stood out from his forearm.

Wizard.

'With those eyes? I'd say so.' The smoke roiled and churned, as though trapped outside some invisible dome. 'Well, the Great Lady will be pleased. Let's get her —'

The crash of breaking glass. The men looked up, and the one holding her loosened his grip, enough for her to tear free. Gwyn toppled backwards ...

And felt hands seize her from behind. Saw a flash of silver as something metallic went streaking through the air. The knife took the nearest man in the shoulder.

A moment of still, shocked silence.

'Don't let her get away!' the wizard bellowed, grabbing at the knife hilt. He tore it free, spraying Gwyn with blood.

'Move,' said a voice in her ear, barely audible over the men's shouts.

Gwyn staggered to her feet, her eyes still streaming, coughing too hard to speak. Her muscles burned as though the flames had already reached them. The man – it was a man, but she couldn't make out his face – hauled her towards the window. The curtains had scorched away, leaving scraps of charred fabric. Broken glass lay in shards across the floor.

The man kicked out the spikes still clinging to the window frame.

And then she was falling.

Flames rushed past her. She hit the ground on her side, breath coming out of her in a *whoomp.* For an instant, the world went dark. She lay dazed, every bone in her body screaming.

Darkness.

'— you well, lass?'

The voice came from far away. Hands. The smell of burning.

Her vision returned in inky, broken fragments. The man was hauling her to her feet. Gwyn blinked at him. Firelight showed a fierce, wild face, the left side cut by a jagged black tattoo from temple to cheekbone.

'Lucian!' she croaked.

He nodded, distracted, eyes scanning the street. There was nobody in sight. The windows of every home and shop were shuttered tight. A corpse lay sprawled in the dirt, soot and a bloom of dark blood staining his Syndicate robes.

'Can you walk?'

At Gwyn's nod, Lucian shoved something into her arms. Her pack. He must have grabbed it just before throwing her out the window.

Throwing me out the ...?

She looked up, gaping, but the smoke was too thick to make out the window, or anything else of the inn. From somewhere inside, timber cracked and groaned, and she heard screams.

'Are there ... people still inside?' she asked. Her voice was a raw whisper. Charred fragments of linen, plaster and paper drifted from the dark sky.

Lucian shook his head. 'The innkeep and his family made it out, and there were only three other guests, all accounted for. Come on, hurry now. One knife canna slow two wizards for long.'

'Where's —'

A tremor shook the ground, made the nearby windows rattle in their panes, and she would have stumbled if Lucian hadn't been holding her. Gwyn whipped around, towards the sound of —

The creature in the middle of the road was bigger than a horse. Bigger than two horses standing nose-to-tail. Its hide was grey-green leather, its head a wedge-shaped monstrosity of swept-back horns and spikes and narrow golden eyes. And its wings ...

Its wings spanned the width of the road, both tipped with a curved claw, like the wings of a bat. But this was a bat the size of Ascepis' wagon; a bat with a thrashing, serpentine tail, with teeth near the length of her forearm.

She didn't notice the man atop the beast until he leaned forward, shouting down at them over the ridged neck. The hot wind ripped at his words.

'Give her up, shapeshifter! No one else has to die tonight.'

Lucian shoved Gwyn behind him, and his warning growl was barely human. 'Not likely! Ye'll need more than a few wizards and a single drake if you think to take her.'

The man laughed, high and cold. 'But we have many drakes, shapeshifter. Even now, more are winging their way here.'

That should have meant something, Gwyn was certain. But the creature arced its long, sinewed neck towards her, and she couldn't think; couldn't breathe. Those yellow fangs seemed to fill her vision.

So she didn't see the moment that Lucian changed. He was there, a solid wall of muscle between her and the beast. And then he was gone, and a striped cat leaped through the air, its full-throated roar making the hard-packed earth shiver beneath her feet like the skin of a struck drum.

Its teeth sank into the monster's exposed throat.

Gwyn yelped, staggered backwards. The cat – was that *Lucian?* – was enormous. If it stood on its back legs, it would overtop a grown man by two feet.

It wasn't standing now. It clung to the creature's thrashing neck, digging in with teeth and claws and rippling muscles. Blood spattered the ground, dark and faintly opalescent in the firelight, flecking the robes of the wizard who half stood in the saddle, shouting something Gwyn couldn't hear over the creature's screams.

But the great cat was struggling. Its paws could

find no traction on the blood-slicked neck. The beast's wings beat the air, forcing Gwyn back a step, and the creature lifted six feet off the ground. Ten feet. Twelve. Its neck whipsawed, trying to dislodge the unwelcome passenger. Lucian's jaws, full of blood and torn flesh, began to slip loose.

The wizard leaned forward, and Gwyn saw *something* forming in his outstretched hands. A crackle of blue fire that made crazy, dancing shadows along the street. The sky was hot and alive and raining ash, blood, embers.

The clatter of hooves made Gwyn whip around, clutching her pack to her chest as though it might offer some protection.

But the figure that emerged from the smoke was Faolan. Faolan, seeming ten feet tall on his black gelding, leading a fully saddled Otani behind him. Faolan, with ash dusting the shoulders of his coat, his face grim and hard and devoid of his usual scathing humour. He held one arm cradled to his chest, as though it pained him. With the other he reached out, palm open and spread towards the sky.

The other wizard and the creature never saw the attack coming. Lucian did, and unclamped his jaws at the last moment. The great cat tumbled through the air and struck the ground – just as a plume of roiling, screaming fire consumed both drake and rider.

For an instant, they were silhouetted. Man and

beast merged: a chimaera of flame and shadow, a smudge of darkness at the very heart of the fire.

In that sharp, searing brightness, Gwyn couldn't be certain what she saw. The flesh sloughing from the bones, perhaps. The blood flash-boiling in the veins, released in a sharp, almost surprised *hiss*. The skin that bubbled and melted and finally burst, like some red, overripe plum dropped from an impossible height. All that, in a single, molten instant, before she could screw her eyes shut and block it out.

But the image was burned onto her eyelids in reverse colours: black flames, sheathing the figure in the centre. The figure that arced towards the sky, mouth locked open in a rictus howl.

That scream still rang in her ears long after the wizard had fallen silent.

'— out of here before the rest turn up,' Lucian was saying. His hands were steady on her shoulder, on the small of her back, and Gwyn opened her eyes. He was a man now, sooty and covered in half-dry blood, smelling of singed fur and somehow – horrifically – the sweetness of cooked meat. Gwyn's stomach came up into her throat, and she clapped a hand over her mouth.

'If they have as many drakes as he claimed,' Faolan said, sparing Gwyn a quick glance. 'Well, what are you waiting for, girl? Mount.'

The word was a whip-crack, and came with a sharp mental command, a tug on whatever invisible yoke bound them. Gwyn hauled herself into the saddle without thinking.

Lucian stepped clear, his form melting and shifting, folding in on itself. She gasped. A heartbeat later, a hawk took flight, wings gusting smoke into her eyes. Smoke, but no flame. The fire lapping at the inn had died completely. In the darkness, Gwyn could barely see the charred scorch mark where the beast and rider had stood. Nothing remained of them but ash.

And then Gwyn was riding. She crouched low over Otani's neck, a few paces behind Faolan. The horses' hooves thundered on the hard-packed road, on the wood-plank bridge out of town.

She looked over her shoulder in time to see the two surviving wizards appear at the door of the inn, one still clutching his shoulder. Their black cloaks swirled around their feet.

Above, the hawk cawed as Gwyn and Faolan galloped out, away from Tønderby, into the night.

CHAPTER 14

A WIZARD OF THE EIGHTH RANK

Lucian dipped his washcloth into the water again. His mouth was set in a thin line, and he wielded the cloth with more force than was strictly necessary.

'Shut yer mouth, necromancer,' he said, dabbing at Faolan's wound. It didn't look bad – just a light slash across the upper arm, courtesy of one of the wizards. 'You're lucky I dinna just leave your arm to rot off.'

Faolan rolled his eyes, but stopped cursing. Gwyn settled back against the tree and wondered if she would ever stop shivering. Whenever she closed her eyes, the image was there. The wizard, twisting and writhing like a candle wick at the heart of the flame. The drake, its eyes liquefying, running down its enormous scaled head in rivulets; its wings crisping in mid-air like autumn leaves tossed into a firepit.

Her eyes snapped open.

Faolan, she thought. Faolan had done that. She had known he was a wizard; known he was a necromancer, even, which was worse. But knowing was different to seeing.

It had been late morning when they finally stopped riding, by the bank of an icemelt stream hidden in a grove of ash trees. There was no food – everything they had was in Faolan's bag, and that was back at the inn, probably char by now. Gwyn, still in her smallclothes, had shivered all the way, the saddle chafing her thighs. She had pulled on her blouse and sarafan as soon as they stopped, but even wrapped in her coat, the chill seemed to have crept into her bones.

A sparrow winged back into the tree with a chirp, cocking its head at them in a sceptical way. Exhausted as she was, Gwyn decided against sleeping. She wasn't sure she'd wake up if she did.

'Are there more of those ...' She swallowed. '... those dragons coming?' Because that was what that beast was, no matter how her mind railed against it. A dragon, as though lifted in full colour from Ascepis' fate cards and made flesh.

'Drakes,' Lucian said absently. 'Dragons are female. And aye, there are more, but they're few in number, thank the Claw. If any do come this way, I'll see them before they see us.' Now he turned to Faolan, his voice flat. 'I dinna ken where you were planning on spiriting her, Faolan, but it stops now. She's going to Idris. My orders were clear.'

Faolan shrugged, rotating his injured arm. 'Oh, we're in agreement there. You're certainly welcome to join us. I do enjoy some *intelligent* company on the road.'

Lucian snorted. 'Is that why you tried to kill me, then? Because our goals are so aligned?'

'Kill you?' Faolan laughed. 'Why, if I'd wanted to kill you, you'd already be dead. As I've told the girl, death and dying are my trade, in a manner of speaking. No, I simply required time alone with young Gwyn here. You were ... an inconvenience.'

'And so you thought you'd be rid of me.' There was a flatness in those ale-coloured eyes. His tattoo was dark as an oil slick, dark as violence; all hooks and thorns and savage angles. Faolan was dangerous, but in a bright, crackling way, like wildfire. In Lucian, the threat was subtler, more restrained.

'You're not the only one to have been given orders,' Faolan said, no longer smiling. 'Idris told me to watch over her. How could I do less? The truth is, I don't trust your methods. You said you meant to take her to Idris, but there you were – stumbling into my cave, scratched and bruised from blundering around in the woods, and with Beheret's mancers and packs of warglings two steps behind you. Hardly a promising start.'

'Idris thought me enough to protect her.'

'Oh, you can fight well enough,' Faolan said, waving his hand as though shooing away a fly. 'But what use is a cat when the warglings come? Can a tiger protect her against a half-dozen enemy mancers? No – the girl needed to go to Idris, and frankly, I was the better choice to take her there.'

'Piss on your choice.' Lucian stood, hurling the washcloth aside. His accent became broader when he was angry, Gwyn had begun to realise – all rolled Rs and quick, growling vowels. 'Ye take too much on yerself. Who are you to contradict Idris?'

Faolan stood, too. He was a head shorter than Lucian, but he looked him in the eye. 'I'm a mancer —'

Gwyn's stomach flipped over. She knew what was coming next, but could do nothing to stop it. She felt as though the ground had just disappeared from under her feet, her legs windmilling in the open air. She closed her eyes. She didn't want to see the shock and fear on Lucian's face, the smug satisfaction on Faolan's. In that moment, she thought maybe she hated him.

'— and so is Gwyn.'

She opened her eyes.

Silence. The sparrow chittered, fluffing its feathers.

Lucian reached for the tree, as though for support. It wasn't fear in his expression. Shock, yes, his hair wild and dishevelled like a man just escaped from prison. But not fear. Gwyn was grateful for that much.

'She ... has the black gift?'

'She does. When I discovered it, I had no choice. I bound her as my apprentice, of course, and —'

'You *what?*'

The sparrow took off in an outrage of wings. Lucian stared at Faolan, face pale as parchment. His hands twitched, and for a moment Gwyn was sure he was going to transform again. She smelled cooked fur; felt her gorge rise. Gods – Faolan was going to kill him, burn him alive.

But the wizard just gave a benign smile, folding his hands together. Ascepis' purloined ring tap-tapped on his knuckles. 'I made her my apprentice. Oh, don't look at me that way, Lucian. Somebody had to do it. She'd kill herself without guidance; any fledgling would. Besides, better me than one of the Syndicate. If they find out about her, they'll be on her faster than wolves on a three-legged deer. If they don't just kill her, that is. They have no love for what they don't understand.'

Lucian scowled and shook his head. He still looked ill, but was trying visibly to master himself. 'What you say ... it's impossible. She's – what? Seventeen? The wizards would have found her long ago.'

'I know that. I could hardly credit it myself. But she *does* have the gift, unbelievable as it seems. I've had her practising every night. Nothing yet, but I feel we're close.'

Gwyn shifted. She had explained about the vision – if it had been a vision – of Ygriel; recounted the things he'd said, the things she'd seen. Faolan had nodded and drawn his eyebrows together and made noises in his throat, had asked questions and passed inscrutable looks back and forth with Lucian. But during all that, he hadn't asked how Gwyn had escaped his unseen ropes. She supposed she had to tell him, although it meant the end of any pretence that she wasn't a wizard. Gods, what was Ascepis going to say?

'Actually,' she said, looking down at her fists. A bug tiptoed across the clumsy stitches of her sarafan. 'I did do something.'

Nobody said anything. She raised her head. The men were staring down at her, blank-faced, as though surprised to find her still there.

'Last night,' she continued. 'I cut through the ropes. Using the ... *sever*. The inn was on fire – I had to.' She shrugged, uncomfortable, and twitched her gaze away. 'I don't know how. I just did it.'

For a moment nobody spoke. The stream burbled and splashed. A wet, woolly skein of cloud came down to cover the sun.

Then Faolan let out a loud *whoop,* making Lucian flinch as though struck. He seized Gwyn by the forearms, pulling her to her feet, and began an impromptu dance around the tree. By the time he let her go, even Gwyn was laughing. He rounded on Lucian, who was still stone-faced.

'And there you have it! Sixteen years old —'

'Seventeen,' Gwyn corrected.

'— and doing her first magic. And the Syndicate none the wiser.'

'I dinna like it,' Lucian said flatly. He seemed to take no delight in her success, if it could be called that. 'Idris will like it even less. If she's really a wizard, he would have wanted to apprentice her himself.'

'Well, he's free to teach her. I'm sure she'll benefit from his experience,' said Faolan. 'Frankly, I'm less concerned with her curriculum and more about delivering her to him in one piece. I'm sure we can agree on that?'

Delivering. Like a package. Like a cart full of beets. Gwyn's flush of pleasure turned cold and evaporated.

Lucian gave the wizard a measured look, then shrugged. Some of the violence went out of his eyes. The beast restrained, for now. 'As you say. You'll have to answer to Idris for what you've done, and if he stripes you up and down the length of Asgerad, then it's no more than you deserve. But if you can agree not to put me down any more holes, I'm willing to work with you.'

They shook hands, looking each other in the eye for slightly longer than was necessary. Gwyn watched, and wondered what new trouble this development would bring.

They kept moving all day, though it was hard to make much progress riding cross-country. The roads were too dangerous now. It was only a matter of time until the wizards caught up. Faolan narrowed his eyes at every dust-tail, but Lucian, flying overhead, saw no signs of pursuit; only lonely farmsteads, and cows with their long hair trailing the ground.

Stop jumping at shadows, Lucian sent. Gwyn had almost toppled out of her saddle the first time he spoke in her head. A shapeshifter ability, he'd explained, though it only worked in his beast forms, and only if he was close enough. *If I catch any glimpse of them, I'll tell you.*

The ground grew harder the further east they went, sloping gradually upward towards the mountains. They passed by steaming thermal vents, and once, a geyser that harpooned a jet of aquamarine water a hundred feet in the air. Faolan said it was hot enough to strip the skin off her bones, and Gwyn believed him.

They waited outside the town of Parvik, hidden in a copse of trees, while Lucian went inside for supplies. With his tattooed face, he was more recognisable than either of them, but his cat form – a sweet-faced miniature version of the giant cat from Tønderby – made it easier to move undetected.

'Nobody kens anything about wizards or drakes in town,' he said when he returned, two hours later, with camping gear, waterskins, bread and cheese. 'They haven't been there yet, far as I can tell, but they must ken where we're headed. The Grimmelvagen Pass is the only way up through the mountains, at least on horseback.'

'So do we leave the horses behind? Go cross-country?' Gwyn asked, stuffing the food in her mouth. She hadn't eaten a bite since Tønderby, and her stomach was tying itself in knots.

'Two weeks past the solstice,' Faolan said, contemplative. 'The snow won't be thick, but ... no. It's hard country. If we abandoned the road, we'd need ropes, hooks – I won't risk either of our necks that way. Better to blast our way through the mancers, if we have to.'

Gwyn shivered, smelling the ghost of smoke and charred flesh. With that sort of power humming under his skin, she doubted Faolan was afraid of anything.

A few weeks ago, neither was I. Mancer Dorin had cracked open her life like an oyster shell, exposing the soft velvet insides. Nights with the bunk swaying beneath her, with the rain pattering against the window. The glow of the potbelly stove, her wool stockings hung over it to dry. The cut-grass smell of fresh herbs – wolfsbane, for protection; meadowrue, for seeing. The clink and rattle of hundreds of glass jars. All gone now.

Since Mancer Dorin there had been no safety, no rest. No home. Just running, and pursuit, and fear sharp and cold as a dagger. Though in truth, it had started earlier than that, with the two boys, with the cards, with the afternoon sun beating down on her neck as she lay prone and dying on the grass.

They rode until night fell, then made camp in a hollowed-out crater, beside a crack that hissed with steam. The steam was good, Faolan said; it hid them from prying eyes. But the smell was rotten and sulphurous, and Gwyn's hair clung to the back of her neck. They ate the last of the bread and cheese, then crawled into their bedrolls without making a fire. Lucian joined them a few hours later, sleeping in his cat form at Gwyn's feet.

'Are they going to find us, Lucian?' she whispered. She couldn't stop looking to the sky. Waiting for the stars to vanish, for the rumble and snap of beating wings.

Nay, lass. Dinna worry yourself. You'll be safe enough once we reach Idris.

She wanted to believe him. But despite her exhaustion, it took her a long time to fall asleep.

Faolan sent another thread of vim towards her, and

Gwyn lashed out clumsily with her new power. His flow fell away in pieces and winked out.

'Good,' Faolan said, nodding. 'Very good. You were quicker that time.' An invisible *thwack* clapped across her shoulders. 'Not quick enough, though.'

Gwyn sighed and rubbed her temples, where an ache pulled at her pulse. The *sever* sign seemed to come instinctively now, like the words of a well-known song. But it was *hard;* hard in a way that made her ears ring, made her knees feel like blobs of jellied eel. Lucian had gone to scout the surroundings, which had left them a few hours before they had to pack up and go. The longest few hours of her life, Gwyn thought.

'Again,' Faolan said.

She saw the power build up around him. Felt, rather than saw, really, but as they practised she found herself less able to tell the difference. The thread of energy he inched towards her looked like a streamer of light, casting wild, flickering shadows against the sheets of steam. Last night the foggy brume had felt like safety, or something close. Now the whiteness played tricks on her mind. She glimpsed enormous scaled wings, the swirl of a dark cloak, the glint of silver sunlight off a smiling mask. A hot, rotten-egg smell scratched at her nostrils.

Slowly, carefully, Gwyn shaped the new area of her mind into a honed edge. The effort made the world swim in front of her eyes, but she gritted her teeth, bore down, and sent her power *out,* cutting Faolan's thread in two. For some reason, the image of the two boys from Vønnerlund – the ones who had almost killed her – flashed in front of her eyes.

Sever. Faolan's thread shivered away into nothing, and Gwyn smiled in spite of herself. She didn't know *how* she was doing it, but it seemed to please Faolan, and that alone was worth celebrating. Not that she needed or wanted his approval – certainly not – but she was tired of being clouted over the ear.

'This doesn't feel like magic,' Gwyn said, swiping the back of her hand across her forehead. It came back damp, and not just from the enveloping steam. 'I thought there would be ... I don't know. Fire. Incantations.' *Like in Tønderby,* she might have said, but thinking of that still made her queasy. Her nerves felt like a bundle of frayed cord.

'Incantations? No. That has nothing to do with magic. Fire, yes, but that's second sign, fourth school.' He cast her a withering look. 'Your skills are far from ... hmm, *sophisticated* enough for that.'

'And the more I practise, the stronger my spells will become?'

'Yes,' Faolan said. 'And no. Strength comes partially from the mancer, but partially from how long they hold the vim before releasing it into a sign. Holding the vim without casting is difficult, you understand, but the longer you can let it gather, the stronger the resulting spell. In the Syndicate, mancers are ranked on how long they can hold the vim. First Rank mancers can hold it for one breath, Second Rank for two, and so on.'

She nodded slowly. Touching the vim and casting *sever* seemed to happen almost simultaneously, for her, but there was always a fleeting impression of ... what? Of something white-hot and scorching, like a ball of lightning. She imagined actually grasping and *holding* that thing, and shivered.

'What rank are you?' she asked Faolan.

'I was an apprentice until the night I left the Syndicate,' he replied, shrugging. 'Apprentices are not ranked. But I could hold the vim for five breaths, then, so I would have been Fifth Rank, had I been free.'

'And now?'

'Now I would be Eighth Rank. The scale goes as high as ten, officially, though few reach that level. Most taper off at four or five.'

Lucian winged down out of the grey sky, shifting back to his human form before he touched the ground. Gwyn tried not to stare, but it was hard. *That* was magic; more so than whatever Faolan was trying to teach her.

'The pass is clear,' he said, shaking rain out of his hair. 'But when I looped back to Parvik, the homes and shops all had their windows shuttered. I dinna think it was a good idea to stop, but my gut says the wizards have been there.'

Gwyn's stomach clenched. Parvik was only a few miles back.

'The sooner we move, the better,' Faolan said. He sounded bored and a little irritated, but Gwyn could feel a thrumming chord of anxiety through the bond. 'We killed three mancers in Tønderby, but there are more out there, and I doubt this Ygriel has forgotten us. Since he only attacked from inside the Lurk, we can assume his physical body is elsewhere. But how close? He knows where we are, now.'

'The Lurk?' Gwyn asked, frowning. Ygriel had mentioned that, but she had made no sense of it at the time.

Ygriel. Faolan had pulled out every possible detail about the masked stranger, but after that, he hadn't seemed to want to talk about it. Even Lucian had only coughed into his hand and changed the subject.

Now Faolan's eyes flickered, and his hands tightened on the gelding's reins. 'Nothing you need to concern yourself with. Come on, girl, get moving.'

There was no point in pressing him, but Gwyn scowled as she pulled herself into the saddle. Ascepis had kept secrets from her all her life. Did Faolan mean to do the same? If so, this year of servitude couldn't end soon enough.

'The rain should help,' said Lucian, squinting up at the grey, roiling clouds. 'Harder to track us. Good for keeping the warglings off our trail, too, if they're still following.'

'Bad for my hair, though,' Faolan said glumly.

They headed northeast, tracing a path through the craggy Geyser Fields. Orange lichen clung to the rocks and mist eddied around the horses' hooves. Now and then, the ground trembled, disgorging a jet of hot steam.

The rain worsened just after midday. Gwyn pulled her hood over her face, but it made little difference. She was soaked almost at once. She crouched down in the saddle, cold, shivering and miserable.

Eventually, they crested a rise and saw winking lights below, barely visible in the gloom.

'Jornholm,' Faolan said. He wasn't shivering. He was barely even wet. The rain hissed when it touched his skin, evaporating into steam that gusted away in the wind. A spell? It had to be. 'The last town before the mountains.'

There were no trees in the Geyser Fields, so they slept in the open, on a rocky knoll that offered no protection from the sheeting rain. Surprisingly, Gwyn slept well that night. The howling wind made it hard to imagine other sounds: the scuff of boots on stone, the soft *ssshing* of blades being drawn. The only time she woke was just before dawn, when she found herself face down in a puddle of water, rousing the others with her coughing and hacking.

The rain eased off that morning, though the wind refused to die down. They skirted wide around

Jornholm, approaching the Grimmelvagen Pass from the south, away from the road. Lucian reported no signs of the wizards, but Faolan was taking no chances.

The ground sloped upwards, growing more heavily wooded as they went, and before long the town of Jornholm was lost far below. Then they reached snow, though it lay sparsely, most already washed away down the slope. A stream passed nearby, its shallow parts filmed with ice. At midday, they ate some dried fruit without dismounting, and Lucian took wing as a hawk, spiralling up and out of sight with a harsh cry. Gwyn watched him go with a touch of envy.

'How does he do that, if he's not a wizard?'

Faolan shaded his eyes with his hand, though the sky was still low and sullen. 'It's a different kind of magic. Old. The native people of Jhabahabi are the only ones known to have the ability. Every second generation, in fact. Fascinating thing. I've known mancers who would have given all the gold in their pockets for the chance to study it, but the Jhabahabians are a notoriously reclusive and insular people. They rarely leave their forest.'

'Why did Lucian leave, then?'

'Exiled,' Faolan said flatly. 'A few years back now. Over a woman, I understand. The Jhabahabians have a strict caste system. The *shamaya* – the shapeshifters – are revered; those without the ability, the *heru*, are considered unclean. I understand young Lucian took up with a *heru* girl.'

'That's forbidden?'

'Forbidden, yes, and taboo as well. I won't pretend to understand the Jhabahabians' culture. I don't think anyone does. They rarely speak with outsiders, and entering the Tanglewood is death for those without a guide. But a relationship between a *shamaya* and a *heru* ... Well, they treat the *heru* as barely human. When Lucian wouldn't put her aside, the girl was killed, and he was exiled.' Faolan shrugged to show what he thought of that.

Gwyn looked up, catching a glimpse of a wingtip through the fog. *Poor Lucian. He lost everything because of love.* There was an undeniable romance to that – like something out of a bard's tale. Gwyn had warmed to him a little since Tønderby. Not many people would have flown through a glass window into a burning inn to save a near-stranger's life. He kept secrets, too, but at least he seemed to have her interests at heart. And he never smacked her with threads of invisible power, or called her a foolish girl.

To be able to take flight like that ... To spiral up and away from all your problems. Feel the cold air on your wings, see the world spread out below you like a child's playthings. Maybe there was a way to do the same through black magic. This Idris might know, if he was really the incredible wizard everyone seemed to think.

That thought stopped Gwyn short. *Wanting* to learn more magic? She must be mad.

But the truth was that slicing through Faolan's threads had made her feel ... good. Powerful. Like she had some small amount of control. Gwyn hadn't realised how much she'd missed that feeling – if it had ever been there to begin with. With Ascepis, she had never been allowed to make even the smallest choices for herself.

There was no sun to mark the passing of time, but it was nearly full dark when they stopped for the night. Lucian led them to a shallow cave, where they tied the horses and started a fire near the opening. At least, Faolan started the fire, with a flick of his wrist that made Gwyn's skin prickle with unease.

'Poor hunting this high up,' Lucian apologised, returning to camp a half hour later, a stringy rabbit slung over his shoulder. 'We'll be at Priory tomorrow, and you'll eat well enough there.'

Tomorrow. She wasn't sure how to feel about that. They said she would be safe from Beheret's wizards there, and maybe that was true. But whoever Idris was, he wasn't her family. Not really. If she had any family, it was Ascepis.

Faolan and Lucian were still talking quietly when Gwyn went to sleep, rolled up in her blanket with her back to the flames. Later, though, she found herself sitting upright, gasping for breath. Her heart hammered in her chest.

Is it you?

In her dreams he never wore the engraved silver mask, but she knew him. Knew the broad, handsome face, aggressively masculine, with laughing green eyes and a mocking smile. *Ygriel.* For a moment she could almost feel him standing behind her, breathing down her neck. He was searching for her, and the cold, cruel laughter in her dreams said it was only a matter of time until he found her.

CHAPTER 15

THE PILLAR OF DUSK

The next day passed without incident. Occasional low growls of thunder echoed down from the peaks, but there was no rain, and the clouds cleared now and again to show a fretful burst of sunlight. By early afternoon, the fog cleared enough to reveal the plains far below, though Gwyn had to twist back in her saddle to see them. They stretched out flat and golden brown, rolling away to the south and dissolving into a pink sky. The Norsvik River was a sinuous line in silvery white, reflecting the hovering inverted triangle of the Pyramid. It was definitely closer, now. Strange.

'Are we nearly there?' Gwyn asked, turning back to Faolan.

He tugged at the reins, ignoring her. The damp weather had him in a foul mood, and he kept glaring at her, as though it had been her idea to come here.

'We'll make it before nightfall,' Lucian said, taking pity. 'I'll fly ahead and tell them we're coming.'

It felt rude to stare as he shifted into his hawk form, like she was peeking at someone changing clothes, but Gwyn couldn't help it. It was hard to say whether it was sickening or fascinating. His broad-shouldered form shrinking, curling in on itself. The pattern of feathers stencilling on his skin, then twisting up into three dimensions. His nose and mouth stretching out, out, like someone pushing their fist through from the other side. A heartbeat later, he launched himself up with a shrill cry, a dwindling speck of brown against the low clouds.

By the time the grass plains disappeared behind the mountains, the sky had begun to darken into purple. A cold wind stirred the gnarled spruces and leather-larch, making chittering, insectile sounds. This was a dead place, too cold to grow more than choked weeds, too cold even for rabbits. And her uncle lived here?

Faolan pointed. A tall column of white stone stood ahead of them, its lower half overgrown with scrub, its top catching the last yellow rays of sunlight. She didn't recognise the symbols carved on its face.

'The Pillar of Dusk,' Faolan said. 'It marks the entrance to the Pale Valley.' He nodded towards a cleft in the side of the mountain, the path leading through it. 'That's where we'll find Idris.'

They filtered into the pass. Cliffs on both sides

leaned towards each other, the sky a thin band of dark grey overhead. There would be rockfalls here, especially in the winter, when the heavier snows came. If this was the only way in or out, the valley would be cut off from the rest of the world for half the year. Perhaps that was why Idris chose to live here.

The gap opened into a broad, flat-bottomed valley of grey slate, ringed by white-capped mountains with flanks red and gold in the setting sun. A river cut the valley into unequal halves. To one side stood an uneven grey-stone building. Two storeys here, three there, like a stack of blocks arranged haphazardly by some clumsy child. On the north side, a squat tower overlooked the river. Smaller satellite buildings huddled around the main house – stables, a greenhouse, a domed chapel with seven sides.

As they approached, the front doors swung open. Lucian had changed into fresh clothes and combed his hair, though he still had a dishevelled look. He took the reins as Gwyn and Faolan dismounted.

'Is he angry?' Faolan asked, almost as soon as Lucian was within earshot. Gwyn could sense his anxiety, a throbbing knot at the back of her mind, like a sore tooth.

'I expect you can find out for yourself. He wants to see you. Your old room is empty, but you might want to air it out some first. It smells none too fresh in there.' Faolan scowled, and Lucian gave Gwyn a wink. 'You'll be in the Little Tower. Severine should be along in a moment, once she gathers some things for you.'

Severine? Another wizard? She didn't want to meet any more wizards. The past few days had given her wizards enough for a lifetime.

But it was too late for that now. Lucian led the horses away, and Gwyn followed Faolan into the house.

Inside the entrance hall it was chilly and dim. The feeling was of a library, and Gwyn found herself treading softly, though her footsteps still seemed too loud. Lucian had mentioned this used to be a monastery, once. She could imagine the monks, hurrying silently on their way to prayer. She could almost see them from the corner of her eye. There was a sense of being ... watched.

Faolan allowed her no time to look around. Disdaining speech, he gave a mental tug for her to follow. Gwyn shouldered her pack and hurried after him.

She was lost within minutes. Dark, furtive corridors and little staircases seemed to loop back on themselves. There was an air of dilapidated grandeur about the place, not to mention a pervasive smell of dust that made her want to sneeze. Someone had been keeping it clean, but Gwyn saw cobwebs up in the roof, and many of the floor tiles were cracked.

At the top of a narrow, winding stair, Gwyn

craned her neck to see over Faolan's shoulder. The cubbyhole beyond was round, with a row of windows overlooking part of the river and a stretch of uneven slate roof. It smelled of lavender and mildew. There was a narrow bed, a chest, a ceramic washbasin and a desk fitted to the curve of the wall.

'Your room,' Faolan said shortly. 'Stay here until somebody comes for you.' He was gone before she could respond, the door banging behind him.

Gwyn stood there for a moment. It was very quiet. She could hear the thud of Faolan's boots down the stairs, and the river underneath her window. Outside, the light was stealing away, turning the shadows on the mountains deep black.

It felt strange to be indoors. The closeness of the walls made her uneasy, though it was only a little smaller than the inside of the wagon. Certainly not so small as the tunnel back in the Warren, with the mountain pressed down around her head, where she had almost ... well. She didn't want to think about that. Gwyn sat on the bed, then stood again, too restless to keep still.

She had managed to get a window open and was fiddling with the prop when she heard the door creak open. She turned, expecting Faolan – but a young woman, holding a bundle of clothes, stood there instead. Golden-skinned and pretty, with upturned grey eyes, black hair and a soft, youthful face, she wore a simple green dress and a dark shawl stitched with creeping vines. Seeing Gwyn, a slow smile spread across her features.

'You must be Gwyn.' Her voice was low-pitched and pleasant. 'I'm Severine.'

She took Gwyn's hand, expertly juggling her bundle under one arm. Her grip was warm and surprisingly firm, the hand lightly calloused along the palm. 'I'm sorry about the room. It's cramped, I know, but we've been having trouble with mice lately. This was the only room without bite marks on the curtains. Here, I brought you some clothes. Just a few of my old things, I'm afraid.'

Gwyn thanked her, putting the clothes down on the bed. This was Severine, then. She had expected someone older. The woman's skin and eyes marked her as Crater Dhavian – the most beautiful people in the world, the tales said. Gwyn could believe that. She felt like a lump of sand next to Severine's graceful, delicate-boned form.

'Do you ... live here?' she asked.

Severine nodded. 'With my brother Alcide, and Lucian, of course. We work for Idris. I'm a healer.' She tilted her head a little, looking closely at Gwyn as though she was some exotic species of bird. Then she shook herself off, laughing. 'I'm sorry. I don't mean to stare. It's only – well, you look so much like him. You have exactly the same eyes.'

'When can I see him?' Gwyn asked, ignoring the nervous clench of her stomach. She had questions.

Questions it seemed only Idris could answer. Though now, being here, she wasn't so sure she wanted to know those answers.

'Soon. He's with Faolan now.' Her voice dropped slightly, and she hugged herself without seeming to notice. 'Idris is angry with him, I think. I couldn't believe it when Lucian flew in and said Faolan was coming. Nobody's heard a word from Faolan in, oh, years now. We half thought he was dead.'

That would have made things easier. Still, without Faolan, Ascepis would have died. Gwyn shifted, uncomfortable. Owing something to the necromancer was ... unpleasant.

'When you say you're a healer, do you mean you use white magic?' Gwyn asked.

Severine nodded, folding herself onto the edge of the bed. 'I've been practising for a long time now, ever since I was a little girl. I suppose I always wanted to help people. I've tried to teach my brother, too, but I don't think he has the aptitude. It's a shame. I think he'd be a great healer. He's so focused, so single-minded. But I suppose he has other skills.'

Gwyn could hear the love and affection in Severine's voice, and she envied it. There had been a kind of love between her and Ascepis, but always of a cool, distant sort. Not like this. 'It sounds ... wonderful,' she said, and she didn't mean the magic.

'Have you ever tried?' Severine asked. 'To see if you can use white magic, I mean. Idris says the ability is more common that people realise. It's just that most never discover it.'

Gwyn looked away, smoothing the front of her sarafan. What could she say? *Yes, I can do magic – but my magic is black. You talk of helping people, but my magic is for killing.* Lucian must not have told her. Gwyn felt ashamed, suddenly – ashamed of the magic, ashamed of herself, ashamed of the dark, hungry thing that lived inside her. Faolan had recognised it in her almost from the moment they met.

'Come on, let's see,' Severine said, reaching for Gwyn's hand. When they touched, a jolt ran down Gwyn's arm, a pain that lodged in her bones like a dark thorn. Severine snatched her hand away at once, laughing ruefully. 'That hurt!'

Gwyn's stomach was trying to crawl up into her throat. She found herself thinking of that night in the wagon, after Vønnerlund, when the old woman had healed her. The pain had been just like that. Sudden, black, annihilating.

If white magic is good, she thought, *maybe my body just can't stand the presence of goodness.* Perhaps it was like pouring milk into a glass of lemon juice. There was no doubt that Gwyn was the lemon juice in this scenario. She felt soiled, and understood now why Faolan had bonded her. Maybe she belonged with him, in the shadows. Not in the world of light and warmth that Severine was part of.

'I'm a wizard,' Gwyn said quietly. Best to get it over with. How foolish she was, to think this girl might have been a friend, or become one. Wizards had masters, and they had slaves. They didn't have friends.

She studied Severine's face, for some sign of the horror she knew must be coming. The widening eyes, the flinching away. She thought of the Churl of Vønnerlund, who had wanted no trouble with the wizards; of the townsfolk who cringed away from their wagon, in spite of the scrawled words: *no magic.*

But Severine only grimaced, slapping her forehead. 'Of course you are! I should have known. You're Idris' niece. How could you not be a wizard? I suppose he found some way to shield you from the Syndicate?'

She didn't give Gwyn a chance to respond, and Gwyn was too gobsmacked to speak, anyway. This wasn't the reaction she'd expected. Severine still sat next to her on the bed, her knee just touching Gwyn's.

'I hope I didn't hurt you,' Severine continued, looking concerned now. 'Black magic and white magic never play well together. Idris lets me practise on him, but it's terribly hard – much harder than healing an ordinary person. And it hurts, too, although he's very brave about it.'

Vønnerlund. Looking into the old healer's eyes, Gwyn had felt a revulsion so deep and instinctive it seemed almost to come from outside herself. Was it her own latent black magic, responding to the healer's white? Ascepis had paid the woman extra, Gwyn remembered suddenly. A scupper for her silence. Nine shills for the healing. Four for the extra risk.

Gods, Ascepis. You knew about me the whole time.

'Gwyn, I hope you haven't been feeling ... well, guilty.' Severine's face was serious now. 'About using dark magic. I know a lot of people say that it's evil, but that's just fear of the Syndicate talking. Magic is only as good or as bad as what you use it for.'

Gwyn wanted to believe it, but she didn't quite dare. Nobody who knew Faolan could say dark magic wasn't evil. He had enslaved her with one sign, and kept her bound and gagged all night with another. He had turned a living man into a screaming inferno. Faolan might always have been a bully, but it was black magic that had made him a monster.

Still, she thought. *He did use magic to save Ascepis.* And magic had helped her escape from her bonds that night, as the inn burned down around her. Gwyn couldn't believe there was anything evil about defending yourself.

If you'd had magic in Vønnerlund, said a voice in her head – a different voice, she thought – *those men would never have been able to touch you.* A real wizard, one who had mastered the vim, wouldn't have ended up a bloody heap on the ground outside some no-name town, just because two sleek, puffed-up boys decided they wanted to make an example out of the hedge-wizard. A *real* wizard would have nothing to fear. Not the random violence of strangers, not the Syndicate, not even Ygriel.

And if a year under Faolan's tutelage would be what it took to achieve that, was it really so bad?

Severine must have noticed her smiling, because she smiled, too, standing up and offering Gwyn her hand. Gwyn took it, and there was no electric jolt this time.

'Come on,' she said. 'Let's take you to Idris.'

CHAPTER 16

QUESTIONS AND ANSWERS

When they reached Idris' study, Faolan was just leaving. More whey-faced than usual, he brushed by Gwyn without a word. Had Idris whipped him, as punishment for binding her against her will? The thought was cheering.

Then the door was opening, and Gwyn stepped into a cavernous, two-storey room, dominated by a heavy desk in front of a round window wide enough to ride a horse through. A tall figure stood with his back to her, looking out over the darkening valley towards the mountains.

Gwyn hoped Severine might stay. She had come this far to meet Idris, but now the moment was here, her stomach knotted with unease. She wiped suddenly sweaty palms on her trousers. What sort of man was he, this Idris, who seemed to be pulling all the strings of her life? Grim and stoic, like Ascepis?

Or like Faolan, capricious and sharp-tongued, prodding and bludgeoning her in turn?

But with a squeeze of her hand Severine was gone, closing the big double doors behind her. Gwyn swallowed hard, aware of the sudden quiet. The man turned to face her.

If she'd had any doubts he was her uncle, they were gone now. Beneath his eyeglasses, his eyes were green as agate, green as springtime. Her eyes. He wore his hair long to halfway down his back, though his was pure white to her white-gold, stick-straight to her loose waves. His skin was pale cream. Despite his dark purple robes, he looked nothing like any wizard she had imagined.

Idris crossed the room to her in a few strides, clasping her hands in his and looking straight into her eyes.

'Gwyn,' he said simply, and she found herself smiling without meaning to. His voice was smooth, rich honey. She understood in an instant why Lucian and Faolan seemed to follow him with such devotion. He had the most magnetic presence she had ever felt.

Idris turned back to the window, leaving her hands suddenly cold. She followed hesitantly. The light was almost gone now. The valley floor and the mountains lay in shadow, only their tips still outlined in fire. The river was a ribbon of darkness, two storeys below.

For a time he said nothing, and Gwyn felt no need

to fill the silence.

The light had gone entirely when he spoke again. 'Lucian told me what happened since he first met up with you, and Faolan filled in the rest. I was sorry to hear about Ascepis. He was a good friend to me. I hope he survives.'

She nodded, though he wasn't looking at her. Ascepis had seemed so small the last time she had seen him, lying on that bed. She had traded a year of her life for the chance to save his. If he survived, that coin was well spent.

'You must wonder what all this is about,' Idris said presently. 'You have a lot of questions, I expect.'

Gwyn had spent hours agonising over what she wanted to ask him. But where to even start? *Am I truly a wizard? Why is Beheret trying to kill me? Why did you bring me here? What do you want from me?*

Strangely, though, all of that seemed suddenly unimportant.

'My mother,' she said, turning to him. 'She was your sister?'

'Yes,' he said, nodding. 'That's a good place to start. At the beginning, then.

'Aislinn was my older sister. I was four when the Syndicate took me. She came to study at the Lower City so she could be near me. Maybe she came for herself, too, because our family had money, but no titles. Father was ambitious enough to marry her off to raise the family name. She would have hated that.'

He turned back to her suddenly, eyes meeting hers. Gwyn was struck again by their queerly hypnotic effect. It was something primal; a force of nature.

'I'm sorry,' he said. 'I forget myself. Would you like some tea?'

She nodded, though she wasn't thirsty, and Idris turned back to his desk. It was a jumble of papers, with a stack of books on one side that looked likely to fall at any moment. He had been writing something, though she couldn't read his cramped script. It seemed to have trailed off in mid-sentence, the ink leaving careless splotches across the page.

A little square teapot, bright green, sat on its stand at the corner of the desk, with small mismatched cups. Idris didn't do anything that she could see, but as she watched, steam started to rise from the spout. He poured the tea, and as he did, his sleeve fell back, showing the tower-and-moon brand on his forearm. Unlike Faolan's brand, Idris' was circled by lines of tiny script.

His marking, Gwyn realised, and shivered. She held her cup closely, cradling its warmth. The tea was hot and fragrant, flavoured with blackcurrant and marigold.

Idris took a long sip. 'Where was I? Oh, yes. Well, I spent fourteen years with the Syndicate, and I suppose I was content enough. I didn't always agree with the mancers, but Ascepis was a good master and encouraged me to think for myself.'

Gwyn gave a small start. She hadn't known Ascepis had been Idris' master. The thought gave her a strange sort of thrill. It still seemed impossible to think of Ascepis – dour, plodding, literal-minded Ascepis – as one of the feared Syndicate wizards.

I never really knew him at all.

'I was sixteen when Aislinn disappeared. We would meet every fortnight, under the Bird Tower in the early afternoon, until one day she just never came. At first I thought she must be ill, but the girl who shared her room said Aislinn hadn't been seen for over a week. Nobody could tell me where she was. The healers who taught her either didn't know, or claimed not to. When I went to the Lord High Physician, he told me outright not to poke my nose where it didn't belong, and when I demanded to know where my sister had been taken, he had me whipped in the public square.'

No emotion in his voice. Gwyn watched him from the corner of her eye and said nothing. Working with Ascepis had taught her a little about how to read people – who was a potential customer, who was wasting time, who looked like trouble. But from Idris she got nothing. He seemed deep and clear as a mountain lake.

'I told Ascepis, of course,' Idris continued. 'He counselled me to stay silent, at first, but he was never one to let an injustice lie. He liked Aislinn, and it troubled him to think she could disappear that way. So he started to ask questions, too. And learned that Aislinn wasn't the only student to disappear. There were others – good students, all of them – who left unexpectedly, with their friends told that they had returned home, or gone to study in the field, or some other excuse that never held up under examination.

'And there were an unexpected number of deaths, too. In a place full of volatile magic and experimentation, there are always accidents. But these were deaths that left no body. Students falling from windows, three thousand feet or more into the chasm below, or else burned to death, leaving nothing but ashes.

'It wasn't just in the Lower City that this happened; not just to the healers. Young mancers, who seemed to be doing well and enjoying their studies, suddenly went rogue. Too many disappearances to be mere chance. And everywhere Ascepis poked his nose, he found people unwilling to talk about it. People who wanted to act like the missing students never existed. He was formally reprimanded by the Archmage for "stirring dissent".'

The hairs on Gwyn's arm prickled. 'So where did they all go?' Her voice sounded very loud in her ears.

Idris smiled without humour, taking another sip of tea. 'That was the question, wasn't it? I was concerned only with finding Aislinn, with or without

Ascepis' help – but by the end he was just as passionate. The questions ate at him. Seeking answers was ever the way of mancers. Where did the students go? And why did it seem that the highest-level mancers and physicians were covering it up?

'We searched for over a year. At the end of it, we did find Aislinn, and some of the other missing students, too, I expect. They were in a cloister to Beheret, not two days' ride from the Clockwork City, and the place had been burned almost to the ground, only hours before we arrived. All that was left was a smoking ruin, and corpses, and a few others, barely alive.'

His voice dropped to a near whisper. Gwyn leaned closer. She had to remind herself to breathe.

'Aislinn was one of those. She did not live long. It was like she was waiting for us to come before she could die.' His face was impassive, but Gwyn thought his cup shook a little as he raised it to his mouth – the first hint of real emotion she'd seen so far.

'In the end, only two survived. You, three years old and big-eyed, covered in soot but unhurt. Aislinn sheltered you from the flames, I think. She named you Yennevere, after our grandmother.'

Yennevere. Sudden foreboding wrapped cold fingers around her heart. Gwyn swayed on her feet, reaching out to steady herself against the edge of the desk.

'Who was the other survivor?'

'A pretty little boy, older than you by some years. When we found Aislinn, he was standing nearby, holding you in his arms. I would have thought him Aislinn's son, if he hadn't been too old, for he looked just like you with his pale hair and bright-green eyes. Aislinn never said anything about him, but when we left we took him too. It was no place to leave a little child. Later I gave him to a family in a village in Nederlund. Perhaps I should have kept him with you, but I thought it safer to keep you separated, and I was asking a lot of Ascepis already. I never learned who the boy's parents were, but he said his name was Ygriel.'

She had known what he was going to say long before he said it, but Gwyn couldn't help the wave of nausea that rolled over her.

Ygriel.

Idris saw her expression, and nodded. 'The Syndicate never knew of him, but he is a mancer just the same, and his gift manifested itself when he was fourteen. When I returned to the village some years later, nobody wanted to talk about him. It was like the missing students all over again. The family who had taken him in was dead, their house a black ruin no one ever went near.

'Eventually I uncovered what had happened. A decade after the boy came, the town was beset by misfortune. Crops failed, animals were born dead or deformed, and plague came where there had been none for fifty years. People died mysteriously. I don't know how, but in time they linked the occurrences to Ygriel. They were frightened of him. He was fifteen when they took him to the town square and burned him.'

Gwyn shuddered. She thought of the face in her dreams – black and grotesque, writhing with maggots under the surface. The room had grown cold.

'What happened next was unclear, even to those willing to talk to me about it. They left the body tied to the stake overnight, as is custom, but when they went to bury it the next day it was gone. The ones who ordered the burning were dead before the year was out, all in seemingly accidental and unrelated circumstances. They believe his spirit still stalks the streets at night, and the town is surrounded by necromantic charms and wards to keep him out, for all that such things are forbidden by Syndicate law.

'But as you know, the reality is worse than their imaginings. The townsfolk burned him, but he is very much alive today, and he serves Beheret as her right hand. I knew Beheret might one day send her servants searching for you, but when I learned that Ygriel had joined her, I was certain of it. Ascepis hid you as best he could, staying on the move, away from the big cities. He changed your name, in case Beheret's servants might recognise it. But we knew it was only a matter of time.'

Without Gwyn noticing, the lamps around the walls had flared to life. She saw her own watery reflection, wide-eyed and pale, in the glass.

Idris set his cup on the desk with a sigh. 'Ascepis paid the greatest price of any of us, in the end. When we left the Clockwork City to travel to the cloister, we were declared rogue. Siver Faiding, who was Exorcist-General of the Inquisition at the time, led a party of Inquisitors to capture us. There was a battle, and several Inquisitors were killed. Ascepis was silenced – cut off from the vim, his power crippled forever. Most mancers would rather be dead than face that. When they were done questioning him, he was exiled, and they must have assumed he would die. But he lived, against all expectations, and even then continued to help me. I wouldn't have blamed him for hating me for what I'd done, what I'd drawn him into.'

Gwyn shook her head and placed her empty cup on the desk. She had wanted answers, but not like this. It was too much to take in. If she'd had anything in her stomach, she might have been sick.

'I don't understand why Beheret would want me,' she said, grasping onto the first concrete thing she could think of. 'Faolan says I can become a wizard, and maybe he's telling the truth ... but if you're right, there are already plenty of wizards on her side.'

Idris pressed his lips together, seeming to consider what to tell her – how much to tell her.

There are still secrets, then. It was almost a relief. The world may have turned itself inside-out in the space of a few days, but some things were the same.

'You and Ygriel were the only children we found alive in the cloister, but there were bodies, many of them too small to be fully grown,' Idris said. 'The adults were kept in filthy cells, no bigger than chicken sheds, and they were thin and wasted when we found them. But you and Ygriel were plump and healthy and seemed well tended. We believe they were breeding children there, for some purpose.

'I found more evidence for it wherever I went. In Crater Deep I learned of three good-sized towns along the eastern rim where every single male over sixteen was taken without explanation. The men who took them wore the uniforms of the Crater Dhavian army, but the new Padshah in Bitter Springs knew nothing of it, and the soldiers were heard to speak with Aranor accents.

'The women and children left behind – those not killed by the soldiers outright – had taken to calling it the Sundering. Severine and her brother lost their father that way. When I met them in Crater Deep some years later, they joined my cause at once. They were sure, as I am, that the men taken during the Sundering were part of the same breeding program as the students who went missing in the south; the same as countless other unexplained disappearances throughout the land. It has been clear all along that Beheret has been working towards a goal.'

Gwyn swallowed, her throat suddenly dry. 'What ... what *goal?*'

But Idris' face had grown cool and remote, and he turned back towards the window. 'That's ... a complicated question.'

If he had been Ascepis, she might have pushed him, might have needled him for *some* kind of answer. But ... uncle or no, he was a stranger.

And a wizard; let's not forget that.

'So that's why my mother was taken?' she asked instead. 'For some ... breeding program?' It took her a moment to recognise the hot, sick swoop in her gut for what it was: anger. Something in her chest, something dark, seemed to uncoil and purr at the feeling of it.

'So I believe.' His voice held no particular feeling now. 'I can't say why they burned the cloister. Perhaps they considered that branch of the program a dead end. I know they have burned others, before and since. I had hoped Beheret might dismiss you as lost, if she ever learned you escaped, but it's clear now that she wants you returned.'

He turned to her, and the lamplight cast long shadows across his face.

'I vowed to Aislinn before she died that I would protect you,' he said. 'And one way or another, Gwyn, I mean to keep my vow.'

PART II

INTERLUDE

THE PRISONER

The girl sagged against the wall. The lamp had started to die, and instinctively, Enoch reached for the vim to relight it.

But there was nothing there, of course. There had been nothing there for months now.

He shivered in spite of himself. The absence was like a dark hole waiting to swallow him.

'This tale of yours,' he said, stomping on the thought. He flipped back through his notes. Ink blots covered the barely legible pages. Well, he hadn't been concentrating on penmanship, had he? 'You must realise how it sounds.' He used his librarian's voice, brisk and no-nonsense. If she realised how off balance he was ...

The girl, though, only smiled, not bothering to open her eyes. 'The best stories are always the unlikely ones, wizard.'

'I'm not interested in stories. Save them for the bards. I'm interested in the *truth*.'

People thought of librarians as woolly-headed dreamers with their heads buried in tales and fancies. Perhaps the girl did, too, if she expected him to believe her words. Oh, there was *some* truth in there; enough to make his blood run cold. But ... dragons, swooping out of the night sky? Mancers in service to a false god?

No – Enoch was a librarian, but he was no fool. The Clockwork City's great library held no tales, no fictions. It was a place of learning, of scholarship, of —

'Truth,' she echoed, and now she did look at him, those demon eyes dead and shadowed. 'I wanted the same thing. Or thought I did.'

Enoch cleared his throat and bent over the notes, heart thundering. He couldn't afford to lose her; not now, when she was finally talking. Best to move on, and quickly.

'This house,' he said. 'Priory. Can you describe the location more clearly? South of Jorvanger, you say? Would that be in the Skaga Mountains?'

Idris Whitemane's secret stronghold. That part, at least, had the ring of truth. The Syndicate knew it was somewhere in the north – all their information pointed there, and the region was a hotbed of dissident activity. Not long ago, it would have been heavily warded, impossible to find without clear directions. All that had changed now.

And if this girl had actually been there ...

A thrill stole over him. To finally capture Idris, the most infamous apostate in recent history, would be something. Enough, perhaps, to see one Enoch Arehi elevated to Chief Librarian.

'I think not, little bird,' the girl said. He could hear the lazy smile in her voice. 'As I told you, there aren't enough biscuits in the world to buy that piece of knowledge.'

Enoch covered his disappointment with a shrug and dared to meet her eyes. 'No matter. There'll be time to deal with him later.'

The look she gave him was coolly amused. Enoch suppressed a flash of annoyance. Who was she to laugh? Sometimes she seemed to forget she was a prisoner and he a Fourth Rank mancer.

'Is something funny?' he asked, not bothering to soften the snap in his voice. Maybe *he* was the one forgetting. Biscuits and soft words? What had they gotten him except a pack of lies?

'If only you knew,' she said. That secret smile again. 'Here you sit, trying to bully me for information, with no idea what's waiting for you. Listen to yourself. Worried about one rogue wizard. Doesn't it strike you as absurd? In a few weeks, like as not you'll be dead, and your Clockwork City will be a smoking hole in the ground. Oh, yes, it's funny. You'll *deal with him,* will you? And how do you plan to do that, exactly?'

Great vim, but her gaze was disconcerting. No girl that age had any business having eyes like those. Even starved, beaten and shackled to the wall, she showed not an ounce of fear. Had her mind cracked? Castlemaine had been at her already, Enoch knew, although the Archmage had ordered only sparing use of the hot irons. Nobody spoke it aloud, but they were all afraid of what would happen if they pushed her too far.

She's trying to throw you off balance, he told himself. She was a *prisoner,* and in no position to be making threats.

It hadn't sounded like a threat, though. More like a warning.

No. The Archmage had told him she was sly. *'Don't let her distract you,'* he had said. Mystery, rumour, speculation ... Those were her weapons. Her only weapons, so long as those chains stayed fast on her wrists.

'With magic,' Enoch said, coming back to himself. He was pleased that his voice only wavered a little. *He* wasn't going to fall prey to the collective hysteria, no matter what her eyes looked like. 'Magic you'll give me, I hope.'

'Indeed?' The girl's tone was feigned surprise. She began to pat herself down, as though searching for her coin purse. 'Am I keeping it in my pocket, then?

No?' Her hands dropped back into her lap. 'You want me to help you so you can kill my uncle? Hardly an incentive, now, is it?'

'Do you need an incentive to do the right thing?'

She smiled thinly. 'The right thing. Mmm. Right for you, I suppose. It galls you, doesn't it – being without your magic? You liked lording your power over the non-talented folk; keeping them in line. You thought it made you better than them.'

'I don't think —'

'And now? With all the magic gone, are you still better? Do you feel safe behind your walls? Do you think —'

Enoch stood, almost knocking over the stool. That guard was right. She was insane. Was she like this when she was captured, or did the Inquisition torture the sanity out of her? Her gaze was calculating, predatory. She should have been afraid.

Why wasn't she afraid?

The woman held up her wrists. The silver chains gleamed, stars and moons flashing in the low light. 'Are you sure these work?' she asked, softly.

Enoch didn't take his eyes off her as he backed towards the door. She made no move. But as he slammed the latch home, he could hear the echoes of her mocking laughter.

CHAPTER 17

NECROMANCER

'I know nothing! Please, m'lord, have mercy!'

Faolan waved his hand, almost lazily, and the woman screamed again. She fell into the dirt, thrashing, and Gwyn's hands tightened into fists at her sides.

When it stopped (an hour later? A day?), the woman was panting, unable to speak, unable even to lift herself out of the slush. Faolan seemed content to wait.

The other tribespeople – those who hadn't fled – huddled a few feet away. They watched with dull eyes. Snow drifted from the blank sky, gathering in the wrinkles and folds of their heavy coats, turning their furs to white. Gwyn heard a child crying.

The woman crawled forward on her belly, stretching out a hand. 'Please, m'lady wizard, please,' she whimpered. 'Tell him it ent so. Tell him I don't know nothing.'

Gwyn took a step back, out of the woman's reach. She felt sick. 'Faolan,' she said, 'I think —'

'Am I paying you to think?' Faolan paused, then laughed. 'Oh – I'm not paying you, am I? Well, my point stands. When I require you to think, I'll give plenty of forewarning, so you have time to prepare yourself.'

Gwyn was silent. She kept her eyes on the ground, jaw clenched. There was nothing she could say. She had tried everything: shouting, crying. Even pleading, once. It only made things worse.

The tribeswoman reached out again, tentatively ... then screamed as an unseen force seized her arm and wrenched it behind her back. Her face was driven into the muck, and she choked.

'Now, now,' Faolan said. 'I don't recall giving you permission to touch my apprentice. If you wish to keep that arm, you won't try it again.'

'I don't know nothing!' the woman sobbed. She was shaking all over. 'Please, m'lord wizard, please, I swear it be so, by Siasr herself I swear it. We ent had a deaths-head priest for nigh on ten years now, since Speaker Rayleigh crossed over the veil! 'Sbones, m'lord wizard, I'd tell you if we had!'

'She's telling the truth, Faolan,' Gwyn said, keeping her voice deliberately even. 'She doesn't know anything.'

'Yes, I expect you're right.' The wizard sounded almost cheerful. 'Well, no matter. Plenty of hours left in the day.' He turned towards the gathered tribespeople, who cringed back, clutching each other. His smile was a slice of cold wind.

'You,' he said, beckoning. 'Yes, you.' Faolan flicked his fingers, and a young man collapsed on his knees in the snow. He didn't scream, but his face was frozen in a rictus howl. The veins stood out in his forehead. The crowd drew back as though the man was infected with plague.

'Now,' Faolan said. 'Let's begin again. Where is Shemeris Morga?'

It was mid-afternoon when they finally left the camp and the huddle of dead-eyed tribespeople.

Gwyn saddled Otani in silence, looking anywhere but at Faolan. She couldn't stand the sight of him – his dour, neat robes, his bland smiles, his otter-sleek hair pushed back from his face just so.

'Clearly you have something to say,' he said finally. 'Please, don't keep me in suspense.'

'Why bother? You don't listen anyway.' The words came out bitter and acrid, but it was too late to take them back, even if she wanted to.

And she didn't. Gwyn's anger was closer to the surface these days, and she found herself caring less and less about tamping it down. What could he do to her that hadn't already been done? Steal her from her family? Enslave her?

'What rubbish.' Faolan pulled himself into the saddle, arranging his robes around him. He still wore her 'wish' around his neck, and the sight of it sent a spike of fury through Gwyn's gut. She caught him toying with it sometimes, watching her with a strange, sidelong smile, and she knew he was laughing at her.

'I pride myself on being a very good listener,' he continued. 'Come now, what's troubling you?'

Gwyn tightened the cinch with a little too much force. Otani flicked her ears back in alarm, and Gwyn patted her apologetically. It wasn't the horse's fault. She took several long breaths before replying.

'You didn't need to torture them like that.' Her voice sounded flat and dull in the crisp air. 'It was obvious they didn't know anything. Vim, they didn't even have a spirit tent. There was nowhere for them to stow a necromancer if they had one.'

'And why should you care?' Faolan asked. He sounded genuinely puzzled, as though even the concept of mercy was foreign to him. 'You don't know those people. If they'd found you out here alone, they would have killed you at the sight of that blonde hair. And eaten your heart, most likely.'

'They don't eat the stone people. Their flesh – our flesh – is meant to be cursed. I read that in a book.'

'Well, that's certainly good to know.' He hauled on

the reins, wheeling his horse around in a flurry of snow. 'Come on. We want to be back before nightfall.'

Clearly he considered the conversation finished. Gwyn mounted in silence and followed him out of the valley. Light snow kept falling, turning everything glassy and grey.

It had been three weeks since she had arrived at Priory. For the first few days, Faolan had ignored her completely, and Gwyn wondered if he had forgotten their bargain. She barely saw him. Despite all the threats and promises, training his unwanted apprentice seemed the furthest thing from his mind.

After the first week had passed, Gwyn could stand it no more, and sought him out. But Faolan was gone. Severine said he'd gone up into the mountains; that he'd been going all week, leaving at dawn and sometimes not returning until after dark. He was investigating something, though Severine couldn't, or wouldn't, say what.

One night after supper, Gwyn was sitting in her tower room when she heard the ring of hooves in the courtyard. She hurried to the stables and found him there, brushing down his horse.

'Where did you go?'

Faolan looked up at her irritably. He had snow in his hair. 'I don't see that it's any business of yours.'

'It *is* my business. I'm your apprentice, aren't I?' She hadn't meant to say that. If he'd forgotten about her, so much the better.

'Feeling neglected, hmm?' He straightened, wincing, and pressed his hand to the small of his back. His usually pristine cloak was travel-stained. 'I should think you'd be glad to see an end to your training. You made it quite clear you wanted nothing to do with magic. Perhaps I've decided to oblige you.'

Gwyn's temper flared immediately. 'Do I miss being called an idiot all the time? And having you box me around the ears every second moment? No. Of course not. And I'm not going to pretend that I wanted ... any of this.' She sucked in a deep breath. 'But I'm a wizard, you say, whether I want it or not. I might as well do it right. If you can teach me anything that might help protect me against Ygriel, I mean to learn it. And if you won't teach me, well, maybe Idris will.'

Faolan looked at her for a long moment. He appeared to be considering. Then he laughed, tossing her the curry comb, which she fumbled and nearly dropped.

'Here. You finish this. And in answer to your question: I was paying a visit to a tribe of hill people near here. You've heard of the Fjallmen?'

Wary, Gwyn nodded. She knew them from books, at least by reputation. Hardly anyone had met a Fjallman in person. They were nomads, living in scattered tribes throughout Asgerad's southern mountains. The original inhabitants of the region, some said, although most were wiped out when the taller, stronger northmen moved in. Nobody knew how many remained. They stayed far away from Jorvanger and the outlying villages.

'Well, they're not easy to track down, as you can imagine,' Faolan said. 'But I've had dealings with them in the past. They revere necromancers, you see. Call them *deaths-head priests.* Some necromancers join up with them after fleeing the Syndicate. I spent a little time with Brilstoltsa's tribe, myself, but I didn't stay long. Not my sort of crowd. Cannibals, you know. Nasty business.'

Gwyn almost dropped the comb again. *Cannibals?* That wasn't in any of the stories she'd heard. The wide-open valley seemed very exposed, suddenly.

Faolan continued, 'A necromancer by the name of Shemeris Morga, though, did take up a position in one of the tribes, and last I heard, she was still with them. It's been years since I saw her – not that I've searched very hard. Shemeris was never a close friend. But unfortunately she has some information I need, which means I'll have to enjoy the pleasure of her company once more.'

'What information?' Gwyn's hand had stopped moving. The horse glanced at her over his shoulder – reproachfully, she thought – and she began brushing again, though with only half her attention. The name *Shemeris Morga* had tweaked something at the back of her mind.

Faolan gave her a measured look. He seemed to be

weighing his options. Finally he shrugged. 'Information about Ygriel. Information especially relevant to you, I should think.'

Whatever Gwyn had been expecting, it wasn't that. She frowned, turning her attention back to the horse. She had tried not to think about Ygriel, and that had worked well so far. Except for the nights she woke screaming, of course, but nobody knew about that. Her room was in a quiet corner of the house.

'Why would this Shemeris know anything?'

But Faolan had told her enough, apparently. His expression became hard and closed-off. He sniffed, flicking an appraising eye over the horse.

'You've missed a spot.' He turned and stalked out of the stable, calling back over his shoulder: 'If you want to come with me tomorrow, make sure you're awake early. I won't wait for you.'

That was how it began. They were on their fourth trip into the mountains, now, and no closer to finding Shemeris.

Privately, Gwyn thought it was a fool's errand. Most days they never found anyone at all. They just wandered the bare, rocky valleys and peaks, crunching through snow while the wind moaned all around them. It was bitterly cold in the passes, the scenery all the same: white and grey, grey and white. They spoke little. The cold always put Faolan in one of his black moods, and he rode stiffly with his coat around his ears. Only the familiar ritual of torture seemed to lift his spirits.

It was always the same. The cowering, fur-swaddled Fjallman crouching in the snow. The questions, always in that pleasant yet indifferent tone – *who is your necromancer? Where are they? Where is Shemeris Morga?* Then the screaming. Faolan made no distinction between man or woman, young or old. Like death itself, he was indiscriminate.

She had tried to stop him, of course – at least the first few times. But how could you fight someone who held such complete power over you? If Faolan didn't like what she was saying, he would simply lock her mouth shut, lash her arms to her sides. Sometimes it seemed her protests only encouraged him.

So Gwyn stopped coming. If she couldn't prevent the torture, at least she didn't have to be a part of it.

That only lasted a few days, which she spent in a lather, pacing the house, imagining what he was doing. Who he was torturing. Faolan didn't seem to care whether Gwyn came along or not, but she cared. Turning her back on what was happening didn't make it any less real. If her presence at least stopped him from escalating torture into murder, it was worth it.

So she came back. Faolan didn't comment on that, any more than he had on her absence. He just gave her a curt nod and a small, knowing smile.

Now, Gwyn watched as he rode ahead of her. His good humour was already evaporating – she could see that in the set of his shoulders, in the way he tugged peevishly at the reins. The horses' hooves scattered loose stones as they went, the clattering sounds unnaturally loud in the stillness of the pass. Broad snowdrifts choked what little grass remained, brown and grey against the rock. The wind tugged at her coat with icy fingers.

'I thought all the hill tribes had their own necromancers,' Gwyn said, more to break the silence than out of any real desire for conversation. She had been scouring the library for mentions of the Fjallmen, learning everything she could. 'But we haven't found any. Why?'

'Not all. The necromancers tend to stick with the bigger and more prosperous tribes. Actually, it's the main reason the Fjallmen are always at war. The necromancers change allegiance quite easily, as you can imagine.'

'And if we find another necromancer, instead of Shemeris? What do we do?'

'Kill him, most likely.' He saw Gwyn's expression, and gave a tight smile. 'Necromancers hold to a treaty when they meet in the Lurk, for the most part. But in the living world …' Faolan shrugged, unconcerned. 'It's a good way of keeping the population down.'

The Lurk. Gwyn shivered. She had gotten an

explanation out of him, finally, a few days after they'd reached Priory. The Lurk was the name necromancers gave to the world of the dead – the Underworld.

'You look surprised,' Faolan had said, smirking at her horrified expression. He had been sitting in the kitchen, nursing a cup of steaming tea with a book open on his lap. 'I don't see why. Did you never wonder where the souls go when they die?'

'To Siasr's realm,' Gwyn had replied, wrapping her arms around her body. Bad enough that the vision of Ygriel back in Tønderby had been real. To know it had taken place in the world of the dead ... Well, that was enough to make her scream herself hoarse. 'But it was meant to be —'

'Yes, yes. Caverns of ice, frozen mists seeping from cracks in the ground, the Seat of Bones. The usual High Country nonsense.' He'd sniffed, looking scornful. 'Stories for peasants. In Padmaphur, they say when you die you're given a ten-thousand-mile-wide field of saffron to harvest. And when you finally manage it – centuries later, presumably – Siasr comes down from the sky herself in a flaming chariot and takes you to paradise. Do you believe that, too?'

She hadn't. But then, she hadn't believed in Siasr, either; not really. *Stories to frighten children.* That's what Ascepis had always said, when he shoved the unwanted prayer books back in the priests' faces, or

– a few times, at least – chased them away from the wagon with a stick.

But if Beheret was real, then the death goddess might be real, too. Siasr, and all the rest of them. Maybe Molech really was sitting on some thundercloud, throwing down bolts of lightning. Maybe Umbrael truly sat at the centre of the world and spun the fates of mortals on her great wheel.

The world was a much larger and stranger place than Ascepis had taught her.

Autumn was barely upon them, but already the trees stood stark and bare against the white sky. A bright wind rattled the branches, depositing snow on the ground with muffled thumps. That wind promised a hard winter. This far north, the cold season would make those winter nights in the wagon, huddled with Ascepis around the potbelly stove, look like lazy spring days in Portuga.

The horses held to a steady pace, but it was dark by the time the red roofs of Priory House came into view. Lamps burned in the kitchen, and as they drew closer, Gwyn caught a snatch of laughter carried on the wind.

'Tomorrow we resume your training,' Faolan said. His voice gave no clue what he thought of that. 'Let the hill tribes stew for a while.' He left her to brush down the horses while he went inside.

Cooking smells drifted out on the night air, and somewhere far off, a barn owl hooted. She moved quickly, jigging up and down on the spot to stay warm. Prior was a white sliver wrapped in a veil of cloud, but the dwarf moon hung fat and crimson over the rooftop. Gwyn couldn't help glancing at it now and again as she worked, trepidation tap-tapping at her heart.

Red moon dawning, heed my warning.

The hill tribes said the red moon was the heart of Siasr. 'Born under Siasr's heart' was the worst insult you could give another person. When it appeared over a roof, it forewarned a death in the household. That was why the hill people chose to live in tents – or so said their legends.

Gwyn shivered in spite of herself. The red moon was hanging directly over her tower window.

CHAPTER 18

THE FIVE TOWERS OF THE ARTS

Gwyn ducked and rolled as the low wall exploded, raining chunks of dust and brick.

Up! She was back on her feet and running before she could catch her breath. From the corner of her eye she saw Faolan's second fireball coming at her. She held up her arms instinctively to shield herself, lashing out at the same time with *scinder*.

The fireball dissolved like mist, and hot sparks rained around her, winking out as they touched the ground.

She stopped running, her hands on her knees, gasping. Her left side twanged with pain in time with her breaths.

'That was better.' Faolan strolled over, a lazy smile on his face. 'You perform well enough under stress.

At this point I expect you could nullify any single sign I sent at you.'

Better. From Faolan, that was high praise. Usually it was a slap on the back of the head, a curled lip, a sneering comment about how a pregnant sow could move faster than she.

But Gwyn was improving, finally. It was getting easier to hone the vim into a sharp edge. Most of the time. If she concentrated too hard, it wouldn't work at all. But when she stopped fighting and let it happen ...

The vim. It still frightened her. Their training ground – the burned-out shell of the old sheep shed – looked like a battlefield: all scorched grass and blown-out sections of wall. The smell of smoke made her want to heave her guts out.

Technically, she was a First Rank wizard now, though Faolan took pains to remind her that apprentices had no rank. She could hold the vim inside her for all of one second before it fizzled away, leaving her sweaty and dazed. Faolan said that without the apprentice bond as a buffer, holding the vim for any length of time would leave her mad and gibbering – if it didn't merely burn her to a crisp on the spot.

She believed him. Even that one hard-earned second felt like trying to hold the sun inside her chest.

'Quick,' Faolan said, clapping his hands and

pointing at her. 'The Five Towers of the Arts. Tell me about the first. Go!'

She sighed inwardly, but pulled herself upright and began to recite, as she had at least once a day for the past two weeks. Faolan believed in rote learning, the duller and more wearisome the better; in drilling and meditating and reciting the same old dry catechisms over and over again. Learning magic, it seemed, wasn't that different to learning herbs and remedies. Though she had rarely ended her lessons with Ascepis covered in soot and sweat.

'The first school of the black arts is nullimancy, also known as the Tower of *Agares*. Nullimancy acts to sever and nullify magical forces. It can be used to stop an enemy's attack, dissolve wards, or cut through another wizard's threads.'

She could name the other schools, too. Metamancy, kinomancy, evocation. And the fifth: necromancy. That part had come as a rude surprise. Early on, she had asked Faolan why he referred to *five* Towers of the Arts, when her uncle had mentioned only four during their regular chats in his study. With a wolfish grin, Faolan had told her that while the milksops of the Syndicate might teach only four schools, there were five, and he wasn't going to pretend otherwise.

'This afternoon we try with two spells,' he said now, brushing the dust off her shoulders. 'You're not ready, of course, but I think it's time we took things up a step, don't you? Now go. Eat. I'm done with you.'

Gwyn tramped back to the house, coat slung over her shoulders. She knew her way to the important places now – the kitchen, her room, Idris' study. But Priory seemed to have a mind of its own, and conspired to keep her lost much of the time. One morning she found herself climbing a staircase that, after turning a corner, ran straight into the sloping roof. There was no hatch. On the second day she had opened a door she was sure led to the entrance hall, only to find a blank stone wall.

That rarely happened now, but in the early days, she had often needed Severine to rescue her. Gwyn had thought maybe the house itself was magic, but Lucian had laughed at that and said it was just poorly built.

That was how she first met Severine's brother, Alcide. For the first two weeks he hadn't been there at all – away on some secret business for Idris, she supposed, though Severine spoke of him often.

Then, one evening, when Gwyn had taken a wrong turn on her way back from the kitchen, she rounded a corner and almost smacked into a tall man she had never seen before. He had the same darkly golden skin as Severine, the same ink-black hair, tied back in two long braids. But his face was all hard angles and planes where hers was softness, and though his narrow eyes were the same pale grey, they held none of her warmth.

'You should watch where you're going,' he said flatly, and brushed past without another word. Gwyn had been too surprised to think of a good response.

She had seen him a few times since, heeling Idris as he walked in the garden, or else running through sword forms in the yard. He spent a lot of time doing that. Once she had found him in Severine's room, sitting backwards on his sister's chair and laughing at something she was saying, but when he caught sight of Gwyn at the door his expression shuttered, and he stalked out without saying anything. What had she done to make him dislike her so intensely?

Fortunately Gwyn saw little of him, for he spent most of his time away from the valley. Lucian went with him sometimes, though most days he would fly out alone in the morning and return before nightfall, tapping at Idris' window with his beak to be let in.

He visited Gwyn's window, too, and she had come to enjoy their discussions. In some ways he was more instructive than Faolan, for though he wasn't a wizard, he had a way of explaining things in simple terms so they made sense. He also knew some of the advanced signs, and unlike Faolan, he was willing to share his knowledge. She had practised drawing them on a piece of parchment she kept hidden under her pillow. None of the signs worked for her yet, but sometimes when she focused on the Fire sign – *sigel*

– she could feel a warm tingle in her fingertips. Once, they had started to glow.

Other times she would sit with Lucian in the drawing room and listen to him play the falcifer. He was very good. Better than the travelling bards in the villages back home. He sang along sometimes, too, in his husky, lilting accent – familiar songs like 'Copper Fields' and 'The Jarl's Privateers', and unfamiliar ones. He started teaching her to play, and after a few lessons, she heard him proudly telling Severine that Gwyn had the worst ear for music of anyone he'd ever met.

She talked to Idris sometimes, sitting across from him in his study, sharing cups of the bitter tea he enjoyed. But when she asked about Beheret's wizards, or what their next move would be, he had little to say. He assured her that the mountains were too vast and too wild for them to locate the Pale Valley, even if they knew where it was. She was safe here, for as long as needed. *Forever* – that was the unspoken word.

Gwyn wasn't satisfied. She should be doing *something,* though she wasn't sure what. Knowing Ygriel was out there somewhere, still searching for her, was like cold fingers running constantly down her back.

Only Faolan seemed to be thinking about Ygriel at all. But his quest to find Shemeris was at a dead end, and he appeared in no hurry to take it up again. Not that he would tell her *why* it was important. That information was for friends, for equals – not for 'witless apprentices with their heads in the clouds'.

Faolan wasn't the only one acting secretive, though. The longer Gwyn spent at Priory, the more she began to feel it.

There was something very strange about this place and its inhabitants.

Initially, it was an absence. Of people, of noise. The wood floors and interlinking corridors tended to carry sound, but from time to time as Gwyn moved through the house, she heard nothing but her own footsteps. Once she spent an entire day without seeing a single person. When she called out, no one answered but the wind. She was sure they hadn't left the valley – it was flat enough outside that you could see a rider coming or going long before they reached the encircling mountains. And when she checked the stables, the horses were all accounted for, including Idris' quick-footed white mare and Severine's placid gelding. Lucian, she allowed, could have left without being seen, but not the others. Wherever they went, they were determined not to let her know.

As far as Gwyn was concerned, that was as good as an invitation. Before winter came, she was going to find out what they were hiding.

CHAPTER 19

OLD GODS AND NEW

Faolan didn't resume the search for Shemeris straight away, so Gwyn spent most of her free time in the library. It was, perhaps, the most natural place for her. She had inherited more from Ascepis than an aversion to settling in one spot. Among the familiar pipe-smoke smell of the books, Gwyn could close her eyes and almost imagine herself back in the wagon.

Almost. Compared to the two rude, sagging shelves that served as a library back home, this was like something lifted out of a fairy story: all plush rugs and crackling fireplace logs and well-mannered dust that never settled on the drapes or the colt-legged writing desks, just hung suspended in the golden afternoon air. A scholar's dream.

'I thought Idris was the only one who *liked* reading,' said Lucian one day, lounging in a leather armchair by the window, his leg slung over the arm. He avoided the library as a rule, but from time to time he would come to visit, seemingly amused by her diligence.

'It's not about liking it or not,' Gwyn replied. She had three books tucked under her arm already, and was standing on her toes to reach the fourth. Lucian sprang to her aid.

'So what is it about?'

'Being prepared.' She arranged the books on the table, frowning down at them. *Commentaries on the Temple of Molech Suun. Faith and Reason. Encountering Iahta. Antecedents of the Cult of Aeshma.* That last one might be useful, but it wasn't enough.

'Am I sensing a theme?' Lucian said, peering over her shoulder. 'Aye, possibly I am. The theme is "an omnipotent goddess is trying to kill me, please help".'

Gwyn smiled in spite of herself. In the ruddy sunlight streaming through the tall windows, it did seem absurd. But Ygriel, at least, was no joke. He frightened her more than Beheret did. Her smile faded.

'You don't think I'm mad for looking into this?' she asked. Faolan certainly did. Last time Gwyn had seen him in the library, he had laughed openly in her face and called her a foolish bookworm – an absurd insult, coming from the man who was rarely seen without a book under one arm.

'I'm not sure what good will come of it,' Lucian

said. 'But I canna blame you. At the very least, it's clear Beheret wants you, and badly. Anything that might help keep you safe is a good thing, at least until Idris figures out how to kill her.'

A shock ran through to her feet. 'Idris wants to kill Beheret?'

Lucian looked as though he regretted having spoken. 'Well, if it's possible, I suppose. Ever since your mother died, it's been on his mind, and I canna blame him.'

Gwyn sank slowly into a chair. Her mind was whirring. *Kill Beheret?* If that were true, it explained a lot. Idris' tight-lipped secrecy, for one. Killing gods wasn't the sort of thing you shouted from the rooftops.

'He hasn't said much about her,' she said. 'My mother, I mean. Just that she was taken from the Lower City, along with a few other students over the years. That he eventually found her in a cloister to Beheret. That sometime during her captivity, she had me.'

'That's about as much as we ken.' Lucian took the other chair. He spoke carefully, as though worried he might hurt her.

'And my father?'

Lucian shook his head, and Gwyn sighed. 'I wish I knew something about him. I don't even know if he was someone my mother loved, or ...'

She didn't want to say it, but Lucian seemed to

understand. 'I think it was ... unlikely to be love,' he said, after a moment. 'It seems producing children was the aim behind the kidnappings, for whatever purpose.' He hesitated, seeming to wrestle with something, then added, 'Idris thinks Beheret was trying to breed sorceresses.'

Gwyn gave a jolt. *Sorceresses?*

'Not you,' Lucian said hastily. 'Sorceresses aren't human; not really. They've glowing eyes, and ... well, it's not you. Besides, Beheret plainly thought you a dead end when she ordered the cloister burned. It was only by chance that you survived. You and ...'

And Ygriel. He didn't have to say it out loud. Gwyn's stomach felt suddenly full of sour milk. 'She wants me now, though, doesn't she?'

Lucian grimaced. 'Aye. You're clearly no sorceress, so what could she want you for? The plainest answer is that she's decided you might be useful in the breeding program after all.'

Gwyn frowned, confused. 'How is that possible? Wizards can't reproduce.' She hadn't given much thought to that since Faolan had told her; had never thought much about having children to begin with. A traveller's wagon was no place to raise a child, and for that matter, life on the road was no place to meet a husband. Still, it stung a little to know the choice would never be there.

'We assume Beheret kens a way around that. After all, she stole wizards from the Clockwork City, not just healers. There's little point if she canna use them for breeding.'

That gave Gwyn pause. It made sense, in a twisted kind of way, but it also opened up a chasm of frightening possibilities.

'We dinna ken anything for sure,' Lucian said firmly, 'so there's no sense speculating.' He hesitated again. 'Ailbhe Ahriddin used to live here, at Priory House – did you ken that?'

'She lived ... here?'

He nodded. 'Centuries ago, obviously. Right before Beheret supposedly destroyed her.'

'Supposedly?' That surprised her. 'You don't believe it?'

Everyone knew the story of Ailbhe Ahriddin, the Last Sorceress. Queen of Ashsalem, she conquered Aranor on the back of her twin dragons; conquered Crater Deep and Shatse, would have conquered Mothmelech and maybe the rest of the world, too, if Beheret hadn't struck her down.

Lucian made a noncommittal sound. 'When it comes to Beheret, it's hard to ken what to believe. There's no record of a body being found. Besides, we're fair sure that all the sorceresses were born through the breeding program. So why would Beheret turn on one of her own creations?'

Severine came into the library then, her face lighting up when she saw them. She headed to their table, a book tucked under one arm. Another romance, Gwyn saw, smiling to herself. She suspected Idris kept ordering them just to keep Severine happy. Certainly she had never seen anyone else reading them.

'Uh-oh!' Severine said, taking in the mood immediately. Her eyes moved from Lucian to Gwyn, then back. 'This seems like a serious conversation.'

'The most serious.' Lucian leaned back in his chair, arms folded behind his head. His shirt had come untucked from his trousers, showing a sliver of flat, tanned stomach. Gwyn looked away quickly, her cheeks growing warm. 'Sorceresses, goddesses, that sort of thing.'

Severine's smile slipped a little. 'Oh – that does sound bad.' She perched herself on the edge of the table and folded her hands in her lap. In her slim-fitting green gown with feather-stencilled embroidery at the sleeves, she looked like an elegant, brightly coloured bird. 'You're not trying to frighten Gwynnie, are you?'

'I dinna think she frightens that easy,' Lucian said, with a wink for Gwyn.

She wasn't so sure. The knot of uneasiness in her stomach refused to go away. Any connection with the sorceresses, even a distant one, was enough to turn her legs to jelly. Still, she had to know.

'So,' Gwyn said slowly, the words coming out almost against her will, 'if Ailbhe was really taken by

Beheret for the breeding program, and not killed ... do you think she could be my ancestor?'

Lucian gave an easy shrug. 'Well, we already ken that.' Seeing Gwyn's stunned expression, he laughed, and Severine punched him in the arm. 'Indirectly, of course. You should ask Idris to see a copy of the family tree. Your grandmother was descended from Ahriddin's younger brother, Gwyllyn.'

And she lived here, in this house. Gwyn's thoughts were suddenly moving at double speed. 'Could she have left anything behind? Ailbhe, I mean.'

'Like what?' Lucian's eyes were bright, now, looking at her with interest. Severine eyed her warily.

'I don't know. A journal, maybe?'

'Well, I dinna ken about a journal.' Lucian ran a hand through his hair, seeming to consider it. 'But the attic is full of crates, from when this place used to be a monastery. The monks were real bowerbirds. That was fifty or so years after Ahriddin's death, of course, but if they found anything she left behind, that's where it would be.'

'Nobody's checked?' That seemed like a gross oversight to Gwyn. 'She could have left chests full of gold and jewels up there!'

Lucian chuckled. 'That's not likely. The monks would have found anything interesting when they moved in. Gold and jewels would have been spent. But a journal? Aye, that's possible.'

'Then I need to go and look,' Gwyn said, standing. Lucian looked up at her in alarm.

'What, now?'

'Why not?'

'It's getting dark, for one, and I'm fair sure you dinna ken how to make a light spell yet. Why the sudden interest, anyway?'

Gwyn sighed and lowered herself back into her chair, energy evaporating. 'I feel like I should be *doing* something.' She couldn't explain it any better than that; not in a way anyone would understand. They weren't the ones being hunted by an evil goddess, were they?

'You moved around a lot, when you lived with Ascepis, didn't you?' Severine spoke gently, tilting her head and watching Gwyn with her grey owl-feather eyes. 'I suppose being stuck here feels a little like being in a cage.'

She had gotten to the heart of it, of course. 'We never spent more than a few nights in one place,' Gwyn said, her voice a little hoarse. That was Ascepis' way of keeping her shielded from the Syndicate and Beheret, she realised now. Not that it had helped in the end. What would he do now that she was gone, his burden lifted? Did he have family somewhere? She had never asked.

'That must be ... difficult,' Lucian said carefully. He looked over at Severine, as if to confirm he was saying the right thing. At her nod, he continued, more forcefully. 'Maybe we can talk to Idris. He should be involving you more in ... um, things.'

'*He* should be teaching you. Not Faolan,' Severine said. It wasn't a criticism of Idris, exactly – Gwyn had never heard anything like that from Severine – but it came close.

'Faolan was the one who bound her,' Lucian said with a shrug. 'It's too late to put that bird back in the coop. Besides, whatever else you might say about him, he does ken his magic.'

Severine's lips drew into a thin line. 'Necromancy.'

'And other things. He's good at what he does. Dinna look at me like that!'

Severine turned back to Gwyn. 'Can you wait for a bit? I'll talk to Idris about getting into the attic. He might be able to move some of the crates around for us. Then I can help you.'

Gwyn nodded. *Assuming Idris doesn't use the delay to hide anything useful.* She couldn't be sure, with him.

But in the meantime, there were books to read, and lessons with Faolan.

Especially tonight. Gwyn's stomach fluttered. The full moon had come around quickly, before she had a chance to think about what she had asked him.

Tonight, she was going to learn necromancy.

CHAPTER 20

NECROMANCER'S MOON

'I want you to teach me necromancy,' Gwyn had said, three days earlier.

Faolan was sitting outside on a bench against the wall, enjoying the last days of sun. The autumn equinox was approaching fast now, the days seeming to slip by in halts and starts. He hadn't looked up when she approached, but now he turned his face to her, his expression unreadable, his eyes curiously bright.

'Why would you ask me that?'

Gwyn pulled her coat tighter. It was chilly, though Faolan seemed not to feel it. From the sheen on his brow, she guessed he had conjured up a heat spell.

'Don't act like you weren't expecting this.' She held out her hand, showing him the marking on her palm. 'I've figured out what this means. A five-pointed star, for the Five Towers of the Arts. Yours only has four points, because you were marked while you were still in the Syndicate. But you gave me five. You intended me to learn necromancy right from the beginning.'

He smiled then – a cold, satisfied smile. 'The four-pointed star is a lie. A comforting one, perhaps, but I would never mark my apprentice with a lie.'

Gwyn stuffed her hand back into her coat. 'If necromancy is one of the Five Towers, it seems foolish that the Syndicate bars wizards from learning about it. I know you can do evil things with it ... but you can do evil things with the other four Towers, too, and nobody tries to ban those.' Again, the smell of roasting flesh. Soot and death on the night air. 'I also think that, seeing as I already entered this *Lurk* by myself – and you say that's not normal – maybe it means I'm meant to learn it.'

'*Meant* to?' Faolan repeated, eyes narrow. 'Do you mean destiny?' His tone was quite serious, with none of the mockery she had come to expect.

'I don't know about destiny.' Gwyn hesitated. She hadn't shared these thoughts – not with Faolan, not with Idris, not even with Severine. But they were playing on her mind, and maybe Faolan's perspective would help. 'Everyone says Umbrael the Weaver controls a person's destiny, and cuts the thread of their life when their purpose is fulfilled. Ascepis never believed that, but if Beheret is real, then maybe

Umbrael is too. I'm not sure what that means about destiny.'

Faolan, for once, had nothing nasty to say. He looked straight ahead, his expression bland. Too bland. Through the bond, she could feel him vibrating like a plucked string. What was he hiding?

'In my experience, your destiny is whatever you make it,' he said finally. 'Gwyn ... I counsel you to think about this first. Necromancy ... changes things.'

'What things?'

Faolan didn't seem to hear her. His mouth was drawn into a thin line as he stared over her shoulder, seeing nothing. Gooseflesh prickled the back of her neck.

Then the moment passed, and his eyes refocused on her. His expression was hard.

'Why do you want to learn this thing? And don't feed me that rubbish about destiny, or about wanting to learn all Five Towers. What is your real reason?'

She swallowed. There was no way to lie to Faolan – the bond prevented that. She had hoped giving him half of the truth would be enough.

'Ygriel knows necromancy,' she said, 'and he wants to kill me. I need to be able to defend myself.'

'If you avoid the Lurk altogether, you will never have to face him there,' Faolan said, though she sensed an ambivalence behind his words. 'Does it not seem foolish to spend time in the very place you know your enemy to be searching for you?'

'I never meant to go there in the first place. But it still happened. How can I be sure it won't happen again?'

Faolan shrugged, as though he had been expecting that answer. 'So you wish to learn because it will give you power.'

'Only to defend myself.'

'Power is power, no matter how noble your intentions.' His smile held no warmth. 'Very well. I have my own business in the Lurk soon enough. When Sadira is full, come to my room after night meal. We'll see if you have what it takes.'

On the night she was to learn necromancy, Faolan didn't appear for the evening meal. Gwyn picked fretfully at a baked potato, drawing worried looks from Lucian and Severine. After a short time, she excused herself and headed for Faolan's room. The full, red moon peered in at her from the high windows.

She had never been inside his quarters before. Part of her expected ... well, she didn't know what she expected. Skulls, perhaps. Black curtains. A blood-stained altar. But the room was cold and spacious, empty save for a hard little bed and a washstand. The heavy drapes on the window were drawn, and the room was illuminated only by a single tapered candle.

The necromancer himself sat cross-legged on the floor. Gwyn wanted to laugh at his undignified position, but his expression forbade it. There was a white circle drawn around him that looked like chalk, but when she came closer she saw it was salt.

'What's the circle for?'

'Protection,' he said coolly. 'From other necromancers. Entering the Lurk sends out a ripple that others nearby can sense. The salt masks the trail. Now come. Sit. Let's begin.'

She stepped over the salt circle, half expecting to smack into some sort of magical barrier. Nothing happened. She sat opposite Faolan, looking around warily.

'The most fundamental aspect of necromancy is the ability to enter the Lurk – otherwise known as Death – at will,' Faolan said. His voice took on a calm, lecturing tone. 'The ability is unique to mancers, but it's not one of the thirty signs, and most are too squeamish to ever learn it.'

Squeamish, or just sensible? But it was too late to turn back now. 'And the Lurk is ... a real place?'

'As real as any.'

Gwyn swallowed. And she had really gone there, back in Tønderby? She had been trying to concentrate, focusing on drawing in the vim, on unpicking Faolan's knots. How had it gone so badly wrong?

'So how do I do it?'

'The first step is to make yourself perfectly still.' He was helping her, she realised, sending calmness and serenity to her through the bond. It was working a little too well. In spite of her racing heart, a part of her was ready to fall asleep.

'Now reach out with your mind,' she heard him say. His voice was strangely muffled.

Reach out with your mind? That sounded a lot like what she had done in Tønderby – making her awareness detach up and away from her body. She tried to remember how she had managed it, but it was hard to do that while also keeping her mind completely empty.

'Not like that,' Faolan said, and his irritation shivered the edges of her calm. 'Reach inwards.'

Gwyn bit back a retort. Any hint that she was being *ungrateful* and he was likely to refuse teaching her altogether. And she wanted to learn this. Didn't she? Well, maybe not, but it was the only way she knew to protect herself from Ygriel. She wouldn't be helpless again, like that night at the inn. Never again.

She pushed the thought aside, focusing on keeping her mind blank. It wasn't easy, but Faolan had gone back to radiating calm and serenity, and that helped. Presently she felt her mind start to float.

Her instinct was to pull up and away out of her body, but Faolan had said that was wrong. She focused her attention on the darkness behind her eyelids, and imagined herself falling inwards.

Instantly, she was sinking, a stone through dark water.

Awareness of her body faded. Her legs had been growing stiff and heavy beneath her, but they were gone now, as though they had never been there at all. There was only darkness, and the sound of her own heartbeat in her ears. In a moment, that melted away too.

Sudden cold hit her, jarring, but it was gone before she was even fully aware of it. She gasped, her eyes flying open.

'You're not trying,' Faolan said. His mouth was pressed into a thin line.

'I am!' Her voice came out raw and scratchy, as though she'd been screaming, though she was sure she hadn't.

'You're not. You were close, but I felt you pull away just as you reached the barrier.' He sighed heavily. 'Let's try again.'

But the second attempt proved no better, nor the third, nor the fourth. Eventually, Faolan threw his hands up in frustration.

'I'd have better luck teaching my horse. At least it can follow simple instructions.'

'I'm trying,' Gwyn protested. 'It's just that —'

Faolan cut her off with a wave. 'Excuses. I've little patience for them. We try again tomorrow night. I suggest you spend the day in fasting, and quiet, *intelligent* contemplation.' That last was delivered with a raised eyebrow.

Gwyn staggered as she left the room. *Tomorrow night.* Maybe now she knew what to expect, it would be easier. She wiped her forehead with the back of her hand. For all that she'd spent the time – how long had it been, hours? – sitting completely still on the floor, it was tiring work. She felt wrung-out.

Quiet, intelligent contemplation – ha, she thought, as she stripped off her clothes and rolled into bed. *Well, I'll show him. I'll ...*

She was asleep before she could finish the thought.

CHAPTER 21

DOWN

The next night proved no more fruitful. Nor did the night after. Gwyn thought Faolan might give up – his frustration flayed at her like a whip – but he simply dismissed her, with instructions to come back at the next full moon, and in the meantime, to spend at least one day every week in fasting and meditation.

Her regular lessons didn't stop, though. When it came to the four traditional schools of study, Faolan worked her harder than ever. Always the First Tower, though; always *Agares*. Gwyn had complained about that, telling Faolan she wanted to learn to *do* magic, not just counter it.

It was no use. The traditional Sequentialist school of thought said the Four Towers should be taught step-by-step; that the student should master the first before moving on to the second. For a practitioner of illegal necromancy, Faolan was strict on following the rules.

One morning in late autumn, there was no lecture to accompany her lesson. Faolan dismissed her brusquely, striding back to the house before she even had a chance to ask why.

That was strange. It was strange, too, that Severine was not in the kitchen, where she spent most mornings. Only she and Lucian could cook, and with Lucian often gone, the task of bread-baking usually fell to her. Now there was no Severine, and no bread, either, leaving Gwyn with nothing but dried fruit and hard cheese.

The cellars would be better stocked. Isolated in the mountains, it was hard to get supplies, and Idris kept enough food underground to last through the winter, warded against rats and decay. Gwyn never had cause to visit the cellars herself, but now seemed a good time.

The heavy trapdoor was easy to find, in the middle of the larder floor, off the kitchen. A thick layer of dust lay on the shelves, but the cellar door was clean and looked recently used. It took all of her strength to lift it.

The stairs stretched down into complete darkness. Gwyn put her face close to the hole. A cold breeze tickled her nose. There was no sign of the bottom.

If it was like the rest of the house, the torches

should light automatically. She decided to take the chance. She was hungry, and ... yes, curious, too. It struck her that this would be a good place to hide things.

Hide what? She didn't know, but ...

When she reached the bottom of the ten or so steps, torches flared into brightness down the length of the cellar. She blinked, eyes watering in the sudden light.

The room must have run the entire length of the house. A high ceiling stretched away in a series of arches. Rushes covered the stone floor, and stacks of barrels were arranged against the black-streaked walls. There was a sooty smell in the air. This part of the house seemed much older than the rest. She could imagine it as a crypt, during the monastery days, with coffins against the walls instead of barrels. Perhaps it had been.

But it was just a cellar now, whatever she had been expecting. The barrels were labelled, and Gwyn soon found herself inspecting one marked 'dried beef' and wondering if she could possibly get it back up the stairs herself. Lucian's strong arms would be useful. Alcide looked strong, too, but she wouldn't ask him for a cup of water if she was on fire. She doubted he would offer one, either. The man was nothing like his sister.

Gwyn was still trying to shimmy the barrel away from the wall when she heard the music.

She froze. It was the same faint, off-key melody she had heard playing now and again since the caves. Louder now, as though just in the next room. Not a song she knew, but familiar all the same, like something half-remembered from childhood.

It was coming from the other end of the cellar.

Gwyn peered down the length of the room. The cellar ended in a blank stone wall. There was nobody in sight.

She began to walk without thinking. The torches flickered as she passed. It seemed to take a long time to reach the end. When she stood before the wall, the music seemed to be inside her bones.

It was a few moments before she realised there was another sound.

The wall was *whispering*.

She couldn't make out the words, but there were voices, and Gwyn knew they were speaking to her. Up close, the wall was not blank at all. There were shapes carved into the stone, so faint and age-worn they seemed a trick of the torchlight. She thought they might be figures, crudely drawn, looking up at the sky. Their arms were raised in worship ... or as though cowering from a blow. Over it all hung a giant moon. While the figures were half hidden by dust and soot, the moon was white; pristine. It was made of something different to the surrounding stone. Something smooth, like polished white glass.

On instinct, Gwyn reached up and pressed her hand to the face of the moon.

There was a sudden, clear sound, like a bell being struck. Before Gwyn could even snatch her hand back, the wall had pulled back and slid away. The music stopped as though cut with a knife.

Torchlit stairs curved down and out of sight. The low ceiling was a jumble of different-coloured pipes, some transparent, with a dark liquid like blood running through them.

Voices came floating out of the dark, carrying the smell of dust and hot metal. Her first thought was to run, but it was too late.

Three figures appeared around the corner, coming up the stairs towards her. Idris, Severine and Faolan. They were speaking quietly, their heads together, and at first they didn't see her.

'I'm not questioning her motives,' Severine was saying, 'but I do think we have to look at what was *meant* and not just what was *said.* We have to guard against putting our own beliefs in place of hers. I think —' Then she looked up, and her words ended in a gasp. She stopped walking.

'What are you doing here?' Both Faolan and Severine spoke at the same time, then looked at each other with matching expressions of distaste. Idris didn't say anything at all.

Gwyn felt suddenly awkward, as though she'd been caught doing something wrong. Her face grew warm. No, they were the ones who were wrong. For not telling her about – whatever this was. They *were* hiding something in the cellar, after all.

'What's down there?' She wasn't going to make excuses. She had every right to be here. 'Is that where you've been disappearing to all this time?'

Severine hesitated, seeming to search for the right words. 'It's complicated, Gwyn. But I suppose you might say we're very ... religious.'

Gwyn said nothing. A tiny flicker of anger – barely an ember – fluttered somewhere in her chest.

Faolan and Idris looked sceptical, but Severine continued. 'We go underground, now and then, so we can ... commune ... with the great spirit.'

That sounded like rubbish, but the back of Gwyn's neck prickled just the same, at the mention of a *spirit.* Was there a ghost in the lower level? Faolan was a necromancer, after all. She had a sudden, horrible image: the three of them, and Lucian and Alcide too, in black robes, chanting and dancing around a blood-stained altar piled with skulls ...

She pushed the image away. *Ridiculous.* The thought of Severine as some kind of demon-worshipper was absurd. As for Faolan, she could already hear him complaining about how the black of the robes was *very* unflattering with his skin tone. No – whatever they were doing down there, it wasn't that.

It made no difference. She knew where the secret

room was now, and she knew how to get inside. Short of confining her to her quarters, they had no way to stop her.

It was just a matter of waiting for the right moment.

CHAPTER 22

THE GHOST OF PRIORY HOUSE

The next day, Gwyn recruited Severine to search the attic. The healer jumped at the chance, apparently anxious to make up lost ground between them. The secrecy surrounding the cellar had made things awkward.

'I'm embarrassed,' Severine said, coughing and fanning dust away from her face. The room smelled like mice droppings and ashes. A bar of light streamed through the dormer window, casting a watery yellow circle on the floor. 'This place is a mess. Someone should have cleaned it out years ago.'

'When was the last time anyone came here?'

'Well, we bring thing up for storage, from time to time.' Severine shrugged and heaved the lid off one of the crates. They were stacked to the ceiling in some areas, but unhelpfully, none were labelled. 'But I don't think anyone has – oh, look at this!'

Gwyn peered over her shoulder. The crate was stuffed with straw the colour of old milk, and smelled like mildew. Severine fished something out and held it to the light.

'Faolan's things,' she said, scowling. The object in question appeared to be a mummified human hand. 'From when he used to live here, years ago. I didn't realise Idris kept it all.'

Gwyn stared at the hand as Severine set it aside. 'Is that really ...?'

'Oh, probably.' The next item in the box was an old-fashioned gold lamp with a delicately curved spout. 'He spent the better part of a year hunting down cursed items. Supposedly cursed, I should say. A lot of them turned out to be fake.' After the lamp came a small brass telescope, a bag of odd-shaped blue stones, and a silver ring inscribed in a language neither of them recognised.

'Is that why he left? To find more cursed objects?'

'That's probably part of it,' Severine said. 'But it was Idris' idea, really. He wanted somebody to go south and keep an eye on you – not that he didn't trust Ascepis, of course. But, well, he knew Ascepis had been severed, and if it came to a fight, he wouldn't be able to defend you. Not against the Syndicate, at least.'

There were a few more things in the box: a carved soapstone wolf figurine, a silver bracelet, a lock of white hair tied with a ribbon. Nothing that seemed important. The second and third crates held old towels and bedsheets, a little moth-eaten now. Severine was moving them aside when she suddenly stopped.

'Is that ...?' Gwyn asked.

Propped up against the wall was a framed painting, about four feet high – a portrait. For an instant, Gwyn thought it was her. The girl was around fourteen, pale-skinned, with jade-coloured eyes and hair the colour of cream. Although the colours had faded, the resemblance was still plain.

But no – this girl was a little slimmer, her features a touch more delicate. Her hair was pin-straight where Gwyn's ended in loose curls.

'Aislinn,' Severine said. Her voice was troubled. 'I didn't know Idris had a portrait of her. Gods, but they did look alike, didn't they?'

They did, Gwyn realised, though she hadn't seen it at first. They could have been twins, rather than plain siblings. Her own resemblance was nothing in comparison – muddied, she supposed, by the contribution of her unknown father.

In the crate next to the portrait, they found a trove of items that could only have belonged to her. An ivory comb. A gold locket, the front carved with the shape of a rose. Women's clothes that somehow, impossibly, still held a ghostly fragrance of woods-lily. Idris must have gathered them from her quarters in the Clockwork City before he fled.

'What about this?' Severine said, amused. She was holding up a slingshot and a bag of stones.

Gwyn laughed, feeling suddenly lighter. 'Idris did mention something about her having a spirited nature. I didn't realise this is what he meant.' She tried to picture the girl with the big, innocent eyes, prowling the corridors of the Clockwork City with a slingshot in her hand. It was difficult.

Deeper in the attic, the wood crates were replaced by other, stranger things – metal drums, boxes made of painted steel, and crates hewn out of some hard, white substance like resin.

'These things are so old,' Severine marvelled, as they cleared room for the containers. Disappointingly, many of them were rusted shut, the lids refusing to budge even when Gwyn tried to pry them with an iron bar. 'They must have been here when Idris first found the house.'

'How did that happen, anyway?' Gwyn was breathing heavily now, sweat soaking through the front of her white shirt.

'How did he find the house?' Severine hesitated, seeming to consider her words. 'Well, that was a good eight years or so before Alcide and I joined him. So I'm not fully certain. But I suppose you could say he had a vision.'

Halfway through trying to screw the lid off one of the white barrels, Gwyn paused. 'A vision?'

Severine came to her aid, nodding. 'Yes. Or a

dream, at least. Here in the highlands, that sort of thing is ... well, not common, exactly, but not unheard of. Idris still has them sometimes. But that night, he was staying at an inn, not far from here, in Kasteberg. That's when he had the vision.' She gave a small, slightly uncomfortable laugh. 'You'll have to ask him exactly what he saw. But the next morning, he got on his horse and rode straight here.'

'And he's been at Priory ever since?'

'More or less. It was just him and Faolan, for a little while. Then Lucian joined him, and a few years later, he came to Crater Deep, where he met Alcide and me. And now you.'

Under both their weights, the lid finally popped off. Gwyn choked on the sudden cloud of stale air. No dust, though. The contents of the drum were still in perfect condition.

At least, I think they are, Gwyn thought, pulling out ... something. It was made of the same substance as the container, shaped entirely of odd curves and bulges, with a small metal tab poking out of one side like a tongue. It was impossible to say anything about the object's condition, let alone what it was or what it might be used for.

More items followed, all equally strange. A sphere, dark and reflective as obsidian, but strangely lightweight. A transparent tube with a spout at the top, connected to a white inner core.

'I think this is a pipe,' Severine said, holding up

something shiny and grey, made up of hard planes and angles. 'See, the pipeleaf goes in here.'

'Could be,' Gwyn said doubtfully. 'What about this?'

It was a looking glass, the border rimmed in ornate gold leaf. The surface was so badly cracked it showed her reflection in slices – a single green eye, a curl of pale hair, the edge of her mouth. But the background seemed wrong, somehow. Darker than the attic should be.

As Gwyn brought it closer to her face, the glass ... lit up. There was no other way to describe it. She gave a yelp and almost dropped it. Severine's eyes looked ready to pop out of her head.

'I've never seen *that* before.'

Tiny words appeared in a curling, white script, as though drawn with an invisible quill:

Hello, Ailbhe.

Gwyn did drop it, then, as though it had become red-hot. The glass should have shattered completely, but the words continued to stare up at her.

'Well,' Severine said slowly. 'I suppose that means we've found the sorceress' things.'

Neither of them wanted to touch the object, and in the end, Gwyn took off her coat and wrapped it up so that no part was touching her skin.

'It's probably safe,' Severine said, as they made

their way to Idris' study. But her voice was unconvincing, and Gwyn noticed *she* wasn't volunteering to carry it.

Safe. As though anything that belonged to the sorceress could be safe.

Idris was sitting behind his desk when they came in, half hidden behind teetering piles of books. Hearing the door open, he looked up and blinked owlishly at them. There were smudges on his eyeglasses. He looked to be in the process of writing a letter, but, seeing their faces, he put the quill away, and his expression cleared.

'We found something,' Severine said.

Gwyn unwrapped her coat, and the thing fell onto the desk with a small *thunk*. For a moment, Idris just stared at it. She could almost see his mind working.

'It's a memory glass,' Severine said.

Memory glass? Gwyn had heard of them in books, she thought, but had never imagined actually seeing one for herself. This would have been old even when the sorceress was young. Relics from the First Era were astoundingly rare, ones that actually worked even rarer. Supposedly the Emperor of Shatse had a construct that controlled the weather – the source of the impenetrable, ever-present fog that surrounded the kingdom. But that was far to the south; further than Gwyn had ever been, or thought to go. Perhaps it was only a story.

Severine was still recounting how they had

discovered the mirror, though Idris seemed to be barely listening. He had already picked it up and was turning it over in his hands, apparently fascinated. Gwyn could still see the tiny, elegant letters. *Hello, Ailbhe.* She shivered and shrugged her coat back on.

'It is essentially intact,' he said finally. 'Damage to the surface, of course, but the memories likely remain.' He put it down and looked up, meeting Gwyn's eyes over the rim of his glasses. 'However, it appears to be locked.'

'Locked?' said a man's voice.

'Protected by a blood seal,' said Idris, looking over Gwyn's shoulder. She turned, and there, coming down the spiral staircase from the upper level, was Alcide. He carried a bundle of scrolls under one arm, sword belted at his hip. His dark hair fell slightly over his face as he glanced at Gwyn. He displayed no particular expression when he looked at her; not even dislike.

Severine gave him a beaming smile, and received a small, fleeting one in return. 'Did you see what we found? Isn't it remarkable?'

'Not if it doesn't work,' Alcide said, coming over to the desk. In motion, he was graceful as a leopard. He glared down at the strange instrument, and Gwyn had the impression he was prepared to draw his sword on it if it proved to be any threat.

'I never said it doesn't work,' Idris said. His mild

tone was at odds with the strange light in his eyes. 'Gwyn, would you come here, please?'

She didn't want to, but she stepped forward almost against her will. The memory glass sat in the middle of the desk, the words glaring up at her like a snake. She could feel both Alcide's and Severine's eyes on her.

'Touch the glass, if you would.'

Slowly, half in a daze, she reached out. Her finger made contact with the edge of the glass. It was cool and hard and thrummed faintly under her touch. Realising what she was doing, she immediately pulled away. The mirror went dark.

Then, rising up from its surface, there came a woman's voice, as smooth and rich as honey.

'This will be my last entry. Tomorrow, I'm getting out of this place.' There was a long pause, then a sigh. *'Umbrael isn't going to be happy with me. Well, trust is a hard –'*

The voice cut off.

Gwyn blinked, feeling as though she was coming up from underwater. Idris had touched something on the glass, making it fall silent.

'That was Ailbhe Ahriddin, wasn't it?' she asked. 'Why did you stop it?'

'The memory has been compromised,' he said, too smoothly. 'I will examine it more closely tonight and see if anything useful can be recovered.'

Compromised, Gwyn thought scornfully. It was

plain that he didn't want her to hear whatever the sorceress had to say. Never mind that she had been the one to find it. Nor that it was *her* hand that had unlocked its secrets. *'Protected by a blood seal'*, he had said.

So I am descended from Ailbhe Ahriddin, after all. She grimaced inwardly. That thought was going to keep her awake at night for a long time.

There was one thing Gwyn was certain of. She needed to get her hands on that glass. Uncle or not, she was sick to death of Idris keeping secrets from her.

Not just Idris, she thought grimly. *All of them. Even Severine and Lucian.* That stung the most. Those two were the closest she had – the closest she'd *ever* had – to real friends.

She knew it was just loyalty to Idris, and the desire to keep her safe, that stilled their tongues. There was no malice behind it; she would stake her life on that.

But it made little difference. A lie was a lie, and they were lying every time they withheld information from her.

'I'm going to get some food,' she said shortly. The others looked at her in surprise, but didn't try to stop her as she turned on her heel and left the study, closing the door a little too firmly behind her.

. . .

That night, Gwyn was reading on her bed when she heard a tap at the window. She reached over and threw it open without looking up.

'You look angry,' Lucian said, brushing off the front of his shirt. He had the ruffled look he always had after changing.

She sighed and smacked the book closed. 'Maybe I am angry.' As she said it, she realised it was true. She seemed to be angry a lot lately. At Idris, certainly, but it was more than that.

'Not at me, I hope?' When Gwyn didn't reply, he laughed. 'I'm wounded. I thought we were friends.' The thought of her anger didn't seem to bother him. If anything, he seemed entertained.

'Friends don't keep secrets,' she said shortly.

Lucian settled himself on the end of the bed. 'Dinna blame Idris for not telling you sooner. Wizards like to keep their secrets at the best of times. And Idris, well, he's the best of wizards. Secrecy is just the way his mind works. I'm sure you understand why we canna tell anyone about her. If the rest of the world found out, it would certainly put a few noses out of joint.'

'I suppose so,' Gwyn said slowly. Who did he mean by '*her*'? Lucian didn't seem to realise how little she actually knew. She hoped he might let something else slip, but instead he changed the subject.

'How are you coming along with everything? I hear Faolan is working you pretty hard.'

'I like the lessons,' she said. Faolan had added three more marks to her tattoo, though only *algiz* – 'ward' – seemed like it would be useful. 'He says I'm learning quickly, that I'll be ready to start the Second Tower soon.'

'Impressive. In the Syndicate, you know, they dinna teach the students anything practical to start. And then they spend a year or more on *Agares* before they move on. You've come a long way in a short time.'

'Idris mastered *Agares* in less than a month.' Faolan had told her that. He had a lot of stories about Idris' time in the Syndicate, most of them making her uncle out to be some heroic, almost mythical figure. Learning all twenty-four traditional signs before finishing his first year. Publishing his own book on theory at fifteen. A secret duel in the Lower City, where he took on five older students and won.

'Well, Idris is Idris. Everyone kens he's abnormal.' Lucian grinned. 'Buck up. Faolan is a bastard, but he's good at what he does. You could do worse than him for a teacher. Just watch out for the ...' He waggled his fingers in a way she supposed meant *necromancy.*

'He hasn't taught me anything like that,' Gwyn said carefully. *Not successfully, anyway.* She was still practising the fasting, the meditation, but without success. 'He said setting me loose in the Lurk would be like "letting a half-wit baby play in the rusty knife store".' That was one of the more polite metaphors he'd used. Still, she could deal with his sulks and his fits of nasty humour if it meant learning to defend herself from Ygriel.

After their last lesson, as she limped out of the training yard, Faolan had called after her – too casually by far – and said that when the full moon came again, she should meet him in the bathhouse. The bathhouse! She wasn't sure what *that* augured, but it could be nothing good.

'Well, he has some sense, then,' Lucian said. 'And if *you* have enough sense to fill a soup spoon, you'll stay well away from that rubbish. Leave the dead in the ground where they belong.'

'Are you worried I'll start raising ghosts, Lucian?' She watched his face closely as she said that, but he just laughed and stood.

'Ghosts I can manage. It's the rotting ones I dinna like. A corpse shambler can stink out a room for a month.' His face grew serious. 'Just keep your head down. Learn as much as you can. You might need it before long.'

He left, and the room seemed suddenly chilly. Gwyn drew her blanket up around her with a sigh.

CHAPTER 23

ECHOES OF THE PAST

Gwyn had two secret projects, now. The first, and perhaps the most pressing, was to find a way into the secret room in the cellar. She had almost put it out of her mind for a time. But Lucian's words had reminded her, and now it seemed more important than ever that she find out what was behind that door.

'*Her*'? Maybe there really was a ghost down there. But whose?

The second project was getting her hands on Ailbhe's memory glass. Presumably Idris kept it in his quarters, which meant she just needed to wait until he was occupied elsewhere, and sneak in.

The trouble was that he never seemed to leave the room for long enough. She saw him in the kitchens, sometimes, though he ate in his study as often as not. Once, she almost ran into him when he was coming out of the bathhouse. Or rather, he almost ran into her – he had his head buried in a book, and didn't see her until they were nose-to-nose.

Whether by intent or design, the others were keeping her busy. There were the lessons with Faolan, of course, which could stretch the entire day if he was in a particularly expansive mood. When he wasn't working her to the point of collapse, he was slapping the back of her head and calling her an idiot girl. Still, as Lucian had said, he knew his magic, and day by day Gwyn could feel her abilities growing.

Lucian himself became more serious about teaching her to play the falcifer. 'When you're on the road, sometimes you might have to play for your supper and board,' he'd said. 'It's useful to have at least some skill.' Gwyn couldn't see that she would ever be 'on the road', so long as they kept her locked away in Priory, but she enjoyed his company. Over time, her playing matured from awful to merely bad.

Surprisingly, she also started receiving lessons from Alcide in swordsmanship. That directive came straight from Idris, who said that it was 'foolish to always rely on magic'. On hearing that pronouncement, Faolan's eyes had almost bugged out of his head. As far as Faolan was concerned, there was nothing that couldn't be solved by magic.

When it came to the sword, Gwyn proved even worse than at the falcifer. Alcide was a more patient teacher than Lucian, in some ways – he never laughed at her fumbles, for one thing – but that flinty glare of his had a way of making everything she had just learned evaporate out of her head. Alcide was never hesitant to press his advantage, and she sported fresh welts to remind her of every mistake.

In the beginning, he simply set her a series of exercises – strike, parry, block. It wasn't much like the stories. For one thing, she found herself exhausted within minutes. Held at arm's length, even a wooden practice sword became heavy as iron. And there was much less leaping and slashing than she had expected.

'Too close.' Alcide tapped her back leg and pushed her shoulder to show her balance was off. 'It's not enough to just stand there like a tree and move the blade. The footwork is just as important. That will get you halfway there. The rest is concentration and practice.'

Concentration, as it turned out, was the hardest part. The kind of responsive, free-floating focus needed for swordwork was the exact opposite of the honed intensity needed for magic. Half the time, when she tried to summon one, she got the other instead. She understood now why so few wizards had any skill with weapons, at least according to Faolan.

Still, every now and again she surprised both herself and Alcide with unexpected bursts of magical ability. More than once, a blow from Alcide's wooden training sword that should have landed across her ribs instead somehow glanced off and sent him sprawling into the fence of the yard. Faolan, who came by now and again to watch them, laughed uproariously whenever that happened.

'She's my apprentice,' he said, smiling like a cat. 'Should she just stand there and let you wallop her?'

She did exactly that, though, most of the time. Alcide had a smooth, liquid grace that made Gwyn wonder if he wasn't secretly a wizard himself. It certainly seemed like magic, the way he could be one place and then the other, without any intervening motion. Sometimes it took her a few moments to even realise she'd been struck.

So Gwyn studied, and she trained. And she waited. Deep inside, she held on to a tiny flame of anger, stoking it every time it threatened to go out.

They want to keep secrets from me? Well, I'll show them that I'm not a bull, being led around by the nose. Cellar or memory glass – whichever opportunity presented itself first, she meant to take it.

Days turned into weeks, and her body began to grow harder and move faster. Her magic improved inch by painful inch. Her fingers on the falcifer became surer, with less fumbles and mangled notes. She grew closer to Severine and Lucian, and even Alcide seemed to warm to her – or at least, he sometimes gave her a grave nod when they passed in the hallway, rather than a scowl.

But still she waited. And in the third week after finding the memory glass, her chance came.

She was in the chapel when she sensed it.

At Faolan's recommendation, Gwyn had been spending an hour there every day, meditating and trying to learn *quiet, intelligent contemplation.* It was getting easier. The seven-sided chapel with its rounded cupola was a quiet place, and after the first frustrating week, she had come to enjoy spending time there. It was the first real peace she had felt in months.

Two days before the full moon, Gwyn opened her eyes and realised she was alone. Not just in the chapel – it was too small to admit more than one or two people comfortably, and they rarely came here anyway, except to sweep out the dust. (*So much for being 'religious',* Gwyn thought.)

No, she was alone in the house; alone in the whole valley, maybe. It was just a feeling, but Gwyn had learned to trust those. A certain hush in the air, more than just the natural stillness of the chapel. She reached out with her senses – something that was second nature, now – and confirmed it. The others had gone into the cellar again. For now, she was completely alone.

Gwyn wasn't going to let this chance slip past. Quickly, she pulled herself up from the ground and brushed off her trousers. The stained-glass windows let in bars of coloured light, illuminating a thousand sparkling filaments in the air. The air smelled of dried flowers and smoke from the candles. The small statue of Molech Suun glared at her as she hurried outside, along the walkway to the main house.

Gwyn had never been in Idris' study alone before. The desk seemed very large, the orange-washed sky behind it casting a long shadow across the floor. On the upper mezzanine level, she could see bookshelves stretching from floor to ceiling. No paintings, no tapestries, no decorations, except a vase filled with fresh flowers on a marble stand by the door. That was obviously Severine's work. She doubted Idris even noticed they were there.

Moving quickly, Gwyn crossed the room. The desk was scattered with papers. Most were news updates, or rumours, collected by various contacts of Idris' throughout the land. The Queen of Chastis was dead without an heir, and the city-state on the brink of civil war. The Syndicate was intensifying its campaign against a rogue wizard faction in the Slumbering Isles. Some kind of conflict had broken out in distant Shatse – nobody seemed to know what, exactly – and the common folk were saying Ailbhe Ahriddin had come again.

She shoved the papers aside. No memory glass. There were two cabinets flanking the window, divided into pigeonholes, but they contained only rolled-up scrolls and charts. Some were held in metal cases, and these she opened, just to be certain. Most of them were maps, showing the land around southern Aranor and the Blighted Rim. She stared for some time before recalling herself and sealing them away again. They weren't what she had come for.

'Where are you?' she muttered. She glanced out the window. The first, faint stars were starting to appear. How long until the others returned from the cellar? Heart beating faster now, Gwyn took the spiral stairs to the upper level.

Idris' bed was narrow and hard, his wardrobe small and filled with a dizzying number of bright-coloured robes. She groped for a secret panel, but found nothing. Moving to the bookshelves, she began lifting down books one by one. Many seemed to be in scripts and languages she couldn't read, or else pure nonsense. Books on other worlds, on palaces in the sky, on men and women made of stone or steel or glass. Gwyn shoved them back on the shelf impatiently.

One book was smaller than the others, with an unmarked black leather cover. The contents were ...

She paused with the book halfway back on the shelf. She couldn't remember *what* the contents were, although she had just flipped through it a moment earlier. She took the book back and opened it again. Of course, it was ...

Again, Gwyn stopped. The book was back on the shelf. Had she put it there? She was sure she hadn't.

In a sudden burst of insight, Gwyn grasped the vim and called up the double circle and curved line of *reveal* – the third sign of *Agares*, another new addition to her marking. The concealment spell shattered into a thousand tiny shards, and then Gwyn was holding the book again.

Only it wasn't a book. It was the memory glass.

Hidden in plain view, she thought scornfully. She took a steadying breath and touched the front of the glass.

Hello, Ailbhe.

Her heart was beating at double speed. Again, she felt that revulsion, that desire to throw the thing against the wall. What had she done last time to unlock it? *I touched it here, and here ...*

'This will be my last entry,' came the voice, making her jump. *'Tomorrow, I'm getting out of this place. Umbrael isn't going to be happy with me. Well, trust is a hard thing to come by lately, and she has her own reasons for what she does. She wants Beheret dead – I'm sure of that – but I doubt she cares much whether I die in the process.'*

There was a pause, then a bark of derisive laughter. *'To the six hells with that. I'm no hero. I got this far by being a survivor. Running and hiding ...'* She trailed off; sighed. *'These days I'm far removed from Queen of Ashsalem. I've fallen a long way. Gilles probably wouldn't recognise me. My nails are all broken, and my hair ... It's better not to mention my hair. It's hard to get Anchoran oils this far from civilisation.*

'Well, it doesn't matter. There's no one to see, except Umbrael, and she's no peach herself. Maybe when I'm settled with the hill people, I'll start rubbing whale blubber in my hair, like they do. At least the smell should be interesting.

'If I do go back to Angharadan – or Harrowing, as they're apparently calling it now – it'll be with an army.' There was a smile in her voice. *'A few ragtag necromancers aren't much to start with, but I've made armies out of less. And there's always the Syndicate. Gabriel loved me once. But if he won't help me for my own sake, maybe he will for Gilles. Blood is thicker than water, after all.*

'If Umbrael knew I was taking the core, I'd be finished. She'd rather keep it here, a gift for the next sacrificial lamb. Ha! The core is my insurance, in case things take a turn. No, I might as well say it: in case Beheret catches me.'

Another long silence. When the voice spoke again, it was grim and hard as ice.

'Let her try. Let her send her servants, her hounds, her drakes, her pet mancers. It's been too long since I spilled some blood. Blood that wasn't my own, at least. The red magic is even harder to give up than the black, and a sorceress has to make do with what she can find.

'Besides, I've faced worse. I broke free of Beheret when

most still thought her a myth. I toppled the Fausarian Dynasty. I razed Kljestervik and left its widows weeping over the ashes. I've spoken with prophets, slewn Archmages, built an empire up from nothing. My magic has shattered mountains and made the gods tremble. I could crack this world like an egg if I wished it. So let them come.'

The voice fell silent, and Gwyn thought it might be finished. The mirror made a crackling sound.

Then: *'I don't even know why I'm leaving this message. If I die, nobody is going to want to hear a sad story from the evil sorceress. At this point, my reputation is more or less set in stone. I suppose it's not undeserved. My list of victims is a long one – though I would have liked to have added one more name to the list. Maybe I still will. Just not the way Umbrael wants.'*

The voice grew tighter, more urgent. *'If I fail, I know there'll be another, sooner or later. Maybe she'll end up right here, in this house – Umbrael has let too many slip through her fingers already. Priss Azarov, Ninde Akvadi, Servenna Namaidhrin, Ailbhe Ahriddin.'* She laughed darkly. *'All almost-good-enoughs. Of course, the next one won't get far without the core. But maybe that's a good thing. If anyone is going to kill Beheret, it should be me.'*

The sorceress was silent again, briefly. She cleared her throat. When the voice returned, it was contemplative. *'That's assuming there is another near miss. She got close with me, I think. Too close. If there was any point in praying, I'd pray the next one isn't the real thing. Because if that happens, this world is finished.*

'Still, I don't intend to die. Even if that means running from Beheret for the next thousand years. If she does manage to breed a true vessel, I'll still be around. And then I'll kill the fledgling myself.'

The voice trailed off at last into silence.

Gwyn stared at the half-shattered glass in her hands, at the reflected slice of her own bright green eye, as though she had never seen it before.

And then I'll kill the fledgling myself.

Ailbhe Ahriddin had intended to kill any product of Beheret's breeding program that she suspected of being 'the real thing'. Gwyn could make sense of that much, at least. But what did it mean? Wasn't breeding sorceresses the point? How could one be more 'real' than another?

She took a deep breath. It made no difference. Even if the sorceress hadn't truly been killed by Beheret – if she had fled and joined the hill people, like the memory suggested – she was long dead by now. And even if she *had* been alive, she could have little interest in Gwyn. *Priss Azarov, Ninde Akvadi, Servenna Namaidhrin* ... Dangerous names, but nothing to do with her. She was a failed attempt; her bloodline a dead end.

Gwyn put the glass back where she had found it. She had no idea how to remake the concealment spell, but there was no helping that. Perhaps Idris would think it had broken naturally. Spells did unravel over time.

If Beheret is trying to breed some kind of new, different sorceress, maybe that's what she wants me for. To be its mother. After all, she was a descendant of Ailbhe. It would explain why the goddess was hunting her so doggedly.

Gwyn's hand went automatically to her stomach. She felt ill. *My child?*

No. She refused to share the same fate as her mother.

CHAPTER 24

TOUCHING DEATH

The stone-walled bathhouse was warmer than the rest of Priory. A deep fireplace occupied one wall, flanked by two tall cabinets containing towels and soaps. Three copper bathtubs sat along the remaining walls, circling a drain in the centre of the tiled floor. The logs blazing in the hearth were the only source of light. Faolan sat cross-legged on the floor, just next to the drain, with his back to the fire.

Without speaking, Gwyn stepped over the salt circle and sat opposite him. The firelight cast his face into shadow.

'Death,' he said. He sounded almost cheerful. 'The necromancer's playground. But a dangerous place for the, ahem ... *inexperienced.*'

'For idiots like me, you mean?'

'Ah! See, you *are* learning.' His voice grew serious.

'The only reason I've agreed to teach you is to give you a sporting chance at defending yourself against Ygriel. Under normal circumstances, a mancer would have spent a decade in the Clockwork City, learning the fundamentals of magic, before even thinking to step foot in the Lurk. Even so, most of them die in the first year – if they're not rooted out by the Inquisition and executed.' He gave a dismissive shrug. 'Carelessness. Many fledgling necromancers fall prey to it. But that's a trait I can beat out of you, if needs be.'

Gwyn was already starting to regret this decision. 'Is there a reason we had to meet in the bathhouse? I thought —'

'Ah, ah,' Faolan interrupted, holding up one long, slender finger. 'I'm coming to that. Patience. Great vim, girl, you expect me to cram ten years of education into a single night, and you refuse to stay silent for even a moment.'

He gave a flick of his wrist, and with a squeal, the tap in the bathtub turned. Cold water began to pour from the spout, filling the tub. 'Death. You already know of the Five Towers of the Arts. Their old names: *Agares, Belphegor, Carnival, Dantalion, Eligos*. These are also the names of the five rivers of the Lurk.'

'Rivers?' Gwyn repeated, frowning. There had been no rivers in her room at Tønderby that night. Aside from the lack of colour and the odd, shifting quality of the air, it had looked little different to the ordinary world.

'There are five rivers in the Lurk, each one the gateway to a deeper level. Now, the veil between life and death is not marked by a river, but it is still the first barrier you need to cross.' He gestured at the bathtub, now just over a quarter full. 'Water helps to, shall we say, lubricate the transition.' He gave a small smile, pleased with his own wit.

'So … you're going to make me sit in the bath?' Gwyn asked, forgetting to stay silent. She frowned, suppressing a shiver. That water looked damnably cold.

'No, no, not at all.' He shook his head, still smiling. 'No – I'm going to drown you.'

There was a long silence. Gwyn wasn't sure she had heard correctly. She stared at Faolan. He stared back, unblinking.

'I'm sorry?' she said, finally.

'Drown. You.' He nodded, as though that settled the matter. 'It should be quick. Possibly painless; I wouldn't know.'

'Oh, you haven't been drowned before?' Her voice was slightly hysterical, but she couldn't help it. He had lost his mind, finally. Playing around with dark forces had finally cracked his sanity.

'Of course not. I'm not a complete fool. I learned to cross the barrier the proper way – *slowly.* It took years. In your case, though, it seems we must, hmm, *accelerate* the process. Oh, cheer up, girl. I don't intend to let you die – at least, not permanently. But the first time entering the Lurk under your own power is by far the hardest, and this is the fastest way to accomplish that – by bringing you right up to the barrier. This is how all necromancers used to learn, before we discovered less ... *barbaric* means.'

'Cheer up?' she said weakly. 'You're asking me to let you *murder* me.'

'*Temporarily.* And I'm not asking. I would have insisted you learn all this eventually, but I thought it better to let you come to me first. Idris agrees, loath as he is to condone any sort of necromancy. Your safety requires it.'

There was no getting away from it, Gwyn realised. If she didn't agree, Faolan would force her. He had the power, thanks to that damned apprentice bond.

'Good,' he said, seeing that she wasn't going to fight him. 'Now, take off your clothes, if you please.' He must have noticed her expression, because he rolled his eyes. 'Keep your shirt, if you must. There's nothing there I have any interest in seeing.'

'I'm absolutely not going to take off my clothes.'

Faolan pursed his lips, but for a wonder, he didn't force the issue. 'Suit yourself. Into the tub.'

She reached one hand into the bathtub, touching the water as though it might bite. It was ice-cold.

'It's better that way,' Faolan said, seeming to sense

her thoughts. 'Cold water slows the heartbeat, stops the breathing and redistributes the blood flow to the heart, lungs and brain. And the cold reduces the body's need for oxygen.'

'How do you know all this?' Gwyn asked, more to distract herself than out of any desire to know the answer. She closed her eyes and lifted one foot into the tub, then the other. The water soaked into her boots. Gooseflesh sprang up on every inch of exposed skin.

'Just part of my studies,' she heard him say, though her teeth were chattering so loudly they should have drowned him out.

Drowned him out. Poor choice of words. She clamped her teeth together to stop herself from breaking into hysterical giggles.

Slowly, slowly, she lowered herself into the tub. It was like being stabbed, everywhere, all at once. Her shirt ballooned up around her armpits. She pushed it down. Her hands had gone an alarming shade of purple.

'Are you ready?' Faolan asked. Too serene by far. He'd probably been waiting to do this since the first time he met her.

'Just ... get it ... over ... with,' Gwyn said, through gritted teeth. She squeezed her eyes shut.

Faolan's hand on her breastbone was like iron. He had the sleeve of his robe rolled up to the elbow, and his bare skin tingled strangely against hers. She felt him push her down into the water. Instinctively, she sucked in a deep breath as her head went under the surface.

She opened her eyes. The freezing water stung them, but she could make out Faolan, misty and indistinct, leaning over the tub.

Ten seconds passed, then twenty. The pressure in her lungs began to build. Flecks of silver and black danced in her eyes.

At thirty seconds, panic set in. She reached for Faolan's arm – or thought she did; her vision had narrowed down to a pinprick. Her hands clawed at him. She was much stronger than him, usually, but it made no difference. Too late, she realised that strange prickling on his skin was a strengthening spell. She thrashed, helpless, and heard the water slopping over the side of the tub.

He's probably stronger than Alcide, now.

That was her last thought before the darkness expanded and swallowed everything.

'Now, that wasn't so bad, was it?' Faolan said.

Gwyn opened her eyes, and immediately wished she hadn't.

The room was reduced to a black-and-white sketch, drawn by some artist with a terrible palsy of the hands. Everything was twisted and wavering, a reflection glimpsed through glass. The effect made her stomach clench. She was still lying in the bathtub, but there was no water now, and her hair, skin and clothes were dry.

'Am I ... dead?'

'You were,' Faolan said, sounding bored. 'For a moment, at least. Long enough. I restarted your heart before I followed you here.' He eyed her in a way that suggested he was regretting that decision.

Gwyn nodded weakly. *Dead, dead, dead.* The words echoed in her mind like a shout in an underground cave. *Only for a moment.* Too long. Her heart thundered in her ears, defying Faolan's words.

'Where's the water?' she asked, looking down at herself. Not even damp. How? Was there no water in this place, in Death? Hadn't Faolan spoken of rivers?

'Where do you think we are, girl?'

'Dea— the Lurk?' she said, swallowing. Was this another test?

'And what do you think this is?' He reached out one long finger to jab her in the chest, just above the breastbone. 'You think this is your flesh? You think you carry your body here with you, like luggage? No. Your body is sitting on the floor of the bathhouse where I left it. You've been disincorporated, girl. Unsheathed from your flesh.'

'I'm not ... here?' She rubbed at the spot where Faolan had jabbed her. Real or not, it hurt.

He rolled his eyes, turned and strode from the

room. Gwyn hauled herself out of the tub and hurried after him. Her legs felt made of treacle.

'This is always the problem with amateur necromancers,' he said, when she'd caught up. 'They refuse to see the body and spirit as separate. You think you *are* your body.' His eyes scanned the blank hallways around them. There was something different about him, something in his appearance. 'Which do you suppose is stronger – the flesh, or the spirit?'

'The ... spirit?'

'Wrong!' He clicked his tongue and gave her a withering look. 'The spirit can access only a small part of black magic. Six signs, no more. Only the Fifth Tower; only *Eligos*. We are badly hamstrung in this place.'

She followed, silent. Priory felt so eerie on this side of death. It was always a cold and empty-seeming place, but she had grown fond of it all the same – of the little twisting stairways, the rambling gardens, the way the stones grew warm in the afternoon.

All that was gone, here. Priory was as hollow and abandoned as the dead city beneath the Warren.

Trotting at Faolan's heel, it came to Gwyn in a flash what was different about him. He was *solid,* as he never seemed in the real world. The faint afterimage that followed his movements was gone here. Seeing him so clearly now, she realised his form in the real world had always been slightly off – just a little out of focus, a little blurred at the edges. Here, he was more concrete than anything around them.

Outside the house, the valley was a grey expanse ringed by mountains white and dry as old bones. She tried not to look at the sky, but it was impossible to avoid entirely. The blackness was vast, unbroken, curiously deep. It was like a hole that she might fall into. It made her want to run screaming indoors.

Instead, she made herself hurry after Faolan, her gaze fixed firmly on the ground. 'Where are we going?'

She expected him to ignore her, as he usually did, but it seemed he was in one of his rare good humours. He turned to her without breaking stride, and he was actually smiling. Gwyn stumbled and would have tripped if he hadn't caught her elbow.

'A meeting,' he said. 'A meeting of necromancers, in fact.'

Gwyn stopped dead, and it took Faolan a few moments to notice she had fallen behind.

'Is there a problem?'

'A ... a meeting of necromancers?' she said, hardly able to believe what she was hearing. '*Why?*'

'They meet at this time every month,' he said, and she had the strong feeling he was misunderstanding her deliberately. 'Necromancers are solitary creatures by nature, but there are benefits to sharing information. A lot of politics too, of course. I usually don't bother to attend. Oh, don't look so frightened, girl. They're friends of mine. You'll be quite safe.' He stopped, rubbing his hands together, though the air wasn't cold. 'This should be far enough. I suggest you take my arm.'

Gwyn grabbed his arm quickly, terrified of being left behind. The world went dark, and she squeezed her eyes closed, her fingers tightening on his sleeve. Her stomach dropped as though she had stepped off the edge of a cliff.

'You can look,' Faolan said, shaking off her grip.

Gwyn opened her eyes. Wherever this was, it was surely not the Pale Valley. Bare-limbed trees grew close around them, grasping and skeletal. There was a faint, flickering light, no more than thirty feet away. She thought she saw movement, and heard ... Were those voices?

Faolan slashed her a grin and began moving towards the light. 'I hope you enjoy parties.'

CHAPTER 25

CONCLAVE

They emerged from the trees into a shallow clearing, ringed on two sides by a steep rock face covered in tough, clinging brush. The ground was clogged with rocks and boulders and dead leaves, the edges thickly forested. A firepit had been dug in the middle of the clearing, though there were no flames. The pale, sourceless light of the Lurk trickled down thinly through the bare branches.

Seeing Faolan and Gwyn, the gathered crowd looked up in alarm, their conversation dying mid-sentence. Those seated on rocks half rose, as if readying to flee. Gwyn counted seven of them – four men and three women. When they recognised Faolan, they sat again, but there was no mistaking the sudden tension in the air.

I thought these were supposed to be his friends? Gwyn tried to position herself behind him, but she had already been spotted. A few eyed her with open curiosity.

'Twice in a row, Faolan?' said a bored-sounding female voice. 'You should be careful. We might start to think that you like us.'

The woman was sitting on the ground with her back against a boulder, her skirt gathered under her to reveal long, terracotta-coloured legs. She, at least, seemed quite at ease. Her eyes held cool amusement.

'For you, Hulin, I would come every month,' he replied with a bow. The woman gave a short, barking laugh. The others seemed to relax slightly at that, turning back to their conversations, though Gwyn could still feel their sidelong glances.

Hulin pulled herself to her feet. She came across and took Faolan's arm, ignoring Gwyn completely. She was taller than him by several inches. Gwyn fell into step behind them, focusing on drawing as little attention as possible. Despite Faolan's promise that it was safe, she couldn't help but think of the salt circle. *For protection from other necromancers,* he had said that first night. It hadn't occurred to her to ask precisely which necromancers he thought they would need protection from.

'— going to come back as long as she knows you're searching for her,' Hulin was saying quietly. They had drawn a little away from the crowd now, towards the edge of the clearing. 'You're not the only one, either. Abulurd has been half crazed, trying to figure out her secret. He has this theory, if you can believe it, that she found a spellbook at the very centre of the Lurk, and it taught her a sixth school of magic. Last night he almost got himself killed trying to get there. He made it as far as Carnival when a grigori found him. I had to help drag him out.'

Faolan whistled through his teeth. 'He tried to cross Carnival? He must be desperate. You were lucky to make it back.'

'He's saying he means to try again.' She jerked her head back towards the clearing, where a squat, barrel-chested man was speaking animatedly to the small group gathered around him. 'He's trying to recruit a party to go with him. Says the reason nobody has ever come back from beyond the Third Circle is because everyone who tried went alone. I think some of them are starting to listen to him.'

'Why is he so convinced the answer is in the Sixth Circle?'

Hulin shrugged, tossing her tight, dark curls over her shoulder. 'He's crazed, like I said. It's an obsession.'

'You don't credit the other rumour?'

'What, that she's the next sorceress?' She let out a bark of laughter. 'Hardly. Yes – Shemeris has become powerful in a way I can't explain. But if she's a sorceress, I'm the Exorcist-General. This is something different.'

Gwyn flinched at that – *sorceress* – but covered it

with a pretend cough. She remembered Faolan's words that first morning after the Warren, tossed down carelessly from horseback as he shaded his eyes from the rising sun. Rumours of sorceresses since Ailbhe Ahriddin. *'The Great Sorceress of the Northern Wastes is the latest, but I've seen no evidence for it.'*

Shemeris. Had he known then? If he had, his opinion must have changed in the intervening months, because now he clearly thought Shemeris was someone worth finding.

'And did you notice anything else, the last time you saw her?' Faolan asked.

Hulin shrugged. 'Nothing in particular. Though that was some weeks ago, before all the talk really started. She had some bruises – I could see those clearly enough, even in the Lurk. And she was walking gingerly. My impression was that someone had given her a real thrashing. That surprised me. With the kind of power she's been wielding, no-one should be able to touch her. What else? She wore a necklace, though she had never cared for ornamentation that I could remember. But it looked like a chip of glass on a leather thong, so I assume it had something to do with her position in the tribes. A mark of status, maybe.'

'It's not much to go on,' Faolan said. 'Clearly Shemeris has learned a lot since her time in the Syndicate.'

Hulin snorted. 'If she learned all that on her own, I'd be mightily surprised. Shemeris was always a coward. I don't think she ever crossed Agares more than once or twice in her life. That's why Abulurd's theory is such nonsense, but he won't be told.'

'And you?' Faolan said. 'What do you think?'

'I think if she stumbled on some undiscovered realm of magic, she did it by pure chance, not through any heroics on her part. But this talk of a sixth school cuts no ice with me.'

'Have you heard of such a thing? A mancer growing in strength so late in life, and so rapidly?'

'No. I wouldn't have thought it possible. But last week I saw a demon with eight legs that floated through the air as though it were water. I wouldn't have thought that possible, either.'

'Some are saying the Hunter has taken her for his apprentice.'

Hulin sighed, rolling her eyes. 'The Hunter. Necromancers have been swapping stories about that one for ten years or more. Strange that no one will ever admit to having seen him themselves. It's always *an old friend of mine down in Mothmelech,* or *a necromancer I met once in Padmaphur.* If he were real, I think someone would have come across him by now.'

'But you must admit, there's been more chatter about him lately,' Faolan said. 'Didn't Sepion claim to have seen him once?'

'Yes – through the trees, for a split second, while

he was bleeding from a chari bite. I don't lend much credence to that sighting. But feel free to ask him yourself.'

Gwyn followed her gaze. Sepion was one of the group clustered around Abulurd – a tall, white-haired man with a long nose and a pinched, unsmiling face. Sensing their regard, he looked across, and his eyes met Gwyn's coldly.

'Faolan,' he called, without looking away from her. 'I see it's true, what Hulin said at the last conclave – that you've bonded a whelp. I said it was impossible; that you'd never be so foolish. It appears I was wrong.'

Faolan went to join them, and Gwyn hung back, trying to stay out of Sepion's line of sight. His face reminded her of Ascepis, a little, but she didn't like those flinty eyes. They were all looking at her now, she realised, even those outside Abulurd's little circle.

'It's true,' Faolan said lightly. 'Wonderful things, apprentices. It's amazing how much time it frees up to have someone doing the dull, tedious tasks for you.'

'No doubt this one is better company than some,' said a short, olive-skinned man standing nearby. He had a thin, pointed beard that didn't quite disguise his weak chin. He looked Gwyn up and down in a slow, speculative way that made her skin crawl. 'Though wasted on you, Faolan.'

One of the outsiders drifted closer – a broad-shouldered young northerner with plaits in his beard. 'I don't remember seeing her around the Clockwork City,' he said, frowning. 'Who was she apprenticed to?'

Gwyn felt Faolan clamp down on the bond, preventing her from speaking, but the warning was unnecessary. A thrill of fear lanced through her.

'Enzo Caelius,' Faolan said lightly. 'I doubt you would have known him. He was a very minor Fourth Rank mancer. The wind swept him off the library bridge one night, apparently. A rather ignominious way to go.'

There was some scattered laughter. The northman was still looking at her in a sceptical, sidelong way, but Gwyn forced herself to breathe evenly. He had no way of guessing the truth. There were hundreds of novices and junior mancers in the Clockwork City at any one time, Faolan said, and the full mancers paid them little mind. The others had lost interest in her already, and in a moment the northman looked away, too.

'Faolan, I hear your attempts to flush Shemeris out of hiding have been ... less than successful,' Sepion said. 'If you're still so intent on finding her, you should speak with Abulurd.'

'Ah, yes,' Faolan said, smiling in that unpleasant way he had. 'I hear you're mounting an expedition of sorts.'

Abulurd frowned, seeming unsure whether he

was being made sport of. 'You might call it that. An undertaking of this magnitude has never been attempted before, certainly.'

'The way I hear things, you attempted it last night, only to have Hulin drag you back by the scruff of your neck like a foolish pup.'

Hulin snickered. Abulurd's cheeks grew dark, but he held Faolan's gaze. 'I was over-eager. I attempted it alone. This time I mean there to be three or four of us at least. No one has ever tried to cross with a group before.'

Faolan's face held almost no expression, but Gwyn could sense how much he was enjoying himself. 'Mmm, but you say Shemeris made it all the way to the Sixth Circle? Did she have a group, then?'

'Perhaps she did,' Abulurd said, and there was some heat in his voice now. He seemed to want to say more, but reined himself in with visible effort. He went on, more calmly: 'We would be glad to have you along, Faolan. I'm not sure what we'll find across the river, but your experience could prove valuable.'

'Perhaps your whelp could serve as bait,' Sepion added.

Faolan dismissed that with an airy wave of his hand. 'Very kind of you to offer, but I intend to confine my enquiries to the other side of the veil.' He turned to Sepion, ignoring Abulurd's look of indignation. 'Rumour is that you've seen the Hunter. What can you tell me?'

Sepion's frown deepened, if that was possible. The look he directed over Faolan's shoulder at Hulin was icy. 'No doubt Hulin told you I imagined what I saw.'

'I wouldn't be asking if I thought you'd imagined it.'

Smirking, Hulin cleared her throat, meeting Gwyn's eyes for the first time. She winked. It struck Gwyn suddenly that the necromancer was young – closer to Lucian's age than Faolan's.

'It was months ago now,' Sepion said. His voice was strangely expressionless. 'I was in the Second Circle, tracking a bathinat that had been eluding me for several nights. I followed it as far as the Samerine Grasslands, but I lost the trail just east of Lake Aralin and got into a minor scrape with a chari. That's when I saw him.'

'Nonsense, Sepion,' said one of the other women. She was Crater Dhavian, middle-aged and very short, with dark, flowing hair that made Gwyn think of Severine. Unlike Severine, though, she had a sharp, no-nonsense voice, and a small rosebud mouth that looked perpetually annoyed. 'You don't truly believe this man has anything to do with Shemeris, do you? There is no Hunter. You saw an ordinary necromancer – nothing more.'

Sepion turned to the woman, looking down at her from his considerable height. He didn't raise his voice, but his tone was cold enough to freeze water.

'You may be right, Amandine. I've never known a

necromancer who wore a silver mask, but – yes, perhaps.' He turned back to Faolan with grave dignity. 'Hunter or no, the fact remains that you've had no success in finding Shemeris. She knows you're searching for her, now, and she's not likely to come out of hiding as long as she feels threatened.'

'You've blundered things, Faolan,' said the woman – Amandine – bluntly. 'Oh, yes, we've all heard about your little adventures with the hill people. Strong-arming tribesmen left and right – what did you expect? That she would just decide to show herself? "Here I am! Come torture my secrets out of me!" You've driven her deep underground – not to mention risked our relationship with the hill people. They've been our greatest resource for hundreds, nay, thousands of years, and now you've jeopardised that. For what? You —'

'See, this is just my point,' Abulurd broke in, sounding exasperated. 'We can't even hold conclave without it descending into bickering. Is it any wonder that no mancer has returned from beyond Carnival? If even two or three were able to work together —'

'This isn't the time for —'

Gwyn felt a mental tug, and drew closer to Faolan. He had to speak directly into her ear to be heard over the sound of raised voices.

'I think we've heard enough,' he said quietly. 'Come on.'

He pulled away from the group, Gwyn following. The others were too busy to pay them any mind. Hulin saw them, though, and raised her hand to Faolan in farewell. Then she looked at Gwyn and, after a moment, nodded at her, too.

The voices faded quickly when they left the clearing, swallowed by the trees. Gwyn had to hurry to keep up.

'Are they always like that?'

'More or less. Sometimes they can be bullied into working together for a time, but mostly it's like herding cats.'

'That's what all this is about, then?' A root caught her on the toe, and Gwyn cursed under her breath, wondering how injuries in the Lurk could hurt just as much as real ones. 'You think this Shemeris might have become a ... a sorceress?'

'I tend to agree with Hulin,' Faolan said. 'The literature is clear on the nature of sorceresses. They practise blood magic. Human sacrifice. Nothing like our magic; nothing like the vim. And sorceresses are born, not made. In the Syndicate, Shemeris never displayed a whiff of anything unusual.'

'And you don't think Abulurd is right – that she somehow went to the centre of the Lurk and ... learned things?'

'Unlikely. No necromancer has been that far, but we have a fair idea what's there from the demons we've been able to question. There's a dense forest on the other side, and beyond that, a twenty-foot-high stone wall.'

'And beyond the wall?'

'Certainly no libraries of secret, arcane knowledge, if that's what you're thinking.'

'This Hunter ...' Gwyn began, feeling sick.

'Yes,' Faolan said. 'You made that connection, too, I expect?'

She had, although it seemed worse now that Faolan had acknowledged it.

A necromancer in a silver mask.

Ygriel was still out there in the Lurk. Searching for her.

CHAPTER 26

THE POLISHED MOON

After the necromancers' conclave, Faolan's training intensified, to the point that Gwyn did little but eat, sleep and cast. Every day, she shuffled like a prisoner from her tower room to the training yard, and by the time he finished with her each afternoon, it was all she could do to crawl straight into bed.

'You're getting sloppy, girl,' he said one morning, as she picked herself off the ground for the sixth time. 'My aged mother could have severed that thread. And my aged mother is *dead*.'

As Gwyn pulled herself to her feet, he lashed out again, and this time she was ready. Her power sheared through his spell like a knife. He rocked back on his heels.

'Better,' he allowed, though the words twisted his mouth as if they tasted bad. 'But still sloppy. You're distracted. It makes you slow. Do you have something else you'd rather be doing?'

Secret room, secret room, secret room ...

'Of course not.'

There had been no chance to even go near the cellar, but Gwyn hadn't forgotten about it. Faolan narrowed his eyes, seeming to sense something, and she grasped for a change of subject.

'Couldn't I learn something *different?* It's been months, and I just keep doing the same severing spell, over and over; maybe a little shielding thrown in. Aren't I ready for something else by now? Another school? What about fire?'

Her talks with Idris and her research in the library had revealed how little magic she knew. Knowing the signs was barely the beginning. Magic was a new language, but understanding the script was very different from being able to form whole sentences, or even whole words.

'You think you're ready for something new?' Faolan asked.

'I mean, don't you think it makes —?'

Gwyn was flat on her back before she could finish speaking. She wasn't even sure what had happened. His attack had been faster than she could follow. For a moment she was too winded to stand, and she lay on the frosty ground of the training yard, blinking up at the featureless white sky.

'No, I certainly *don't* think it makes sense,' Faolan

drawled. 'When you can prove you're not a lazy, undisciplined child, then we'll talk about teaching you something else. When you can show me you're not the total imbecile you appear to be. You'd pop your own head like a melon if I taught you how.'

Stupidly, Gwyn felt tears prickling at the back of her eyes, though they were tears of anger.

'Don't take it to heart,' Severine said later as they sat in the kitchen, passing Gwyn half of the apple she'd just sliced. 'He's like that with everyone, and he's probably twice as hard on you, being his apprentice. Remember, the bond works both ways. He can control you, up to a point, but *you* can sense his emotions. He's been alone for a long time. Now he has you living inside his head, seeing all the parts of himself that he keeps hidden. It must frighten him.'

Gwyn liked that about Severine. She understood people. And had compassion for them, even the ones she disliked. Gwyn herself was not so generous.

'He hauls me out of bed before the sun is even up,' Gwyn said, shifting in her seat. Her bruises throbbed. 'Then thrashes me all day, tells me I'm the stupidest person ever to live, and orders me to bed. When I agreed to learn magic, I didn't think it would be like this.'

Severine nodded. 'Fear is a bad way to teach anything, I think. Ascepis was strict too, but he always treated Idris like an equal, even when they were first bonded. That seems like a better way.'

Thinking of Ascepis as Idris' master – thinking of him as a wizard at all – was still hard for Gwyn. He was so different to Idris, or even Faolan. There was nothing abstract or dreamy about him. Ascepis had always been solid as stone.

Like stone, he could be cold, too. But Gwyn couldn't blame him for that – not knowing what she knew now. Ascepis had sacrificed everything, had given up his power, his friends, his entire old life. There hadn't been much left to give to the small girl in his care. Least of all love.

Well, at least he was alive. He had sent a letter, just as Faolan had promised. It had shot out of the fireplace last week while they sat for evening meal, almost clipping Lucian in the back of the head. Alive and fully recovered, the message said. He had taken the wagon south, laying a false trail for any of Beheret's wizards who might still be seeking her. *I hope to see you again,* the letter had said – the last words. Now it sat on Gwyn's nightstand, the edges slightly charred from the flames.

Not all of Gwyn's time was taken up with training. Getting her hands on the memory glass had convinced her that to make anything happen around here, you had to do it yourself. And so, in the long hours between Faolan's lessons, between Alcide's swordwork and Lucian's falcifer classes, between talks with Idris and helping Severine in the greenhouse – then, Gwyn thought of the secret room.

Secret room, secret room.

At first it had been simple curiosity. But now – maybe because every other part of her life seemed to have slowed to a crawl – it had become vitally important. She saw that white, polished moon every time she closed her eyes; saw it in her dreams, sometimes.

Whether by chance or by design, the others seemed to sense what she was planning. Every time she thought of slipping away to the cellar, a distraction appeared. Severine, asking for help in the kitchen. Lucian, dropping in at her window for one of their chats. Idris, wanting to show her something in a book. Alcide was the only one who ignored her completely, outside of their lessons.

It was all too convenient. She was sure they were keeping her occupied deliberately.

That knowledge did nothing to improve her temper. She was so sick of being passed around like a plaything. Was this how they expected her to spend the rest of her life? Stuck in this valley, just reading and training and never doing anything worthwhile?

She had asked Idris the same thing one day, as they sat in his study drinking tea. He had put down his cup with a sigh, looking at her over the rim of his eyeglasses.

'You are doing something worthwhile, Gwyn,

even if you don't know it. Have faith. Every day you stay out of Beheret's grasp is a victory for us.'

'Running and hiding doesn't feel like much of a victory,' she said, and was dismayed at how sulky her voice sounded. 'We should be doing ... something. There are two fully trained wizards here. Lucian is a shapeshifter, Severine a healer, Alcide a swordsman. Between us we have enough power to ... I don't know. To take the fight to Beheret.'

Ever since Lucian had planted that idea of killing Beheret, it had started to bloom. Gwyn didn't know if a god could be killed, but she did know that with Beheret alive, she would never be safe.

Idris didn't understand, of course. Staying in the shadows had been his life for too long. He had spent years hiding – first from the Syndicate, now from Beheret and her allies. And the others worshipped him. She could see it in their faces. They would never disobey him. If Idris ordered it, they would all stay in their valley until they wasted away.

More than once she considered just packing her belongings and leaving, and damn her promise to Faolan. Ascepis' letter hadn't said exactly where he was heading, but she could find him.

Those plans never lasted long. The others would never let her leave. Gwyn knew that without having to ask. And the bond with Faolan made it impossible to defy him, so there was no hope of packing up and fleeing in the night. He would call her back to Priory the next morning without having to stir from his bed.

And then there was Ygriel. He was still out there, him and the wizards, and she knew all the things Faolan had taught her would be nothing if she came face to face with Ygriel again.

Of one thing Gwyn was certain: Ascepis would never have sat around for months at a time, doing nothing. His habit of staying on the move had been impressed deeply into her. The longer she stayed here, the more her anxiety began to stir. The days were getting shorter and colder. The snow on the peaks was creeping slowly downward, and when it reached the valley, Gwyn knew her chance would be lost. With the pass snowed over, only Lucian would be free to come and go. That seemed not to bother the others, but for Gwyn it was like a noose slowly tightening around her neck.

Somehow, she knew that the key to her escape was locked in that secret room.

Gwyn wasn't sure what had woken her.

She sat upright in the darkness, her blanket wrapped around her and her heart beating almost out of her chest. A dream? She couldn't remember. But she was awake now, and Sadira's reddish light poured through her window like blood.

Get up.

She was half dressed before she even stopped to think why. It was the middle of the night; where was she going?

The answer came immediately. Everyone was asleep, even the unblinking and ever-watchful Alcide. The cellar was unguarded. She could feel Faolan through the bond, fast asleep in his room. His presence in her mind had the fuzzy, indistinct feeling she associated with his excursions into Death. He had been a necromancer for too long – even sleeping sent his spirit halfway into the Lurk.

Now. She had to go now. There would never be a better time. Why hadn't she thought of it before?

Because they keep you so exhausted every day that you fall asleep as soon as your head hits the pillow. By design, it seemed now. Everything they did was by design. She was exhausted tonight, too, but ...

The cellar. Gwyn felt it pulling at her. The polished white moon seemed to swim before her eyes, a lighthouse glimpsed through fog.

Just the same, as she pulled on her boots, she almost changed her mind. The cold sank iron jaws into every inch of exposed flesh. She had more clothes now, thanks to Severine – snug breeches, tunics with billowing sleeves, a few brightly coloured dresses – and she contemplated piling on every coat she owned. If this was only the beginning of winter, what would it be like in a few weeks? With Ascepis, she had always spent the colder months further south, sometimes as far as Wayhaven. Even so, she remembered mornings where the caravan's windows were frozen shut; where she had to climb onto the roof and sweep off great drifts of snow. This far north, the winter must be worse than she could imagine.

With luck, I'll be gone by then. She wasn't sure where the thought came from, but it felt right. Even if she had to slit Faolan's throat in the night, she would leave this place before the winter came. If she stayed, she would die.

Gwyn's teeth chattered as she eased her door open and crept out into the stairwell. At the bottom, though, she paused. There was a torch on the wall in the hallway that she knew would flare to life when she walked past. It was doubtful anyone would notice, but she couldn't take the chance.

Gwyn reached out with a thread of power and felt for the knot. Yes, there it was. She unpicked it carefully, and the spell melted away. She did it almost without thinking, now. Had it really been only a few months ago that the thought of magic had terrified her? That she'd resisted everything Faolan had tried to teach her, resisted even the idea of being a wizard?

She knew the way to the kitchen by heart now, but it was slow progress in the near-total darkness. The house seemed too still, somehow. Beyond the windows, Sadira was full and fat in the sky, Prior a waxing sickle half smothered by clouds.

The creak of the cellar door was impossibly loud, and Gwyn froze. But there was no cry of alarm, no sudden thud of footsteps coming to stop her. She felt for Faolan. Yes, he still slept. She crept down the stairs. When the torches came on, she had to shield her eyes.

The music was playing again, though Gwyn hardly noticed it now. She stood before the carved wall, and the whispering voices seemed to fill her mind. There was something primal and terrifying about that carving, but something *familiar,* too. For some reason, it made her think of her mother. Stupid. She didn't even know her mother.

Gwyn put her hand to the white moon. The wall opened.

In the stairwell, the air smelled like the inside of a smithy. With the music and the whispering gone, she could make out another sound. A faint hiss, like escaping air. And a low thudding as well, coming from somewhere below. A heartbeat, it sounded like, keeping perfect time with her own.

Something about this place felt ... alive. There was a presence that she couldn't identify. A heaviness in the air. A whispering breath on the back of her neck.

The sensible part of her wanted to turn and flee. She could be back in her bed with the blankets pulled tight, and nobody would ever know. But the compulsion was strong, and her feet moved down the stairs. Torches, burning with a cold, blue flame, did little to hold back the creeping darkness.

It seemed a long way down. She must be deep underground. Old – this place was old beyond anything she'd seen, beyond even the lost city in the Warren. The smell was metal and blood and the inside of a tomb.

Thump-thump, thump-thump. Louder now.

The stairwell opened into madness.

CHAPTER 27

UMBRAEL

A woman dangled in the centre of the room.

At least, she resembled a woman at first glance. But the head was wrong: elongated, somehow, with pure black eyes that seemed too big. Insect eyes. She was tall, but her arms and legs hung shrivelled as a starving child's, the fingers oddly boneless, and far too long. And no woman had skin like that – blue-tinged, so fine that the delicate tracery of veins showed through.

The worst part, though, was the pipes.

They sprouted from her body like twisted flowers, from her stomach, her chest, the back of her head. Dozens, in different colours, with liquid running through them, circulating through and outside her body with a soft *sigh*ing noise that filled the room. Those pipes held her upright and pinned, like a heretic at her own crucifixion.

The woman was alive, but she definitely was not human.

Black-on-black eyes met Gwyn's own. They were bottomless. Fathomless. They were pools of night sky, cold and infinite. Gwyn stepped forward as though compelled.

The errant child returns home.

The voice vibrated in her head. It was multi-layered – low, emotionless, but overlaid with the high screech of breaking glass, the cracking of ice, the outraged thrum of a beehive. A dozen voices speaking – *screaming* – at once.

Come closer.

She obeyed without thinking. There was no way to defy that voice. It was too powerful.

Do you know who I am?

Her hair was long and deep black, bound into thick ropes like the legs of a spider. Gwyn looked up into that long, pale face, and still saw nothing human there.

No, she thought. *Who are you?*

I am Umbrael.

Umbrael. Shock punched Gwyn in the chest, left her gasping.

Umbrael – one of the Void Gods, the demons imprisoned by Beheret at the time of creation. Umbrael the Weaver, the patron of destiny, the spinner of fate.

Severine's words came back to her. *'We're very ... religious.'*

Do I look a demon to you? the creature asked, although Gwyn hadn't spoken aloud.

She looked like nothing Gwyn had ever seen. It was clear she couldn't move – not hanging there, connected to those pipes that must be the only things keeping her alive. Her skin, thin as beaten silver, had never seen sunlight. Her frail legs had never supported her weight.

No, not a demon. But her presence ... It was overwhelming. A sense of terrible *age* radiated from her. She seemed outside of time. Outside of anything.

Does this make me a god? Her voice was the skitter of black, furred legs down Gwyn's spine. The gleam of cobwebs beneath cold moonlight. The space between the stars. Awareness of the world faded, and nothing existed but the two of them, alone in the void. She could feel Umbrael in her mind, a heavy presence, cold and steady as the tip of a knife. Could feel her emotions, her amusement. Curiosity, caution, *anger.*

But it was different to her bond with Faolan. Faolan was a little ball of sensations and feelings at the back of her awareness, a tether of lightest silk. Umbrael *was* her mind. No boundary stood between them. She barely remembered her own name.

What are *you?* The question came slowly, and from very far away; somewhere outside herself.

Nothing but one of the original watchers of humankind. Perhaps this makes me a god in truth. Not creator, but created. An immortal crafted from the rib of man. Perhaps this makes you the god. I have thought on this, but I cannot say.

She felt Umbrael reluctantly pulling away from her as she spoke. Selfhood began to return. Gwyn; she was Gwyn. She remembered who she was. She remembered where she was. The sudden separation left her cold and horribly empty. She fought for clarity.

Beheret is ... like you? she asked. Her voice sounded so small, even in her own mind. *And all the other gods too?*

Beheret. Yes. She was the first among us. Mother, elder, wisest of the wise. Beheret, the betrayer. Beheret, the eater of hope.

But ... what are you?

Because ... this wasn't a god. Not like the murals she'd seen daubed on the walls of chapels across the High Country. Not like the statues of Molech, smooth-limbed and stormy-eyed, holding his thunderbolt aloft. Not like Aeshma, stamped in profile on every silver coin minted south of Chastis, with a crown of stars circling her brow.

The creature – Umbrael – just stared at her for a long moment. Unfeeling. Unmoved.

We are Scions.

Gwyn's mouth opened, but nothing came out. Her

head was swimming, her tongue dry as an old leaf. Her ears felt packed with earth.

Scions? A nonsense word. Dreaming; she had to be dreaming.

You feel it, do you not? Umbrael said in her mind. *The kinship?*

The …?

You are not one of mine, Umbrael continued, seeming to speak to herself now. *Not like your uncle. One of Aeshma's, that is certain; I sense her touch on you. The blood runs strong, even now. But one of Beheret's … Yes. That you are, most of all.*

The words jolted Gwyn out of her trance. Blood rushed back into her head in a giddy wave, and she swooned and almost fell.

'I am *not* Beheret's,' she said aloud, the sound of her own hoarse voice shocking in the near silence.

All the sorceresses are Beheret's. Umbrael's mind-voice was … not cruel. Not even cold, in any deliberate way. Just remote. The voice of a distant star. *Nimet Greeves, first and unmourned. Virani of the Wheel. Priss Azarov, the Red Priestess. Yrian, the Silent Queen. Ninde Akvadi, Deathwalker. Falien the Dread. Servenna Namaidhrin, the Muse of Massacres. Ailbhe Ahriddin, the Beloved.*

Every name was like the sharp blow of a hammer. Gwyn was on the floor. Her palms smarted. Had she fallen? She had no memory of it.

Umbrael couldn't be saying what she seemed to be saying. It was impossible.

You did not know?

Gwyn shook her head, mute. She was supposed to a wizard, not ... *this,* not ...

Sorceress. She was a sorceress.

Even Lucian hadn't known, hadn't suspected. His own words, back in the library: '*Sorceresses aren't human; not really. They have glowing eyes, and ... well, it's not you.*'

But hadn't *she* known? Hadn't she suspected? Perhaps some part of her, perhaps ...

Why? she demanded. Her eyes were full of tears, fracturing the Scion into a hundred tiny glimmering shards. The question was meaningless – an angry shout to the heavens. Wasn't it enough to be one of the wizards, those feared creatures of nightmare, a legend to frighten children? And now ...

Sorceress. Vim help her. Was she destined to half destroy the world, too, like the sorceresses before her? *Why?*

Because of Beheret's rage, Umbrael replied, and the answer seemed to cover every possible question. *She was the first, and she was created too human. Her dreams are human dreams. She wishes to walk among her children.*

Make no mistake. All these long years, Beheret has nursed her anger to her breast like a child. Her mind is a shadow of what it once was. All her longing, all her fury, all her misery, has been twisted into evil. Where she walks, she will destroy. She will punish all of creation for her suffering.

All she requires is to create the perfect sorceress. When she succeeds – and she will; every generation brings her closer – she will inhabit the vessel. She will wear its skin as her own, and all will be lost.

A terrible hunger filled the Scion's mind-voice. Hunger to cast off the frail, dependent body with its tubes and tethers. To run barefoot on the grass under the moons and smell the air, sweet with night-blooming jasmine.

Do not fear. Perhaps I have become too human myself, to think such things. You, though ... You have a purpose beyond my own desires, little sorceress.

The words settled around Gwyn like a cold shroud.

A purpose?

Yes. Beheret must be ended. She will have no rest until she makes this world weep.

The words sounded like a gong in her mind. It was so hard to think. The voice clouded everything. Umbrael was so powerful; so vast. She was like the seasons, or the tides, or the mountains. How foolish, how small, Gwyn felt. Who was she to deny this being, this god?

But who was she to defeat one?

There is a way. Only one way. In Beheret's great temple lies the Well. When you immerse yourself in it, you will join with us, like the sorceresses of old. The Well gave them power, but bound them to Beheret's will, to her service. That is where she will take you. And that is how you will overcome her.

Gwyn frowned, or thought she did. Her body was so far away, a prayer kite flapping at the end of an impossibly long tether. She might drift away, soon, and part of her thought it would be a relief.

No. She had to focus.

Beheret's temple? At first, the shape unfolding in her mind made no sense. Harsh lines, flat black planes like polished glass. Then ...

There was no mistaking that image. The obsidian Pyramid hanging inverted in the sky, tip brushing the clouds, its long shadow like a dagger over fields of corn and barley. A relic from the ancient times – even the smallest child knew that.

And Beheret was inside it?

You will not sneak in, Umbrael said, reading the words in her mind. *You will walk in. Understand, Gwyn, that Beheret wants nothing more than for you to come to her willingly. You are to be the mother of her prized vessel. She needs you alive, needs you whole.*

I ... I don't understand, Gwyn thought desperately. *Even if I could reach the Pyramid ... how could I defeat her?*

But before Umbrael could answer – if she meant to answer, if there was any answer to give – somebody behind Gwyn spoke.

CHAPTER 28

THE SECRETS OF WIZARDS

'You must have some questions.'

Gwyn almost leaped out of her skin. She tried to stand, but her legs wouldn't listen, and she only managed to pull herself to her knees, to half turn towards the doorway.

Idris. Still in his nightgown, spectacles halfway down his nose, hair long and loose like a skein of white silk. He didn't seem angry to see her, or even surprised. Just tired.

'Questions?' Gwyn echoed, when her heart had stopped hammering, when her throat had unclenched enough to speak. *Questions.* She had a hundred, a thousand, all clamouring for space, tripping over each other like rats fleeing a burning building. The *thing,* the Scion, burned in the centre of her vision like some dark star, black-on-black eyes expressionless. The room was quiet except for the gurgle of fluid in the pipes, the soft sigh of the Scion's breath.

She wants to know what I am, Umbrael said.

A shudder ran through Gwyn. Was the question written on her face, or had the Scion plucked it straight from her mind?

'Of course,' Idris said, nodding. He looked so ... calm. Unruffled, even now. 'A fair question. But one that may take some time to answer.' He raised a hand to forestall her protests. 'This isn't an attempt to waylay you, Gwyn. I mean to tell you everything. Would you come to my study in the morning? Please?'

Gwyn had never heard him say that before; *please.* It unsettled her. 'Please' meant you wanted something, and Idris had seemed so far above that, above *wanting.* But his eyes were steady on hers.

After a moment, she nodded.

Umbrael's blue lips twitched in what could have been a smile.

Gwyn returned to her room, but sleep was a long time in coming. Images whirled through her mind, autumn leaves caught in a furious gust of wind. Memories – but not her own. Some leftover impression, an echo from the Scion beneath her feet. Like a handprint on fogged glass.

Flash.

A stern-faced woman with skin the colour of teak, her white shirt covered in blood. Figures seated at a round table, shouting, slamming fists so the surface cracked into whirling, spinning shards. The same woman, gripping something in her fist, her face wet with tears. Or was that blood, too?

Memories gave way to dreams. She was back in the Scion's chamber. The thing in front of her was clearly Umbrael, with its long ropes of dark hair, its black-on-black eyes, like boreholes to the centre of the world. But it was a human Umbrael, clad in a filmy, colour-shifting dress instead of a tangle of cords and pipes. The woman stood before her with hands folded – *human* hands – and in the logic of dreams, this seemed perfectly normal.

'Nimet gave her life,' Umbrael said. Her voice was dry and harsh as a crow's. Instantly, all around the room, the lights went out.

'She was betrayed,' Umbrael continued, from somewhere in the dark. 'As we were betrayed. As you will be betrayed.'

Gwyn started to back away. Her shoulders came up against something solid, something cold.

She spun around. The light returned. Yellow light, pulsing like some great jaundiced heart. It flashed off a smooth surface of glass – a giant vessel. There was water inside, and something else. A dark shape. She put her nose to the glass.

The shape moved.

Two hands appeared, pressed against the glass. Blackened, charred hands. The skin was peeling off them in reams. Floating away like potato peels.

And then a face. Oh, gods help her, it was a face.

'Is it you?' Ygriel said.

Morning found everyone gathered in Idris' study.

Gwyn was almost asleep on her feet, and only several cups of bitter tea, drunk standing up in the kitchen that morning, kept her upright. After the dream, she hadn't slept; had just lain awake in the dark with the blanket drawn up around her head. Was it her own blood whooshing in her ears, or the sound of fluid running through pipes in that coldly lit room beneath the house?

Faolan lounged in the chair across from Idris, examining his nails, while Lucian perched on the edge of the desk. Severine stood with her hands behind her back, chewing on her lip. Even Alcide was there, though he brooded at the window, looking out over the valley and the fire-capped peaks, and didn't glance at Gwyn as she came in.

'I want to know everything,' Gwyn said, planting herself in front of the desk. She had silently rehearsed this speech as the sun crept inch by inch through her window that morning. Though in her head, her voice hadn't sounded so small, so shaky. 'No more secrets. No more lies.'

Idris had the grace to look uncomfortable at that, but he didn't protest – just took a steadying breath and folded his hands atop the desk. 'Then you may wish to sit.' Faolan rose with ill grace and offered her his chair, and Gwyn lowered herself into it, her heart racing.

Idris continued, watching her from over the top of his spectacles. 'To understand the Scions, you must go back to the beginning.'

'The *very* beginning,' Lucian put in, giving her a smile and a wink. 'Pre-history.' His appearance was ruffled, as always, and he needed a shave, but he looked in good humour. Relieved, perhaps, that all those secrets were finally spilling out.

'You mean the Dawn Times?' she asked carefully. Thanks to Ascepis' relentless tutelage, her knowledge of history was better than most might expect. But the Dawn Times ... well, that period was a blank, a white space in the history books. There *were* no history books from that time. Only legend; only myth.

'The Dawn Times,' Idris agreed. 'Before the first year of recorded history. Much of that time remains a mystery, even to us. But thanks to Umbrael, we do have some knowledge; enough to put together a sequence of events, a series of decisions and moments and personal grudges that lead, inevitably, to ... you.'

Gwyn blinked and rubbed her arms, but said nothing. Part of her was afraid to speak. As if it might break the spell that had been woven, might make Idris snatch back the information he was offering – finally offering! – to her.

'It started with the aether,' Faolan said, after a glance at Idris, who leaned back in his chair, content to let Faolan speak. 'A ... force, I suppose. Similar to the vim, but rougher. Purer, in a way. A kind of wild magic.'

Gwyn straightened, her reticence forgotten. 'Another vim? Is it more powerful?'

Faolan barked out a laugh, and Severine shot him a cold look. 'Yes,' he said. 'You might say that. Those who tried to wield it likely thought so, as it incinerated them from the inside out.'

Gwyn recoiled as though slapped. That scent was in her nostrils again, the scent of Tønderby, of flesh shrivelling in the crisp night air. It had been some time since she'd thought of it.

'Enter the first players in this game,' Lucian said. 'The Friends of Shedet. Dinna ask who or what Shedet was – we've no idea. Not even *she* kens, or she isn't telling.' He jerked his head towards the floor, and the thing that lay beneath it.

'The Friends were a group o' men and women. The strongest practitioners of the aether in their time – though they were only able to wield it through the help of devices and contraptions, and then only roughly. The human body was too frail to channel the aether in its raw form. The Friends shared a single goal: to dilute the aether into a form that humans *could* wield.

'We dinna ken whose idea it was to create the Scions. Nor do we ken the how of it, save for one thing: that the Friends used their own blood in the process. And we —'

'Wait,' Gwyn said. She hadn't meant to cut him off, but she couldn't stay silent, not until she was certain she understood. 'You're saying that these humans in the Dawn Times, these Friends of Shedet ... They *created* the Scions?' But hadn't Umbrael said the same thing, last night? *Not creator, but created. An immortal crafted from the rib of man.*

'Beheret was the first,' Idris said, nodding. The sunlit window behind him turned his pearl-frost hair into a halo of silver. 'And we know that the woman who created her, the one whose blood was used, was named Nimet Greeves.'

Nimet. That name tickled something in the back of Gwyn's mind, but she couldn't place it.

'Beheret was considered a failed attempt,' Faolan said. 'The purpose of the Scions was to help the humans harness the aether. Beheret exhibited no power at all, and the aether seemed lifeless and unresponsive in her hands.

'And so the process was refined, and the "true" Scions were created: Iahta, Siasr, Umbrael. Yotha and Molech Suun. Each one lovingly crafted with rudimentary aether and the blood of one of the

Friends. While none were able to tap the aether in the way the Friends expected or hoped, they apparently exhibited *some* form of power; enough to justify the research continuing. In Aeshma, the last of the Scions to be created, the Friends finally achieved their stated aim.'

Their stated aim. To dilute the aether. To tame it, change it into something safe. Something that could be harnessed.

'The vim,' Gwyn said, stunned, as the pieces clicked into place. Beneath her feet, the earth itself seemed to shift, and for a moment she was sure she felt the Scion turn its blank eyes up towards her.

'The vim,' Faolan said, nodding. 'Through Aeshma, using her as a sieve, the aether could finally be moulded into a workable form.'

'But not by everyone.' Severine, who had joined her brother at the window, turned back to them. 'The Friend whose blood was used to create Aeshma was named Porter Sabine. An older man, well respected, with four grown sons and several grandchildren. Porter and his direct descendants ... They were the only ones able to tap this new power, this vim. The other Friends remained locked out.'

'We can't be sure exactly what happened next,' Faolan said. 'Only that, at some point, the Friends fractured, each taking their respective Scion with them. They believed themselves tricked, you see. The Friends dreamed of a new golden age – a time of peace and prosperity, a time of wonders. The new power was meant to be free for any to use. But instead, it was locked away, locked behind bloodlines, only granted to a chosen few.'

'The wizards?' Gwyn asked, looking at Faolan now. Her mind felt oddly sluggish. It was all too much, too fast. When she'd demanded answers, she had expected ... well, not this. 'They're ... we're ... all descended from Porter Sabine?' Vim, that meant she and Faolan were *related*!

'Distantly,' Faolan scowled, seeming to sense her thoughts. '*Very* distantly. This was well over two thousand years ago. Wizards weren't sterile back then, and so they spread to every corner of Caerwyn. The blood ties are barely threads at this point.'

'You're telling the story out of order,' Severine said, a little sharply. Ignoring Faolan's rolled eyes, she pushed a cup of steaming tea into Gwyn's hands. The powder-blue dress she wore this morning would have suited a kindly nursemaid; one skilled at soothing frightened children. Severine laid a quick, steadying hand on Gwyn's shoulder, and she wondered what her face must look like.

'A few hundred years after the Scions were created, the war began. We don't know who started it, or why. Only that the descendants of the Friends brought all six powers to bear, and the world was almost destroyed.' Her voice hitched there, at the destruction, the senseless death.

Gwyn took a long sip of her tea and realised her hand was shaking. She sat on it quickly, before anyone noticed. In the face of their calm, their seriousness, she felt suddenly very young. A child who had walked in on something she wasn't supposed to see. 'So ... what happened?'

'Nimet Greeves happened,' Lucian said, hooking his ankle over one knee. 'As it turned out, Beheret wasn't such a failure as the Friends believed. Because when all of them were naught but dust and bones in the earth, Nimet remained unchanged, year after year.'

Gwyn sat silent, thinking. Her eyes wandered over the bookshelves lining the room, over the rows of stiff, jewel-coloured spines. She had always believed anything worth knowing could be found in books. Now she wondered if she knew too much. So much information, so many moving parts ... It was hard to make sense of any of it.

'Beheret's power was ... immortality?' she asked slowly. The only immortals she knew of were the liches, locked away in their stone city at the edge of the world, and even they were more fairy story than fact.

'There's more to it, but I'll come to that,' Faolan said. 'Nimet wanted the war to end. Perhaps she tried negotiating with the others. We don't know. But in the end, only Darro Sabine – Porter's descendant, and Nimet's lover – agreed that the Scions should be destroyed. The other bloodlines had no intention of giving up their powers, and Nimet, with no true power of her own save her immortality, had no way to force them.

'And so she came up with a plan. A way to bind all six of the other Scions to Beheret, and *through* Beheret, imprison them forever.'

'We'll spare you the details,' Lucian said. 'The binding worked, and the six Scions were locked away in an enchanted sleep. But to destroy Beheret herself and ensure the Scions could *never* be woken ... Well, that was a mite trickier.

'You see, by now Nimet had figured out the key to unlocking Beheret's powers – not just the immortality, but the rest of it. Too late for her to take part directly in the war, and perhaps that's for the best. The world barely survived the other six.'

'Blood,' Faolan said, seeing Gwyn's confused expression. 'The key was blood.'

'Blood?' That took a moment to sink in, and when it did, she shot up out of her chair so fast it made her head spin and her heartbeat thunder in her ears. 'You mean ... Beheret's power was *sorceress magic*?'

'Right you are,' Lucian said, and now his easy smile had slipped a fraction. 'Red magic – the power of the sorceresses. To destroy Beheret, Nimet would need to wield the Scion's own power against her. But a magic like that could only come at a price.'

'Her life,' Severine said into the silence. 'Nimet gave her life.'

'Which brings us to the personal drama in the story,' Faolan said. His eyes danced, and he practically rubbed his hands together. He had a surprising weakness for tragedy and melodrama – Gwyn had seen him sneaking Severine's romance books out of the library when he thought no one was watching. 'Broken hearts! Betrayal! A tale for the ages.'

Lucian pushed himself off the desk and snorted. 'A tale for swooning girls. In short: Nimet used her own death to create a blood curse; one aimed specifically at Beheret. She drained her life essence into a stone —'

'— the core of a fallen star,' Faolan said under his breath.

'— and left instructions with Darro that the stone be cast into the Well where Beheret lay sleeping. That, it seemed, would have been enough to destroy her – and the Scions bound to her – forever.

'But Darro betrayed her and kept the stone. And instead of destroying Beheret, he woke her. With her help, he was able to wake Aeshma – his family's patron Scion. Just Aeshma; none of the others.

'The vim was restored, and the other powers locked away, their Scions sleeping. The balance shifted. The descendants of Porter Sabine – those who would one day be called wizards – became the dominant power in Caerwyn.'

Silence fell. Silence like a yawning precipice, threatening to swallow her.

Gwyn sank back in her chair. Names danced through her mind. Nimet Greeves. Porter Sabine. Darro Sabine. Players in a game that was over thousands of years before she was even born.

Idris spoke, his voice cool and distant, like starlight reflected on a dark lake. 'Beheret believes Gwyn essential to her plan – which is, of course, to breed a suitable vessel. Likely she intends Gwyn to be its mother. If she succeeds ...' He let the words trail off into silence.

If she succeeds, she'll walk the earth in human flesh and take her revenge.

The bread and cheese Gwyn had snatched from the kitchen that morning turned to lead weights in her gut. Was there anything Beheret wouldn't do to free herself? The light streaming through the window cast a chequerboard pattern on the rug that made her think of a steel cage. She shivered. The Scions weren't behind bars, but they were trapped just the same, in their own frail and useless bodies.

'So that's why you're all here?' she asked, looking from Idris to the others in turn. 'To ... what? Kill Beheret?' Noble, perhaps, but how did you defeat something so ancient, so powerful? How could a mortal slay a *god?* 'You said only Nimet's stone – her life essence – could do that. And Darro stole it.'

'He did,' Faolan said. 'And went on to become the

very first Archmage of the Syndicate. He founded the Clockwork City, where the stone remained for over a thousand years, until it was finally stolen ... by Ailbhe Ahriddin.'

Gwyn flashed back to the memory glass, to the sorceress' voice, raw and harsh in the silence of Idris' study. *'If Umbrael knew I was taking the core, I'd be finished. She'd rather keep it here, a gift for the next sacrificial lamb. Ha! The core is my insurance policy, in case things take a turn.'*

'Umbrael told Ailbhe about the core; that the wizards still had it,' Gwyn said, thinking out loud. 'Told her that it could be used to defeat Beheret. Told her to steal it!'

'Yes,' Idris said. 'But instead of taking the core to the Well, to Beheret, she carried it with her when she fled.'

'To the hill people.'

Faolan, floating himself a cup of tea from Idris' desk, nodded. 'And they may still have it, if the rumours about Shemeris Morga's newfound abilities have any truth to them. Nimet's sacrifice, her blood curse, was intended to destroy Beheret – but that kind of power can be harnessed in many ways. If Shemeris has learned how to tap the power of the blood curse, it would certainly explain her sudden ... proficiency. And the hill people have long told a tale of a magic relic – the Amulet of Cambulan. Just a tale, or so I believed. Now I suspect that the amulet and Nimet's core are one and the same.'

Idris slid an open book across his desk towards Gwyn. The full-page illustration showed a lump of some rough-hewn crystal, wrapped in delicate wire filaments and suspended at the end of a long chain. *The Amulet of Cambulan.* It didn't look like anything special – certainly not the vessel for some long-dead woman's soul.

Gwyn looked up at Faolan, eyes wide. 'But you're saying ... if you can get the core back, and throw it into the Well, Beheret can be defeated? Like Nimet originally intended?' The rest of it – the aether, the sleeping Scions, the Friends of Shedet – all of that was unimportant. But the core ...

Faolan sniffed. 'It's a little more complicated than that, girl. Do you even know where the Well is located?'

She did know. Umbrael had shown it to her, though the thought still turned her insides to water. 'It's in the Pyramid – isn't it?'

'The Pyramid, yes. Hardly a place one can stroll into for tenth-day tea and cakes. And my attempts to locate Shemeris have born no fruit these past months. So you see our predicament.'

His face was quite expressionless, but Gwyn sensed ... something, down the bond. A glimmer. She leaped on it like a wolf on a fleeing rabbit.

'You have a plan to find her, don't you?'

Faolan looked startled for a moment, then clicked his tongue, eyes narrowing. 'It's considered rude to spy on your master through the bond.'

She ignored him, leaning forward in her seat. 'Do you know where she is?'

'Where she's going to be, more like,' Lucian said, ignoring the cold look Faolan shot him. 'Have you heard of the Clansmoot?'

'Lucian, I hardly think —' Faolan began.

'No secrets!' Gwyn said, baring her teeth at him. 'Idris promised.'

At Idris' nod, Lucian continued, though he still eyed Faolan warily. 'The Festival of Bones – that's what the hill people call it. It's a yearly gathering of all the tribes, held on the last night of autumn. We think Shemeris will be there, assuming Faolan's wee jaunts into the mountains haven't frightened her underground.'

Faolan's lip curled at the barb, but he only nodded and folded his hands. 'It was only after we visited my – ahem – colleagues that it came back to me. Amandine, for one, was far too interested in the goings-on of the hill people. She seemed very perturbed at the idea I might have shaken them up. It got me to wondering. I happen to know Amandine has spent the last three years in Mothmelech. What the Fjallmen are doing shouldn't matter to her one way or another.'

'So ...' Gwyn said, trying to understand, 'you're

saying that other necromancers know Shemeris will be at this festival? They're all looking for her too, aren't they?'

'I can handle them, if it comes to it. Amandine has some strength in the vim, but nothing out of the ordinary.'

Her heart began to beat a little faster. 'Then I want to come.'

Faolan laughed at that; actually laughed. 'Oh, yes, you'd be a great help. Such prowess. Unless you mean to annoy Shemeris to death, of course.'

But Gwyn barely heard him. She was electrified. This was it, what she'd been searching for. A purpose.

And ...

And they meant to shut her away from it.

A sudden vision came to Gwyn, clear and certain as prophecy. *If you can't make them agree, here and now, you're going to spend the rest of your life in this house. Training in the yard. Research in the library. Little rides out into the valley – but not too far. You'll never meet another person besides these five, and you'll die having accomplished nothing.*

'I'm the one Beheret wants,' she said. Her voice had risen, and she saw Severine flinch. 'I'm the one she means to breed like some farmyard sow.' The words tumbled out, faster and faster. Tea, cold now, slopped over the rim of her cup. 'I'm the one who's been chased through the woods, who almost burned to death, who's had some crazed man in a mask stalking me in my *dreams*! You want Beheret dead, but it's not personal to you. It is to me. As long as Beheret is awake, she's going to keep sending her servants for me. Wizards, warglings, Ygriel himself. This is *my life*. Do you truly think I can hide forever?'

'Aye, I do,' Lucian said. His voice was steady enough, but the tension around his eyes was close to fear. Fear for her? 'So long as you bide in this valley, at least.'

'And it's *your life* that Beheret will snuff out once she's done with you,' Faolan said. His mouth was tight with anger ... but he hadn't used the bond to cut her off. A small mercy. '*Your life* that we're protecting ... though at the moment, I can't imagine why. And it's —'

'Faolan.'

Idris' voice was quiet and even, but it made Faolan bite off his words mid-sentence. Everyone turned to look at him.

'Gwyn is going to the Clansmoot.'

A long silence.

Faolan surged to his feet. His face had gone suddenly pale. 'Idris, there's no reason she should go – none at all. It's too dangerous, especially for her. I can go myself, or with Lucian, or Alcide, or both. The girl would be nothing but a liability. If she —'

'I have seen it, Faolan,' Idris said quietly, and Faolan fell silent as though poleaxed. 'I have seen her kneeling among pillars of ice, the core in her hand. Not you. Not Alcide. Her.'

Five sets of eyes swivelled back to her. Idris and Alcide, cool and emotionless. Lucian and Faolan, their faces masks of surprise. Severine, looking on the brink of tears.

Gwyn's stomach tightened as though she'd been punched.

Idris has dreams. Visions. Severine had told her that, as they pawed through the boxes in the attic together. And now it was Idris' vision that had freed her. At last.

When she spoke, her voice hardly shook at all.

'I'm ready. Tell me what I need to do.'

PART III

INTERLUDE

THE EXORCIST-GENERAL

The hollow boom of the cell door woke her. Gwyn squinted into the sudden glare. A prune-like face above a frayed robe swam into focus behind the torch. Enoch. He looked chastened.

The Archmage sent him back with his tail between his legs, Gwyn thought with some humour. He hadn't come willingly, either – that was clear from the way his feet dragged as he stepped over the threshold.

'How are you feeling today, Gwyn?'

She wasn't sure how long it had been since he left. There was no day or night in the cell – just an unbroken expanse of blackness that went on and on. Little things had a way of taking on an almost hallucinatory significance in that darkness. The chitter of a rat, somewhere in the corner. The feel of dried blood under her grimy, chewed-on nails. The scrape of her manacles on the stone.

'I feel splendid,' she said, forcing a smile. Her voice was a weak rasp, but she saw how Enoch shied away from it. A band of sweat circled his brow.

He really is afraid of you. She had worked hard at that, but it gave her less pleasure than expected. The man reminded her of Ascepis, somehow. It was in the clipped accent, in the way he folded his hands when he spoke.

Would Ascepis be afraid of me too?

The smile faded.

Enoch sat and looked at her in silence for a moment, then stood again. He seemed to be locked in some internal struggle. His fingers rubbed absently at the brand on his forearm. Ascepis used to do that, too, over the lopsided burn scar where his brand used to be.

'I wish to speak with you further about Beheret.'

Enoch's voice jolted Gwyn back to the present. He had forced himself to sit, apparently, but he still looked on the verge of fleeing. White-knuckled, he fiddled with his stack of notes, avoiding eye contact. The common people said looking a sorceress in the eye would turn you to stone.

'You don't believe in Beheret,' Gwyn said, amused. He had been covering a smile when Gwyn first mentioned her. Most wizards were the same. Oh, they followed their patron goddess Aeshma, at least in name. But in the end, magic was a science, not a religion, and the Clockwork City held few true believers.

'I try to keep an open mind.'

'Isn't it a little late to start believing in the power of prayer?'

Enoch gave a shrug that was only half denial. 'There is a great deal of concern in the Syndicate. Some say Aeshma has withdrawn her favour because the mancers have lost faith in her. They would see us turn from mancers to something more akin to priests.' His voice showed what he thought of that. He had some fire in him, stuffy little creature that he was. 'There are others who say that you *are* Aeshma, come to Caerwyn in mortal form.'

'And what do you think of that?'

He had calm eyes, this wizard, when he could actually bring himself to look at her. They were the brown of old leather. 'I think a god would not have allowed herself to be captured and imprisoned. And I see no reason those shackles should work on a god.'

'Ah. So I'm just an ordinary mortal, after all.'

'I didn't say that.'

She leaned forward – as much as the chains would allow – and was pleased to see that he barely flinched away this time. He smelled of dust and dry parchment.

Better if he did flinch. Their fear of you is the only thing keeping you alive.

But did she deserve to live? That was the question, wasn't it?

'It seems you don't know what I am,' she said. 'Not a god, not a mortal. I imagine the name "sorceress" has crossed a few lips in the Clockwork City, but that doesn't quite fit either, does it? After all, you know what to expect from sorceresses. You've fought them before. Servenna Namaidhrin almost laid waste to your city in the Second Era.' Those last words came out before she had time to think, and Gwyn immediately wondered where they had come from. She hoped her face masked her confusion.

'There is still some ... debate,' Enoch said. He didn't seem to have noticed anything.

'And the Archmage?' she said, giving herself a little shake. 'What's his view?'

That was a mistake, Gwyn saw at once. Enoch's expression shuttered, and he leaned back, suddenly businesslike again.

Very like Ascepis. I wonder if they knew each other?

'The Archmage believes we need more information before reaching any conclusions. I am in agreement. I think that —'

The cell door crashed open, cutting off his words. Enoch leapt to his feet as though scalded.

'Here, now, what is this about? This is an interro—'

He trailed off, and a moment later Gwyn saw why.

There was no mistaking the figure standing in the doorway. He was seven feet tall, or near enough, and ridges of muscle bulged from neck to calf. His hairless skin, criss-crossed with scars, had the dark, glossy look of obsidian. She could barely make out his eyes, obscured under a low, heavy brow. His head was round and bare as a river stone.

The Exorcist-General.

'I'll take over from here, Mancer Arehi,' Castlemaine said, not bothering to look at him. His beetle-black gaze was focused on Gwyn, in a curiously detached way that made her skin crawl.

Enoch swallowed hard, both hands pressed to his stomach. 'The Archmage has said —'

'The Archmage has authorised a more robust interrogation. You will not be required.'

Even in the torchlight, Gwyn could see Enoch blanch. But he made no move to leave, and for one wild moment it seemed he might refuse. He took a little step forward, lifting his chin.

'I —'

Castlemaine looked at him – just a slight turning of the head – and Enoch quailed at once, rebellion forgotten. Gwyn let out the breath she had been holding. She was grateful for that moment of defiance, brief as it had been. Enoch left the room without looking at her, and she heard the scuff of his boots on the stairs, fading fast. He was almost running.

A moment later, there were only the two of them in the room. Saire Castlemaine, Exorcist-General of the Inquisition. And Gwyn – whatever that meant, now.

'It's time we had a proper talk,' Castlemaine said.

CHAPTER 29

OUT OF THE VALLEY

'You know, you don't have to do this,' Severine said on the third morning, seeming to read Gwyn's thoughts. Her expression was sympathetic. 'Here. Eat.'

Gwyn bit into the slab of bread she offered, barely tasting it. She chewed mechanically as she looked out over the valley. It was still dark, though the tops of the mountains were starting to turn from purple to pink. A longspur appeared on the windowsill, its feathers fluffed against the cold. 'Yes, I do. There's nobody else, is there?'

Severine had no answer for that. They sat in silence for a time as dawn outlined the black, sheer faces of the mountains in gold. Details appeared: drifts of snow, the bare skeletons of white birch and aspen. When Severine spoke again, the peaks were all ablaze.

'I was fifteen when I first met Idris. After our father ... disappeared, we fell in with a local warlord, Salomon, and moved around from village to village. It wasn't much of a life, especially for a young girl. I studied under the band's Wise Woman, but I hated the death, and the battles, and the towns we left burning behind us. Alcide ... well, he was happy to live with a sword in his hand, but I knew that killing for gold and spoils was killing him, too. I just couldn't see any way out.'

Gwyn covered her surprise by taking another bite of her bread. Severine, part of a raider band? She could imagine it of Alcide – he seemed half wild even now – but ... *Severine*?

'And then Idris came?' she asked.

'Yes,' Severine said, smiling. 'Right into our camp, in fact. He seemed almost surprised when Salomon ordered him captured. He didn't fight back, but the warriors beat him anyway, and Salomon gave him over to me to tend, rather than leave him lying half dead in the desert.

'That was how I first got to know him, and how I learned of his work, his research. It was the first time somebody had given us real answers. And it changed everything. We had hope again; a purpose. Some reason to get up in the morning, besides razing the village over the next hill. It made all the difference.'

Gwyn nodded. She could understand that. *A purpose.* That was what Umbrael had given her, and it was why she had to take this first step. Getting inside the Pyramid, actually defeating Beheret – those things might prove impossible.

But if they could recover the core, at least there would be a chance.

By midmorning, everything was in order, and the horses stood saddled in front of the house, laden with bedrolls and leather panniers. It would take five days to reach Jorvanger, where they could replenish their supplies, then four more through the hard, unforgiving Asgerad wilds. Gwyn was almost as worried about that part as she was about the Clansmoot. When she had ventured to Faolan that it would probably be very cold north of Jorvanger, wouldn't it, he had just given her a dry look and kept cramming more furs into the saddlebags. Now they bulged so much the straps hardly closed.

Idris waited at the front door as everyone mounted up. He said something quietly to Alcide that Gwyn couldn't make out, then turned to her.

'You will do well,' he said, his gaze dispassionate. 'Your role is small, and Faolan, Lucian and Alcide will be close at hand. I wish you good fortune.'

'Thank you,' Gwyn said. Everyone was looking at them now, and she shifted, uncomfortable. *I have seen her kneeling among pillars of ice, the core in her hand.* A true vision of the future, or just a possibility?

Idris nodded, and Gwyn mounted Otani in silence. It seemed an abrupt end to the flurry of preparation, and to her time at Priory. Was it only three months since she'd first come here? It seemed an age ago.

Faolan said nothing to Idris before they left; just clamped down so hard on his emotions he was practically vibrating. He never looked back. Gwyn did, in time to see the house vanish behind the curve of the mountain. A surge of excitement made her heart flutter in her throat, but there was uneasiness in it, too. She couldn't shake the image of Umbrael, alone in that vast space beneath the house, watching with her dark, fathomless eyes.

The road north tracked gradually upwards, winding back on itself as it passed higher into the mountains. The ground was a muddy slush, except where the snow had drifted, almost knee-deep in places. Trees pressed in tight at their sides, leaving a narrow, walled route that had them riding single file. At the tail end of autumn, the birches, aspens and rowan were bare-limbed. But at this elevation it was mostly pine forest, and the trees grew thick enough to turn the day to grey darkness. The wind howled, shaking snow off the branches, and Gwyn shivered, even through her fur-lined coat.

'There's an inn further along the road, at Kasteberg,' Severine said, pulling her horse up alongside Gwyn's. She had insisted on riding out with them, at least for a few hours. 'You can spend the night there.'

'Full of fleas, of course,' Faolan said glumly. The words came out a pale mist in the frigid air. He wore a wide-brimmed, floppy hat, pulled down low over his eyes, and had his coat tight around his ears as though disgusted with the whole affair. His gelding snorted agreement.

'Then you should feel at home, shouldn't you?' Severine said, sniffing. She nudged her horse and moved away, joining Alcide further up the road. He leaned down and said something to her that Gwyn couldn't make out, and Severine shook her head stiffly.

'She really doesn't like you, does she?' Gwyn noted. That much had been obvious from the beginning. At the dinner table, Severine would watch Faolan with barely disguised suspicion, as though expecting him to leap out of his seat and start raising corpses on the spot.

'She doesn't appreciate my work,' Faolan said, echoing her thoughts. 'Healers are hypocrites. Oh, yes, it's fine to pull somebody back from the brink of death and close up their wounds and heal their fever and knit their broken bones. But as soon as they actually cross over, well, then it becomes evil and unholy to help them.'

This impassioned defence caught Gwyn by surprise. 'But necromancers don't use their powers to help people,' she said. 'I mean, you raise dead bodies, and summon demons, and ... I don't know. But it doesn't seem the same.'

'I didn't see you complaining when it was Ascepis I was saving. Or when you were begging me to teach you, either.'

Gwyn fell silent. She couldn't argue with that. Maybe the power was evil, but it could be used for good, too. Faolan had proven that. He was many things, but she didn't think he was evil. That word seemed bigger than his petty cruelty.

The road twisted along shadowed cuts in the mountainside, protected from the snowfall but strewn with dead leaves that scattered in the persistent wind. They passed narrow, frozen waterfalls; crossed a wind-eaten stone bridge that dropped into a jagged ravine on either side.

'Are you going to be alright, Gwyn?'

That was Severine, of course, sensing her mood, if not the cause of it. It was past midday, and time for her to head back to Priory.

Gwyn summoned what she hoped was a brave smile. 'Of course. Lucian and Alcide will be with me. And Faolan.'

Severine nodded as though she believed her, though she didn't have her brother's gift for studied blankness. She gave Gwyn's hand one final squeeze before wheeling her horse around.

'I've told Alcide to watch out for you,' she said.

Her voice was only a little tremulous, which Gwyn was grateful for. If Severine started crying, Gwyn was sure she would too. 'I'll see you back home in two weeks.'

Gwyn nodded, but as her friend turned away, she couldn't suppress the sudden, powerful feeling that she would never see her again. Her arms had broken out in rashes of gooseflesh that had nothing to do with the cold air.

In a moment, Severine was gone.

Spindly blue-green pines gave way to dark spruce and thickets of peashrub, and by late afternoon even those had disappeared. Dim flakes of snow began to appear, settling on Gwyn's coat and falling faster and thicker as they went on. She wished she could summon up a warmth spell, as Faolan had obviously done. She had asked him about it, on some of the more frigid nights back in Priory, but Faolan had only laughed and said that it *would* be amusing to see her burn herself to death.

The town of Kasteberg appeared suddenly, like the prow of a ship rising up out of the mists. Stone houses lined the main road, window lights barely visible through the flurry of snow. The streets were empty, but laughter and music drifted on the air, along with cooking smells that made Gwyn's mouth water.

Outside the inn, they stopped and dismounted. The lamp cast a pool of light into the courtyard, illuminating a signboard that squealed on rusty hinges: The Windy Peak Inn. It was well named, for a chill, persistent wind swirled the fog around their feet, and blew the snow sideways as it fell.

'Let's get inside,' Alcide said – the first words he had spoken since leaving the valley, at least within Gwyn's hearing. They gathered their saddlebags and blanket rolls, and the stable boy led the horses away while Gwyn followed Lucian, Faolan and Alcide into the inn.

The next morning, a persistent drizzle followed them out of Kasteberg. This part of Asgerad would not have looked out of place in a nightmare. The ground was a slushy brown ice that cracked under the horses' hooves. No grass or flowers here: just pale, gnarled trees clinging to the side of the road, bowed down under the weight of snow and wind. They must have been five thousand feet above sea level at least, but the rain and the grey cliffs obscured any view. Alcide's dark-maned stallion, Guarin, was barely visible.

A very wet bundle of feathers swooped down suddenly out of the rain, transforming ten feet off the ground into an equally wet Lucian.

'Nice day for a spot of flying,' Faolan observed.

'I've had worse.' Lucian shook himself off like a dog, but with the rain it made little difference.

'Road's clear all the way to Jorvanger. Bit o' traffic up the farthest end, but nothing that smells like trouble. No sign of Ygriel or Beheret's wizards, either.'

'How about a wine merchant? Any of those?' Faolan rubbed his hands together and exhaled a puff of white steam. The temperature had dropped rapidly in the last hour or so. Gwyn thought she might have actually frozen to her saddle.

'Oh, aye,' Lucian said. 'A half-dozen, to be sure. They're lined all along the road, crying their wares. "Free wine for murderous necromancers," I think they were saying. It was hard to tell from the air, o' course. Maybe you should run ahead and have a look.'

Faolan made no reply to that. Instead, he raised his hand and summoned a small flame that crackled around his fingertips. It flickered wildly in the high wind, but didn't die. The shadows it cast on his face were dark and jagged. He turned to Gwyn.

'Do you like roast chicken, girl? I find the chill in the air has given me quite an appetite.'

'*I find the chill in the air has given me quite an appetite,*' Lucian echoed, putting on a high, affected voice. 'Pish. Hope you choke on my bones.' He turned his back on them and went to join Alcide at the front of the line.

It grew colder still as they travelled north, and the

days seemed to take on a sort of lurching slowness. On the second night they stopped at Volheim, leading the horses down the muddy streets of the village, past rows of grey-stone houses with roofs of dark slate. Pale woodsmoke curled from their chimneys, and the glow of hearth fires spilled between the slats of shuttered windows. The wooden stalls surrounding the market square stood empty.

In Brunna, where the moonlight glittered on the icy river and the dark bulk of its silent waterwheel, the innkeeper at The Frozen Barge spoke of trouble to the south – of armies massing on the border and towns put to the torch. 'You can expect no less from those Surudar folk,' he muttered darkly. 'Be lucky if there's anything left of Asgerad come the spring. Now, how many rooms did you say you need?'

After Brunna was Kilvik, nestled in a dimple near the top of a steep hill; then, finally, Jorvanger, which they reached near sunset the following day. The tall lamps that lined the side of the road were the only sign of human habitation. Snow fell lightly, turning to slush underfoot.

The road sloped gently downward, into a wide cleft in the rock – almost a cave. Mud and dirt gave way to rough cobblestones. Narrow openings were set into the walls at intervals, and light poured from inside. Gwyn could glimpse people seated at their tables, or warming themselves by crackling fires.

'Outer limits of the city,' Faolan said. He jerked his

head towards the nearest doorway, where a rangy dog lay gnawing on a bone. 'Most of the city is built into the rock. There's a reason they call it the City of Stone. This high in the mountains, timber is hard to come by. Harder still to keep wooden houses from blowing away in the winter storms.'

The passage widened from time to time, allowing snow to fall. In the relative warmth, though, it melted quickly, and the water trickled into drains set into the road.

'Are we staying at an inn?' Gwyn asked quietly. People packed the street, some on horseback, all bundled to the eyes in cloaks and coats. None paid them the slightest heed, but just the same, she felt exposed and uneasy.

Faolan nodded. 'On the outskirts. Better not to take you into the city proper. The Syndicate has eyes and ears in all the great cities.'

The road narrowed into a lamplit tunnel, stretching in both directions. There were more people here, many of them soot-smudged, with pickaxes hefted over their shoulders.

At the end of the street, the way widened into a large plaza, with merchants' stalls, empty now, arranged in a ring around the outside. A double-storey inn stood at the junction of two streets, and when the horses were unloaded, Alcide handed them across to the stable keeper, along with a few coins. Otani had her head in a trough before they had even left the yard, wearing an expression that looked a lot like relief.

Gwyn swallowed. The interior corridors were warmer than the open air, but even through her layers of fur and hide, her bones ached. How much colder must it be out there, in the wilds? They would leave their horses here until they returned, taking only one sturdy packhorse. North of the city, Alcide said, the roads hardly deserved the name. Four days of pitiless trekking through some of the most dangerous country in the world. And at the end of it, if Shemeris really had the core, if they could actually take it from her ...

No. I'm not going to think about that. One problem at a time.

Gwyn shivered and pulled her cloak tighter. The chill she felt now had little to do with the cold.

CHAPTER 30

NORTH WIND

The next morning they rose early, trekked north in the near dark, and pitched camp ten miles from the city. It was only a few hours past midday, but already the sky was beginning to darken again. They hobbled the packhorse, furs drawn up tight around their necks against the insistent, shredding wind. Alcide's face was stone as he set up the tiny stove.

'We leave before first light,' he warned, as Gwyn, Faolan and Lucian sat nursing cups of hot tea. 'We have three days before the Clansmoot begins, and a ways to go if we're to make it in time.' He stood up, shrugging off his blanket. He barely seemed to notice the cold, and paid no mind to the wind except to keep his cloak clear of his sword arm. 'I'll take first watch.'

'You look troubled,' Lucian said to Gwyn, edging

closer so their hips touched. The sudden warmth made her shiver. 'May as well spit it out.'

Gwyn frowned into her battered tin cup. Lucian knew what she was – what Umbrael claimed she was – but she hadn't talked about it; not with anyone. Lucian was the closest she had to a friend, along with Severine, and the thought of him treating her differently, or looking at her with fear in his eyes ... That was more than she could stand.

'I'm a sorceress,' she said finally. Some wounds had to be dressed, but others healed better in the open air. 'I suppose I'm still trying to figure out what that means.'

'I dinna think it means a damn thing.'

The heat in his voice made her look up, surprised. His gaze was bright and intense and held no fear at all. Her breath caught in her throat.

'It was bad enough when Faolan told me I was a wizard,' she said, when she could speak again. 'I grew up frightened of wizards. Hearing stories about them stealing children in the night, burning down villages ...' She swallowed, a sudden memory flooding back: the wizard and the drake, aflame in the night sky. 'But Ascepis was a wizard himself, once. And then there was Idris, and Faolan, and neither of them seemed evil. And so eventually I accepted it.'

'But being a sorceress is different?' Lucian asked, and the look on his face said he understood.

She nodded. 'There's no one to learn from. No

one who can teach me. Just stories ...' Her voice faltered. 'Stories of what the sorceresses have done. Ailbhe Ahriddin, conquering half of the world. Priss Azarov and the Councillors' War. Ninde Akvadi and the razing of Coventry.'

'And you're worried that you'll be the same? A conqueror? A tyrant?'

'Not because I want to be. Vim, if I could forget about being a sorceress, forget I ever heard about it, I would. But ... what if it means I'm evil? What if I can't help it? What if I can't stop it?'

She wanted to take the words back as soon as she spoke them. There it was, out in the open: the great fear. Fear of that humming, fizzing, dark power that she sometimes felt – thought she felt – nestled behind her breastbone.

'Hey,' Lucian said, taking her hands in his. She jerked and almost pulled away. 'Gwyn ... you're not evil. I ken evil; I've seen it.'

Of course. His own people had executed his lover, cast him out of his home. Gwyn had never asked him about it, and she supposed this wasn't the proper time. She cleared her throat, reclaiming her hands.

'Remember,' he continued, 'all the other sorceresses were created by Beheret.'

'So was I!'

'Aye, but she had nothing to do with raising you. That was all Ascepis. The other sorceresses, the things they did ... That all came from Beheret. And you canna forget: Ailbhe Ahriddin rebelled against her in the end. Even if she was born a slave, she didn't die one. She had free will.'

Yes, she wanted to say. *Ailbhe turned on Beheret. The memory glass made that clear. But she did it to save her own skin, not for the good of the world. If she'd really cared about anything but herself, she wouldn't have bartered away the core. She would have used it to defeat Beheret and end the breeding program forever.*

Now that task fell to Gwyn. But unlike Ailbhe, she didn't mean to run from it. She would do what had to be done.

'You're right.' She felt her face close like a fist. Lucian didn't pull away, but he didn't reach for her hand again, either. 'I'm just gnawing at nothing, I suppose.'

When they turned in for the night, the cold seeped up through the ground and wormed inside Gwyn's layers of blankets and furs. She found herself lying awake long after the others had fallen asleep. An aurora veiled the stars. Ribbons of pale green and rose, drifting on some unseen wind.

Gwyn felt cold all the time. Cold in a dragging, bone-chilling way she was sure had nothing to do with the thin northern air. The Lurk felt ... close, somehow. Back in Priory, at night in her room, she sometimes swore she could see those dim, flickering shadows at the edge of her vision. How many trips before she became like Faolan, a creature with one foot in this world and one in the next? Once or twice, as she wiped the fog off her looking glass in the morning, she was sure she caught a faint afterimage, gone before she could be certain it was there.

The Lurk is already changing me.

Worse, that thought didn't frighten her nearly so much as it should.

Each morning, they roused from their blankets and set off before first light, stopping only when twilight deepened. Often, their campsite was little more than a patch of coarse heath, pressed flat by snow, amidst rocks and scrubby conifers. By the third night, even the trees had disappeared.

The road wound over icy ridges, around wind-blasted peaks and down through hidden fissures of tumbled stone. They forded shallow, half-frozen streams that even Lucian could put no name to. There was little sign of civilisation – little evidence, aside from the road itself, that humans had ever come here. From time to time, Gwyn caught a glimpse of the high-peaked thatch roof of a barn, or smelled the distant smoke of a chimney, but Alcide circled them wide to avoid any villages or farms.

Even rarer were other travellers on the road. They passed a few hard-driving trader caravans, a guard patrol returning to Jorvanger, a bard with a lute strapped to his back. But for the most part, their only companions were the wind and the low sky.

They made fifteen miles on the first day out of Jorvanger, but on the morning of the second, the road turned sharply west, and they left it behind entirely. The snow was deep here, up to their knees in places, but even so, they were forced to make constant detours around upthrust rocks and shaded crevices where the snow had failed to settle.

Faolan might have helped them – he could melt snow, or blast handholds into the rocks to help them climb – but he had turned in on himself, walking with his head down, a grim and silent shadow. At night, he took tea and hardened chunks of road bread, grumbling about the cold and the slowness of their progress. Then he wrapped himself in his furs and fell instantly asleep, his snores bouncing off the rocks.

During the day, Lucian would scout ahead, wings beating hard against the ripping wind, or fall behind to check their backtrail. There was no sign of pursuit, but Alcide was cautious. Not out of concern for Gwyn's safety, she was sure – he rebuffed her attempts at conversation, speaking only when it was necessary to give instructions. And so they struggled across the snowfields in silence, save for the crunch of their boots. There were no birds, not even ravens. The sun hid behind the flanks of the mountains, except when it stood directly overhead, so much of the time they tramped along in shadow.

The weather grew steadily worse. Snow fell on and off through the day, matting Gwyn's hair to frozen, waxy strands, no matter how she pulled her hood forward. Her breath steamed the air. She had to tie her waterskin to the inside of her coat to keep it from freezing, and even so, it was like cradling a lump of ice.

On the third day, they followed a narrow, snow-packed trail that snaked upwards along the side of the mountains. It was wide enough for them to walk side-by-side, but only barely, with out-thrusting shoulders of stone and deep cracks filled with frozen water. The air was thin here, and the mountains surrounded them on all sides, an unbroken chain from east to west.

They pitched camp beneath an overhanging rock fringed with icicles, though it was on the sheer side of a north-facing ridge and offered little protection from the keening wind. At Alcide's direction, they had gathered sticks throughout the day and tied them to their packs, but it was a meagre collection, the resulting fire barely warm enough to melt a little snow for drinking. Dinner was a knob of hard bread and a few slivers of damp cheese. They were down to the last of their rations.

First light revealed a long, wedge-shaped valley, narrowing on one side into a frozen waterfall hundreds of feet high. Below, the glinting ice shelves dropped away into a glassy lake that mirrored the encircling white-tipped peaks. The distance was obscured by haze.

The Fimbulvang Valley, Lucian sent faintly. He was barely visible, a dark speck against the salmon-coloured sky. *The Court of Bones lies alongside Lake Nilvanger. Not far now.*

The path broadened as it began its descent towards the valley floor, smooth and featureless under its blanket of snow. For a wonder, the sky was clear, the air so clean and crisp it made Gwyn's nose stream. Across the lake, she could make out the razor peak of Mount Tilgis. Beyond, Alcide said, were the Northern Wilds, where even the Fjallmen rarely ventured. There, the maps grew hazy, showing the outline of mountains that tapered off into nothing. Further north, at the edge of the world, was Necropolis, the city of necromancers – or so the stories said. Nobody had ever been there and told of it; not even Faolan. The only reports were from whaling ships circling Cape Providence. Sailors had glimpsed a stone city wreathed in fog, high up on the bluff – gone before they were even certain it was there.

Stories to frighten children, Gwyn thought. She didn't want to think about necromancers; not now.

But she would have to think about them soon. It was Saman Night – the last day of autumn. The

Festival of Bones was tonight. Whether she was ready for it or not.

They came out of the mountains into the teeth of the wind. Not just wind, but sleet, carrying sharp fragments of ice that stung Gwyn's cheeks and made her squint. A screed of powdery snow covered the field, clinging to their boots so they had to stop every few minutes and shake off the excess. Even with her coat pulled tight, Gwyn shivered constantly.

We're nearly there, Lucian sent suddenly, a few hours after midday. Gwyn looked up, but she could see nothing but glaring white.

How far?

Less than half a mile.

Even so, it took them over an hour to reach it, and by then the sky had turned inky. There was no sunset in the valley, no twilight. Night fell with the suddenness of a door slamming.

Among the tents, the snow had been stamped down into a muddy slush. There were perhaps a hundred tents in total, ranging from plain burlap affairs barely large enough to fit a single person, to house-sized pavilions with decorative fringing and woven mats at the entrance. Lanterns strung up between some of the trees cast a greenish glow. Fires burned in heavy metal braziers, and the main path between the tents was lined with stalls selling hot food and drink, among other things. An appealing scent of grilled meat and mulled wine wafted on the night air, and Gwyn's stomach growled appreciatively. There had been no midday meal that day, and only a stale end-of-road bread for breakfast.

'Just stay quiet and try not to make eye contact,' Alcide said. 'You might have a Fjallman's hair now, but you don't have a Fjallman's eyes.' Severine had brewed her a hair dye just before they left Priory – a thick, sludgy concoction that turned her hair from gold to black.

Do you see Shemeris? Gwyn sent into the night.

For a moment there was no response. Then, *Nay – she'll be in one of the tents. I'll see if I can overhear anything. Just try to look natural.*

Gwyn followed the direction of his mind-voice. She could just make him out, perched on an outcropping of stone away from the fires. He was clearly trying to stay as still as possible. Crows and ravens were sacred to the hill people, but any other bird might find itself in a cookpot.

'Spirit beads?' came a voice. An old woman, no taller than Alcide's hip, had fallen in beside them. She was so swaddled in dark furs that she looked like a moss-covered boulder. The wicker pannier on her back was stuffed with an amazing array of items, including what looked like human bones.

Gwyn shook her head, not trusting herself to speak. On the road, her attempts to practise the

Fjallman accent had been met with uproarious laughter from Lucian. She kept her gaze lowered. She was white-skinned enough to pass as a Fjallman, but a flash of green eyes would give the ruse away.

'You take bones to deaths-head priest, you need! Proper gift.' The woman's speech was disjointed. The hill people were one of the few societies that didn't primarily use the common tongue. Each tribe spoke its own dialect. Fortunately, meetings between tribes were always held in the common tongue, or a near approximation of it.

Alcide grunted in response, pressing something into the woman's hand. She held the coin up to the light, then bit down on it.

'Northern filth,' she said. Gwyn jumped, but the woman was referring to the coin, not them. She looked displeased, but she pocketed it just the same and scuttled away, leaving Alcide holding a string of bones. He passed them to Gwyn, looking bored. They were too small to be human bones, fortunately. Though you could likely buy those, too, for the right price.

'Do you sense anything?' Alcide asked Faolan quietly.

'There are mancers nearby,' he said, shrugging. 'Where, I couldn't say.'

There's activity around the tent with the red mat outside, Lucian sent. *I just saw two men come out carrying a coffin. That could be it.*

By now they had reached the main path through the camp. It was crammed with people, so they moved at a crawl. The three of them stood head-and-shoulders taller than most of the crowd, but although they drew a few curious looks, nobody challenged them. Someone was playing a drum nearby, a wild, insistent beat that made Gwyn tap her feet involuntarily. To her surprise – though she wasn't sure why it should be a surprise – this place felt no different from any other bustling town, the familiar patterns playing out: buying and selling, pushing and shoving, voices raised, fights always falling just short of actual violence. The peace of the Clansmoot was sacred.

Gwyn wanted to stare at everything, but that would only have drawn attention. She kept the hood of her coat raised, shading her face.

In a clearing near the centre of the camp, a small stage had been erected, and masked men and women were performing a play. A comedy, from the screaming laughter of those gathered nearby. But they spoke one of the hill tribe languages, and Gwyn could understand none of it.

All the tribes will put on performances, said Lucian. *Of course, most of them only speak their own dialect, so the effect is somewhat lost on anyone from outside the tribe.*

I was expecting the Festival of Bones to be more ... solemn, Gwyn sent back.

Aye, some parts are. But aside from consecrating the dead, the Clansmoot is the only time of the year when the tribes can mingle without the threat of violence. There's trade, marriage pacts agreed to, alliances formed. By midnight they'll all be drunk as Anchoran pirates.

Some had already gotten started on that. Many of the younger Fjallmen stumbled as they walked, clutching clay jars full of something that smelled like fish oil. Drummers made quick, lively music for laughing crowds doing a shuffling dance that seemed to have no agreed steps. Around the larger firepits, overturned logs served as seats, and people sat drinking and chatting in the firelight, hoods thrown back to show their pale faces. Gwyn caught snatches of too-loud conversation as they passed by.

When they reached the tent with the red mat, though, the laughter had died away. A few people squatted on the ground, rubbing their hands together against the cold and looking glum. The tent flap was closed, but Gwyn could make out the sound of quiet conversation inside. There was something hanging on either side of the entrance. Skulls, she realised, when she drew closer. Not human skulls, for a wonder, but the skulls of small animals, strung together with pieces of thin rope.

Is this it, do you think?

It's a necromancer's tent, Lucian sent back. *Though it may not be Shemeris'. Faolan said the hill people had six necromancers, didn't he? It could be any of them.*

'We can't afford to make any mistakes,' Alcide said out loud. 'We'll mingle for a while and see what else we can find out.'

Gwyn nodded, and they worked their way back into the crowd. They were drawing less attention than she had feared – only a few quick glances in passing. Some of the hill people were tall, if not as tall as Alcide, and Gwyn even caught a glimpse of grey eyes here and there. The hill tribes were known to raid outlying Asgeradan villages at times, carrying away prisoners, so there was some northerner blood mixed into the tribes' bloodlines.

Still, they had to look as though they belonged here, and she doubted Alcide or Faolan would agree to dance. Before long, Gwyn was carrying packets of dried herbs, a copper teapot and three more strings of 'spirit beads'. She had tried to swap a stone bit for one of the clay bottles of drink, but the seller had rejected her coin, and she had ended up trading her first set of beads for two bottles. She gave one to Faolan, but she hadn't seen him drink it yet.

'Too serious to have a drink?' Gwyn asked. In spite of the danger, she was starting to enjoy herself. It was exciting to be out in the world for once. Ascepis would never have set her loose in a crowd like this. She took a swig of the drink, and immediately spat it out. Was that *herring*?

'I don't seem to be missing much,' Faolan said. 'It

—' He broke off, seeing Gwyn's face, or perhaps feeling her alarm through the bond. 'What is it?'

She swallowed hard, barely noticing the foul taste of the fish-wine. Carefully, trying not to draw any attention, she nodded at the couple standing nearby, examining a cookware stall.

The woman was short and raven-haired, with a small, pouty mouth. The man was much taller, almost as tall as Alcide. A long nose dominated his pinched, unsmiling face. His hair was close-cropped and dark, but she knew that under the dye it would be white.

That's Amandine and Sepion, Gwyn sent urgently. *They're necromancers.*

There was a brief pause, then Alcide nodded to show that Lucian had passed on the message. There was no outward change to his body language, but Gwyn could feel him sizing them up for a fight.

Faolan pulled his hood forward, although the necromancers didn't seem to have noticed them. 'I expected they would be here. I doubt they'd break the peace of the Clansmoot, but ... best to keep clear of them.'

I've found Shemeris' tent, Lucian sent. *Alcide says we should go now, before those necromancers get there. If she has the core, we can't risk them getting their hands on it first.*

Sepion and Amandine had moved closer now. They spoke quietly, their heads together, and Gwyn could just make out the words.

'... if we have to,' Sepion was saying, 'but I think she will cooperate, with the right leverage.'

'That depends on her mysterious patron,' Amandine replied. 'If the ...'

They moved out of earshot, still affecting an air of casual indifference. Sepion picked up a piece of rough-hewn cloth from one of the stalls, turning it over in his hands. Amandine continued whispering in his ear, low and intent.

They're going to ruin everything, Gwyn sent back. She could see the plan evaporating in front of her eyes. *Where is Shemeris' tent, Lucian?*

On the west side of the camp. A couple with a jar of ashes went inside a few moments ago. I can hear them talking.

We're coming now.

By the time they reached Shemeris' tent, the couple with the ashes was just coming out. The man was crying softly, clutching the jar to his chest, and the woman had her arm around him. Alcide never paused; just strode into the tent, pushing the curtain aside.

'Go,' Faolan said, nodding after him. 'I'll follow in a moment. I don't want to alarm her.'

Alarm her? That was laughable. Before her nerve abandoned her, Gwyn followed Alcide into the tent.

The woman seated in front of the brazier was not what Gwyn had expected. She was no taller than a child of twelve, though her face put her closer to mid-thirties, and she had a stocky build. Not plump, but muscular, like the short-haired dogs merchants used to guard their caravans. Her hair was a thatch of reddish-brown, cropped close like a boy's. Her tough, no-nonsense face was at odds with Hulin's description of her as a coward.

'From what tribe have you come?' Shemeris asked. Her face was unsmiling, but not unfriendly. She had glanced at Alcide when they came in, but now her attention was focused entirely, unsettlingly, on Gwyn.

'No tribe,' Faolan said, stepping into the tent. Shemeris' eyes snapped to him at once. 'Hello, Shemeris.'

CHAPTER 31

FESTIVAL OF BONES

Shemeris leaped to her feet, face stark with fear. The air shimmered around her. Wards. At the same time, her hand shot up, and something ice-cold hammered into Gwyn's shoulder, hurling her to the ground.

She blinked, suddenly staring at the canvas roof of the tent. The side of her body was a ball of pain, her robes white and stiff with – was that ice? Yes, though it was rapidly melting in air that had grown uncomfortably hot. Shemeris had drawn the cold out of the air itself and directed it at her, like a lance. At the last moment, by pure instinct, Gwyn had tried to sever the spell. She had only half succeeded, but the attempt had probably saved her life.

Faolan will be pleased, Gwyn thought distantly. Her head felt woolly, dark flecks shimmering in her vision. Why was she on the ground, again? She sat up, blinking to clear her eyes.

Shemeris was pressed against the far wall of the tent, her hands raised. Somebody stood in front of her, somebody who held a sword at her throat. Who was ...?

Alcide.

Gwyn scrambled to her feet, ignoring the stiffness in her arm and leg. Her entire left side felt like it was on fire.

'You could,' Alcide said, in response to something Gwyn hadn't heard. 'But you'd be breathing through the hole in your throat before you could finish.'

What's happening? Lucian sent, his voice coloured with alarm. *I felt something in the tent. Are you well?*

She attacked me – no, I'm alright, Alcide and Faolan have got her pinned.

'This is hardly the greeting I was expecting,' Faolan was saying, his arms folded behind his back. 'Are we not old friends, you and I? Come, stop your blubbering; I only wish to talk.'

Damn Faolan to hell, Lucian sent. *I kenned this was an ill idea. But Gwyn, you've got bigger problems. I canna find those two necromancers. I was following them, but I've no idea where they went. They would have sensed what just happened. You need to get out of there!*

Gwyn nodded, though he couldn't see her. It would be too much to hope that Sepion and

Amandine had left the Festival empty-handed. How long until they arrived?

'We know all about you,' Gwyn said, throwing caution aside. Faolan's head whipped around, but he didn't use the bond to silence her, for a wonder. Her voice came out raw, and she rubbed her throat, still freezing cold where the ice had struck her. 'We know you've found Ailbhe Ahriddin's lost relic. We know you've been using it. Now tell us where it is.'

Shemeris began to lower her hands, but hastily raised them again when Alcide jerked the tip of the sword. A point of blood welled in the hollow of her throat.

'You're not from the Syndicate,' she said, managing to sound scornful despite her position. 'You're not even a mancer.'

'It doesn't matter who she is,' Faolan said, stepping in front of Gwyn. He spoke quickly; Lucian must have relayed the message about Amandine and Sepion. 'The core, Shemeris. What do you know about it?'

But Shemeris wasn't looking at him. Her eyes were still fixed on Gwyn, mingled fascination and fear in her expression.

'Impossible,' she whispered, as though to herself. Then, louder: 'I sense nothing from you. How do you —'

'The Amulet of Cambulan!' Faolan barked,

clicking his fingers in her face. 'Do you still have it, or did you give it to Ygriel?'

Gwyn, Lucian sent. *Are you there? You need to hurry. I found the necromancers. They're coming straight for the tent.*

'Amulet ... What amulet?' Shemeris turned to him, finally, her mouth twisting in fury. She seemed to have forgotten Alcide's naked blade pressed to her neck.

'The lost relic of Ailbhe Ahriddin.' Faolan spoke quietly, harshly. 'We know she fled to the Fjallmen in the year prior to her death. We know she had it with her. We know the hill people have held it all this time. Where is it, Shemeris?'

She blinked at him, and for a moment she looked utterly lost. Then her expression cleared, and she laughed, reaching into the front of her shirt.

'Slowly, necromancer,' Alcide warned.

She scowled at him, but obeyed. Inch by inch, Shemeris pulled a leather thong from the inside of her shirt. And dangling at the end of it ...

'That's it!' Gwyn said. Exactly as it had looked in the book, wrapped in gold wire and winking in the firelight. To finally see it in person ... It couldn't be that easy, could it?

'That's it,' Faolan agreed, and his face hardened. 'Give it to me, Shemeris, and I'll let you walk away from this.'

'The sorceress' lost amulet,' she mused, barely seeming to hear him. The core hung loose in her fingers. 'I wondered what it was. Now why would you want this, hmm?'

'That's none of your concern,' Alcide said. 'Hand it over. Now.'

She looked at him, then, and her mouth compressed to a hard line. The core disappeared into her clenched fist. 'No. I don't think I will. This is a Fjallman relic, and you're no Fjallman.'

'Neither are you,' Faolan said, taking a step closer. Alcide's body tensed as though preparing for violence, and Gwyn reached instinctively for the vim, holding back just on the brink of touching. Of course Shemeris wasn't going to give it up without a fight. But there were three of them, and one of her, and Faolan had said Shemeris was weak, as far as wizards went.

That ice of hers didn't feel weak, though. More like getting struck with a bolt of frozen lightning.

'Not by birth, perhaps,' Shemeris was saying. 'But they've accepted me; they trust me. More than the Syndicate ever did. So no, Faolan Ladimore. If you want Ailbhe's amulet, you'll have to take it from me.' She unclenched her fist, and the core disappeared back into her shirt.

Faolan met Alcide's eyes, and nodded.

Alcide surged forward, but Shemeris ... Vim, she

was fast; impossibly fast. A wall of *something* slammed out from her, and Gwyn was thrown back, barely catching her footing before she fell. The flame in the brazier snuffed out, plunging the tent into near darkness. Light filtered through the canvas from the fires outside, casting silhouettes: Faolan, stumbling; Alcide, sword raised. Where was –

The inside of the tent exploded.

Gwyn didn't know her feet had left the ground until she felt her cheek pressed against snow. She thrashed, sucking air that had suddenly gone from warm to scalding. Her left arm was numb, her mouth full of blood. She pushed herself up onto her knees. Her hearing was oddly muffled, as though she was listening from one end of a long tunnel.

Gwyn, get out of there!

Lucian's voice in her mind, faint but still clear. She shook her head. The edges of her vision had gone grey. Around her, the tent lay in bloody, flaming tatters. Smoke obscured everything, choking and acrid. People were screaming, flailing, just smudges of black against the flames. She saw tribesmen scrambling over piles of debris. Bodies lying in the snow. Some stirred weakly, but many didn't. Already the fire had spread to nearby tents. The air had cooled enough to breathe, but it smelled of a charnel house.

The whole place is going up in flames, Lucian sent.

He felt close, though she couldn't see him. *Are Alcide and Faolan there?*

I don't know. I can't see anything.

Oh, damn it, damn it, that twally-heided ... He trailed off into inaudible cursing, then returned, clear and sharp. *I've got to find them. Stay there. Dinna move. I'll be right back.*

She nodded, though she wasn't sure if he could see her. There were figures moving among the rubble. Through the smoke, Gwyn could catch only glimpses, but she thought – yes. Amandine and Sepion. Had they attacked, or was it Shemeris? It had happened so fast.

Gwyn wormed her way towards a nearby pile of crates, staying low to the ground, out of their eyeline. She wasn't sure she could stand, anyway. And Shemeris? Escaped, or dead? Gwyn shook her head again. If only her ears would stop ringing! She was bleeding heavily, from scrapes on her legs, from long, painful gashes on —

She sensed the attack a heartbeat before she saw it, a blinding flash of hot, crackling light, and only months of practice with Faolan made her pull up a ward in time. The impact nearly rattled the teeth from her head. A second volley came on the heels of the first, and she rolled, lashing out with *sever*. The crates next to her exploded, raining chips of charred wood.

Gwyn leaped up, not waiting for the third attack. She drew in the vim and felt it roar to the surface, hungry, *furious.* The heat of it wanted to boil her blood, wanted to sear the flesh from her bones. She cleaved another attack from mid-air.

'Not bad, apprentice,' said a female voice.

Gwyn peered through the smoke, coughing into her sleeve. The smoke stung her eyes. Not Shemeris; the voice was too high-pitched for that, too wild.

'She's quick,' said someone else – a male this time. Familiar, that voice. Gwyn's eyes darted, but she could make out nothing but smoke and shadow, lit by the occasional flash of fire.

'But so green!' said the female, laughing. 'Like a newly harvested novice!'

Gwyn saw her outline in the smoke an instant before the woman struck, lashing out with tongues of black flame. The heat scorched her, and she threw up a ward just in time, stumbling backwards.

Lucian, where are you? she sent, desperate. No response but empty sky.

'Has Ladimore trained you at all, girl?' Sepion asked. He stepped closer, and the smoke glowed red from the flames wreathing in his hand. 'Come! Show us what you can do.'

Amandine struck again, whipcords of dark, fizzing fire. Gwyn flung up an arm to cover her face; called up a ward to shield herself. The black flames exploded against it, raining sparks onto the snow. The impact knocked her back several steps, and her knees buckled. Too fast to even think of severing those attacks. For the first time, she realised Faolan had been going easy on her, letting her build up her strength, her confidence. Next to a real wizard ...

'Are you going to stand there blocking us all day, girl, or are you going to fight back?' Sepion demanded. He raised his hand, and a torrent, a cyclone of flame was spinning towards her.

Gwyn shouted – something. She didn't know what. She reached down into herself, grasping at the vim like a lifeline. The ward glowed in front of her, a hazy distortion of the air, rippling like the surface of a pond as the flames hammered at it.

And kept hammering. Sepion moved closer, though she could barely see him through the wall of flame and the clouded surface of her own weakening ward. Three seconds ... Four seconds ... She couldn't hold it —

Her power snapped, and it was all Gwyn could do to throw herself aside. Flames whooshed past her head, and the last half-inch of her braid turned to ash. She landed hard in the snow.

'Pathetic!' Amandine spat.

She sensed the next lash of flame coming, but could do nothing to stop it. The vim had abandoned her. She reached for it anyway, one last attempt.

And the flames, still five feet away, turned to hissing sparks in mid-air.

Gwyn blinked. Had she ...?

But no. The vim was still as distant as the moons. That was someone else. Someone ...

'Get up,' Faolan hissed, appearing at her side. Across from them, Sepion hurled a spear of pure flame, and Faolan knocked it out of the air with one slash of his hand. 'Get up, girl.'

Her legs were shaking, but Gwyn pulled herself to her feet. Faolan was – vim, he was fighting both of them at once.

Amandine struck with ribbons of dark fire that seemed to suck in the light. Sepion brought pure flame, white and hot and so dazzling it made his shadow seem to stretch for miles.

And Faolan met every attack. Most exploded harmlessly in the air; the ones that made it through fizzed to nothingness against his wards. He held one arm raised, as though gripping a shield. The other twisted in the air, capturing balls of dark, crackling energy that he flung towards his opponents. Around them, the snow turned to slush. He was pulling the cold out of the ground, funnelling it into ... whatever that was.

Sepion hissed as one of Faolan's attacks struck home. He was still standing, so he must have severed it, at least partially. But he clutched at his shoulder, arm hanging loose at his side, and blood appeared between his fingers.

Faolan didn't relent. He took a step forward, sending a barrage of dark energy that Amandine barely managed to sever.

Gwyn could hardly follow what was happening. She didn't know these signs; didn't have them marked on her skin, even if she had recognised them.

But she knew how to sever. When she called on the vim again, it responded, spiralling up from some hidden reservoir of strength. Eyes stinging with sweat, feet planted a step behind Faolan, she sent her power snaking out, severing Amandine's attacks before they could land. Not all of them – not even half. But some. Enough to help, at least.

'Get out of here,' Faolan said, his teeth clenched. He raised his arm, and Sepion's fireball hammered against his ward.

'Faolan, I don't —'

'Find Alcide and Lucian! I can't hold these two off forever.'

And he couldn't, she realised. He was stronger than either of them, but the strain made the bond vibrate like the skin of a drum. He was nearing the end of his strength. Her help wasn't enough to tip the balance; not nearly enough.

She turned and ran. Stumbled through the smoke and the darkness, through piles of burning rubble.

She couldn't see anyone now, or at least no one living. Humped shapes lay among the wreckage.

Lucian! Can you hear me?

But there was no reply. Nothing but the crackle of flames, the sound of distant screams. And behind her, the sizzle and hiss of spells striking Faolan's wards. A man bellowed in pain. Sepion; it had to be Sepion. The bond wavered.

Lucian! Where are —

I'm here, lass!

Gwyn sagged with relief, and might have fallen, if not for the set of powerful arms that caught her. Alcide, soot smudged along his cheekbone. And behind him, wreathed in smoke, a gigantic striped cat with eyes of liquid flame.

'Faolan,' she gasped, pointing back the way she'd come. 'He's fighting Sepion and Amandine, but he can't —'

Calm yourself, Gwyn. We're here. Now, where is he?

'That way. You have to hurry. He's strong, but there are two of them, and he —'

A shape moved in the darkness behind them, and both whipped around. A stocky figure, a flash of reddish hair, gone as soon as it appeared.

'Was that ...?' she whispered.

Aye, Lucian sent back, grim. *That was Shemeris. I recognise her scent.*

'We can't let her get away,' Alcide said, looking down at Lucian.

It took Gwyn a moment to register. Shemeris was the reason they were here. They were going to follow her – and leave Faolan to his fate.

'No,' she said, and her grip on Alcide's arm tightened. 'Forget Shemeris! She —'

'We came for the core,' Alcide snapped. 'That's our priority. Not Faolan.'

No, no, this was all wrong. Faolan ... He couldn't hold them off for much longer. The bond was practically on fire.

'Help Faolan,' she repeated, and her voice was steady. 'I'll follow Shemeris.'

Absolutely not! Lucian's voice in her head was a whip crack. She saw his teeth bared in the firelight.

'There's no time to argue! I won't get close to her – I'm not a fool. I'll follow from a distance. She can't get far; not on foot in the dark. After you help Faolan, he can use the bond to find me again.'

Lass, if you think for one minute that —

'Let her go, Lucian,' Alcide said, pulling his arm free. 'She's right.'

Gwyn tensed. Support from Alcide? But he wasn't even looking at her, now. His eyes scanned the wreckage, at the place where flashes of rumbling fire illuminated the smoke.

If anyone should track her, it should be me, Lucian said. *I can stay out of sight far easier than —*

'You can help Faolan,' Gwyn snapped, and the dark power coiled and hissed in her breast. They were always doubting her, all of them; always trying to protect her when she didn't need or want their protection. 'I can't. Go, Lucian!'

'Stay well clear of her, girl,' Alcide warned. He unsheathed his sword. 'I don't need to tell you how dangerous she is.'

'I'm not a fool,' she said again.

Alcide nodded, then loped off into the darkness. Lucian stared after him, then turned to look at Gwyn, the firelight gleaming off his golden eyes.

Gwyn, I dinna like this. It's reckless and foolhardy.

But she didn't stay behind to listen. She turned towards the place where Shemeris had been. Dark, utterly dark, except for ...

Yes; those were footprints in the snow. A single set, leading away from the mess of the camp, into the trees. Narrow – a woman's footprints. Shemeris? It had to be.

Gwyn followed them. As she left the tents behind, she turned back in time to see Lucian vanish into the dark, tail lashing the cold air.

Good. She ignored the sudden tightening in her chest, the brief sting of abandonment. Faolan was still alive; she could feel that much. But he was weak. They had to get to him in time. If he died ...

She squashed that thought and focused on the snow. In the light of the two moons, both waning crescents riding high above the trees, it seemed almost to glow. The prints led uphill, weaving among the trees, towards the foothills of the mountains. How far had Shemeris fled? The argument with Alcide and Lucian had only taken a minute, so she couldn't have gotten far.

But she is strong, whispered a small voice in Gwyn's head. *Stronger than expected. Strong enough to be ...*

No – Shemeris wasn't a sorceress. Beheret wouldn't have left a sorceress free to join the Syndicate, free to do whatever she wished for thirty-odd years. It was the core that made Shemeris so powerful; it had to be. The core, and whatever power Nimet's sacrifice had imbued it with. No wonder she hadn't wanted to give it up.

But ... Shemeris had barely seemed to know what the core *was.* And there had been a lie in her voice when she called it a Fjallman relic.

No time. She had no time for this. Not while Shemeris was out there making her escape.

The ground was steep here, so slick with ice that Gwyn had to climb hand-over-hand where her boots threatened to slide from under her. Overhead, a thousand knifepoint stars glittered in the dark. And woven among them, like wisps of sheer silk, the aurora.

Gwyn halted, breathing hard. She looked behind her, at her own dragging footprints shadowing Shemeris' lighter ones, disappearing into the dark and the trees. No one following; no sign of Alcide or

Lucian, no Faolan. The bond ... Well, the bond told her nothing, save that he was alive.

And ahead of her ...

She cursed under her breath, but there was no mistaking it. The rock face ahead opened into a cave, wide enough to sail a ship into, its top lined with drips of frozen water. Inside was only blackness, swallowing up Shemeris' footprints.

CHAPTER 32

THE MISTRESS OF MAGIC

If only Faolan had taught her a light spell. She knew there was one. The first sign of *Dantalion,* the Fourth Tower. But what it looked like, or how to call on it – no. That was for better, stronger wizards, not for the likes of her.

So Gwyn stumbled in the dark, bumping into down-thrust stalactites of rock and ice. Foolish; this was foolish. Shemeris could be hiding five feet away.

That thought made her halt in her tracks, the blood pounding in her ears. She listened for the scuff of boots on stone, for breathing. Nothing but the drip of water on stone, and, far beneath her feet, the rushing of some subterranean river.

Lucian? she sent out, not expecting an answer. None came.

I should wait for them here, she thought, grabbing a

column of stone to steady herself. *There's no sense wandering around in the dark until I twist an ankle.*

But if these were true caverns like the Warren, and not just a single passage through the mountains, then how could they hope to find Shemeris? The others could be a minute behind her, or an hour, and by then Shemeris could be long gone, taking the core with her. No – she had to follow. *No choice.* Faolan could find her later.

If the others save him.

And if they don't?

Perhaps her eyes were beginning to adjust, because there was light in the cave, of a sort. A pale, greyish light. She followed where it seemed brightest, boots whispering across the ice-slick stone. The air was dry and smelled faintly of ... oil? Something else?

There *was* a light, she realised, as she crept deeper into the cave. Not the natural light of the stars, or the moons, or even the pale ghost-light of the aurora. This was harsher, somehow.

Gwyn gasped; froze. That sound – she knew that sound. Would know it anywhere.

It was the faint, discordant twang of the Scions' music.

'It was as he said,' Shemeris was muttering. 'Just as he said.'

Gwyn crept closer, as close as she dared. Her heartbeat was like thunder in her ears.

It can't be, it can't be, it can't –

But it was. No matter how many times she rubbed her eyes, or shook her head, the vision refused to dissipate. It was real.

The figure hanging in the centre of the room, illuminated by glowing glass spheres, could only be a Scion.

Not Umbrael, though the shape was similar. Shrivelled limbs, elongated head, delicate, near-transparent skin. But the eyes were pure white instead of black, the skin red-tinged where Umbrael's had been blue, the hair a skein of copper. And tangled among it were links of metal that looked like ...

Chains.

The Scion was in chains.

'I can't!' Shemeris said, rounding on the Scion, her hand slashing the air. 'Stop saying it, damn you! You know why I can't.'

Gwyn pressed herself against the rock. She was trembling all over, trembling so hard she feared she might vomit. *How?* More importantly, *who*? This Scion was female, so ... Siasr? Aeshma? Beheret herself? No, surely not.

The eyes. The eyes are different.

White eyes. White, the mirror opposite of Umbrael's black. Umbrael, Siasr, Iahta, they were Void Gods – the demons that myth said had chased the Old Gods across the heavens to Caerwyn. In art and sculpture, they were always shown with black-on-black eyes. But the eyes of the Old Gods – those were always white-on-white.

The Old Gods, Gwyn thought, hugging the rock. *The Old Gods.* There were four of those, including Beheret herself. Molech Suun, the god of storms and sky. Yotha, the fiery-eyed god of wisdom and warfare. And Aeshma.

The Mistress of Magic.

'Shut up, shut up, *shut up!*' Shemeris screamed, clapping her hands over her ears.

This wasn't Shemeris' first time in the cave – not even close. Even half wild with anger, she moved surely, confidently. How long? How long had she known the Scion was here?

'If you won't shut up, I'll make you,' Shemeris said. She faced the Scion now, her back towards Gwyn, but her hand reached up to pull something from inside her shirt. Something small and gold-wrapped, dangling on the end of a leather thong.

The core!

'You did this to yourself,' Shemeris said, stepping closer to the Scion. She slipped the loop around Aeshma's neck, so the core hung between her withered breasts. No reaction from the Scion – not even a flicker in those all-white eyes – but Shemeris stepped back, sighing in apparent relief.

'Done,' she said, seeming to speak to herself now. 'My part is done. Lord Ygriel can do whatever he —'

Gwyn clapped a hand over her mouth, but it was too late. The gasp had escaped before she could stop it.

Shemeris whipped around, eyes trained on the spot where Gwyn crouched. Staring straight at her.

Gwyn leaped to her feet, turned to flee —

And sprawled onto the rocks as invisible ropes lashed her ankles.

She snatched at the vim, desperation making her clumsy. The ropes tightened and began to drag her across the floor, towards Shemeris, towards the Scion.

No, no, no!

Her hands clawed at the rock, scrabbled for purchase and found none, leaving ten long streaks of blood. Then the ropes hauled her upright, and she found herself nose-to-nose with Shemeris.

'So you're the girl,' Shemeris said. There was no pleasure in her eyes. Just cold, grim satisfaction. 'You're the one Lord Ygriel is so desperate to get his hands on.'

The vim! Gwyn hurtled at it with every ounce of strength, and for an instant, Shemeris' eyes went wide. She felt something go up between her and the vim, some kind of shield. Too late. Gwyn *punched* through it, grabbed the vim and held it like a blazing sun in her chest.

Sever. The ropes around her legs parted like cut threads, and she stumbled forward, almost knocking Shemeris to the ground. She barely noticed. The light in her chest was bright – so bright it was searing her, melting the flesh from her bones. The light, the *light!* Gwyn thought she was screaming, but she didn't know anymore.

And then ...

And then the vim was gone.

Gwyn's knees sagged, and she would have fallen if Shemeris hadn't caught her with fresh bindings. Invisible cords pulled her upright, so she faced the necromancer once more. But Shemeris was breathing hard, too, the front of her shirt torn, her hair in disarray.

'That was ... unexpected,' Shemeris said. Her eyes narrowed. 'You drew straight from her. How did you do it? Who showed you?'

The vim! Gwyn reached for it once more, strained for it. But something stood in her way. An unseen shield, like a glass wall, cutting her off. The vim was there, on the other side – oh, she could feel it – but it was hopelessly out of reach. She scrabbled at the invisible wall until sweat stood out from her face.

'Stop that,' Shemeris barked, and a lash of cold air struck Gwyn across the face, made her head whip to the side. She tasted blood.

Think ... She had to think.

'What do you want?' Gwyn asked. Her tongue was thick in her mouth. She'd done something just now; something dangerous. The vim had never seared her like that before. So powerful – for a moment, she'd forgotten her own name.

'From you? Nothing,' spat Shemeris. 'Lord Ygriel is the only one who can give me what I want. What I need.'

Gwyn coughed, swallowed blood. 'What do you need?'

Shemeris stalked away, peering into the Scion's empty face as though looking for something.

'What do I need?' she repeated. 'I need some *peace and quiet.* From *her*!'

Gwyn stared, trying to control her trembling. The Scion made no sound at all, not that she could hear; not even that strange music, now. So what was ...?

'Lord Ygriel wanted to take her with him,' Shemeris continued. 'He was going to kill me, just for the crime of digging her up. Two thousand, one hundred and twenty-five years, she's rested here. And for most of that time, no one even remembered. But *I* found her.'

Around the room, the glowing lights went dark for a moment, then flared.

'He made a bargain. I could keep her, he said. Use her. He'd even show me how to shut out the voice.'

Voice? Gwyn could hear nothing but the drip of water, the distant keen of the wind.

'But he wanted something in return. A small thing, he said.'

She stalked towards a corner of the room, towards an iron grate half hidden in gloom. The hinges screamed as she heaved it open, revealing a round, dark hollow with no bottom. Alarmed, Gwyn pushed against her restraints, but they were tight; tighter than Faolan's had ever been.

'If the girl with green eyes ever came here, he said I was to capture her. No matter what.' She shook her head. 'I certainly never expected you to appear with Faolan Ladimore. Back in the Syndicate, we were – not friends; not really. But I always respected him.'

Shemeris stepped towards Gwyn, seizing the back of her shirt in one fist. Gwyn thrashed, but she couldn't escape that grip, any more than she could escape the invisible bonds around her legs, her arms.

'Lord Ygriel never said what he wanted you for, so I won't silence you,' Shemeris said. 'Not if he intends to make use of your magic. I won't risk his anger. But until he arrives, I'm afraid you'll have to stay put.'

And before Gwyn could do or say anything, Shemeris shoved her forwards into the hole.

CHAPTER 33

CELL

Gwyn wasn't sure when she awoke.

The darkness was so complete it seemed a physical thing. Opening her eyes was no different to keeping them closed, but she opened them anyway, staring into the dark and listening to her heart trying to beat out of her chest.

The ground was cold. Stone, she thought, with a slick coating that felt like moss. Her hands, reaching out to either side, came back damp. She pushed herself upright, and her limbs yowled at the sudden pain. Nothing broken, but ... vim, she hurt all over.

As her eyes began to adjust, Gwyn sat up and examined her surroundings. She was in a narrow, circular room, or perhaps a pit. The walls stood twenty feet high at least. It was too dim to make out anything clearly, though the top of the pit was a little lighter. That was good – it meant Shemeris hadn't covered over the grate, locking her away in the dark.

Gwyn forced herself to take deep, steadying breaths. It made little difference, but it was better than giving in to the panic that she felt bubbling beneath the surface.

Out. She had to get out. Because if Shemeris really meant to hand her over to Ygriel ...

The others will find me, she told herself, though the thought did little to calm her. The bond felt ... strange. Dimmed, somehow. She would have felt it if Faolan was close, surely.

Feeling her way through the dark, Gwyn got up and began slowly circling the room, stamping her feet as she went. As she suspected, the floor was solid, oil-smooth rock, and by the time she reached the centre again, she had only succeeded in bruising her feet. It seemed to be all of one piece, without even a crack to wedge her fingers into.

The walls, then. Slowly, like a drunkard, she crossed to the edge of the room and began exploring with outstretched hands. This, she discovered, was more promising. The wall was made of stone that was crumbly in places. If she could dig space for her toes and fingers, perhaps she could climb to the top. She would need a tool to pick the stone, though. It was too dense to make any progress with just her fingers. Something metal, preferably, or even a piece of jagged rock.

Nothing. She had nothing. Not even a coin – Alcide and Faolan always carried those. All her supplies were in her pack, probably ashes by now.

What, then? The vim? Even the thought of touching it made her shy away. The vim had *burned* her. But she would touch it again if she had to, if it meant getting out of this pit before Ygriel showed up.

Gwyn looked up at the dim circle of grey light with a sinking heart. Another fall from twenty feet could kill her. And even if she could scrape out fingerholds and climb to the top, Shemeris could be waiting for her.

There's no way I can pick out handholds with my fingers, she thought, fighting the bleakness. *Unless ...*

She ran her hands along the wall at waist level. Perhaps there was a way. Not with the signs tattooed on her palm – even after months with Faolan, she had only earned three new markings after *sever,* and none of them would help her here. But she knew some of the other signs, even if she wasn't marked with them, even if Faolan would box her ears just for knowing. She had no parchment here, no quill, but ...

It was easy enough to draw fresh blood. The gash on her arm, when the necromancers' attack had hurled her clear of Shemeris' tent, had clotted over now, but Gwyn scraped at the scab until blood flowed once more. Then she painted the mark on the back of her hand. A simple inverted triangle. The sign of *sigel.*

Then, before she could think about what she was doing, Gwyn touched the wall, reached for the vim, and called up the sign of fire.

There was a small crack, as though someone had stepped on a nut. Gwyn drew her hand back. A rain of dust fell to the ground, revealing a thumb-sized chip in the stone, and a tiny spiral of smoke coming out of it.

Behold the power of a wizard.

She looked up towards the opening again. At this rate, each step would need a dozen blasts with *sigel* to carve out room for her feet and hands. That meant casting *sigel* hundreds, maybe thousands of times. Could she do it? Even the first casting had left her feeling weak and shaky.

No choice, she thought. *Whatever happens, I won't just lie here and wait for Ygriel to come find me.*

Steeling herself, Gwyn laid her hand on the stone and reached for the vim again.

After casting *sigel* for the three hundredth time, Gwyn stopped counting. There didn't seem to be any point.

As it turned out, casting signs one-handed while clinging to the wall was much more difficult than casting from solid ground. After she had blasted away enough stone on the first few rows, she had to begin climbing, and after that her progress became much slower. As she tired, it grew harder and harder to call up the vim.

She had been doing this for several hours – climbing, casting, scraping, climbing – when she finally slipped. The distance was less than six feet, but she fell badly, landing hard on her rump and scraping the palms of both hands as she scrabbled for purchase. The pain was incredible.

After that, she was too spooked to climb any more, at least for a while. There was no water to wash her scrapes with, but she cleaned them as best she could with the edge of her shirt, then lay down to rest.

Where are the others? Faolan, Lucian, Alcide – they should have come for her, should have been able to follow her footprints, and Shemeris'. And the bond ... The bond was quiescent. It said that Faolan still lived, but nothing more.

After relieving herself in a corner, away from her sleeping area – the best she could do – she felt strong enough to resume work on the wall. It was impossible to say how long it took her to dig out the final seven feet. The stone felt denser here somehow, and her castings were weakening as her exhaustion grew. More than once, she froze, clinging to the wall in terror, certain she had heard Shemeris' footfall on the floor above.

By the time she reached the top, her throat was too dry to swallow, her lips so cracked they had begun to bleed. Wedging her toes into the wall as firmly as possible, and trying not to look down, she heaved the grate open, and hauled herself up and over the side.

Gwyn stood, her knees so weak they could barely hold her weight.

Stood, and met the all-white eyes of the Scion Aeshma.

There was no recognition in the Scion's face. No emotion at all. The eyes were glassy and unfocused. Only the slow rise and fall of her chest showed that the creature was alive. So different to Umbrael, to the sharp, piercing intelligence of the Weaver's gaze.

Gwyn's eyes moved downwards. The core ... It was still there, hanging around Aeshma's neck.

Oh, she didn't want to touch the Scion. The thought made her skin crawl as though covered in flies. But the core ... The core ...

Gwyn reached out and grabbed it.

And the Scion's voice *exploded* in her mind.

It was the same layered, shattered-glass screech as Umbrael's, filling Gwyn's head, making her stagger back as though from a blow. But the Scion wasn't talking. She was screaming.

GETMEOUT GETMEOUT GETMEOUT GETMEOUT GETMEOUT –

Gwyn clutched at her head, barely aware that the

sound had driven her to her knees. The core she had forgotten she was holding slipped from her hand and pinged against the stone floor.

FREE FREE NEED TO BE FREE GETMEOUT NEED TO AIR SWEET AIR FREEDOM GETMEOUT –

Over the screams was another sound, one that threatened to drown the Scion out entirely. Music. The same music that had followed Gwyn, in hints and snatches, for months now. Again and again she had heard it, distant and strangely familiar. In the Warren, like a breath of cold air on her cheek. In Priory House, drawing her down towards Umbrael's hidden lair.

Now it was all around her, hammering her, so loud she felt her eardrums must be bleeding. It was coming from the Scion, as discordant as the flow of senseless screams.

GETMEOUT SETMEFREE AIR AIR FREEDOM SETMEOUT GETMEFREE FREE FREE FREE –

Stop! Gwyn sent back, hands clapped over her ears as if that could somehow dampen the sound. *Stop, you're killing me!*

On and on the screams went, laced with madness and desperation and a seething hate that made Gwyn want to vomit. And under it all, pictures, each one exploding into Gwyn's mind with the force of a cyclone.

Flash.

Awakened from darkness, hands pulling her up, up, *out*. Choking and gasping as the liquid heaved its way out of her lungs.

Flash.

Grey eyes, human eyes, cold and unfeeling and rheumy with age, looking into her own. Porter Sabine. Her ... father? Creator? God?

Flash.

Darkness again, darkness everywhere. A great yawning *nothing,* like the heart of a dead star. But there was peace in that darkness. An end to the slow drain, to the hundreds of tiny hooks that tugged on her power.

Then a crack of light appearing, widening. Voices – human voices – low, murmuring, too faint to understand. A hand fumbling at her neck, grey human eyes that glittered with youth and malice ...

Flash.

Caverns of ice. A temple of stone and water. Shrieking wind blown straight from the frozen north, straight from her half-dead sister. Siasr's voice whispered down it, but she couldn't make out the words. And fire, fire in the torches of the fur-swaddled humans who gathered around her, fire in the hand of the red-haired witch who laid a noose around her neck.

She was in chains. And the voice in her head, mocking, laughing. The voice of the First Scion. *Beheret.* The traitor.

Flash.

Gwyn reeled against the onslaught, certain she was going to pass out. Underneath the images were other things, other thoughts and impressions, and in a blinding instant Gwyn understood everything. Saw the truth there, half buried under the whirl of images and thoughts and desperate, pleading screams.

Beheret had sold Aeshma to Darro Sabine – sold her in exchange for her own freedom. And the hundred hooks had become thousands as the wizards spread and multiplied. Aeshma felt every hard, insistent tug. Too long – she had lived too long. The pain. *The pain!*

Then Ygriel had sold her again, sold her to Shemeris in exchange for ... what? Nothing. A power play. A game. And now it was worse, worse than she could have imagined, because Shemeris was drawing on her power directly, and the pain, the *pain*. Not a trickle, but a flood. For months, Shemeris had gorged herself on Aeshma's very essence.

Her power. The emanations of a trapped and tortured Scion, waiting to be tapped by those who shared the blood of the Sabines. The ability was inside the wizards and the healers, inside that bloodline, but the power itself came from here. From Aeshma.

The source of all the vim.

FREE SETMEFREE SETMEFREE

NEEDTOGETOUT KILL ME KILL ME KILL ME KILL ME —!

Gwyn lashed out with *sigel,* and the glowing glass spheres around the room exploded outwards, raining down sparks and fragments of glass, plunging the chamber into darkness. But Gwyn didn't need to see. She knelt, snatched up Nimet's core with one hand. With the other, she grabbed a shard of glass, as long as her palm. The jagged edge sliced at her fingertips, but she hardly felt it.

KILL ME KILL ME KILL ME KILL —

When she drove the glass shard into the Scion's neck it was like watching somebody else's hand move. Aeshma's blood was green, seeming almost to glow in the dark. The white-on-white eyes met hers, and as the ancient creature's life drained away, Gwyn heard the voice in her head again for the last time.

Thank you.

And all the magic in the world winked out.

CHAPTER 34

BROTHER

Gwyn had no memory of leaving the Scion's chamber.

When she came back to herself, she was leaning against an ice-slick outcropping of rock, panting in harsh, ragged breaths that sounded like a saw cutting wood. Had she been running? Her hands, still gripping the glass shard, were covered in the Scion's blood.

Fighting the urge to gag, Gwyn dropped the glass and forced herself to take deep, steadying breaths. Vim, but her head hurt. So did everything else. She thought she might have tripped and fallen during all that running, perhaps more than once. The memory was a vague, vaporous thing. She found herself wiping her hands compulsively on her trousers, leaving streaks of luminous green. One thought kept chasing itself around her head.

The magic is gone.

She had never felt the presence of the vim before. Not really. She had sensed the edges of it during those long nights practising *sever;* had understood it better once she started learning the more advanced signs. But it had always been a background thing, something she was only aware of when she went searching for it.

But oh, she felt the absence now. It was a hollow inside her chest, in the place once filled by the invisible, thrumming power of the vim. In that moment she would have given up a leg and both arms to have it filled again.

But the magic was gone.

Gwyn didn't feel the tears streaming down her cheeks, but she had to scrub her eyes before she could see clearly enough to go on. There was light, and the taste of snow and pine in the air. The way out.

The magic is gone.

The voice in her head was shrill and insistent now, nearly a scream, demanding attention. There was nothing she could do about it, no way to undo her actions. She still wasn't convinced it had been the wrong choice.

But the magic is –

She forced the voice down and stamped on it firmly. Light; she had to follow the light. How long until Ygriel came for her? She had to get as far away as she could, even if it meant fleeing into the Northern Wilds with nothing but the core and the clothes on her back. A death sentence, but better that than waiting here for Ygriel or Shemeris to find her.

Then ... daylight!

She stumbled towards it, almost weeping. Not the main entrance. This was narrower, barely more than a cleft in the rock. But that was daylight on the other side, and the gleam of sun on snow.

Gwyn burst into the open, panting, sucking in gulps of frigid air that burned her lungs and made her nose stream. Free! The magic was gone, and Ygriel was coming for her, and Faolan was who-knew-where, but ... she was free.

Then Gwyn looked up, and almost tripped as a wave of vertigo washed over her. She recognised the dark, segmented shape hovering above, impossibly huge, like the greatest mountain ever imagined. Her blood ran cold, and her knees almost buckled beneath her.

The Pyramid.

It was moving. Already, the downward-thrusting tip had cleared the mountains. Only the furthest side was still visible, and as she watched, that began to recede too. But it shouldn't be here at all. The Pyramid never drifted this far north; never! Unless ...

'Hello, Yennevere.'

A hand of ice gripped Gwyn's heart.

She spun, reaching for the vim – and finding nothing. Of course.

The man who stood by the mouth of the cave, leaning against the rock, was no one she knew. Certainly not Ygriel, as she had feared. Plain-faced, his nose red with cold, with heavy eyelids and hair like coarse, dark wire. And overhead, perched on an overhang of rock —

Gwyn reeled back, and her boot heels slipped on the damp stone, so she landed hard on her backside. Her teeth clicked together. She tasted blood.

'It's a pleasure to finally meet you,' said the stranger, folding his hands into the pockets of his dark, high-necked coat. His speech was the smooth, precise accent she'd come to recognise as Syndicate.

Her mouth was too dry to speak, so she simply stared without answering. Stared at the *thing* glaring down at her. At the leathery hide, covered in parts with dark, interlocking scales. At the massive wings, both tipped with a claw that it used to cling to the rock. At the wedge-shaped head, the prominent brow ridge, the narrow, golden eyes with their slit pupils. And at the curved fangs, dripping saliva onto the snow.

'Don't let my drake frighten you,' the man said, baring his own teeth at her. 'It won't attack unless ordered. And I don't intend to give that order, if you cooperate.'

Gwyn shook her head, mute. She couldn't take

her eyes off it. The drake stared back at her, steam curling from its nostrils in the frozen air.

'Come,' said the stranger, and he straightened, reaching out to take her by the arm. 'Lord Ygriel wishes to speak with you.'

The words snapped her out of her trance. She fought, then, with a manic rage that frightened her – fingers slashing out like claws for his face, his hair, anything she could reach. Her training with Alcide was completely forgotten. She snarled like a beast, twisting in his arms, trying to bite. But the man was wrapped deep in heavy winter clothes, and her fists might as well have been pounding at a steel door.

Then the stranger's heavy backhand took her across the face, and she would have fallen if he hadn't held her.

'Stop that,' he hissed, shaking her so her teeth clattered together. 'Otherwise you'll make the trip in the drake's mouth. And he's none too careful where he puts his teeth.'

Gwyn wanted to keep fighting, but the blow had winded her. The world swam in and out of focus, and the tang of blood was on her tongue. The man hauled her up the sheer slope, towards the *thing,* the drake. And then he was bundling her up into the saddle, fastening leather straps around her legs, tying her in place. The creature's body was cold against her legs.

'Any trouble when we're in the air, I cut the straps and let you fall,' the man said as he settled into place behind her, feet tucked into the stirrups. 'Understood?'

She couldn't have answered, even if she wanted to speak. Nor did she have the chance. At a click of the man's tongue, the drake began to move. It turned, gripping the rock with its claw-tipped wings, and began to climb, and Gwyn would have slid right off the back of the saddle if the man hadn't been seated behind her.

Up and up along the sheer face of the mountain, like a spider. She would have pressed her eyes closed if they hadn't been locked open in terror. Up, with the wind biting at her cheeks, her breath misting the air in front of her.

And then the drake turned, forked tongue tasting the air ... and launched itself off the cliff face.

The flight to the Pyramid took less than half an hour.

When they reached the tip, barely visible among low cloud cover, Gwyn saw the opening. The drake angled straight for it, wings beating hard against the thin, frozen sky.

She had closed her eyes, in the end. The air whipping past made them burn and stream, turning the rapidly vanishing landscape into a blur of snow-scoured peaks, columns of cloud, white-limbed trees no bigger than her fingernail. She thought she must have screamed, too, because her throat was raw, though she had no memory of it.

The drake banked left, caught an updraught of wind, and arrowed into the opening in the tip of the Pyramid, folding its wings at the last second. And then she was in a dark place that smelled of damp and mildew, silent but for the scrape of the drake's claws on the obsidian floor.

The stranger unstrapped her legs and shoved her from the saddle. Gwyn landed awkwardly, her ankle giving a bark of pain as it twisted beneath her. A few feet away, the wind keened up through the open shaft and whipped her hair back from her face.

'Come on,' said the man, grabbing her under the arm. The drake stayed behind, its enormous head turning to watch them go.

'Where are you taking me?' The place was a labyrinth of twisting stone stairwells, of dark corridors illuminated by torches that burned with cold light. She saw no one, heard nothing but the distant howl of wind and the scuff of their boots on the floor.

'As I said,' the stranger replied. 'Lord Ygriel has words for you. He sent me to fetch you. You'll show him the proper respect, if you know what's good for you.'

Lord Ygriel. He hadn't even bothered to come for her himself. Perhaps she had overestimated her importance to him, to Beheret. Did he know what she had done to Aeshma?

'He's going to fix it,' said the man, seeming to hear her thoughts. The light of fanaticism burned in his voice. 'What you did to the vim. He knows how to fix it. Lord Ygriel is a great man.'

'He can't fix anything,' Gwyn said, stumbling as the man yanked on her arm. 'I can. If you let me go, I know how to bring back the vim.' A trained Syndicate wizard, he must be feeling the loss of it even more keenly than she. Perhaps he could be persuaded.

But the man only snorted, not bothering to look at her. 'I think not, Yennevere. Lord Ygriel was quite specific.'

Gwyn grasped for another lie, anything that might help. Though what hope she had of escaping the Pyramid without a drake of her own ... Well, she wouldn't think about that. Get away from the wizard: that was the first step.

'Ygriel is a monster,' she said. Ahead of them, a door groaned open. 'He doesn't —'

The words died on her tongue.

She had expected another corridor, another stairwell. But this space was cavernous, with a ceiling that must have been seventy feet high at least.

And in the centre ...

It was the Well.

A crystalline tube, twenty feet wide and filled

with a white light so bright it made her eyes stream. It hung suspended in the centre of a vast, open space, criss-crossed with obsidian walkways polished to a high gleam.

Gwyn held her forearm up to shield her face. The light ... There was no heat, but even so, it was like looking into the sun at noon.

'Quite the sight, isn't it?'

Not the wizard's voice. He released her arm, bowed, turned on his heel and left without a word. Gwyn looked up, towards where the voice had come from.

And there he was, of course, just as she knew he must be: standing on the walkway above, regarding her with those cool, amused, familiar eyes.

But the rest of him – oh, that was different.

Gwyn stared. She was asleep; she had to be. She had hit her head back at the Festival; was having a fever dream as she lay on her bunk in the wagon.

But she wasn't asleep, and she knew that. It was all too real.

He was fifteen when they took him to the town square and burned him. In the heat of the pyre, his skin had burst like an overcooked sausage casing, turning his flesh to a nightmare patchwork, melted and charred. Above his dark trousers, spindly arms hung limply from a bare, bloated torso. Knotty scars roped the purple neck beneath the mask. Both ears had burned away like candle wicks. Only a few strands of pale hair remained atop the ruin that was Ygriel, drooling over the surface of the silver mask and its pleasant, slightly vacant smile.

'Mother is displeased with you,' he said. 'And by extension, displeased with me.' His booted feet crossed the floor towards the nearest stairwell, making a hollow *clunk* against the walkway, and Gwyn had to stop herself from cowering.

If you have to die, then at least do it with some dignity. Strangely, the voice in her head sounded like Alcide. She wished she had had time to thank him for the sword training, for all the good that had done her in the end.

Up close, Ygriel's mask was the same as it had been in the Lurk, the same as in her dreams – but it sat lopsided here, hugging whatever remnants of his face lay beneath.

Gwyn forced her spine straight and looked him in the eye. *Die facing him, not cringing on the ground like a dog.* In that moment, she missed all of them so much – even Alcide; even Faolan – it was like a fist clenching her heart.

'Mother had known Aeshma for over two thousand years,' Ygriel continued. 'She was angry when she learned what you had done. And I share in the blame. When the dog Shemeris dug her up, Mother wanted Aeshma brought here, where she could be kept safe. But I counselled her to wait. Better to use Aeshma to ensure Shemeris' cooperation. The mancers are useful servants, but to have one more powerful than the rest, one granted the ability to drink the vim straight from the source – yes, that would have been a boon.'

'Aeshma was a *slave*!' The barely contained fury in Gwyn's voice stunned her. It had come out of nowhere, a sudden blast of furnace heat scorching away her fear. She took a step towards him, hardly knowing what she did.

Ygriel seemed unperturbed, though it was impossible to say what was happening beneath the silvery mask. He gave a little gesture, half shrug, half nod. 'Can you imprison something that was designed at birth to be a slave?'

'The wizards have been draining her! For thousands of years!' No wonder Aeshma had gone mad. Even now, pity made Gwyn's throat tighten.

'The ancients would have called that the entire purpose of the Scions. Nimet Greeves certainly wasn't squeamish about siphoning Beheret's power, once she realised its value.' He nodded at Gwyn's left palm, at the spiralling black wizard marking. 'And you've supped at Aeshma's teat yourself often enough these past months, haven't you?'

She stepped back as though slapped. 'I didn't know —'

'You didn't *care.*' Ygriel laughed, a light, pleasant sound that made the hairs on the back of her neck rise. 'Not where the power came from, nor who had to suffer for it. Besides, Mother wasn't the one holding poor Aeshma captive, sweet sister. That was the humans, the mancers – your own kind. Starting with Porter Sabine; with Darro Sabine and his precious Syndicate, and every generation since. You've put a stop to that now, of course. The Syndicate will be most unhappy.'

'And I'm *glad*,' Gwyn said. Her jaw ached from gritting her teeth. 'I'm glad it's over. Even if it means ...'

She couldn't finish. She *was* glad, even with that gaping, hollow place inside her chest where the vim should have been. It had been the right choice. To allow the Scion's enslavement to continue, just to hang on to her own magic ... That would truly be an act of evil, one worthy of her sorceress forebears.

'Indeed, the time for regrets has passed,' Ygriel said. He was standing close now, so close she would have felt the heat of his breath, if not for the silver mask. 'Come. It's time for you to do what you were made for.'

Gwyn stepped backwards until she felt the cold stone of the door behind her. No knob, no keyhole. No escape. A numb, recoiling horror crept up from the pit of her stomach.

'I won't let you use me,' she said, and her voice trembled. 'If Beheret wants to breed a vessel out of me, I'll fight her every day of my life, if I have to.'

Ygriel tilted his head at her; blinked. 'Breed a

vessel? Why would she wish that, sister? Mother's vessel has already been perfected. Her work is done.'

'What?' Gwyn shook her head, struggling to make sense of his words.

Her work is done.

No, no, he couldn't mean ... *No!* It was impossible. He was lying, trying to throw her off balance, confuse her.

'Umbrael told me —'

'That you weren't the vessel?' Ygriel nodded, conciliatory. 'I'm not surprised. If you had known, you hardly would have dared leave your precious valley, would you?'

Umbrael tricked me? Gwyn's blood was ice in her veins. Lying – Ygriel had to be lying. She had merged her mind with the Scion's, in that dark room under the house. Could Umbrael truly have held anything back, let alone lied outright? No – Gwyn couldn't believe that.

But if she *had* lied ...

'Why?' Gwyn whispered. Her hands were shaking now, a tremor that had started at her feet and was creeping higher with each breath. Why would Umbrael lie? She was Idris' ally; how could she turn against him?

The question wasn't intended for Ygriel, but he answered anyway. 'Umbrael is no friend to our mother, but I expect she has her own reasons for wanting you here. Perhaps she seeks to purchase

Beheret's forgiveness with your life. No matter. When Mother is free, perhaps she will travel to your valley and slay the traitor Scion with her own hands.'

Umbrael lied. Her mind wanted to shy away from it, but there was no point. She believed Ygriel. Vim help her, she believed him.

I am the vessel.

Her dream of stopping Beheret had turned into a nightmare, had crumbled to dust in her hands.

Ygriel's fingers closed around her arm, cold and impossibly strong, digging into the flesh. And then he was hauling her up flights of stairs, along walkways that circled the outside of the Well. She moved with no more will than a puppet. Her instinct screamed at her to reach for the vim – but of course, there was nothing there; not now. Aeshma's death had seen to that.

Ygriel's hand moved from her arm to her neck, tight and cold as a manacle. It drove her to her knees on the walkway.

They had reached the top.

He forced her head out over the edge, so she was looking down into the Well. The top was open to the air, and the surface roiled and churned only ten feet below them, moved by some unseen current beneath its surface. It was unlike anything Gwyn had seen before, but the strangeness could not account for the surge of revulsion that filled her, or the sudden knowledge that she would rather die than dip so much as a single toe into that pool.

'I look forward to spending more time with you, Yennevere,' Ygriel said, his voice low and crooning. 'We were such good friends, once. Do you have anything you wish to say before you meet your destiny?'

Destiny ...

'Yes,' Gwyn said. She stared straight ahead into the Well, into that white and burning circle. The light that radiated from it sizzled the tears on her cheeks to vapour. Slowly, Gwyn's fist opened on the gleaming thing inside, dangling from its leather thong. She felt Ygriel's eyes go to it.

'What is —?'

'Give my best to your mother,' Gwyn said, and tossed the core into the Well.

The core containing all of Gwyn's hopes traced a graceful arc through the air, flashing in the light that streamed from the Well. That light was too bright, near to blinding, and so Gwyn didn't see when it struck the surface. She only heard it, a distant *plop* that seemed to echo throughout the whole room.

Gwyn sucked in her breath.

And Ygriel began to laugh.

'Oh, sister!' The hand at her neck loosened, and she twisted to face him, incredulous. Her heart was hammering in her chest, a drum beat in time with the pulsing of the Well.

'What —?'

'Sister,' he said, still laughing. 'What other lies did Umbrael spin you? Did you imagine it to be some kind of weapon? Yes, I see you did. Foolish, foolish. Let me tell you about that amulet, Yennevere. The hill people have guarded it for centuries. A relic handed straight down from Ailbhe Ahriddin.' His mouth twisted on the name. 'It was a small matter to lay an enchantment on it to silence Aeshma's ranting. Shemeris begged for it, and I deemed it a fair price for her aid in capturing you.'

Gwyn's eyes moved from him, back to the surface of the Well. She felt numb. The core had been her last hope.

But it had been a lie, the same as everything Umbrael had told her. Had the core ever held Nimet's soul? Was Nimet even real? There was no blood curse, no weapon. No hope. She wished she could have warned Idris. He was devoted to the Scion; would never have expected she might be working against them. Too late, now.

'A fine thing, isn't it?' Ygriel said, pulling Gwyn to her feet. His eyes followed hers, down into the roiling depths of the Well. The opalescent white surface popped and bubbled like sludge. 'On the other side of Death, it looks quite different. Sometimes I wonder which is the *true* face of the Well. This, or ...' He trailed off; sighed. 'Well, no matter. The time has come.'

Gwyn sensed the finality in his words. No more talk. No more explanations. No more chances.

'What was it you said?' Ygriel asked. His hand moved up to her neck, tangled in her hair. 'Ah, yes. Give my best to Mother.'

And he pushed her in.

CHAPTER 35

THE WELL

Drifting.

Gwyn couldn't see her hands or feet; she wasn't even sure she *had* a body, here. She floated in a place outside of time, a sea of pure light. It was peaceful, in a way. No Ygriel. No terror. Just the light.

Where am I? The Lurk? There was nothing to say so, but ... it felt like the Lurk, somehow. Or as though she had been smeared across the surface of it. Did that mean she was dead?

You are afraid, said a voice.

It seemed to come from nowhere. Perhaps it was just inside her head. Or maybe it was her own voice, though it sounded different than Gwyn remembered. Harsher. Older. It was a comforting voice, though. She listened with the rapt attention of a child.

I have waited a long time for this, the voice continued. *Your kind take your human forms so much for granted. Did you know I have never seen sky with my own eyes? I think I will like it very much. No, calm yourself. I would speak with you, first.*

She did feel calm. She felt sure she was supposed to ... well, *care.* But it was impossible. The light around her was warm – a shaft of sunlight, thick as syrup.

Should I lie to you? Should I say there is honour in fulfilling the purpose for which you were made? That the greatest accomplishment is to accept our lot? It is a type of destiny, after all, and the drive to achieve one's destiny is, I think, very ... human.

The light stirred – an ocean, rippling from the passage of some titanic, scaled thing beneath the surface.

You think it your purpose in life to see me destroyed. Who put such ideas in you? Not the Caretaker, I think. Nor the Uncle, nor the Claw, nor any of the others who surround you now. Who, then? Show me.

There was no resisting. Images burst into her mind like savage flowers. Umbrael hanging. Umbrael whispering in her head.

Yes, I see now. The Weaver lives, then. I suspected Ailbhe Ahriddin was in contact with another Scion. So, that one was responsible for her defection. I always thought it was Iahta. No matter. Ailbhe was punished, as Umbrael will be.

The light was red, like blood.

You place your trust very easily, Yennevere. The people

of this world think us gods, but they know no better, and cannot be blamed. But you – you surprise me. You, who have seen our true nature, still cleave as tightly to Umbrael's words as though she were a god in truth! The great and magnanimous Umbrael. She sent you straight to me. A sly choice, as befits the Lady of Prophecy. I expect I know why. Shall I tell you for what price your soul was sold to me?

Umbrael wishes for her freedom, child, the same as all of us. Did you never think it strange, that I would wish to walk among humankind, but she would not? I may have been the first to dream of green fields and open skies, but I was not the only one. Umbrael wanted it too, only she was willing to lie and manipulate to achieve it. To manipulate a child, no less. What a benevolent god she is!

Gwyn floated, untethered from her flesh, from everything. Beheret's words twined around her, ribbons of fire and starlight.

Freedom. I am the First, Yennevere; I control the Scions. Nimet bound them to me herself. When I am free, it is within my power to free them, too.

There was nothing but red. She was the heart, suspended in some arterial chamber. *Thump-thump. Thump-thump.* The light passed into her, and when it flowed out, it was red.

And what would happen, if I allowed this? I think you would not like it. A free Scion might inhabit any *descendant of their bloodline. With the way man has spread over this world, they would hardly be lacking in choice. The others – they are not bound by the same limitations as the First Scion. To walk free, I need something very special, something very rare. But* they *need only to be released.*

The sound was enormous; catastrophic. *Thump-thump. Thump-thump.*

It is a dark future to imagine. Five lesser Scions now survive. Molech Suun; Yotha. Iahta, Siasr, Umbrael herself. And to have each of them free, walking this world wearing human flesh? One can easily imagine the consequences. I doubt very much that they would be content to simply live out their modest human lives. What new powers would spring from the other Scions, should they ever be wakened? And how many of mortal kind could harness the essence of each?

Does that future appeal to you, then? Five Scions, each at the head of an army wielding powers unknown? No, I thought not.

Be at ease, Yennevere. I have no desire to share my freedom; not with any of them. When I walk the skin of this world, I will see each of them destroyed for good. This, at least, I promise you.

But you have indulged my weakness for conversation too long. I apologise. It is lonely here at times, and Ygriel is poor company. You and I, though, we have work to do. And the first task is ...

It was the only warning she had. Pain exploded along every nerve, and the strange, dreamy lethargy shattered. Gwyn knew who she was. Knew *where* she was.

And worst of all, she knew what was happening.

Beheret's voice was gone, but her presence was still there. Gwyn felt it boring into her skull.

The blood curse, she thought desperately. The mounting pressure in her head made it hard to think. *I have to ...*

But no – the curse was a lie, wasn't it? She had already thrown the core into the Well, and it had done nothing. Or had that not happened yet? Past and future unspooled, winging away from her in every direction like startled butterflies. Past, present, future. Then, now. Gwyn, Beheret, the voice, the *pain.*

The pain.

The pain ... stopped.

Blood curse? Beheret whispered. *What is –*

And then the screaming began.

CHAPTER 36

A SILVER BRACELET

Gwyn no longer knew where she was. The corridors all looked the same, black and grey and empty, save for the smoke and the occasional shuddering burst of flames. There was blood on her hands, and only the bright redness of it told her this was the waking world, not the Lurk. The blood was hers, from the foot-long gash in her side where the broken lip of the Well had cut her open as she climbed out. There was a lot of it. Gwyn wondered if she might not be dead, after all.

'Easier if you were,' she said out loud. The bitterness in her own voice made her stagger. Or was that the loss of blood? Did it matter?

Easier if she were dead, yes. And better for everyone. Gwyn knew what she had done. The truth of it, the enormity of her failure, had hit her the moment she pulled herself from the Well.

I am the First, Yennevere; I control the Scions. Nimet bound them to me herself. When I am free, it is within my power to free them, too.

Beheret had warned her. Beheret, who had started all of this. Who had stolen her mother away from the Clockwork City; who had taken hundreds, thousands of others, all in the hopes of eventually creating *her*.

A free Scion might inhabit any *descendant of their bloodline. And with the way man has spread over this world, they would hardly be lacking in choice.*

To walk free, I need something very special, something very rare.

But they *need only to be released.*

And she had felt it. Oh, she had felt it. In the dark nothing of the Well, they had been with her, inside her. Umbrael, Molech Suun, Iahta, Yotha, Siasr. Even Beheret, defeated, catatonic.

She knew, then. Umbrael had never intended to bargain with Beheret. The core had been nothing; a diversion to get Gwyn to where she needed to be. To the Well.

The curse, though ... The curse had been real. Real, and locked in Gwyn's blood since before she was even born. Had Nimet always intended it that way? Had the core ever existed? Maybe she had distrusted her lover Darro at the end; known he would betray her. Maybe. It made no difference now.

Five lesser Scions now survive. And to have each of them free, walking this planet wearing human flesh? One can easily imagine the consequences. I doubt very much that they would be content to simply live out their modest human lives.

The blaze of triumph she had felt then was not her own.

It was theirs.

With Beheret gone, they had no need to beg the First for their freedom. One by one, they broke free, their ancient minds winging away to find new human forms.

Umbrael was the last. Before she winked out, she had seemed to touch Gwyn's mind, softer than the wing of a moth. There was sympathy in that touch. Almost apology.

Then she was gone too, and it was just Gwyn, alone in the Well with Beheret's comatose consciousness.

So what new powers, then, would spring from the other Scions, should they ever be wakened?

Gwyn wasn't sure what had happened then. She remembered pulling herself out, her hands shredded by the jagged edge of the Well. It had erupted like a boil, black sludge churning, roiling, spilling across the stone floor. She remembered the pain in her side. Then nothing.

Does that future appeal to you, then, Yennevere? Five Scions, each at the head of an army wielding powers unknown?

They were free, as they had planned all along. All

of them. Already, somewhere out there, five Scions were opening human eyes for the first time.

Whose eyes? There was no way to know, and no warning for the five men and women who had just lost ownership of their bodies. Beheret was gone, for now; removed from the game.

But in her place, Gwyn had unleashed something far worse.

The walls still trembled, and Gwyn hurled herself to the side as a piece of ceiling above her exploded, raining sparks that singed at her hair, her coat. The fall took the wind out of her. She lay for what seemed a long time as smoke wrapped loving fingers around her lungs, making spots swim in front of her eyes. She considered not getting up at all.

You did this, she thought. The voice in her head was cold, accusing. *You wanted to be a hero. You wanted to be* important.

Why had she come? That night in Priory, looking up at Umbrael's suspended form, hearing the Scion's voice in her head ... It seemed so long ago, now. Why had she trusted her?

You trusted without reason, like a fool, the voice continued, merciless. *All your life you've lived on the fringes, and when you saw the chance to be the hero of the tale, you leaped at it.*

That voice barely sounded like her at all. For one wild, irrational moment, she thought it was Lucian, whispering into her mind. But no – he wouldn't speak to her that way, his voice tight with hate, with rage. Even now. He would forgive her.

Wouldn't he?

Gwyn forced herself up onto her knees and scrubbed at her eyes. The Well had taken everything she had worked for ... but it had given something, too. She reached out one hand, calling up the sign that burned in her mind, the sign still written in the dry blood on the back of her hand. The sludge of the Well hadn't touched that blood, though it had stripped the black dye from her hair, now clinging to her neck in pale, wet clumps.

Sigel. Flames erupted from her hand. A white-hot fireball floated two inches above her palm; a tiny sun.

Not sorceress magic. A wizard sign, carried straight to her on the wings of the vim.

The power that linked the Scions together was ancient, and simple in many ways. It saw that Aeshma was gone, and it saw that a new Scion – or something not much different – had been added. What came next was only logical.

The vim was back. But, gods help her, it wasn't coming from Aeshma any longer.

It was coming from *Gwyn.*

And in the Well, she had seen ... what? She knew, but her mind didn't want to circle back to it. It was too much, too big.

Everything. I saw everything.

Every memory, every thought, every emotion,

from every living being that had ever touched the Well. She had *been* them. Ygriel. The sorceresses, all eight of them, from Ailbhe Ahriddin all the way back to the first days, to Nimet. Everyone. All in a single moment.

No human mind could contain that much. Already it was fading. Who had come before Ailbhe Ahriddin? Raven-wing hair, a thin and beautiful face with eyes of wildfire ... No, it was gone. She was losing them all. In her hand, the flame winked out.

The corridor shuddered. Another crack echoed through the hallway, and above her, the roof groaned and bowed inwards. Gwyn leaped to her feet and started to run, hand pressed to her side to staunch the blood. It was hard to breathe, and she stumbled, half blind, down twisting corridors that all looked the same.

No sign of Ygriel. She didn't know what to make of that. Was he dead? What had happened here? Destruction – flame and smoke and scorching heat. Her doing? Of course. It was all her, every bit of it.

The corridors echoed with distant crashes and booms. She staggered, fell, pulled herself upright; staggered and fell again. She was going to die here. Maybe she was already dead, and this was Siasr's deepest hell.

Then ... a whisper of cool, sweet air.

There was light on her eyelids. Gwyn blinked away dust, and saw a circle of brightness. Behind her, the hallway groaned as though dying. She surged through the doorway and stepped out into blinding sunlight.

She blinked to clear her eyes, struggling to make sense of what she was seeing.

There was wreckage all around her, some of it still on fire. A wide-open field of scorched grass, of leafless trees that still burned and cracked. Behind a curtain of choking smoke, the sun was blood red.

A hand seized the back of her coat.

Gwyn was spun forcefully around, coming face to face with a stranger. He was in his middle years, lantern-jawed, with streaks of white in his hair. Brown eyes surveyed her dispassionately.

'This one is human,' he said.

Behind him, another man approached on horseback. There were six of them in total, four mounted and two afoot, all close in age and with the same grim and humourless faces. Their coats all bore the tower-and-moon sigil.

Wizards.

'Human?' said the nearest man. He urged his mount closer, reaching down to grasp Gwyn's face in one hand. His fingers felt hot, and smelled faintly of ash. Inside his wrist she could make out the neat script of his marking. He turned her head left and right, as though inspecting a horse he was thinking of buying. 'Are you sure? Her eyes look funny to me. Look, here.'

Gwyn tried to pull away, but his grip was like iron. Another man came over and peered down at her.

'Yes, you're right. Strange. She's not one of ours, but we should take her, I think, to be safe. Castlemaine will want to have a look.'

The first man snorted and released her. 'Not much to show, is it? Some burning wreckage ... and one captive. A servant, I imagine. Perhaps she knows something useful.'

Both men turned back to her. Behind them, the other four circled outwards, searching for ... what? Survivors?

'You there,' one of the wizards barked. 'You came from inside, yes? In the Pyramid? Tell us, what do you know of what happened? Why did it fall? Speak, girl.'

'I don't know anything,' Gwyn said. Her voice sounded hoarse, strained. *The Pyramid ... fell?* But it was the only thing that made sense, the only explanation for the apocalypse surrounding them. 'I'm from Asgerad. I was kidnapped. I don't know anything.'

The mounted man snorted. 'A likely story. Well, never mind. You'll talk to Castlemaine, if you won't talk to us.'

'Why would the Syndicate care what happened?' Gwyn asked. Anger stirred in her breast, unexpected, but no less potent for that. She had faced Beheret, had entered the Well, had likely killed Ygriel ... for what? To be stopped by wizards? Who were they, to question her? Mere children. She should strike them down where they stood.

Then the feeling was gone, as quickly as it had come. She felt cold, sick, empty. Frightened, too, though she tried not to show it. The men were looking at her now with renewed interest.

'Look at her *eyes,*' the black-haired one whispered. The other nodded slightly, but made no reply. Instead, he stepped closer to Gwyn.

'So you know who we are, hmm? Well, *servant,* the truth is we have little interest in this place, except as a curiosity from an earlier age. It was bound to fall from the sky sooner or later. But we *are* interested in the magical disturbance that was felt here some hours ago. And more interested still in the hour that preceded it. The hour when, despite all logic, it seemed that the vim – our magic – simply disappeared. Tell me, then, would you know anything about that?' His eyes were razor-sharp under bushy white brows.

'I don't know anything.' Gwyn said. Her voice was barely a whisper.

The man turned away, lips pressed together in apparent disappointment. 'Very well. Perhaps you will feel more cooperative later. Trask – the bindings, if you would?'

The one called Trask nodded and strode towards

her. There was something silver and shining in his hand, something that jingled slightly with each step. Gwyn had time only to flinch backwards before the man grasped her forearms. Before she could stop him, he had clamped something around each wrist. Two silver bands, joined together with a long silver chain hung with little stars and moons.

As the bands locked, Gwyn felt a tearing sensation somewhere deep inside her.

Trask's eyes widened.

'Vanna?'

The mounted man turned. 'Hmm?'

'It's gone again.'

'What?'

'The vim.' He stared into Gwyn's face, stared with a sick, dawning horror. *'It's gone.'*

EPILOGUE

TOWER AND MOON

Gwyn swung her wrist, watching the dim light flash off the silver chain. It was hard to make out much of anything in the cell, and she took what little amusements she could.

Three days since Enoch had last been here. The memory of him scuttling backwards out the door still brought a smile to her face. Poor Enoch. Syndicate wizard he might be, but she couldn't help feeling sorry for him.

Clink-clink. The silver charms made a pretty sound. They reminded her of the chimes that hung outside her bedroom window as a girl. When the wind blew, it carried the scent of oranges.

Chimes?

Gwyn sighed. Not her memory. Her bedroom had been the little bunk at the front of Ascepis' wagon.

No chimes there. Just the rumble of wheels and the clop-clop of Pepper's hooves on the road.

It seemed to happen a lot lately. The confusion. Perhaps it was because she spent so much time in darkness. Sometimes it was hard to tell where her memories ended and the others began. They were fragments, mostly, like reflections caught in a hundred shattered pieces of glass. A garden, filled with graceful, splashing fountains. A man's face, dark-haired and laughing. The smell of white fig and juniper. Tiny slivers of memory from lives not her own, left over from her time in the Well.

Sometimes they were more than fragments. Like when Castlemaine came. He never smiled, except when the hot irons were brought out.

The welts on her arms and legs told what had happened next, but Gwyn remembered none of it. When Castlemaine grasped the iron, it seemed that something snapped in her mind, and suddenly she was standing in a vaulted hallway with high, soaring windows, hung all over with drapes and tapestries.

'Do you like it?' she heard herself say.

'A little much, perhaps,' said the man next to her, laughing. *'But you always did have expensive taste.'* There was something familiar about him. The eyes, maybe – slate-grey under a heavy, hawkish brow. His hair was the colour of coal, winged with white at the temples.

'I think it will be good for us,' she said. *'Though perhaps –'*

She broke off as the man smiled, seizing her around the waist and pulling her close.

'Hush. It's perfect.' And then he kissed her, and the hall faded away in a roar of white.

Gwyn was laughing when she awoke, propped up against the wall of her cell.

The burns had scabbed over now, though she still moved stiffly, when she had the strength to move at all. Castlemaine had not returned, and when the guards brought food, it was slid to her through the slit in her cell door. After all this, maybe they simply meant to let her rot down here.

Her wrists were almost thin enough now to slip right out of the silver bands. Perhaps she should start refusing food. That would be easy enough. She barely felt hungry now; barely felt anything at all.

Gwyn dropped her hands to her lap, too weak to hold them up any longer. Her nails were ragged, too. Faolan would scold her for that, if he could see her now.

Faolan. In the first weeks, she had dreamed of rescue. Some nights she awoke in the dark, heart hammering, sure she had heard his voice calling to her. Any minute she expected to see him outlined in the cell doorway, reaching down his hand for her.

'I've come to take you home,' he would say.

But Faolan, if he had survived the Festival, likely

thought her dead. There would be no rescue, no going home. Gwyn wasn't even sure where home was anymore.

And the disc ... Well, she still wasn't sure what to make of that. The last time she'd seen her 'wish', it had been hanging around Faolan's neck. The sight of it dangling from the librarian's fingers had shocked her to the core. How had it gotten here? She still had no idea, but she was glad to have it back, a cool and comforting weight against her heart, even if it did mean selling her story to the wizards. Doubtful they would believe her, anyway.

She sighed, running the length of the chain through her hands. There was blood on them, mostly dry, but some fresh. Her wrists were raw where the inside of the cuffs had chafed them.

Blood. There was something about that. Something to do with the redness of it. Something she should remember, something that seemed important. What was it? Her eyes narrowed. Oh, it was infuriating. She could almost —

There was an abrupt sucking noise, and Gwyn started back in surprise, dropping the chain. Everything went dark – a crushing, *squeezing* dark, like being yanked at high speed through some impossibly long tunnel.

Then Gwyn was on her feet, with a sound like a whip crack ringing in her ears. Her head spun.

Behind her, she heard the silver shackles clatter to the ground.

Gwyn looked at her wrists, hardly daring to believe.

There were two angry strips of red where the bands had chafed at the skin. The heavier chains that tethered her to the wall were gone, too, and the manacles lay empty where they had fallen. For a moment, she stared, uncomprehending.

Blood.

She remembered. Faolan, sitting astride his horse and smirking at her, on the road to Edge.

'A sorceress – well, nobody knows what they are, save that their power is blood magic.'

Ailbhe Ahriddin, her voice speaking to Gwyn from the memory glass, echoing down through the centuries.

'It's been too long since I spilled some blood. Blood that wasn't my own, at least. The red magic is even harder to give up than the black, and a sorceress has to make do with what she can find.'

Red. Sorceress magic was red magic.

Blood magic.

And then she knew. Yes, the chains were enough to block a wizard's powers, enough to sever her connection to the vim. Bound in silver, any wizard would be powerless.

But she wasn't just a wizard. She never had been.

And no shackle ever forged could hold a sorceress.

A warmth was invading Gwyn's body. She knew that feeling. It was as simple and vital as breath. With the bindings gone, the vim had returned.

For me, yes – but for every other wizard, too.

If she stood still, Gwyn thought she could actually feel it radiating off her skin. A sizzling, crackling power, like the air before a storm.

Well, no matter. That would only make things more interesting.

Her lips curved in a smile. In the darkness, it hardly looked like her at all.

ACKNOWLEDGMENTS

I started writing this book in its current form back in 2006, during my undergrad degree. But its origins go back even further, to the old days of online fanfiction, and to my Year 10 English major work – the story of a green-eyed girl named Gwyn. I lovingly refer to this book as my *Big Ugly Baby,* and I've been giving birth to it for almost half my life.

In all that time, I've been lucky enough to receive encouragement and help from a lot of people. Being very aged and very absent-minded, I'm sure I've forgotten half of them. Sorry! These are the ones I can remember.

Firstly, to you. To all the readers who decided to pick up an unknown author's debut and give it a spin. Without you, I'd just be a weirdo writing alone in my bedroom. I'm still that weirdo, but now I'm an author too. I can't thank you enough.

To the team at Talem Press: thank you for taking a chance on my book and making the Big Ugly Baby a bit less big and ugly. Helen and Claire, your boundless enthusiasm for this project made me believe I can really do this author thing after all.

To my writer friends at Thursday Night Novelists: George, Terry and Alf. You don't read fantasy, and you often stare at the page in bafflement when I start talking about *wizards* and *necromancers*. If I can win you guys over, I know I've done a good job. Thanks for putting up with me!

To my family. Not one of you ever told me that being an author was a stupid dream. That means a lot. And to my long furry son, Percival Hector – no amount of pigs' ears can repay your faithful and sometimes smothering love, but I'll certainly try. Thank you.

To my second family, the Evendens, who have been cheerleading from the sidelines since I was five. Sue, for endless cups of tea. Graeme, who read an extract to the puzzled crowd at his own daughter's wedding – if that's not a vote of confidence, I don't know what is!

I can't list all my friends, but here are a few: Ally, Alex, Marianna, Alyce, Emmy, Mercedes. I hope you're reading this at my launch party, because you're there and you've all bought six copies. No freebies! And of course, thank you to my boss, Cambeez, who never gives me too much grief when I say I need a week of leave to 'work on my art'.

Lastly and most of all, thank you to my mum, who asks me ominously, whenever she gets a cough or cold: 'Have I been a good mother to you, Bonnie?' You have. This book is proof.

ABOUT THE AUTHOR

Bonnie Wynne studied Writing and Cultural Studies at UTS, and completed her law degree at the University of Sydney. After a brief stint in legal publishing, she now works for the Australian government, deciphering ancient law tomes.

She lives in Sydney with her cocker spaniel, Percival Hector (Canine Inspector). When she's not reading or writing, she can be found playing video games, booking her next holiday, or elbow-deep in flour.

The Ninth Sorceress is her debut novel and the first book in her series, *The Price of Magic*.

DID YOU ENJOY THIS BOOK?

You can make a difference.

Reviews are one of the most powerful tools for an author. They help bring books to the attention of new readers.

If you enjoyed this book, the author would be incredibly grateful if you could spend a few minutes leaving a review on the Amazon page for *The Ninth Sorceress*.

Made in the USA
Coppell, TX
13 February 2021

50301667R00288